Christine Merrill lives on a farm in Wisconsin, USA, with her husband, two sons, and too many pets – all of whom would like her to get off the computer so they can check their e-mail. She has worked by turns in theatre costuming, where she was paid to play with period ballgowns, and as a librarian, where she spent the day surrounded by books. Writing historical romance combines her love of good stories and fancy dress with her ability to stare out of the window and make stuff up.

Regency Surrender

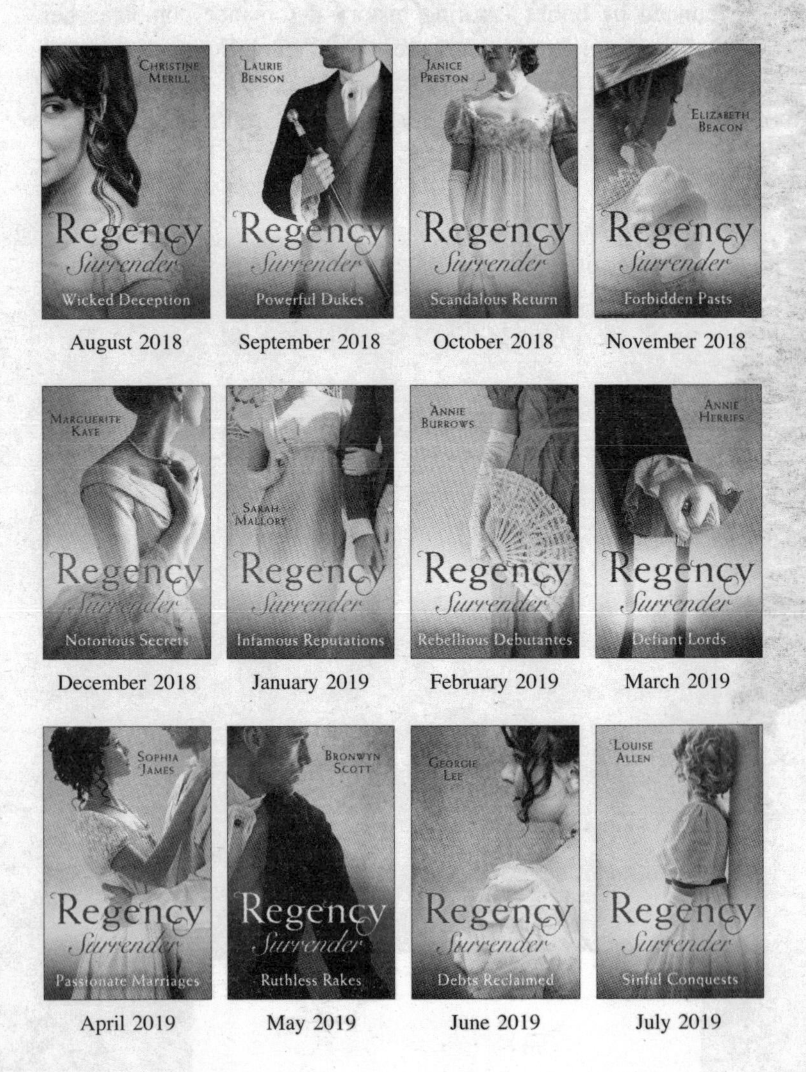

August 2018 | September 2018 | October 2018 | November 2018

December 2018 | January 2019 | February 2019 | March 2019

April 2019 | May 2019 | June 2019 | July 2019

Regency Surrender: Wicked Deception

CHRISTINE MERRILL

MILLS & BOON

First Published in Great Britain 2018
By Mills & Boon, an imprint of HarperCollinsPublishers
1 London Bridge Street, London, SE1 9GF

ISBN: 978-0-263-26787-7

52-0818

This book is produced from independently certified FSC™ paper to ensure responsible forest management.

For more information visit: www.harpercollins.co.uk/green

Printed and bound in Great Britain
by CPI Group (UK) Ltd. Croydon, CRO 4YY

THE TRUTH ABOUT LADY FELKIRK

To Jim: after thirty years, you must be near to sainthood.

Chapter One

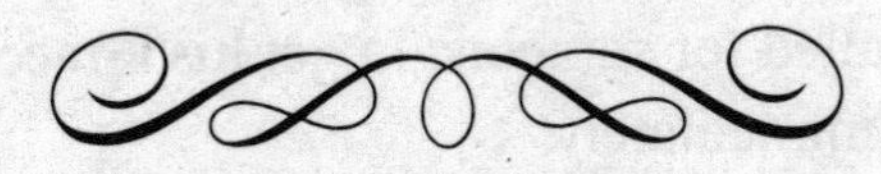

Everything hurt.

William Felkirk did not bother to open his eyes, but lay still and examined the thought. It was an exaggeration. Everything ached. Only his head truly hurt. A slow, thumping throb came from the back of it, punctuating each new idea.

He swallowed with effort. There was no saliva to soothe the process. How much had he been drinking, to get to this state? He could not seem to remember. The party at Adam's house, which had been a celebration of his nephew's christening, was far too sedate for him to have ended like this. But he could not recall having gone anywhere after. And since he was in Wales, where would he have gone?

His eyelids were still too heavy to open, but he did not need vision to find the crystal carafe by the bedside. A drink of water would help. His arm flailed bonelessly, numb fingers unable to close on the glass.

There was a gasp on the other side of the room and the shatter of porcelain as an ornament was dropped and broken. Clumsy maids. The girl had been cleaning around him, as though he was a piece of furniture. Was it really necessary to shout 'He is waking!' so that anyone in the hall could hear?

Then there were hurried footsteps to the door and a voice called for someone to get his Grace and her ladyship immediately.

He opened his eyes at last and tried to sit up, but the room was still a blur and his back did not want to support him. He stared at the ceiling and what little he could see of the bedposts. It was still his brother's house. But Penelope had never been a ladyship, even before marrying Adam. Even now, she laughed about not feeling graceful enough to be her Grace, the Duchess of Bellston. Though she was just out of childbed, she was not so frail as to cede her duties as hostess to another. Who the devil was *her ladyship*?

He must have misheard. But the rueful shake of his head made the pain worse, as did the thundering of steps on the stairs and in the hall. Could not a man bear the shame of a hangover in privacy? He tried to sit up again, and as he did, he felt an arm at his back and hands lifting him, like a child, to settle him against the pillows.

'There's a good fellow.' Adam was treating him like an invalid. It must be even worse than he thought. 'A drink of water, perhaps?' But instead of the cup he expected, there was a damp rag pressed to his lips.

Will spat and turned his head away. '…Hell?' He must be parched for he could not seem to speak properly. But it had been enough to make his displeasure known.

'You want a glass?' Adam seemed to find this extraordinary. 'Where is Justine? Find her, quickly.'

The rim of the cup met his lips. He reached for it, felt his arm flop, then tremble, and then the hand of his older brother was there to steady it so he could drink.

Crystal goblet. Crystal water. Cool and sweet, trickling, then coursing down his throat, which still felt as though it was full of cobwebs. Some of the pounding in his skull subsided. He paused. 'Better.' His voice croaked, but it was clearer.

There was another feminine gasp from the doorway.

'He is waking,' Adam said, softly, urgently. 'Come to his side.'

'I dare not.' It was a woman's voice: a melodious alto, with the faintest hint of an accent to it.

'After so long, you must be the first thing he sees.' He could feel Adam rise, and, as he watched, another hand came to guide the water glass.

Something smelled wonderful. No. It was someone. Roses, and cinnamon, close at his side. Muslin leaning against his bare arm and warm silky skin touching his shoulder, then smoothing the hair on his brow. His senses were returning to him, in a series of pleasant surprises.

When his vision could focus past the fingers on the cup, he saw a perfect, heart-shaped face, looking worriedly into his. It was the sort of face that made him wish he could paint, or at least draw, so that he might carry a copy of it with him for ever. Her eyes were the strange green gold of coins at the bottom of a fountain and he could not seem to stop staring at them. They were sad eyes and fearful. For a moment, he thought he saw the beginnings of a tear in one. Her pink lips trembled. Her hair was a mix of sunset golds and reds, partially obscured under a plain muslin cap. The curls swayed gently, as though their owner was eased away from him.

'Do not be afraid,' he said. Why was she here? And why was she so hesitant? He was not sure of much, least of all who this might be. But he was quite sure he did not want her to be in fear of him. Adam had been right. To wake to this was a gift, especially when one had such a damnable headache.

'After all that has happened, he is concerned for you?' Adam gave a short, satisfied laugh. 'You have not changed at all, then, Will. We had so feared…' His brother's voice cracked with emotion.

'Is it true?' Adam's wife, Penny, was here now, somewhere by the door. She was out of breath, as if she had rushed to the room.

Adam hissed at her to be silent.

'The more, the merrier,' Will muttered, still without the energy to turn away yet another visitor to his bedside. But when he turned his face to the duchess, something was wrong. Very wrong, in fact. She appeared to be pregnant. That could not be right. Just yesterday, he'd thought her rather thin. He'd enquired after her health and had listened to his brother's complaints that the recent birth had taken too much from her. Today, she stood in the doorway of his bedroom, plump and healthy.

Will frowned. If it was a joke, it was both elaborate and pointless. The whole family was watching him, as though waiting for something. He had no idea what they expected. His head was swimming again. He went to rub his temple, but it took all his strength to lift his own arm.

The woman at his side grasped the hand and brought it down again, rubbing some feeling back into the fingers, flexing joints and massaging muscles. Then she laid it carefully on the counterpane and brought her own fingers up to stroke his forehead. Damn, but it felt good. If he were not still so tired, he'd have sent the family away, to test the extent of her familiarity with his body. Though she had hesitated at first, she did not seem the least bit shy now.

He relaxed back into the pillows that had been leaned against the headboard and sighed. Then, slowly, carefully, he flexed the fingers of each hand. It was difficult, as was moving his toes. But when next he raised his hand, he was able to gesture for the water without embarrassing himself. His beautiful nurse brought the glass to his lips again.

He licked a drop off his dry lips and swallowed again. 'Is someone going to explain to me what has happened, or will you leave me to guess? Did I take ill in the night?'

'Explain?' Adam, again, speaking for the group. 'What do you remember of the last months, Will?'

'The Season, of course,' he answered, wishing he could give a dismissive wave. 'That blonde chit you were forcing on me. Why you think you can choose my wife, when I had no say in yours, I have no idea. And coming up to Wales with you for the christening. What did you put in the punch to get me into such a state? Straight gin?'

He meant to joke. But the faces around him were shocked to silence. Adam cleared his throat. 'The christening was six months ago.'

'Certainly not.' He could remember it, as clearly as he could remember anything. It seemed distant, of course. But he had just woken up. When his head cleared…

'Six months,' Adam repeated. 'After the party you left and would not tell us where you were going. You said you would be returning with a surprise.'

'And what was it?' Will asked. If he was here now, he must have returned, with a story that would explain his current condition.

'We heard nothing from you, for months. When Justine brought you home, you were in no state to say anything. There had been an accident. She thought it best that you be with your family, when…' Adam's voice broke again and he looked away.

'Who is this Justine?' Will said, looking around. But judging by the shocked expression on the face of the woman holding his hand, the question answered itself.

'You really don't remember?' she said. And he did not. Although how he could have forgotten a face or a voice like that, he was not sure.

'I remember the christening,' he repeated. 'But I have no recollection of you at all.'

The gold eyes in front of him were open wide now, incredulous.

Adam cleared his throat again, the little noise he tended to make when he was about to be diplomatic. 'It seems there is much you have lost and much that must be explained to you. But first and foremost, you must know this. The woman before you now is Lady Felkirk.' He paused again. 'William, may I introduce to you your wife, Justine.'

'I have no wife.' He'd had more than enough of this foolishness and swung his feet out of the bed to stand and walk away.

Or at least he tried. Instead, he flopped on the mattress like a beached fish, spilling the water and sliding halfway out of bed before his brother could steady him, and muscle him back to the centre.

'It is all right. As long as you are getting better, it does not matter.' There was the voice of the ministering angel again, his supposed wife. What had they called her? Justine?

The name, though it was as beautiful as its owner, held no resonance.

Adam leaned over the bed again, smiling, although the grin was somewhat stained. 'Justine brought you home some two months ago, and you have lain insensible since then. I feared you would never…' There was another pause, followed by a deep sigh. Perhaps fatherhood had made Adam soft, for Will could not recall ever hearing him sound near to tears. 'The doctors did not give us much hope. To find you awake and almost yourself again…'

So he'd cracked his skull. He did not remember it, but it certainly explained the throbbing in his head. 'What happened?'

'A fall from a horse.'

That seemed possible. He sometimes overreached himself, when in the saddle. But his old friend, Jupiter, was the most steady of beasts, as long as he held the reins. And a wife… He stared pointedly at the woman leaning over him, waiting for her to add some explanation.

'We were on our honeymoon,' the woman said, gently, as though trying to prod the memory from him. 'We met in Bath, at the beginning of summer.'

Still, nothing. What had he been doing in Bath? He abhorred the place, with its foul-tasting water and the meddling mamas of girls who could not make a proper match in London.

'I am sure marriage must have been in your plans when you left us,' Penny said, encouraging him. 'You did promise us a surprise. But really, we had no idea how welcome it would be. When Justine returned with you…' She gave an emotional pause again, just as his brother had done. 'She has been so good to you. To all of us, really. She never lost hope.' Under the guise of wiping her fogged spectacles, Penny withdrew a handkerchief and dabbed at her eyes.

Only the woman, Justine, seemed to take it all calmly, as though a husband returning from death's door with no memory of her was a thing that happened to everyone. When she spoke, her voice was unbroken and matter-of-fact. 'You will be all right now. Everything is better than we could have hoped.'

'As if being concussed and losing half a year of one's life is a thing to be celebrated.' He glared at her. Perhaps this lovely stranger had done nothing to deserve his anger. Or perhaps she had got him drunk and knocked him on the head so she could pretend to be his wife.

But that made no sense. He lacked the money and title necessary to be the target of such intriguing. If she meant him ill, why did she bring him home, afterwards? Why bother to nurse him back to health?

The mysterious Justine ignored his dark look and smiled down at him. 'It is to be celebrated. The physician said you would never wake, yet, you did. Now that you can eat properly, you will grow stronger.' But did he see a fleeting shadow in her eyes, as though his recovery was something less than a blessing?

Perhaps she was as confused as he, after all. Or perhaps he had hurt her. He had taken the trouble to marry her, only to forget her entirely. Now, he was snapping at her, blaming her for his sore head. Had he treated her thus, before the accident? Perhaps the marriage had been a mistake. If so, he could hardly blame her for a passing desire that his prolonged illness would end with her freedom.

When he looked again, her face was as cloudless as a summer day. The doubt had been an illusion, caused by his own paranoia. When he was stronger and had a chance to question her, things would be clearer. For now, he must rein in his wild thoughts and wait. He shook his head and immediately regretted it, as the pain, which had been ebbing, came rushing back.

She leaned closer, reaching across him for a cool cloth that lay beside the bed, pressing it against his forehead.

How did she know it would soothe him? It did not matter. If she guessed, she guessed correctly. He took her hand and squeezed it in what he hoped she would know as gratitude. But though the pain was lessening, his doubts were not. There was nothing the least bit familiar about the shape of the hand he held. Surely, if he had married her, the joining should not feel so entirely alien. As soon as he could do so without appearing awkward, he withdrew his hand.

She made sure the compress was secure and withdrew her own hands, folding them neatly in her lap as though equally relieved to be free of him.

While the two of them were clearly uncomfortable with each other, the rest of the room was ecstatic. 'Whenever you are ready, we will bring you downstairs,' Penny said. 'Perhaps we can procure a Bath chair so that you might take sun in the garden.'

'Nonsense.' The compress slipped as he tried to struggle to his feet again. This time he made slightly more progress. He was able to swing both legs over the edge of the bed and sit up. Almost immediately, the dizziness took him and he felt himself sliding to the side.

Once again, Adam rushed in, taking his arm and holding him upright. 'Easy. Do not try too much at once. There will be no Bath chair, if you do not wish it. You may go at your own pace. I am sure you will be walking well on your own in no time at all.'

'But you do not need to do it now,' Penny insisted. 'Rest is still important. And quiet. For now, we will leave the two of you alone.'

'No.'

'Yes.' He and the woman spoke simultaneously.

'You need your rest,' Justine said, laying a hand gently on his chest to try to ease him back down to the mattress. 'There will be time later for us to speak.'

'I have had more than enough rest,' he said. 'If you are all to be believed, I have been asleep for months.'

She was probably right. His head ached from even this small bit of activity. He needed time to think. But before that, he needed answers. Despite the innocent look on the beautiful face in front of him, Justine knew more than she had said.

'Leave, all of you. Please,' he added after noticing the shocked looks on their faces at his short temper. 'But send for my valet. After all this time in bed, I want to wash and dress. Until he arrives, I will talk to my wife.'

'Of course,' his brother said, with a relieved smile. 'If you are well enough, you can come down to dinner, or we will have a tray sent up. Either way,' he stepped forward again and clasped Will's hand in a firm grip, 'it is good to see you recovering. Come, Penny, I am sure they have much to discuss that does not concern us.'

Once they were gone and the door shut behind him, he was alone in a room with a woman who claimed to be his wife. He suppressed a rush of panic. He was still too weak to defend himself, should she not be as kind as she appeared. But why could he imagine such a sweet-faced thing as a danger to him? If she'd meant him harm, she'd have had ample opportunity before now.

Still, should not a new bride be happier to see her husband recovering? If she loved him, why was she standing at the side of his bed, mute like a criminal in the dock? There was something wrong about her. It was one of many things he could not place.

She seemed to realise this as well, for she attempted a hesitant smile and slipped easily back into the role of caregiver. 'Is there something I can get for you? Anything that might give you comfort?'

'What a good little nurse you are, to be so solicitous.' he said, not feeling particularly grateful for it. 'At the moment, there is nothing I need, other than an end to this charade.'

'There is no charade,' she said, looking more puzzled than frightened. 'We are not trying to trick you. You were injured and have been unconscious for several months. Come to the window and you shall see. The christening was at Easter time. It is no longer spring, or even summer. The leaves are falling and the night air is chill.'

'I do not need for you to tell me the weather,' he grumbled, glancing at the grey sky beyond the glass. 'I can see that for myself. And I know I was injured, for I still feel the pain of it.' He ran a careful hand through his hair, surprised at the crease in the scalp. 'But that does not explain the rest.'

'What else is there?' she said, though she must know full well what he meant.

'It does not explain you. Who are you, really? And who are you to me?' He looked full into the wide green eyes. 'For I would swear before God that you are not my wife.'

'William,' she said, in a convincingly injured tone.

'That is my name. And what is yours?'

'Justine, of course.'

'And before you married me?' he said, unable to help sneering at such an unlikely prospect.

'My surname? It was de Bryun.' She paused as though waiting for the bit of information to jar loose some memory. But nothing came.

'So you say,' he replied. 'I suppose next you will tell me you are an orphan.'

'Yes,' she said, unable to keep the hurt from her voice.

In a day, he might regret being so cavalier about her misery. At the moment, he had problems of his own. 'So you have no one to verify your identity.'

'I have a sister,' she added. 'But she was not present at the time of our wedding, nor was your family.'

'I married without my family's knowledge?' Penny had hinted at as much. But it still made no sense. 'So neither of us considered the feelings of others in this. We just suddenly…' with effort, he managed to snap his fingers '…decided to wed.'

'We discussed it beforehand,' she assured him. 'You said there would be time after. You said your brother had done something much the same to you.'

As he had. That marriage had been as sudden as this one. And Adam had admitted that he could not remember his wedding either. But while circumstances were similar, he had more sense than Adam and would never have behaved in that way. 'You could have learned the details of Adam's wedding anywhere,' he said.

She sighed, as though she were in a classroom,

being forced to recite. 'But I did not learn it anywhere. I learned it from you. You told me that your father's name was John, your mother's name was Mary. They were Duke and Duchess of Bellston, of course. You had one sister, who died at birth. And you told me all about your brother. It was why I brought you here. Why would I have done that, if not for love of you?'

This was a puzzle. He rubbed his temple, for though he was sure there was a logical explanation for it, searching for it made his head ache. 'You could have got any of that from a peerage book.'

'Or you could have told me,' she said, patiently. 'And it is not so unusual that I have no parents. You have none either.'

That was perfectly true. So why did it seem somehow significant that she had none? He shook his head, half-expecting it to rattle as he did so, for he still felt like a broken china doll. 'I suspect I can quiz you for hours and you will have an answer for everything. But there is one question I doubt you will answer to my satisfaction. What would have motivated me to take a wife?'

'You said you loved me.' Her lip trembled, though she did not look near tears. 'And I did not wish to lie with you, until we were married.'

It was not a flattering explanation. But it made more sense than anything else she had said. 'I can believe that I might have wanted to lie with you. My eyesight is fine, though my memory is not.' He stared up at the magnificent hair, still mostly obscured by her very sensible cap. Tired and confused as he was, he still wanted to snatch the muslin away, so that he might see it in all its glory. 'You are a beauty. And you know it, do you not? You are not going to pretend that you are unaware of the effect you have on men. Why did you choose me?'

'Because I thought you were kind and would be a good husband to me,' she said. There was something in her voice that implied she had been disappointed to find otherwise. Then she cast down her eyes. 'And you are right. I cannot help the way I look, or the reaction of others.'

'I do not see why you would wish to,' he answered honestly. But when he looked closely, her face held a mixture of regret and defiance, as though she very much wished she were plain and not pretty. Her clothing was almost too modest, nearly as plain as a servant's. The cap she wore was not some vain concoction of lace and ribbons, but undecorated linen. If she was attempting to disguise her assets, she had failed. The simple setting made the jewel of her beauty glow all the more brightly.

'You are acting as if, now that you have what you want, it is somehow my fault that the results do not please you.' She absently straightened the cap on her head, hiding a few more of the escaping curls. 'I did not seduce you into a marriage you did not wish. Nor did I injure you and leave you to your fate. I doubt I can prove to your satisfaction that things are just as I claim. But can you prove that I have done anything, other than to give you what you wanted from me, and care for you when it resulted in misfortune? You are alive today because of my treatment of you. I am sorry that I cannot offer more than that.'

To this, he had no answer. If she truly was his wife, she was a very patient woman. She had reason to snap at his harsh treatment of her. But there was no real anger in her voice, only a tired resignation as she accepted his doubt. If it weren't for the troublesome void where their past should have resided, he would have believed in an instant and apologised.

'I will admit that I owe you my gratitude,' he said. 'But for the moment, your help is not needed. Please, go and prepare for dinner. Perhaps I will see you at table. We can speak again later.'

'I will welcome it, my lord.'

She was lying, of course. She rose from the bed and offered an obedient curtsy, before leaving the room. But there was an eagerness in her step that made her simple exit seem almost like an escape.

Chapter Two

He did not remember her.

Justine de Bryun stopped just beyond William Felkirk's door and tried to contain the excitement and relief she felt at this convenient amnesia. She must channel that tangle of emotion into an appropriate response for a woman whose husband had awakened like Lazarus, before someone saw and questioned her. Felkirk had asked more than enough questions during the difficult conversation that had just occurred. She did not need more questioning from the duke and duchess. At least not until she could discover a way out of the mess she had created.

Penny was waiting for her, a little way down the hall, trying to pretend that she was not interested in a description of what had happened, when she and William had been alone together. She must try to come up with something that was not a total lie. Since coming here, she had lied too much to her hostess and felt guilty each time. What had Penny ever done to deserve such treatment? From the first, the duchess had offered the hand of friendship and the sympathy of a sister.

While Justine had reason enough to hate the Felkirk family, there was no reason her animosity need extend to a woman who had married into it. Nor did it feel right to hate the heir, who was nothing more than an innocent babe. The duke, who was the true head of the family, had been kindness himself as well and earned some measure of forgiveness.

That left only William Felkirk. His meddling in her affairs had earned him the whole share of any punishment for the family's past sins. His slow recovery had been more than sufficient to satisfy her desire for vengeance.

It had been too much, if she was honest. Her father had died a quick death. But William Felkirk had lingered on the brink for months, wasting away in endless sleep. On several occasions, she'd been surprised to find herself praying that God would be merciful and release him. When the prayers had gone unanswered, she had given him what Christian comfort she could.

Or she had until the moment he'd awoken and begun causing trouble again.

Penny was coming towards her now, hands outstretched, ready to celebrate or console, as was needed. Justine discovered she did not need to dissemble much, for her lip actually trembled in what was likely the beginning of tears. Once again, she was alone and helpless in a situation she had done little to cause and was not able to control. While the Duchess of Bellston did not appear to wish her ill, Justine had seen how quickly supposed friends became enemies when they knew one had nowhere to turn. She must be on her guard. 'He does not know me,' she said, softly, glancing back at the bedroom behind her. 'And he does not believe we are married.'

The duchess enfolded her in a motherly hug. 'There, there. It will be all right, I'm sure. Now that he is recovering, it will only be a matter of time before he recalls what you once were to each other.'

'Of course,' Justine answered, as though that was not another reason for tears. Felkirk's total absence of memory was the best news she'd had in ages. He had forgotten the worst of it and she might still escape punishment. One could not be complicit in an attack on a noble family and avoid the gallows. She had known her fate was sealed the day that she had found him on the salon floor in a pool of blood. Even if she had wished him ill, William Felkirk both recovered and amnesiac was a gift straight from God.

Of course, it also meant he could not recall the things she actually wished to know. And that was most vexing. Without that, why had she bothered to save him?

Penny patted her shoulder. 'As soon as he has recovered his strength, you can return to the old manor.

That is his house now and will be yours as well. We will be less than a mile away if you need us. Familiar surroundings will have the memories flooding back in no time.'

A flood of memory was the last thing she needed. Moving to Felkirk's own home would draw her even deeper into the ruse she had created. They would be alone, with no duke and duchess to help her deflect Lord Felkirk's endless questions. 'It will be quite different, being alone with him there,' she said, trying to keep the resignation from her voice.

'We will be just down the road,' Penny replied cheerfully. 'We can come for visits or for dinner, as soon as you are ready to receive us.'

They would come, and leave again, before bedtime. Justine would be left to manage the nights, alone with a strange man who would expect more than nursing from a beautiful woman who claimed to be his wife. What had he said to her, just now? *You are not going to pretend that you are unaware of the effect you have on men.*

Montague had said something similar, when he had informed her of what her future would be. Now, it would be happening all over again. When he was unconscious, William Felkirk had been as pale and beautiful as a statue. But awake she could see the virile strength that had been dormant. The blood was returning to his lips and the observant blue eyes turned on her already sparkled with interest. Soon there would be another, very male response to her presence in his bedroom. She could not help herself, she shivered.

Without a word, Penny slipped the shawl from her own shoulders and wrapped it around Justine. 'You are tired, of course. You have worked so hard to make him well again. And it has not turned out as you expected.'

'No, it has not,' Justine admitted. She had assumed, no matter what she did to prevent it, he would die. She would enter the sickroom some morning to find the patient stiff and cold. It had made her search all the harder for evidence of her father, or a sign that he had delivered the jewels he'd been carrying, when he'd died. If she could have got her hands on them, she might have disappeared before anyone discovered her lies.

Then, it had occurred to her that, if William Felkirk died, it might be easier just to stay as she was, allowing the duke and duchess to comfort her in her mourning. Montague would not dare tell his half of the truth, for fear that she would tell hers. In a year, when she'd cast off her black, there might be holidays, and summer, and a Season in London with balls and parties…

And where would that leave Margot? As usual, the thought doused all happiness like cold water. How unfair was it that any thought of her beloved little sister should be wrapped in negatives?

As they walked down the hall and towards the main stairs, Penny continued to chatter on, filling the tense silence with descriptions of a happy future that could never be. 'Above all, do not worry yourself over his behaviour today. I am sure he loves you. But the truth was quite a shock to him.' She hesitated, then added, 'The doctors said there might be changes in his character, because of the accident.'

'True,' Justine agreed. How could she tell? She knew nothing of his character, after only one brief meeting. When he had entered the shop, she had thought him handsome and pleasant enough. But his initial smile had faded, when he'd realised who, and what, she was.

Penny sensed her unease and added, 'He will remember you, in time, I am sure. You have nothing to worry about.'

'I am sure you are right.' The words were true, even if the smile that accompanied them was not. He would remember her. She must be long gone before that happened, even if it meant returning to the life with Montague that she had hoped to escape.

They were at the door of her bedroom now and she gave the duchess a light kiss on the cheek to prove that it was, indeed, all right. 'I think I should like to lie down before dinner.'

'Of course,' Penny replied. 'Now that your husband is better, you must take care of yourself. And you will want to look your best for him, should Will be able to come to down for his meal.'

Justine smiled and nodded, and prayed he would not. It would mean another inquisition, nearly on the heels of the last one. She needed time to plan and create answers for the questions he would ask. She wasted no time, once the door was closed. A moment's hesitation might cause her to doubt the wisdom of what she had done so far. And that doubt would lead to weakness, and eventual doom. Had not bitter experience taught her that only the strong survived?

She would be strong, even if it meant that she would not be happy. She went to the bedside candle and lit it, carrying it to the little table in front of the window, where she was sure it could be seen from a distance.

It was still burning when she left the room for dinner.

Chapter Three

Will was beginning to fear that Penny had been correct in her suggestion that he use a Bath chair. If he lacked the strength to walk across his own room, there was no way he could manage the stairs to the ground floor without help from the servants. If he had to stagger to get down them, it would take all his energy to avoid the indignity of being carried back upstairs after.

As if it was not enough to lose memory and strength, he seemed prone to nerves—he started at the least little thing. He'd lain in bed, straining to hear the conversation in the hall, as Penny assured the mysterious Justine that everything would be fine. As he'd done so, he was overcome with the fear that the family was plotting against him, with the stranger. Even the entrance of his valet, with clean linen and shaving gear, set his heart to pounding. He'd been so sure of himself, before. Perhaps the blow had addled his brain, and the confidence would never return.

He refused to believe it. He would not spend the rest of his life hiding in his room and starting at shadows. If he worked to make it so, his life might be as it once was.

But now, he had a wife.

He did not wish to think of her, either. After he'd composed himself, it was a comfort to see his valet, Stewart. It was good to be clean, shaved and dressed in something other than a nightshirt. But it embarrassed him that he'd had to be helped into a sitting position and moved about like a mannequin when his limbs would not stay steady enough to help with trousers and coat.

His man had made no comment on it, other than to examine his cheek and remark that her ladyship was nearly as good with a razor as he, and might have made an excellent valet, had God blessed her enough to make her male.

'She shaved me?' Why did it bother him to imagine that graceful hand holding the blade to his throat?

Stewart smiled. 'She did everything for you, my lord. She was so attentive that all breathed a sigh of relief when she was not in the room. We feared she would exhaust herself with the effort.'

The man had said *all* as though he referred to both servants and family. It seemed that everyone in the house was taken with the love and dedication that the mysterious Justine had brought to her nursing. 'What else do the servants say of my new wife?' If there was any below-stairs gossip, Stewart would know of it. Hopefully, he owed enough loyalty to his master to give an honest opinion.

The man broke out in a grin. 'She is quite the finest woman in Wales, my lord. Gentle and kind, with a way about her that makes all in the household easy about the change. She has not spent much time with us, as yet. Your brother deemed it easier to keep you here than in your own home.' Will smiled to himself. For the first time in the discussion, there was the slightest hint of disapproval, and it was because a duke had the gall to overrule his servants in doing what was best for him.

Stewart was smiling again. 'We shall soon have you back with us, now that you are better, and all will be right again. And we shall have her ladyship as well.' The smile grew even broader, as though this addition was not so much a bother as the candied violet on top of a sweet.

Very well, then. All of Wales adored his wife. Logic dictated that he should as well. Had it not been pleasant to see her face, to hear her voice and to feel her gentle touch as he awoke? If he was still whole in body, he should have found it arousing to think that this lovely creature was familiar with the most intimate features of his anatomy. Those soft white hands had touched him as a lover, even as he'd lain helpless.

'Be careful, my lord.' His shudder at the thought had brought a caution from Stewart, whose scissors hovered near to Will's ear as the hair around it was trimmed.

Will took a deep breath and steadied himself. 'That is my intention, Stewart. From now on, I will be very careful, indeed.'

Despite the difficulties involved, Will took supper in the dining room with the family. Though his legs were still too watery to hold him, he could not stand the thought of a meal on a bed tray. Nor could he repress the nagging suspicion that if he was absent, he would be the main topic of conversation. On his way to the ground floor, he held tight to the stair rail and managed to ward off the sudden vertigo as he walked. A footman supported his other arm. While crossing the hall, he'd tried and rejected a walking stick, for his arms were not strong enough to hold it. By God, he would practise in his room, all day if necessary. He would be himself again.

Once he was seated at the dinner table, he felt almost normal. He'd practised sitting up in a chair until he was sure he was steady. And while he might not have an appetite for all the courses, he was still damned hungry. According to Stewart, they'd been giving him nothing but gruel from a pap cup for weeks. The very act of holding knife and fork was enough to raise his spirits, though the use of them was problematic.

It was after dropping yet another bite of fish, as he tried to guide it to his mouth, that he realised the hush that had fallen over the table. They were all watching him intently, as he ate.

He threw his fork aside. 'It is not any easier, when one is being stared at, you know.'

'Perhaps, if I were to cut your…' The woman, Justine, was leaning towards his plate, ready to slice his food as though he were too young to manage it himself.

'Certainly not,' he barked at her. In response, there was a nervous shifting of the other diners and his brother cleared his throat, as though to remind Will of his manners.

'I am sorry,' he grumbled. He was annoyed with her offer and even more so with himself for behaving like a lout. 'It is difficult.'

'Soon it will be easier,' she promised and signalled a footman, whispering a request.

With that, another course appeared, just for him. A ragout of beef had been poured into a tankard and there was a soft bit of bread as well. It was peasant fare and his table manners were a match for it. His hands shook as he brought the mug to his mouth and he wiped away any spillage with the bread. It embarrassed him to be so careless. But the others at table seemed so happy that he could eat at all, they ignored the manner of it and conversation returned to normal.

He could feel his strength returning with each bite. By the time he had finished, his hands had stopped shaking and he felt warm and comfortably full inside. Though it annoyed him to have to do so, he gave Justine a brief nod of thanks.

In response, she gave a modest incline of her head as if saying it was her honour to serve him. He might not know what to make of her sudden appearance in his life, but she seemed to feel no such confusion. Though she barely looked at him over dinner, she was ever aware of his needs and quick to see them tended to. The moment she'd realised his problem, she had moved to help him, while allowing him some small amount of dignity.

Would it be so bad to find that he had married a beauty willing to devote her life to his health and happiness? Tonight, she was wearing a dinner gown of moss-green silk. It might have seemed dull on another woman, but it brought out the colour of her eyes. The cut was lower than her day dress had been, but still quite modest. While it revealed a graceful neck and smooth shoulders, the hint of bosom visible made a man wonder all the more about the rest of her. And on her head was the same starched cap from the afternoon, hiding most of her curled hair.

It was hardly fair that he could not remember knowing her before she'd put on the modest trappings of marriage and covered her head. His brother's wife rarely bothered with such things. But that was less from a desire to display her white-blonde hair and more from a total uninterest in fashion.

In Justine's case, such attire felt less like modesty and more like a desire to hide something that he most wanted to see. It was the same for her pretty eyes that were cast down at her food instead of looking at him, and her beautiful voice, which did not speak unless spoken to. She was like a closed book, careful not to reveal too much. She stayed so quiet and still until the dessert was cleared away. Then she offered a curtsy and retired to the sitting room with Penny, leaving the men alone with their port.

'Can you manage the glass?' Adam asked, pouring for them both, 'or will it be too difficult?'

'For your cellars, I will make the effort,' Will said, wanting nothing more than a stiff drink to relieve the tension.

'See that you do not snap my head off, if you fail,' his brother added with a smile. 'Your wife may not mind it, but if I have any more trouble out of you I will call for the governess to put you to bed like your infant nephew.'

'Sorry,' Will said, still not feeling particularly apologetic. 'I have the devil of a megrim.' He frowned. 'But do not call for laudanum. If, as you say, I have been asleep for months, I do not relish the thought of drugged slumber tonight.'

'If?' Adam looked at him with arched eyebrows and took a sip of his drink. 'Tell me, William. You have known me all your life. In that time, have I ever lied to you?'

'Of course not,' he said, staring down into his drink and feeling foolish for sounding so sceptical. Then he added, 'But I have known you, on occasion, to believe the lies of others.'

Adam nodded. 'Who do you think is lying to me now? And how could they have managed, against such clear-cut evidence? I have watched you insensible in that bed upstairs for nearly two months. There was no question about the severity of your injury, or your nearness to death.'

'But you were not there at the time of the accident,' he prodded.

'No,' Adam agreed, 'I was not.'

'And you believe the story told by this Justine de Bryun?'

'Yes, I believe her story,' Adam replied. 'But her name is Lady Justine Felkirk. Because she is your wife.'

'How do you know that?' Will slammed his fist down on the table in frustration, making the crystal glasses shudder. I know that you were not at the wedding. 'Have you seen the licence?'

Adam did not hesitate. 'You married in Gretna, just as I did. No licence was necessary.'

'Then why do you believe her?' Will pressed him. 'What evidence do you have, other than the word of this stranger? How do you know that she is not responsible for the state I am in?'

His brother responded with a quelling look and said, 'Because I can find no reason to explain why she would injure you, then arrive at my home, exhausted from days spent in a coach, cradling your broken head in her lap, so that she might nurse you back to health.'

'Perhaps she is not at fault,' Will admitted, feeling even more foolish. 'But that does not mean I married her. If I experienced a grand passion that moved me to act so rashly as to wed, I would hope to feel some residue of it.'

'Residue?' Adam was smiling now. 'You speak of love as if it were a noxious mould.'

'Is it natural that I should forget a woman who looks like that?' Even his happily married brother must have noticed that Justine de Bryun was a beauty worthy of memory. 'Is it normal that I feel nothing, when I look at her?'

'Nothing?' his brother said in surprise.

Will shrugged. That last had not been precisely true. There was not a man alive who could look at his alleged wife and feel nothing. But surely he should not feel such a strange mix of suspicion and desire.

'Nothing about these last few months have been natural,' his brother said as though that explanation would be any comfort. 'But I can tell you that the one thing we have all grown to count on, since you were returned to us in such an unfortunate condition, was the love of your Justine. She never wavered in her loyalty to you, no matter how unlikely recovery seemed.'

'I do not fault her for her devotion,' Will said. 'But a compassionate stranger might have done the same for me.'

'She is more than that to you, I am sure,' Adam said. 'Once we knew her, I could not help but love her, as I am sure you did. She is not simply devoted and beautiful, she is talented as well. Good company, well mannered, the very opposite of the sort of empty-headed chits that sought you out in London.'

'It is all well and good that you love her,' Will reminded him. 'But you have a wife of your own.'

'Do not be an idiot,' Adam said with a snort. 'Penny loves her as well. They are practically sisters. In two months she has become like a member of our family.'

'That does not explain why I married her,' Will announced. 'Nor does it explain why you were willing to take her into the house with such a sham story as the one she brought. Sudden elopements? Riding accidents? That does not sound at all plausible. Have you ever known me to make major decisions on a whim? Do I drink to excess, bet foolishly, race my horses, or take up with strange women?'

'You are the most sensible of men,' Adam agreed. 'Almost too sensible to be a younger brother. It is I who should be lecturing you. I remember the way you scolded me, when I brought Penny to London…'

'Let us not speak of it,' Will said, holding up a hand. 'I was wrong. But as you say, I am almost too cautious. That is why I doubt the events as they have been presented to me. It is totally out of character for me to behave in such a way as Justine de Bryun ascribes to me. And you have only her word for the truth of it.'

Adam frowned and then admitted, 'We did doubt, at first. But once we knew her, all doubts were gone.'

'For what reason?' Will said, frustrated almost to anger.

'Because once we had spoken to her, it was clear she was exactly the sort of woman you'd have chosen for yourself. She is level-headed, wise, calm in adversity and has a quick wit. Her tastes and opinions, her sense of humour, and the hours she keeps? All are a perfect match to yours.' Adam shook his head in amazement. 'She is obviously your soul's mate, Will. How could you have married anyone else?'

'You cannot be serious,' he said. He thought back to his interactions with the girl, who would barely look him in the eye, much less speak aloud, and wondered if that was truly what others saw in him.

Adam smiled. 'I know it is difficult, at the moment, But you must have seen these qualities yourself, when you met her. It was clearly a matter of like attracting like. Trust me, Will. More accurately, the two of you are like iron and a lodestone. She has been nearly inseparable from you since the first moment she arrived. She allows herself a brief walk each morning, but other than that, she was never far from your side.'

'Except at night,' Will added. The thought of such constant scrutiny felt almost oppressive.

'Most nights, she slept on a cot in your dressing room,' Adam said. 'She wanted to be near if you awakened. There was no part of your care too lowly that she would not at least attempt it.'

There was that thrill of fear again, that he had felt as he'd thought of her holding a razor. She was certainly as lovely as Delilah. Could she not be as dangerous as well?

But it seemed that Adam had no such worries. 'She has worked, from the first, as though she already possessed your love and admiration. I am sure you will find it again, once you are fully recovered. In the mean time, if you cannot trust your own heart, trust your family. All will be well. Now finish your drink and let me help you to your room. No doubt you will feel differently in the morning.'

And when had he ever trusted his heart when making such a momentous decision? As Adam shepherded him up the stairs, there was no point in telling him the futility of that advice. The heart was a capricious organ, likely to say the opposite of his poor dented skull. As his valet helped him prepare for bed, he still felt headachy and weak, and utterly confused. He did not dare tell Stewart, or even his brother, that, now that it was dark, he dreaded returning to the bed he had lain in for so long. Suppose he closed his eyes and opened them to discover that he had lost another half a year?

Surely that would not happen. He had improved since the afternoon. While the pain and confusion remained, the blank slate of his memory had begun to fill again, even if the scrawls he imagined on it were written in someone else's hand. Now, he must sleep, even though he did not feel tired. In the morning, he would walk, though he had no real desire to move. Little by little he would fight off the stupor and force body and mind to function at his command.

Stewart departed and there was the softest of

knocks on the door. Without waiting for his answer, Justine entered, silent as a ghost in her plain linen nightdress.

And here was another appetite that had nothing to do with the condition of heart or mind. When he looked at Justine, desire did not need memory, just the evidence of his eyes. Her body would be soft and warm under the fall of thin white cloth and she would press it to his, should he demand it of her. They could dispense with the gown entirely and the ridiculous nightcap she wore with it. And for a time, he would forget any fears of past or future and revel in a glorious present. Perhaps a repeat of what they had already done would jar some knowledge in him.

Or would it be as feared? Even after a night together, she might be as much an enigma as she was now? There was something disquieting in those deep-green eyes and that placid smile. It was like a beautiful mask that could come off at midnight and reveal something totally unexpected.

The thought of bedding her had him as nervous as a bridegroom. If the stories were true, he had been that once already. On that night, his body would have performed as he commanded it to. If he was too weak to walk unaided, how was he to manage with a woman in his bed? Would she measure him against previous experience?

Perhaps she had fears as well. She looked rather like a virgin sacrifice in the undecorated white gown with her hair, a touchable river of gold, flowing down her back in a loose braid. In the firelight, she seemed younger than he'd thought, no more than two and twenty.

It made him feel strangely guilty to have suspected her of anything. She looked too innocent to be harbouring some dark secret. There was nothing in her demeanour that said she looked forward to a physical reunion with him. Now that they were alone again, the shyness he had seen at dinner was all the more noticeable.

Then, suspicion returned. If she was truly his wife, should she not be more excited to find him awake and alive, and to renew the physical relationship between them? Perhaps he had married her and discovered the ardour he felt was not returned. She had called him good, and kind, before. But she had not spoken of desire, or hung about his neck showering him with relieved kisses. The smile she gave him now was pleasant, but cool.

The one he returned to her was tight and unwillingly given. 'What are you doing here?' he said, not bothering to hide his doubts.

'I thought, now that you were awake…'

Did she think that she would climb into bed with him and make everything better? That they would rut busily for a time, for no other reason than to prove that his lack of past did not affect either of them? Were men really so easily manipulated as that?

She walked past him and sat on the opposite edge of his bed, perched like a perfectly formed wooden doll on the very edge of a shelf. If he touched her, she would fall on to her back with that same distant look in her eyes, spread her legs and let him do as he wished with her.

The thought made him feel strangely sick. A little awkwardness after all this time would not be unusual. If the couple were in love, it might be laughed away after a whispered conversation on the need for patience and the assurance that nothing mattered more than their time together.

But he could not imagine having such a talk with her. When he looked at Justine, he felt nothing but a vague, unsettling desire. He wanted to see what lay under that prim gown she was wearing as much as he'd wanted to see under the cap and touch her hair. Most of all, he wanted to come inside her, feeling the past return in a rush, turning the past day into nothing more than a horrible dream.

But what did she want? She was gazing at him with a look of placid acceptance that was not encouraging. Perhaps proper women did not take pleasure in the marital bed. If they did not, then what real joy could there be to lie with her? He envied Adam and Penny, so obviously two sides of the same coin. Perhaps that was not what was meant to be for him. Adam had said he and this woman were alike. If she was cold and apathetic, what did that make him?

He had gone too long, staring at her without answer. So she started again. 'While you were ill, I never slept far from your room. I have a cot, in the dressing room. In case you cried out in your sleep, I wanted to be nearby.'

'That will no longer be necessary,' he said. It was probably meant to be a comfort, but he wanted nothing more than to be alone, to puzzle out what had happened to him.

She bit her lip. 'I wish to remain close, should you need me. But as my husband, it is up to you to decide where you wish me to be.' She glanced significantly at the bed beside her. It was the only moment of spirit in her too-perfect subservience.

It made him want to bed her even less. He remained blank for a moment more. Then he gave a laugh of mock surprise. 'I am sorry to inform you of this, my dear, but it does not matter to me in the least where you wish to sleep tonight. I am far too tired to manage anything so strenuous as a loving reunion.'

As he had feared, she looked more relieved than disappointed by his refusal. She stood up mechanically and turned first towards the hall, then towards the door that led to a connecting bedroom. 'Then I will return to my room and leave you to your rest. If you need anything in the night…'

'I shall ring for a servant,' he said firmly. 'You do not need to trouble yourself any further, or sleep at the foot of my bed like a hound. If I need you specifically, I shall walk across the room and knock upon your door.'

A certain type of woman might have snapped at his rudeness, or burst into a torrent of foolish tears.

This one gave him an impassive nod and answered as a servant would, 'Very good, my lord.'

A nagging voice at the back of his head demanded that he stop being foolish. Even if they were not two halves of one heart, it gave him no reason to treat her like a footman. 'I will see you in the morning,' he said, trying to use a kinder tone. 'In the breakfast room.'

'Of course.' And once he saw her there, would she eat when he told her, drink when he told her and in all other ways behave like an automaton? If so, it did not matter what Adam thought. Justine was the exact opposite of the wife he would have wanted. There was no spirit in her at all, no challenge. There was nothing in her to learn, no exciting discoveries to make. The woman leaving his room was perfectly beautiful, totally obedient and dull.

Then he was rewarded with a fleeting memory of the past. He had been watching Adam at the christening, who was full of pride over his son and his duchess. The boy had been crying and his mother near to panic at her inability to maintain order. But Adam could not have looked happier. The room had seemed almost too full of life. For the first time in his life, Will had found something to envy. He had wanted a wife. And he had, indeed, resolved to marry within the year.

The fact that he could not remember bringing it about was a moot point. The thought had been in his mind when he left the house. He was going south. There were any number of fashionable women who would welcome his offer, now that he had decided to make it. He would choose one of them, after…

After what? There had been something else he'd meant to do. Only afterwards had he intended to marry. He must have achieved his goal, whatever it was. He had carried out the second part of his plan and found a wife.

Now, he would have to make the best of his choice. He leaned over to blow out the candle settling back into a bed that was familiar, but strangely empty.

Chapter Four

In the weeks she'd spent at Bellston Manor, Justine had come up with a dozen excuses for her early morning walks. She enjoyed regular exercise. She had a love of the outdoors. She wished to become familiar with the area that would be her home, after the unlikely recovery of William Felkirk. She had caught Penny and the duke discussing her regular exercise with approval. They had been nodding sagely to each other about the need for poor Justine to escape the sickroom, even for a short period of time.

It pained her that they were so willing to accept what was nothing more than another lie. There was only one reason that truly mattered. In a regular series of lonely rambles, it was easy to disguise the few times she did not walk alone.

It took nearly ten minutes to cross the manicured park around the great house. Beyond that, the path wound into the trees and she was hidden from view.

Most mornings, the concealment gave her the chance to let down her guard and be truly herself. That brief time amongst the oaks was all hers and it was a novelty. How many years had it been since she had called her life her own, even for a moment?

But this was not most mornings. Today, the privacy meant nothing more than a change of façades. She was barely concealed before she heard the step behind her. Even though she had been expecting it, she started at the sudden appearance of John Montague.

That he invariably startled her was a source of annoyance. He made no effort to blend with the wood or the countryside. He wore the same immaculately tailored black coats and snowy white breeches he favoured in town. The patterned silk of his waistcoats stood out like a tropical bird lost amongst the trees. His heavy cologne was devoid of woodsy notes. His body and face were sharp and angular, his complexion florid to match his wiry red hair.

The only subtlety he possessed was his ability to move without a sound. Whether walking through the leaves, or over the hard marble of the jewellery shop they ran in Bath, she never heard the click of a heel or the shuffle of a foot to mark his approach. Like a cat, he was suddenly there, at one's side, and then he would be gone. After each meeting she spent hours, starting at nothing and glancing nervously over her shoulder, convinced that he might be nearby, listening, watching, waiting to pounce.

As usual, he laughed at her fear as though it gave him pleasure. Then he pulled her forward, into his arms to remind her that it was not William Felkirk to whom she belonged. She permitted his kiss, as she always did, remaining placid. If one could not summon a response other than revulsion, it was best to show no emotion at all. When she could stand no more of it, she pulled away, pretending that it was the urgent need to share information that made her resist his advances.

He cocked his head to the side as though trying to decide whether it was worth punishing her for her impudence. Then he spoke. 'I saw the light in your window. You have news?'

'Felkirk is awake.'

Montague gave a sharp intake of breath and she hurried to add, 'But he remembers nothing.'

'Nothing?' He smiled at this miraculous turn of events.

'Not a thing from the last six months,' she assured him. 'He does not remember his investigations. He does not remember you.' *Nor me*, she added to herself. 'Most importantly, he does not remember the injury. I told him it was a riding accident.'

'Did he believe you?' Montague said, with no real optimism.

'I do not know.'

'What will happen if circumstances change?'

'It will be a disaster,' she said. 'I must be gone before then.' Her plan to escape Montague was an utter failure, if she must run back to him now. But better to return to the devil she knew than to experience what might happen should Lord Felkirk remember the truth.

'What of the diamonds?' Montague asked. 'You have been in the house for weeks. Am I to believe you found nothing?'

'Not a thing,' she admitted.

'Did you examine the Duchess's jewel case?'

Justine sighed. 'Have I not told you so already? I feigned feminine curiosity and she showed me all. There are no stones in any of the pieces that match the ones my father was carrying.'

'They must be hidden elsewhere.' Montague insisted. 'When he came to Bath, Felkirk was sure he'd found the hiding place.'

'Then the information is locked in his brain along with the reason for his condition.' Justine resisted the urge to tug upon his arm, to lead him further from the house. He seemed to think even the most innocent contact between them gave him permission to take further liberties. 'You must get me away from here,' she said.

Montague grunted in disgust. 'But we will not have the diamonds. Without them, we have gained nothing from this little game you suggested. You might just as well have let me finish him, while we were still in Bath.'

'Suppose he had told someone of his plans?' She took the risk of stroking his arm to distract him.

'Isn't it better to know that there is no trail leading back to you?'

'You discovered that almost immediately,' he retorted. 'If there were no diamonds to find, then you should have done as I suggested and smothered him while he slept.'

'You know I could not,' she said, as calmly as possible. To hear him speak so casually of cold-blooded murder made her tremble. Even knowing that her life might be at stake, she could not bring herself to do such a thing.

'I fail to see what stops you,' Montague replied. 'His family was responsible for the death of your father, who was my closest friend.' He beat his breast once to emphasise the connection. 'He was murdered on their property, delivering stones for a necklace that the duchess did not give two figs for. They did not keep their land safe for travellers. They did not offer a guard to escort him to the house. And once the crime had occurred they made no effort to catch the killer. Even worse, they may have been complicit. If Felkirk is right and the stones are still on the property, what are we to believe?'

'I doubt that is the case,' she said. It made no sense. What reason would a duke have to rob a jewel merchant, when they could easily afford to pay for the stones?

'Perhaps not,' Montague allowed. 'But some justice is owed, after all this time.'

'True,' she said, cautiously. 'But it was very dangerous to take that justice into your own hands by attacking the brother of the duke.' Had her father known there was this strain of madness in his partner, when he'd made him guardian to a pair of helpless orphans? It did not matter, for there was little she could do about it until Margot was of age. 'Since he survived the attack and cannot remember what occurred, you will be safe from prosecution.'

'All well and good,' he said. 'But when you suggested this ruse, you promised you would find the diamonds Felkirk was searching for and bring them to me.'

It had surprised her that he would believe such a thing. If she had uncovered the stones her father had lost, her plan had been to sell them and escape with her sister to a place where neither Montague nor Felkirk could find her. 'As I've told you before, I can find no evidence of them. The plan is a failure. You must help me quit this house, before it is too late and Lord Felkirk remembers who I am.' Then she sighed and offered herself as an incentive. 'We might take a room at an inn on the road back to Bath.'

'Do you miss me?' he asked, with a smile that made her shiver. 'How flattering. Do not worry. You will return to my bed soon enough, and it will be just as it was before Felkirk sought us out. But I think, for a time, you had best remain where you are. His memory might return. Perhaps you can coax forth the information we need and we will still succeed.'

'It will require me to convince him that I am his

wife,' she said. 'You know what he will expect from me.' She held her breath, praying that Montague's possessiveness would finally do her some good.

He grabbed her by the arm and she thought he meant to punish her for even suggesting such a thing. But then he kissed her, forcing his tongue into her open mouth, thrusting hard, as though the idea of her laying with another excited him. Or perhaps he meant to frighten her into submission.

That would have been pointless. She had learned, at times like this, to feel nothing at all. She had but to wait and it would be over, soon enough.

Eventually, he pulled away and whispered, 'You must use your talents on him, my dear. I swear you are woman enough to give speech to a dead man. How hard will it be for you to turn Felkirk inside out and extract what you need from him?'

'But suppose I cannot?' she said. 'Suppose he remembers seeing me with you. In Bath, I am sure he guessed I was your mistress. I could see it in his eyes. Do not make me do this, for it is sure to fail.'

'You had best see that it does not,' he said. 'For your own sake and your sister's.'

'Do not mention Margot again,' she said, yanking her arm free from his grasp as the fear he wanted to see flooded back into her.

'I will speak of her, or to her, whenever I wish.' He knew her weakness and exploited it, relishing her reaction. 'Until she is of age, Margot is still my ward.' Then he took her hand back, more gently this time, running his fingers along the skin in a way he must think would excite her. 'Without you, my life is so very lonely, Justine. Perhaps I should bring Margot home from school. She could take your place, working in the shop. She could keep me company, until you return.' He raised her hand to his lips, running the tip of his tongue along the knuckles. 'I swear, she is very nearly as lovely as you.'

Her mind went blank again, blocking out the feeling of his lips touching her skin. 'It will not be necessary to summon Margot,' she said, in a calm, agreeable voice. 'I will do exactly as you say. I will discover what it is that Felkirk found. Then, I will return to you and things will be just as they were.'

'See that you do,' he said, looking up into her eyes. 'You are to do whatever is necessary to gain the knowledge we want. I will have those stones, Justine. And then I will have you back.'

Whatever was necessary. She would lie to William Felkirk and lie with him as well. Perhaps there would still be a way to find the diamonds and get away. But until then, she would lose a little bit of herself, just as she did each time with Montague. How much was left to lose, when one already felt empty? 'Of course,' she agreed, listening to the sound of her own voice as if it came from a great distance. She thought of Margot and the need for her to stay safe at school, and innocent, for just one more year. 'I will do whatever is necessary.'

Then she let Montague kiss her again, making her

mind a blank as the kiss grew more passionate. But now he was pulling her away from the path, deeper into the woods so that they could be alone. There was no time for it.

She pushed him away and straightened her dress. 'They expect me back at the house. It was only to be a short walk. I will be missed if I tarry. And if Felkirk comes down to breakfast, he will want to see me there.' Then she kissed Montague once, gently on the mouth, hoping that he would believe she was not simply avoiding him.

'Of course,' he agreed, smoothing her hair and straightening her bonnet for another excuse to touch her. 'Go back to the house. Do not arouse suspicion. But do not take too long about it. Remember, Margot is coming home for Christmas. If you cannot be with us, I will send your love…'

She turned and hurried back to the house, surprised, as she always was, at the way that her guardian could turn a simple, parting phrase into a threat.

Chapter Five

Will slept uneasily, waking often and with a start, as though proving to himself that it was truly possible to open his eyes again. But by morning, the ache in his head had diminished. He was able to take a few shaky steps around the room before calling for the crutches that the servants had found, to help him.

In the breakfast room, he found other servants, already clearing away a plate that still held a half-eaten slice of toast slathered with the marmalade from Tim Colton's orangery. It was his particular favourite. The pot on the table was half-empty.

His brother barely looked up from his coffee. 'If you are looking for your wife, she is up and out of the house already. She favours a morning walk, much as you do when you are in the country.'

'Oh.' He stared out the window at the fading green of the park and the coloured leaves swirling in the breeze. 'That particular habit will be quite beyond me for a time.'

Adam nodded, then smiled. 'You have no idea how good it is to see you on your feet again, even if you are a trifle unsteady.'

'Probably not,' Will agreed. 'For me, it is as if no time has passed at all.'

'It is a blessing, then,' Adam said. 'You do not remember the pain.'

'That is not all I have lost,' Will reminded him, glancing at the marmalade pot.

'And as I told you, there is nothing to fear. Unlike my own darling Penelope, Justine is the most patient of women. She will not be hurt by your forgetfulness.'

'I had not thought of that,' Will said. If he had married her, then the hardship was not all on one side.

Adam looked even more surprised. 'How inconsiderate of you. While you were the one who was injured, there were others who bore the brunt of the pain and worry. And over something so uncharacteristically foolish as a fall from a horse.'

'Exactly,' Will said. 'What would have caused me to do such a thing?'

'Showing off for Justine, I expect,' Adam said, moderating his voice to sound less like a scold. 'All men are idiots, when they are in love.'

On this, Will agreed. 'That is why I have always avoided being so.'

'Until now,' Adam finished.

'And that is one more thing I do not understand,' Will said, feeling more desperate than he had before. 'You claim she is just like me. Perhaps it is true.

But why did I not take the time to bring her home to meet you, and to marry properly, in a church? If she is so like me, why did she not insist on it? It is not reasonable.'

His brother laughed. 'You cannot think of a single reason to marry such a woman in haste? You poor fellow.'

'She is pretty, of course,' he allowed.

'Was your vision affected?' Adam asked, drily. 'She is a damn sight more than just pretty.'

'A beauty, then,' Will admitted reluctantly. 'But the world is full of those and I have resisted them all.'

'Until now,' his brother replied.

'But I have no clue as to what caused this magical change in me? And what took me to Bath?'

Adam frowned. 'It will come back to you in time, I'm sure. If not, you can ask Justine.' Adam gave him a searching look. 'You have spoken to her, haven't you?'

'Briefly,' Will admitted.

'Which means that you have exchanged fewer words with her than you have with me.'

William shook his head. 'I would rather hear your version of events first.'

'You will find her story is much the same as mine,' Adam said. 'While you cannot remember her, there is no reason to assume that she will not be forthcoming if you ask these questions of her.'

Will paused, unsure of how to explain himself. Then he said, 'It is not just that I have forgotten our marriage. I have the strangest feeling that she is not to be trusted.'

Adam stifled an oath before mastering his patience. 'The physicians told us that you might be prone to dark moods, if you recovered at all. Do not let yourself be ruled by them.'

'Suppose I cannot prevent it?' he said in return. 'You claim I will love her as I once did, given time. Suppose I do not?'

'Then I would assume that you are not fully recovered from your injury and tell you that even more time was required.' Adam seemed to think it was much less complicated than it seemed to him.

'Then you must ready your advice,' Will replied. 'For when I look at her, I do not love her, nor can I imagine a time when I did.'

Adam sighed. 'You always did lack imagination.'

'Perhaps that is true. But I do not wish to develop it, simply to create a likely scenario for my previous marriage. If I cannot remember her, would an annulment not be a possibility? Surely a mental deficiency on my part…'

Adam's eyes narrowed. 'There is no sign that you were mentally defective when you met her. The accident happened afterwards. A declaration of mental deficiency on your part would cause other problems as well. Do you wish me to take on the management of your money and land, since you are clearly unable to make decisions for yourself? Will you seek to marry again? How will we guarantee to the next woman that she will not meet a similar fate? Unless you want to be declared my ward for the rest of your life and treated as though you cannot manage your own affairs, you had best own what wits you have.'

Will had no answer to this.

'Far better that you should meet your wife as if she were a stranger and grow to feel for her again. I suspect the answer to it all is quite unexceptional. Standing up at the christening put you in mind to marry. You went to Bath, where you knew many young ladies were to be found, chose the most likely candidate and made your offer. Since you were so adamantly opposed to my own sudden marriage, when it happened, you would not have entered into a similar union had the bond between you not been strong.'

It sounded right. But Will still could not manage to believe it. 'What if I was driven by some other reason?'

'Then I would tell you, if you cannot love her, there is nothing about her that is unlikeable. She is beautiful, talented and quite devoted to you. Many marriages are built on less. You could do worse than to keep her.' Adam was using the matter-of-fact tone he used when settling disputes amongst the tenants. It was the sort of voice that said there would be no further discussion.

So the decision was already made. He was married. His brother did not seem to care if he wanted to be. Nor could Will explain the nagging feeling, at the back of his mind, that something was very wrong with this. 'How am I to go about growing this feeling? What advice do you have, oh, wise Bellston?'

Adam gave a confident smile. 'I would advise that you find your wife immediately, and spend the day with her. Then you must remove yourself from my household as soon as you are able.'

'You are turning me out?' Will said with surprise. 'I am barely recovered.'

'Your own home is less than a mile from here,' Adam said with a calming gesture. 'The doctor is even closer to that place than he is to here. It is not that you are not welcome to visit. But the sooner you stop making excuses and isolate yourself with Justine, the sooner you will come to love her again. The pair of you must stop using the rest of us to avoid intimacy.'

'You expect me to bed a complete stranger, hoping that I will rise in the morning with my love renewed?'

He could see by the narrowing of his brother's eyes that Adam was nearly out of patience. 'Perhaps the bump on the head has truly knocked all sense out of you. You talk as if it were a hardship to lie with a beautiful woman. But I meant nothing so vulgar. You must be alone with her. Talk. Share a quiet evening or two and discover what it was that drew you to her in the first place. I predict, before the week is out, you will be announcing your complete devotion to her.'

'Very well, then. Today I will discuss the matter with her. Tomorrow, I will take her home, and make some effort to treat her as if she were a wife by my choice. But I predict we will be having the same conversation in a week's time. Then I will expect you to offer something more substantive than empty platitudes about love.'

So he finished his breakfast and, with his brother's words in mind, sought out Justine. But she seemed no more eager to talk to him than he was to talk to her. The servants informed him that, directly after her walk, she'd gone out with the duchess to call on the sick and needy of the village.

Penny returned without her. It seemed she had been invited to luncheon with the vicar, to celebrate the miraculous recovery of her invalid husband. That they had neglected to invite Will to the event was an oversight on their part.

By afternoon, she had returned to the house, though Will could not manage to find her. When he went to visit his nephew in the nursery, he was told that the boy was just down for a nap. Her ladyship had sung him to sleep. The nurse assured him his wife had the voice of an angel and was naturally good with children. Apparently he had chosen the perfect mother for his future brood, should he find it in his heart to make them with her.

It was hard to accuse her of dark motives when she seemed to fill her day with virtues. It explained why his family was so taken with her. But to Will, it seemed almost as if she was deliberately avoiding him. Wherever he went in the house, her ladyship had just been and gone, after doing some kindness or proving her own excellent manners.

In the end, he did not see her until supper, after they had both dressed for it on opposite sides of the connecting door. Adam was entertaining the Coltons, claiming it as a small celebration welcoming him back to health. More likely, it was an attempt to put Will on his best behaviour. Tim and Daphne were old family friends. But that did not give him the right to bark and snap at them, as he had been doing with his own family.

At least this evening he was able to manage food and drink without subtle aid from his new wife. Though he was fatigued, a single day out of bed and a few hearty meals had worked wonders on his depleted body.

As the conversation droned on about Tim's latest experiments in his greenhouse, Will lifted his glass and looked through it, across the table at the woman he supposedly loved. Today, her gown was white muslin shot through with gold threads, her warm gold hair falling in inviting spirals from another dull white cap. But for that, she'd have looked like one of the more risqué angels in a Botticelli painting, pure but somehow a little too worldly.

She noticed his gaze and coloured sweetly, keeping her own eyes firmly focused on the food in front of her. Perhaps it was simply that he felt better today. Perhaps it was the wine. Or maybe leaving the confines of his room changed his mood. But he wondered what it was that had made him distrust her, when there was nothing exceptional in her behaviour.

She seemed shy of him, of course. But could she be blamed for it? Since the first moment he'd opened his eyes, she had shown him nothing but kindness and patience. He had responded with suspicion and hostility. Even a real angel would grow tired of such treatment and draw away.

Almost as an experiment, he looked directly at her, long past the point where she could ignore him. Slowly her face rose, to return a nervous smile, head tilted just enough to express enquiry. Then he smiled at her and gave the slightest nod of approval.

She held his gaze for only a moment, before casting her eyes down again. But there was a flicker of a smile in response and tension he had not noticed disappeared from her back and shoulders. If possible, she became even prettier. She was more alluring, certainly. She had seemed almost too prim and virginal, perching on the edge of her chair.

But as she relaxed, her body looked touchable, as though she was aware of the pleasures it offered. If he had been married to her for even one night, he knew them himself. He would not have been able to resist. But it was an odd contrast to the woman she had been last night. As she'd sat on his bed, near enough to touch and waiting for intimacy, she'd been as stiff as a waxwork and just as cold.

After the meal, he'd been hoping for a relaxing glass of port with Adam and Sam as the ladies retired. But they took that hurriedly, wanting to join the women in the parlour and using the comfort of the chairs, and his semi-invalid status, as an excuse. At first, he thought it a trick to throw him back into the presence of his wife and force some memory from him. But it seemed that, as their bachelor days receded into the past, his brother and friend had grown used to spending their evenings in the company of their wives. They were less willing to forgo it, even after his miraculous recovery. Now that he was married, they expected him to behave the same.

Married.

It always came back to that. Once again, his feelings were in a muddle. Perhaps he was still avoiding her. He should be able to engage Justine in easy conversation as Adam and Sam did with their wives. But he could not think of a word to say to her, other than the thought that was always foremost in his mind: *Who are you?*

No one else wondered. They all seemed to know her well. She was settled into what was probably her usual chair beside a screened candle, chatting amiably as though she belonged here. She reached into a basket at its side to take up her needlework: a complex arrangement of threads and pins on a satin pillow. The other women smiled at her, admired her work and discussed children and households.

Adam and Sam seemed to be in the middle of a political conversation that he'd had no part in. How long would it take him, just to be aware of the news of the day? Probably less time than to discover the details of his own life. He could read *The Times* for a day or two and find everything he needed. But no matter how he prodded at the veil covering the last six months, it was immovable. If the present situation was to be believed, there was a trip to Bath, love, marriage and who knew what other events, waiting just on the other side.

His headache was returning.

He struggled to his feet and manoeuvred himself to a decanter of brandy that sat on the table by the window, pouring a glass and drinking deeply. That he had done it without spilling a drop deserved a reward, so he poured a second, leaning on his crutches to marshal his strength for a return to his chair. The trip across the room had brought him scant feet from Justine and he paused to watch her work.

There was a scrap of lace, pinned flat to the pillow in front of her. It took him a moment to realise that this was not some purchased trim, but a work in progress. The finished work was held in place with a maze of pins more numerous than spines on a hedgehog, the working edge trailing away into a multitude of threads and dangling ivory spools. As though she hardly thought, she passed one over the other, around back, a second and a third, this time a knot, the next a braid. Then she slipped a pin into the finished bit and moved on to another set of threads. The soft click of ivory against ivory and the dance of her white hands were like a soporific, leaving him as calm as she seemed to be. Though he was close enough to smell her perfume, he saw no sign of the shyness that was usually present when he stood beside her. There was no stiffness or hesitation in the movement of her hands. Perhaps their problems existed outside the limits of her concentration. She worked without pattern, calling the complex arrangement of threads up from memory alone. There was hardly a pause in conversation, when one or the other of the women put a question to her. If it bothered her at all, he could not tell for her dancing fingers never wavered.

Though he stood right in front of her, he seemed to be the last thing on her mind. Now he felt something new when he looked at her. Was this envy that she gave her attention to the lace, and to the other women, while ignoring him? Or was this frustration that he'd had her attention, once, and slept through it.

Slowly, the roll of finished work at the top grew longer. No wonder she had nursed him, uncomplaining, for months at a time. She had the patience to measure success in inches. Penny noticed his interest and announced, 'Her handwork is magnificent.'

It brought a blush to the woman's fair cheeks, but she did not pause, or lose count of the threads. 'In my homeland, lacemaking is quite common,' she announced. 'My mother was far better at it than I.'

'Your homeland?' he prompted, for it was yet another fact that he did not know.

'Belgium,' she said, softly. 'I was born in Antwerp.'

'And we met in Bath,' he added. It did not answer how either of them came to be there. But perhaps, if repeated often enough, it would make sense.

'You may think it common, but your work is the most delicate I have seen,' Penny reminded her with a sigh. Then she looked to Will. 'It is a shame that you did not bring Justine to us before the last christening. I would so have liked to see a bonnet of that trim she is making now.'

'For the next child, you shall have one,' Justine replied, not looking up.

'It is too much to ask.' Penny smiled at Will as though he had a share in the compliment. 'The collar she made for me last month makes me feel as regal as a duchess.' Fine praise indeed, for it was rare to hear Penny feeling anything other than ordinary.

'The edging she made for my petticoat is so fine it seemed a shame to cover it with a skirt, Daphne added. 'I've had my maid take up the hem of the dress so that it might be seen to good advantage.'

'Because you are shameless,' her husband added with a smile. He was glancing at her legs as though there were other things that were too pretty to be hidden. It was probably true, if one had a taste for girls who were buxom and ginger. Daphne was as pretty as Penny was sensible.

Will glanced at his own wife, his mind still stumbling over the concept. The candlelight was shining copper in her hair and bringing out the green in her eyes. In museums, he'd admired the technique of the Flemish painters and the way their subject seemed to glow like opals in the light. But if this woman was an indication, perhaps they had simply learned to paint what they saw before them. Though she sat still and silent in the corner, the woman he had chosen seemed illuminated from within, like the banked coals of a fire. Perhaps that was what had drawn him to her. For now that he had seen her in candlelight, he could not seem to look away.

There was a knock on the parlour door and Adam all but leapt to his feet to open it, breaking the spell. He turned back to Will with a grin. 'Now, for the highlight of the evening. We are to have a visit from your namesake, William.' He opened the door and the nurse entered, carrying a plump toddler that Will assumed was his nephew.

It was almost as great a shock as discovering he had a wife. When he had last seen little William, they had been in the chapel and the infant had been squawking at the water poured over his head. That child had been but a few months old and had cared for nothing but milk and sleep. The baby that was brought into the room was fully three times the size of the one he remembered and struggling to escape, his arms outstretched to his parents, demanding their attention.

Penny had already set aside the book she'd been holding and took the baby, making little cooing noises and interrogating the nurse about his day. Next, it was Adam's turn. But instead of coddling the child, he knelt on the floor and demanded that his son come to him. The child did, once he was free of his mother's arms. It was done in a series of lunges, combined with some industrious crawling and ending in an impressive attempt by little Billy to haul himself upright on the leg of the tea table. He was properly rewarded by his father with a hug and a sweet that appeared from out of Adam's waistcoat pocket, which Penny announced would ruin the boy's sleep.

Will felt a strange tightening in his chest at the sight. Six months ago, he had given little thought to his nephew, other than a natural pride at sharing his name. But to have missed so much in the boy's development was like losing a thing he'd had no idea he'd wanted.

Adam scooped the child from the floor and wiped the stickiness from his hands and mouth before announcing, 'And now, young Bill, it is time to meet your uncle. Can you say hello for him? Come now,' he coaxed. 'We have heard the word before. Uncle. Show your godfather how brilliant you are.'

But as they approached, Billy showed no interest in speech. In fact, he'd wound his little hands tightly into his father's lapel and turned his face into the cloth. The closer they came, the more shy Billy seemed to become. By the time they were standing before Will, he could see nothing but the boy's hunched shoulders and curling blond hair.

'Hello, Bill,' he said softly, hoping that the boy was only playing a game with him. 'Peek-a-boo.'

Instead of laughing at the sound of his voice, the boy let out a scream and burst into tears, butting his head into his father's shoulder as though demanding to be taken away.

'I don't understand,' Adam said. 'He has seen you before. We took him to your room, each day. We would not have him forget…'

'It is all right,' Will said. But it was not. Had the time he'd lost turned him into a monster? What could the boy see that the others were not remarking on?

Now Penny was fussing over the child, taking him from Adam with a dark look. 'This is too much excitement. I will take him back to the nursery. It is time for bed, if it is possible to calm him.'

Will's head was pounding and the screaming boy was making it worse. 'No. I will go. Leave him be.' One crutch slipped out from under him for a moment and he nearly stumbled. But at least as he staggered it was in the direction of the hall. He allowed the momentum to carry him from the room, not bothering to shut the door behind him.

Chapter Six

There was a moment of shocked silence in the room, after William Felkirk's sudden retreat. Even the child was quiet, other than to heave a wet sigh of relief. And then all started for the door at once.

'I will go,' said Justine in as firm a voice as she could manage. Apparently, it was strong enough. Everyone relaxed. Even the duke took a step away from the door and offered an equally quiet, 'Of course. It must be you.'

She did not particularly want to follow, if it meant being alone with Lord Felkirk again. His refusal of her on the previous evening had come as a relief. She had half-feared, even before receiving Montague's orders, she might have to feign affection for a man she wanted no part of.

While nursing him, she had not bothered to think too much about the character of the man she was caring for. The feeding, washing and changing of linens had been little more than a series of tasks to be completed. It was good to be busy and to occupy her mind with the routine of duty.

But that was over now. Tonight, she might have to lie still in his bed, her own thoughts and fears clamouring loud in her head, while he did whatever he wished…

She had hoped for continued indifference, for at least a little while longer. If they could live as strangers for a while, she might think of some way to escape before the inevitable occurred. But he had been watching her, all during dinner, and in the parlour as she'd worked. And he had been smiling. Although it was better than his continual suspicion, it had been the sort of warm, speculative smile she had seen on the faces of men before. It was likely the first step in a chain of events that would lead to the bedroom and trap her even deeper in the lie she had told.

She put the fear of that aside as she went out into the hall. At the moment, he needed her. He needed someone, at least. His wife would be the logical choice to offer comfort. The poor man had quit the room like a wounded animal after his godson's rejection. Even with the complications it would add to her life, she could not abide the sight of suffering.

'Wait!' She needn't have called out after him. She caught him easily, for he'd had to struggle with the crutches and his own limited strength. He'd travelled as far as the end of the hall to the little, round mirror that hung there and was staring into it, as though expecting to see a monster.

She came to his side, allowing him to know her presence by her reflection. 'You must not think too much of that. Billy is normally the most agreeable of children. But even the best babies can take fright when they are startled.'

'Have I really changed so much?' Will touched his own face, as though doubting what he saw.

'Not really.' Much as she did not wish to admit it, he was even more handsome than he had been in Bath. His hair was as black as ever, except for the small streak of white near the scar. His skin, pale from illness, added to his dramatic good looks. And the easy smiles and relaxed manners he used at home were much less intimidating than the distant courtesy of the gentleman who had walked into the shop wishing to speak with Mr Montague about a crime committed in Wales nearly twenty years ago.

She had taken an instant dislike to him, for bringing up a subject that was still very painful to her. But amongst his family he seemed younger and more open. He had barely smiled at her and she had not yet seen him laugh. But she could see by the lines around his mouth and eyes that he did so, and frequently. He seemed like a most pleasant fellow. It was a shame to see him doubt himself now.

'When you went away, after the christening, Billy was too small to know you,' she assured him. 'Since I brought you home, he has seen you often, but never with your eyes open and never standing up. You frightened him because he does not understand the change.'

'Neither do I,' Will said softly, almost to himself. Then he added, 'He has no reason to fear.' He turned to look at her, as though to reassure her as well. 'I am not such a great beast, once you get to know me.'

She fought back her fears and laid a hand on his arm. 'He will learn that, in time.'

He gave the barest of nods. 'I hope you learn the same. I have not treated you very well, since I have awakened. But everything is so strange.' He turned back to the mirror, staring into it as though he expected to see something in her reversed reflection that was not apparent when he looked directly at her.

She resisted the urge to search her own face in the glass. How should one look, at a moment like this? She had learned for most of her adult life to be good at dissembling. But was anyone this good of an actress, to pull off such a stunning performance for an audience of one who would be watching her closely, searching for clues that might lead him to his own truth?

For her sister's sake, she had no choice but to try. She gave him a hopeful, watery smile and managed a single tear to indicate that her heart was too full for words. It gave her a few more moments to compose her thoughts before speaking. 'I do not fear you,' she lied. 'And I understand that it will take time before you can feel truly yourself again.'

'I am told my recovery thus far is thanks to your

care.' His brow was still furrowed as he repeated what must be rote acknowledgements of the situation as it had been told to him. 'But in truth, madam, I can remember nothing before yesterday, of you and our marriage. Please enlighten me. How did we come to be together?' His questions today lacked the accusatory tone of yesterday. He was not so much demanding answers, as honestly curious. It was as though he expected Scheherazade with a story so captivating he could not resist.

What could she tell him that would set his mind at rest? 'You arrived in Bath, after the crocuses were finished blooming, in May,' she said, trying to focus on a happy memory.

'In what month did we marry?'

'June,' she replied. It was a fine month for weddings, real or imaginary.

'Adam said we married in Gretna.' He said this almost to himself, as though calculating miles between the points.

'But we met in Bath,' she repeated, searching for a likely story. 'We met in a shop.' It was true. But she could not exactly tell him it was Montague and de Bryun, Purveyors of Fine Jewellery. 'I taught needlework, in a school for young girls. I wished to sell some of the handiworks there.' Hadn't that been her dream, at one time? To make a modest living with her hands.

'What was I doing in a lady's haberdashery?' he said, obviously surprised.

'You followed me there, I think,' she said, smiling at her own carelessness for choosing such an outlandish meeting place. 'I saw you enter the shop and everything changed.' That was very true. But it had not been for the better.

'You were taken with me?' Apparently, his ego had not been damaged, for she saw the slight swell of pride.

'You are a most handsome man.' Again, it was truth. She remembered the little thrill of excitement she'd felt, at seeing such a dashing man enter the salon. It was followed by the crashing realisation that he was a Felkirk.

'And what did I think of you?'

That had been obvious as well. She had introduced Mr Montague as her employer. But William Felkirk had seen the low-cut satin gowns she wore and the possessive way Montague treated her and known that her duties for the man were not limited to modelling the wares they sold. Then his lip had curled, ever so slightly, with contempt. 'I think you felt sorry for me,' she said, wishing it were true.

'So I offered to rescue you from your dreary life?' He raised an eyebrow.

'I refused you at first,' she embroidered. If she was to create a fairy-tale romance, there should be details. 'I did not think your offer was quite proper.'

'But I won you over with my charm and sincerity,' he said with such obvious doubt that it made her laugh.

'You took me on walks around the Crescent. We

met again in the assembly rooms and tea shops. You made it clear to me that your intentions were honourable.' Hadn't she envied many young couples, courting in just such a way on the other side of the shop window? Sometimes she saw them later, in the showroom, admiring the rings. 'When you made your offer, of course I accepted.'

'Of course,' he said dubiously. 'But what was I doing in Bath? I loathe the place.'

This was a wrinkle she had not accounted for. 'What were you doing in Bath? You did not say. What do most people do there? Take the waters. Attend parties.'

'I have managed to resist such activities thus far,' he said sceptically. 'Why would I decide to do them now?'

'I really have no idea. You did remark that you were bored,' she allowed. 'But that you liked it better, once you had met me.'

'And then we eloped.' He must suspect that this was unlikely. Having met his family and seen how close he was to them, she was sure, when he found the perfect wife, he would bring her to them, immediately.

'You were unwilling to wait, even for the reading of the banns, or the time to procure a special licence. And I was…' She took a deep breath and plunged forward with the biggest lie of all. 'Your affections were very difficult to resist. Impossible, in fact. Afterwards, you deemed it best that we marry with all haste and inform the family afterwards.'

'I see.' Now he was the one who was blushing. Let him think he had taken advantage and owed her some reparation. It would be true, soon enough. He was staring at her reflection in the mirror again. 'I do not doubt that I was insistent, once I set my cap for you. You are quite the prettiest woman I have ever seen.'

'Thank you.' She had grown used to accepting the words as a compliment, though they sometimes felt more like a curse. How different might her life have been had she been plain and undesirable? She might have gone unnoticed through life and kept her virtue. She certainly would not be in a ducal manor, flirting with a peer's brother. 'I was honoured by your attentions. I am sure there were others more appropriate for the brother of a duke, than an *émigrée* without family or fortune.'

He touched a finger to her lips. 'Do not speak so about yourself. You have proven more than worthy, since the accident.' The moment of spontaneous intimacy shocked them both and he carefully removed his hand.

'Thank you,' she said, wishing she could take the compliment as it was.

'But the accident,' he added. 'Tell me about it.'

She gave an honest shudder at the memory of him lying broken on the floor. Then she lied again. 'You were trying to impress me. A jump went wrong.'

'But what of Jupiter?'

For a moment, she was completely puzzled. Was this some obsession with astronomy that she had not known? Perhaps he was the sort who thought his life was ruled by the stars. Then she realised that he was referring to the horse. What had become of the horse? She had no idea. If Montague was aware of it, he had surely sold it by now. Or perhaps it was still in a stable in Bath, waiting for its owner to return. 'I am sorry, but his leg was broken. There was nothing that could be done…' It was kinder that he think the animal dead, than to realise that no one had cared enough to find it.

He held up a hand and turned his face away from hers, as though unwilling to let her finish. The weight of his body sagged against his crutches, as if he could not support himself. When she reached out to steady him, and to offer comfort, she felt the shuddering sob even as he shrugged off her touch.

In a moment, he straightened and composed himself. 'Then I deserved what I got,' he said, in a voice full of self-disgust. 'Taking foolish risks and putting another life in jeopardy. What the devil was I thinking to harm an animal that had been a faithful friend to me for seven years?'

If she had hoped to comfort him, she had failed completely. Felkirk was even more upset than he had been when leaving the parlour. And he grieved for a horse? When she'd met him, she had assumed that he and his family cared for nothing but their money and themselves. They certainly had not cared for her father, as he'd lain dying on their property so long ago.

But the duke and Penny had not been as she'd expected and had treated her as a long-lost sister. Now, the man in front of her was practically undone over the death of a beast. She wanted to take back the words and assure him that, somewhere, the horse was alive and well. Fine blood stock, like Jupiter probably was, would not have sold for hide and hoof to pay a stable bill.

Instead, she remained silent and let him lean upon her, as he struggled to regain his composure. 'Do you wish me to call for Stewart?' she said softly.

He shook his head, once, emphatically. Then he pulled himself upright and took a deep breath. 'This is too embarrassing. But so much of my life is, it seems.'

'It is not your fault,' she assured him. 'And I have seen you worse. Let me help you back to your room.'

He gave a very weak laugh as they made their way to the stairs. 'That does nothing to console me. The last thing a man wants to be is helpless in the presence of a beautiful woman.' He stopped for a moment and wiped a hand across his face. 'And weeping over a horse. You must think me mad as well as crippled.'

'The physicians did say you might not be yourself,' she reminded him.

He gave her another wry smile. 'It does not reassure me to hear I might run mad and no one will think twice about it. I am sorry to inform you of this, my dear. But I cannot blame a head injury on my tears over the loss of old Jupe. He was a fine horse and my truest friend. I must have told you how long we were together.'

'I understand,' she said, trying not to appear relieved. His upset, no matter how unjustified, had been a help. He was too busy trying to save some scrap of dignity to ask any more questions of her.

He paused, took a firm grip on the stair rail and gave another quick wipe of his eyes with the back of his hand before moving up another step. 'All the same, I apologise. If I am still not the master of body or mind, I am unfit company. It was a mistake to inflict myself on others this evening.'

'You cannot be expected to hide in your room for ever. And you are doing much better than yesterday,' she added, since it was perfectly true. Now that he was awake, the speed of his recovery was impressive. 'The family is eager to see you and will be patient.'

'Not too patient,' he said, wiping the last moisture from his eyes. 'I am barely on my feet again and Adam means to put us out.'

'No.' She had no right to think it. Had she forgotten she was an interloper here? This was not her home and she must not think of it as such. But if she did not live here, then where was she to go?

Felkirk gave her a wan smile. 'I said something similar, when he suggested it. But he is right. I have a home of my own, less than a mile from here.' He paused, then said, 'We have a home. It is where we belong. Tomorrow, you shall see.'

'But…' What was she to tell Montague? And how was she to tell him? There was no time to leave a signal.

They had reached the top of the stairs and Felkirk balanced carefully on a single crutch and draped his free arm about her shoulders. 'You have nothing to worry about. Adam was right to suggest it, as you were just now. I cannot hide in my room for ever, assuming I will improve. And we cannot use the size of this place, and the presence of Adam and Penny, to hide from each other.'

Had it been so obvious that she was avoiding him? She could not think of an answer to it, so busied herself with helping him the last few feet down the hall to his room. They were standing outside the door to his sickroom. The valet was no doubt waiting inside to help him to bed. If he did not need her any longer, she could make her excuses and escape to the ground floor to tell the family that he had retired. He might be sound asleep by the time she returned. He was right that she could not avoid him for ever. But was one more night so much to ask?

She dropped her gaze to the floor and offered a curtsy. It was probably not the way a loving wife was supposed to behave. She should be warmer, bolder and unafraid to catch his eye. But when he was near like this, she could not think clearly. What was to become of her, once they were out of this house and had only each other for company? She turned away, glancing back down the hall. 'If you do not need me any longer, I will return to the parlour and explain to the family.'

'There is one last thing,' he said, as though something had just occurred to him and gestured her close again, as though about to whisper.

She leaned in as well.

Then he kissed her. It was just a buss upon the lips. It was so quick and sweet that she gasped in surprise. And for a moment, her mind was calm. Not empty, as it was when she was with Montague. It was as placid as a lake on a windless day. Then she felt the faintest ripples of expectation. Was she actually hoping for another kiss?

'Thank you, for your help. And your devotion,' he said. There was no indication of his feelings on the matter, other than the faintest of smiles.

'It was…' Why could she not find her words? And why could she not draw away from him? She was leaning against him, as though she was the one who needed crutches. Montague would not have approved. He had sent her here as a seductress. He did not want her behaving like some moonstruck girl…

The second kiss that she had been hoping for came in a rush of sweetness, soft as the wing of a moth. William Felkirk braced himself against the doorframe of his room and pulled her body to him, letting the wall support them both. Then he touched his lips to hers and moved them slowly, tenderly, before closing them once, twice, three times, against her mouth.

Why did she feel so breathless? Montague would have laughed and called her a fool. But she did not want to think of him, just now. Instead, she focused on the slight cleft in the chin that hovered before her eyes as those same gentle lips kissed her forehead. There was a faint shadow there, where his valet had missed a whisker or two. She wanted to kiss him there, to trace the crease with her tongue and feel the roughness of the stubble.

She had waited too long. Felkirk was setting her back on her feet, smiling down into her face. And for the first time, she saw the easy smile and friendly nature his family assured her was his by habit. 'You are right, my dear. You must go back to the parlour. And I must rest. Much as I would like to say otherwise, I fear there are things I am simply not yet capable of.'

He meant bed play. She did not know if it was proper for a wife to do so, but she blushed at the thought.

It made him laugh. 'Although, with you here, looking as you do, I will pray most fervently for a return to health and strength.'

'I will pray for you, as well,' she agreed.

'And pray for my memory,' he added. 'I cannot recall what we have meant to each other. But I am sure, once you are in my arms, it will all come back to me.'

She thought of the beads she kept in her dresser. She would tell them tonight, several times over, and hope that the quantity of prayer for a selective memory might counter anything he had asked for.

Chapter Seven

Now that William Felkirk was awake, Justine was discovering the inconveniences of married life. When he had been in a coma, there had been little question as to who made the decisions. On the rare occasions she had been overruled by the duke as to the best method to tend the invalid, it had been the result of discussion and not flat mandate. But now that he was awake, Lord Felkirk expected not just an equal share in his recovery, but the deciding vote in all matters.

After the discussion in the hall, she had hoped that there would be some time to persuade him of the need for caution before a change of location. But when she awakened the next morning, the arrangements for the move back to his own home were already in progress and would be done before noon. The valet seemed relieved to be packing up the limited supply of garments and his lord's shaving kit. Her own garments were only slightly more troublesome, for she had brought a single trunk with her, when she'd come north. Penny offered her the use of the maid she'd had, until she was able to choose someone from her own household. The girl had already gone ahead and was probably already hanging gowns and pressing ribbons in their new home.

In the midst of the activity, William Felkirk paced the floor as though he could not wait to be under way. Though he had claimed to be reticent, he had obviously warmed to his brother's advice and meant to act on it immediately. 'It makes no sense to maintain a second household, less than a mile from the first,' he said. 'It is unfair to expect servants to fetch and carry items between the two. I have a perfectly good home, just down the road from here. I mean to live in it.'

'But you are still so weak,' she said. She cast a sidelong glance at the crutches in the corner and wondered if their kiss in the hallway had given him this burst of energy.

'It is not as if I intend to walk the distance,' he informed her. 'A carriage ride will be no more strenuous than sitting in a Bath chair. The air of the journey will likely do me good.'

'The doctor—' she said plaintively.

'—lives closer to the old manor than he does to this one. And do not tell me that the stairs will be unfamiliar, or the rooms inconvenient. It is the home I grew up in and I know each step of it. It is also a damned sight smaller than this cavernous place of my brother's. It feels like I must walk a mile here, just to get from bed to breakfast.'

His words stopped her objections. 'You did not always live here, in the duke's manor?'

'Heavens, no.' William shook his head and smiled. 'Mother did not like the old house at all. It had been fine for ten generations of Bellstons, but she wanted a ballroom and a grand dining hall. It is good that she did not live to see Adam nearly burn the place to the ground a few years ago. She would have been appalled. But that is another story.'

'How long ago was that?' she asked, trying to suppress her excitement.

'The fire?' he asked.

'No. The building of the new manor.'

'A little less than fifteen years,' he said, taking a moment to count on his fingers. 'In the end, it was a sensible decision. I am able to stay on the family lands without living in my brother's pocket. The two manors are close enough to share the stables, the ice house and the gardens.' He grinned. 'I have all the advantages of being a duke and none of the responsibilities.'

Fifteen years. Her father had been dead for twenty. If there were clues to be had about the murder or the missing diamonds, she had been searching the wrong house for them. Surely they must be at the old manor, the place where she would soon be living.

'I think you are probably right, then,' she said, trying not to sound too excited. 'A change will do you good.' And it would give her an opportunity to search the rooms there that she had not already seen. When she found a way to get the information to him, Montague would be pacified. It would give her time to think of a next step that might keep Margot safe from his threats.

It also meant that she would be alone with her husband. There would be no duke and duchess to fill the days and evenings spent in company with him. The odds increased that his memory might return, or she would let slip some bit of the truth that could not be easily distracted by turning it to another subject.

But when darkness fell, there would be no reason for them to talk at all. As she had on the previous evening, she felt a strange anticipation, like the stillness in the air before a storm.

'You will like it,' he said, mistaking her silence for more understandable worries. 'Just wait. You shall be mistress over your own home. In no time at all, you will have arranged everything to suit yourself and we shall return Adam and Penny's hospitality.'

Her own household. What a strange idea. While she had experience in managing servants for Mr Montague, she had seen the way they looked at her, half in pity and half in disapproval, as though it pained them to take their instructions from the master's whore. Now she was to be the lady of a manor and no one would doubt that it was her proper place. If the situation weren't so dire, she might have been excited at the thought.

Once they were underway, it appeared that William was right about his need to make the move. As she sat in his side in the carriage, she could see his mood lightening with each turn of the wheels. He stared out the window so intently that she almost thought he was avoiding her gaze. At last, he said, 'It is good to be coming home again. There is much about the current situation that is strange to me. Having to deal with it in my brother's house made it no easier.'

'They have been very kind to me, during our stay there,' she remarked.

'I would expect nothing less of them,' he said. 'But when we married, I am sure it was not our intent to live out the remainder of our lives in someone else's house.'

'True,' she agreed.

'We are barely out of our honeymoon, are we not?' It was a perfectly innocent remark and a logical reason to wish to be alone together. But they both fell silent at the thought.

'We have not known each other long,' she answered. 'And it has been a very unusual few months.'

They both fell silent again.

He took a breath and began again. 'I will be frank with you, since it makes no sense not to be. I do not know you, as a husband should.'

'Your accident…' she said, searching for a way to explain the perfectly logical absence of romantic memories.

'Is in the past,' he finished for her. 'I do not remember you. But if we are to be married, it does no good for me to be dwelling on that fact. I… We…' he amended. 'We must move forward with what is left. And it will be impossible if we continue to avoid each other, relying on family and friends to fill the gaps and sleeping on opposite sides of a closed door.' Then he exhaled, as if it had taken an effort to state the obvious.

'It was you who sent me away,' she reminded him, careful to keep the censure from her voice. If they had truly been married she likely would have been hurt and angered by his rejection. But the sensible reaction was the one most likely to reveal her lies.

'I was wrong to do so,' he replied. 'If we are married…'

'If?' she countered.

'Now that we are married,' he corrected, 'we must accept the fact that the last six months change nothing. I have spoken to my brother and I do not think an annulment is possible.'

How could one dissolve a marriage that did not exist in the first place? She ignored the real question and chose another. 'Did you wish to cast me off, then?'

She could see the change in his face, as he realised how cruel his words had been. When he spoke again, it was after some thought. 'If I did, it was unfair of me, just as it was when I sent you from my bedroom. When we arrive at the house, I will instruct the servants to place your things in the room beside mine, for the sake of convenience. But from this point forward, I expect you to share my bed.'

'As you wish, my lord.' When Montague had informed her of her future, he had done it with a similar lack of passion. She had been foolish to imagine, after a kiss or two, it would be any different with this man.

Beside her, Lord Felkirk swore under his breath. 'I did not mean it to sound like a command.'

'You are my husband,' she said, with as much confidence as she could manage. 'I have promised to obey. It shall be just as you wish and I will do my best to give you no reason to be unhappy.'

Apparently, she had failed in that already. He was frowning. Despite his earlier excitement, he looked no happier when they reached the house. 'My home,' Will said in a tired voice, and waited for her comment.

She was not sure what she had expected, but it had not been this. It was not the thoroughly modern manor that the duke inhabited, with its large windows and perfectly matched wings. The old manor still held traces of the fortress it had once been. On the left, a square tower ended in wide crenellations. There was nothing left of the right tower but a low wall of grey stone to mark the edge of the kitchen garden. Though a Gothic stone arch remained around the iron-bound front door, the rest of the main building had been rebuilt of brick by some misguided architect of another century.

It was a hodge-podge of styles and Justine could see why the previous duchess had been eager to build a new manor. She understood, but she could not agree. 'You live in a castle,' she announced, then scolded herself for stating the obvious.

'Part of one,' he said. 'There is not much of the old building left.'

'It does not matter.' She stared up at the tower in front of them. 'It is magnificent.'

'You like it?' He seemed surprised at her enthusiasm.

'You do not?' She stared back at him, equally surprised.

'Well, yes, actually. I do. But I grew up here. Perhaps that is why I am willing to overlook its obvious flaws.'

She stared back at the old manor and could not help smiling at its lopsided grandeur. 'Well, I see no problems with it. It has character,' she said, wondering why he could not see it.

'As you wish,' he said, giving a dismissive nod of his head and turning away from her again. The servants had lined up at the door, eager to greet the master on his homecoming and to officially welcome the lady of the house. William walked unsteadily before her, smiling more warmly at the butler than he ever had at her, and accepting the arm of a footman to help him up the last steps and into his home.

Though he had claimed the trip would be an easy one, it was clear that the activity had tired him. 'I think, if you have no need of me, that I shall retire to my room for a time.'

'You must do as you see fit,' she said. 'We will have more than enough time to talk, now that we are home.' The word stuck in her throat, but she forced it out.

He nodded and muttered something to the footman at his side, who took his arm and helped him to climb the stairs to his room.

Which left Justine alone with the servants and the house. She gave a sigh of relief at being free of him, if only for an hour or two. Then she gave instructions for the unpacking of their things and discussed the luncheon menu with the housekeeper. Then she enquired, oh so casually, about the best room to find pen, ink and paper. She wished to write to tell a friend of her move.

The housekeeper, Mrs Bell, directed her to the morning room without further enquiry and left her to pen a hurried note to Mr Smith, the *nom de guerre* that Montague had chosen for his stay at a nearby inn.

She imagined the way it would travel to him, on the road to the village, which lay equidistant between the two manors. Her father had travelled that road, on the night he died. At the turning, he had gone left and not right, as she'd assumed. She had thought, on her morning walks, that she had been retracing his last footsteps, but she had not gone far enough.

His goal had been this house. His death had been on these grounds. Any clue to the murder, or the missing jewels, would be under this very roof.

She had but to find it and then the jewels. Then, she would rescue Margot and they would run away, all without revealing the truth to either William Felkirk or John Montague.

When put that way, it was hard to be optimistic.

Chapter Eight

Justine was already seated at the luncheon table when Will came down from his nap. He found it faintly annoying. He was unaccustomed to seeing anyone across the table from him, much less a person who would arrive before he had so that she might be ready to attend him. Here she was, fresh, cheerful and inescapable in a muslin gown and starched cap, offering to prepare his plate or help him in any way she could.

He did not want help. He wanted to be left alone to understand what had happened to him. It was an urge he must learn to ignore. After his brave words in the coach about facing troubles and moving forward, he had taken the first opportunity to escape to his room for a sulk.

At least, now that he was free of his brother's home, he would not have to see the ring of happy faces about him, convinced that everything was fine when he was sure it was not. There was only one face before him now. Though it was beautiful, it had the same detached expression it had worn since the first. If they were truly so alike as Adam thought, she should be as angry with him as he was with himself. He had ordered her to bed as though her wants and needs meant nothing at all. She had responded as though she had no feelings to hurt.

Perhaps she was waiting for the same thing he was: a sudden rush of memory that would explain all. But it seemed she viewed it with the strange dread he did. 'Are you not going to ask me if I have remembered anything, now that I am home?' he said, watching her intently as she poured the wine.

She took a sip from her glass. 'I expect, if you do remember anything, I will be the first to know. You do not mean to hide the truth from me, do you?' Her eyes were wide and innocent as though the idea that he might not share all his thoughts had never occurred to her.

It made him feel like a cad for barking at her. 'Of course not,' he said hurriedly. What reason would he have to conceal what he knew? After his talk of annulment, she must think he meant to negate their marriage by feigning ignorance of it. Even if he did not wish for a wife, he would not abandon this one to her ruin, just to avoid a forgotten bad decision.

He spoke again, in a gentler tone. 'It is good to be home. I found the attention at Adam's house to be rather oppressive.'

'It is because they care for you,' she said. 'They

cannot help but crowd you. Would you not have done the same for your brother, in a similar situation?'

He thought back for a moment. 'I suspect I already have. There was a time, a few years back, where Adam had difficulties. I suppose I've told you that the scars on my arm came from a fire that he caused?'

She seemed to consider for a moment, then nodded as though his statement had answered an unasked question.

Surely he had explained the damaged patch of skin to her on their first night together. She must have noticed it. The smooth red mark stretching from elbow to shoulder was impossible to miss. He was self-conscious about it and quick to offer explanation, so as not to alarm the women he took to his bed. But his own wife was looking at him as though he had said not a word to her on the subject. It was strange.

But it was just one of many strange things that had happened in the last week. He willed himself to forget it, and began again, cautiously. 'I wanted to help Adam then and was told on several occasions to go to the Devil. I questioned his wisdom in marrying Penny as well.'

'You disapproved?' Now Justine's eyes were round with surprise.

'I was wrong, of course. But that did not stop me from speaking. Tim Colton went through his own dark time, after his first wife died. He is a particular friend of Adam's, so I did not have to bear the brunt of his moods. But apparently his behaviour was extreme. He also refused the help of his friends.'

'So you are telling me that all men are difficult?' Justine said, with a slight arch of her eyebrow.

'All men around here, at any rate. Perhaps it is the climate in Wales that leads us to be melancholy and pigheaded.'

She nodded. 'Then if you snap and grumble, I shall not blame myself for it.'

'You needn't. It is my problem, not yours,' he said. He thought back to his suspicions of the previous day and wondered if that was true. If she was the one keeping secrets, he would be quite justified in blaming her. But to look at her now, fresh and pretty in the afternoon sunlight, it seemed churlish to find fault with her.

He took a bit of cold salmon and a swallow of wine, and admired her over the rim of his wine glass.

She was nibbling on a bit of roll and glanced up to catch him staring at her. She put it down and spoke. 'Now that you are home, what are your plans? I assume that I am not oppressing you by enquiring.' There was the faintest twitch at the corner of her mouth and he wondered if she meant to be amusing.

It was rather amusing to think of her attention as a heavy burden. She seemed to work at being unobtrusive. Beautiful to look at, but quiet as a ghost, she hovered barely noticed on the fringe of any conversation. When he needed her, she came just close enough to help, then disappeared again, like a sprite.

Perhaps that was why he had married her. To find a woman willing to fit herself seamlessly into his life was a rare piece of good fortune.

She was enquiring after his plans. What were they? Many of the activities he might have favoured were quite beyond him, until he regained his strength. 'I don't have any,' he admitted.

'Then might I trouble you to show me around your home?' she said. 'The housekeeper will do it, if you do not wish to. But I suspect it would be more interesting to hear the details of the place from you. It is many hours before you mean to bed me. We must find some way to pass the afternoon.'

He choked on his next swallow of wine. When he could compose himself to look at her again, there was no sign that she had been laughing. But he was quite sure she had been. It was a promising sign.

He would enjoy walking the halls of his own home, again. And to show it to one of the few women in England who seemed to appreciate its design. Even Penny, who had few strong opinions about anything outside of her books had proclaimed the place an eyesore and suggested that he tear it down and rebuild from the foundation up.

Perhaps Adam had been right all along and he had simply married a woman who suited his character. It would be interesting to see if her opinions matched his on the interior. For though the decoration was not the current style, he liked it very well. He might regain some of his strength as they walked from room to room and pause to rest as needed, under the guise of telling her old family stories.

And why did he suspect that she knew just that and had found a perfect way to preserve his dignity while encouraging him to exercise his wasted legs? 'A tour sounds like an excellent idea,' he agreed. 'Let us finish our meal and we can begin.' Perhaps if he spent the day with her, he would learn something of her as well.

But, after an afternoon of walking the house, he knew no more about her than when they began. She was an attentive audience and he took pleasure in regaling her with childhood tales about growing up in the old manor. But she offered no similar details of her own youth. It was nearly time to dress for supper and the sum total of his knowledge was no greater than when they had begun. She was beautiful. She was Belgian. She was an orphan. She had impeccable manners and made lace, though he had never seen her wear any. And she was most grateful to be married to him and eager to see to his comfort in all things.

As they walked, she seemed to sense when he was tiring and took his arm, as though she was too shy to walk alone. When she suspected that they had gone too long without a break, she claimed exhaustion and requested they sit for a time, in the conservatory, or the music room, which she had guessed were his favourites. In all things she supported him, while persuading him that he was, in fact, supporting her.

She was the perfect wife.

Or nearly perfect. Should it be so disquieting to have such a devoted helpmeet? He could not find fault with her looks. She was quite the loveliest woman he could imagine. But it was as if a painting had come to life, or a statue. There was no passion in her. Her red-gold hair was contained beneath a cloth cap. Her shapely body hid beneath a modest gown. At the table, she had shocked him with her frank acceptance of tonight's possible activities. But once they were in bed, would she be an enthusiastic lover? Or would she be as mild as she was here in the drawing room, listening intently as he described the family members in the portraits and the history of each ornament on the shelves? Did she truly have no character other than the one she assumed he wished to see?

He was sure his married brother could explain to him the dangers of a wife who wished to be contrary. But to have found one that was nothing more than a mirror reflection of his own opinions was not as pleasant as it sounded.

They had walked nearly back to the bedrooms, now, and were standing in front of the nursery. He paused, strangely unwilling to open the door. 'We needn't bother with this,' he said, stepping back from it. 'There is nothing within but old playthings. But you will find the rooms to be most sensible, when we need them for our children.'

'Of course,' she said. And just as strangely, she stepped away as well.

'Now that Adam has started his family, we can be reasonably sure of the succession,' he remarked. 'The need for a son is not pressing.'

'We needn't rush,' she agreed. 'Unless, that is what you wish,' she added hurriedly. Once again, there was the slight, acquiescent bow of the head, as though she would try to produce an entire family for him, right now, should that be his desire.

As if he wished to raise children with a stranger. Despite her looks, he was not even sure he truly wanted to bed her. There would be no joy in it if her response was apathetic acceptance of the act. What was the point of marrying a beautiful woman, if one had to find an equally pretty mistress who would at least feign enthusiasm for his lovemaking?

Then he looked forward, into the nursery again, remembered the reason for wives and retreated. 'We will discuss such matters again when I am fully recovered.'

'Of course,' she agreed, turning away to return to her room.

Justine did her best to maintain her composure in the hours that followed, but her new husband made it more challenging than she'd expected. When she'd first hit upon this scheme, she had not thought that such an evening was in her future. Though she would do her best to save him, William Felkirk was going to die.

She had been sure of it. She'd felt terror mixed with pity at the sight of his bleeding head and Mr

Montague's dispassionate expression as he raised the poker for a second blow. Before he could strike, she'd hurried to convince him that the man would be better off in the bosom of his family than as a corpse on the floor of their salon. What would happen if the Duke of Bellston appeared in Bath, enquiring after his missing brother?

Worse yet, suppose he sent the law? There was no question that they would both hang for murder. Margot would be left alone, with nothing but the scandalously false broadsheet confession of Montague's mistress: the salacious details of a good woman brought low by her own depravity.

She had insisted that further violence against William Felkirk was unnecessary. If the blow did not kill him, the trip north likely would. If he survived that? Then she would linger for a time, until she had discovered the diamonds and could disappear.

But now he was across the dinner table from her, eager to rebuild his imagined past. Escape was impossible, if he meant to watch her every bite. What would he expect of her, now that they would have so many hours together? The tour of the house had been helpful and she had seen a half-score of rooms where she might search for information about her father.

But they could not spend each day in rambling about the house together. Nor would he wish to spend his evenings thus. Along with the letter to Montague, she had scribbled a hurried note to Penny and begged her to come to dinner, hoping to alleviate this awkward togetherness.

The duchess had sent an equally hurried response. 'You need time to get to know one another again,' she had said. 'You do not need the distraction of others. In a week, perhaps, we shall come to see how you are getting on.'

A week? Penny might as well have said a year, for all the help that offered. Justine had sighed and informed the housekeeper that all meals would be served 'for two.' And that was a problem in itself. She had no idea what her husband's favourite foods were, his schedule when home, or even what rooms he took his meals in. She would have to rely on the servants. With the instruction, she had added a shy flutter of her lashes and a worried look. Then she had remarked that he had been sick for so long she'd feared ever having this opportunity…

The housekeeper had rushed to her aid, promising that every effort would be made to help her learn the likes and dislikes of the master, and the proper running of the house. The woman's eagerness to help her made her feel like even more of a liar than usual.

But trusting Mrs Bell had led to the table in the main dining room, facing an excess of silver and crystal, and a banquet clearly meant as a triumphant celebration of their return home. The man who could barely lift his fork two days before was enjoying nine courses and three wines.

Though he ate with obvious relish, she could feel

his eyes upon her, just as Montague's were, when they were alone together. His gaze was possessive, as though he was admiring some lovely ornament on a shelf, still surprised that he had come to own it. Soon, he would take it down and run his hands over it, to learn its every contour and detail. She shivered again.

He glanced immediately to the far side of the room, to the unlit fireplace. 'You will find that old houses such as this are draughty. It is as if the chill settles into the stone, even in summer. Shall I call for a servant to light a fire?'

'It is not necessary,' she assured him. 'We will not be here for long. If it bothers me again, I will remember to bring a shawl to dinner.'

'Oh.' There was a faint downward inflection, as though the idea that she might hide her bare shoulders disappointed him. Why did he not simply refuse her the comfort? She had long ago learned not to make such requests of Montague, for fear that he would insist she must wear even less, to show her obedience. When one had been given the choice of just a gown, or just a shawl, one learned to ignore the cold.

Now, Lord Felkirk pushed his dessert away. 'There is no need for an ice so late in the season, no matter how beautifully it is presented.' He stared down at the china ice-cream pot on the table, its lid heaped with ice to keep the contents cool. The butter, as well, rested in a basin of ice so that it might keep its perfect mould of the Felkirk family crest. He stared at the display and shook his head. 'So cold, all of it. Cold as the grave.'

As Justine watched, his attention slipped from her. He had gone oddly pensive, of a sudden, his expression darkening as though his mind wandered in a cavern somewhere, further and further from the light of day. It was almost as unsettling as his earlier thoughts. 'Let us retire to the salon,' she suggested. 'There is a fire laid there. I am sure it will be most cosy.' She feared that was rather an overstatement of the truth. Although the old manor was smaller than the new one, it was still too large to house a single couple. At the very least, it should hold two rambunctious boys, as it had in William's youth.

But the man before her was no longer an energetic child. When he stood, he offered his arm. But they both knew that what appeared an ordinary courtesy was a subtle request for her support so that he might manage with just a walking stick and not crutches. As she had in the afternoon, she came to his side and they proceeded together down the hall.

In the formal sitting room, she led him to a divan and poured him his port. Then she took her own place in a chair opposite, where her lacemaking pillow had been arranged for her. The evening was likely to be a silent affair, as full of thoughtful glances and mutual speculation as dinner had been. They were strangers, after all. There was little they had to converse about.

Necessary though it was, she could not bring herself to create any more memories out of whole cloth, demanding that he believe anecdotes from their courtship and elopement. There was only one thing she wished to discuss and the topic was unreachable. What was it about his house that had set him looking for a diamond pouch that had been missing and forgotten since late in the last century?

She made a covert study of the room: fireplace and mantel, landscapes on the wall, rug thick, but flat. There were no obvious hiding places here. She could not imagine herself stomping about the place, sounding for loose floorboards and hollow compartments. As her husband stood and approached her, she could not help but listen, hoping that one of his steps might sound different from another, revealing a trapdoor in the planking. But each sounded the same as the other, until he stopped just short of her, staring down as she worked.

She paused and looked up, expecting to see the censure she received from Montague when she occupied herself with something other than his needs. 'If you wish, you have but to say the word and I will put it away.'

'No. No, certainly not.' He took a step back as though surprised at her response. 'If it gives you pleasure, by all means continue.'

She offered a nod of thanks. Though she had not given it much thought, it did give her pleasure. While her hands were busy, her mind was free as a bird to think whatever she liked.

She felt him shift uncomfortably, foot to foot, and wondered if he wished for a similar pursuit. Perhaps he was as unsure of his place in this new world as she was. She raised her eyes from the mechanical motion of her hands on the bobbins and said, 'What do you normally do, of an evening, to pass the time?'

'You do not know?' he asked, almost suspiciously.

Her mind raced for a moment, then settled on an answer. 'We were together only a short while. You had little time or interest in domestic pleasures. In fact, I did not pick up my lace again until after we arrived in Wales and I knew you were settled comfortably. There simply was not time for it.' She waited for him to infer the obvious.

'We spent more time in the bedroom than the drawing room?' he said, then laughed at her blush. 'It need not embarrass you. We are married and our behaviour was quite normal.'

'Of course,' she responded. Now that she had put the thought into his head, he would likely demand that they retire immediately to return to their old diversions. At least the suspense would end and she could settle her nerves. Lying on one's back in silence was easier by far than trying to think of what to say while sitting up.

He looked at her thoughtfully for a moment, then said, 'I am sure, with practice, we can learn to sit together in the parlour as well. You asked how I spend my evenings when at home?' He paused again. 'I like to read. Not very exciting, I suppose. You may have noticed that my brother is happiest pacing about the room and debating politics. And while Penny is a great reader, she is often translating from Greek or Latin as she does so.' He paused, as though it were some sort of guilty secret. 'But I prefer novels.'

'Do you read aloud?' she asked. It was a solution that would solve no end of trouble. He might be happy and conversation would be rendered impossible.

He thought for a moment. 'I have not done it thus far. Until recently, I have not had an audience.'

'I should be happy to listen,' she said, 'if you wish to do so.'

'It would not distract you?'

'It would be a welcome addition to the evening,' she assured him. 'Perhaps you could choose one of your favourites, to share with me.'

He had responded to this with a relieved smile that made her wonder if the ensuing hours weighed as heavily on him as they did on her. When he had taken up his cane to go to the library for a book, he had waved away her offer of help. Both his spirit and his step had seemed lighter.

The answering warm glow she felt inside on seeing the change surprised her. Perhaps she had grown so used to thinking of him as her patient that she took credit for his success. Or maybe it was the equally unexpected knowledge that she did not like seeing him unhappy. Before he had come into the shop in Bath, she had felt only bitterness at the thought of him and his family. But the man before her now was what her father might have described as *tabula rasa*: a blank slate on which anything might be written. It did not seem fair to hold the past against him.

When he returned from his search, he was barely winded by the trip down the hall and holding a battered copy of *Gulliver's Travels*. She could barely remember the story, but she was sure she had read it some time in childhood. But it was plain that she had not understood the finer points of the narrative. The passages, though very funny, were too bawdy to be read aloud in a drawing room. She did not know whether to laugh or blush, doing both by turns. What must he think of her?

Then she remembered that she was supposed to be his wife and should not be shocked by his choice of subject. Perhaps he meant to relax her and put her in the mood for what was likely to follow, once they had retired to his room. It was strange. If he meant to flirt with her, he needn't have bothered. He had but to command and she would do whatever he wished.

Or he could give her another kiss. The memory of the kiss in the hallway of his brother's home was far more shocking than anything he was reading and left her so flustered that she confused her twists with her crosses on a whole row of bobbins and had to undo them and start again.

What was she to make of him? It would be a lie to say she did not like his company. She had not expected to enjoy this time alone, or to be so entertained by a thing that obviously gave him pleasure. It made her think longingly of the library. There were enough books in it for a lifetime of evenings just like this one.

She had enjoyed listening to him this morning as well. His stories of home and family had been so interesting that she had almost forgotten the reason she had wished to hear them. Her father's fate, and the location of the gems, had seemed unimportant compared to the history of a place that would never be a true home to her.

She suspected it was its master who fascinated her, not the house itself. She liked to look at him, with his pale skin, black hair and fine features. Even as he'd lain in the sickbed, she'd had more than a nurse's interest in the naked body concealed beneath the sheet. Though it was wasting from prolonged illness, she could imagine the vitality that had been there. As he read to her tonight, she could see the vigour she had assumed was there. His enthusiasm for the book filled the room. His voice was expressive, his whole body animated, so she could imagine the scenes playing out before her. She had been right to bring him home. What a waste it would have been for someone so alive to die violently, alone and unloved.

She let herself relax into the sound of his voice and the flicker of the candle behind the screen at her side, her fingers working methodically on the trim in her lap. When he shut the book with a snap, she was surprised to hear the clock strike eleven. She looked up at him and he returned her gaze with a surprised smile.

'I did not think it had got so late,' she said.

'Nor had I.' He yawned and stood, setting the book aside. 'I think, perhaps, it is time for us to retire. Let me escort you to your room. When you are ready for bed…' he paused, as though he was as nervous as she. 'Come into my room by the connecting door. You need not bother to knock. I will be waiting for you.'

'Of course,' she agreed.

Chapter Nine

She did as he suggested, letting the maid that had come with her from Penny's household dress her in her nightgown and comb and braid her hair. With each stroke of the brush she reminded herself that it was foolish to be so nervous. She was not some fainting virgin, unaware of what was about to occur. Her time with Montague had prepared her for any request Lord Felkirk might make.

William, she reminded herself. His family called him Will. So must she think of him, for she was his wife. If the stories she had told him were true, they had been intimate for some time. They would be so again. It was only natural.

She fought down the depression that the thought caused. It was bad enough to be the plaything of Montague. But to open herself to a stranger in the hope of gain? It was a dangerous precedent.

The best she could hope for was that this would be the last man to use her so. But it was a shame that it had to be this particular man. He was kind. He was funny. And he was most certainly handsome. At one time, it had been her dream to find such a man. More accurately, she had wanted to be found by him. If only he could have come five years ago, before it was too late…

She dismissed the maid and took one more glance in the mirror, watching her own eyes go blank as she put such foolish thoughts aside. Then she went to the door that connected their rooms and turned the knob.

He was already in bed, smiling at her as she closed the door behind her. He had propped himself up on the pillows, bare arms folded behind his head. The covers pooled in his lap, exposing his equally bare chest. She suspected he was naked beneath them. For a moment, she wanted nothing more than to turn and run.

Foolishness. She had seen a naked man before. She had seen this man naked. She'd been bathing him for weeks. There were no surprises here.

He unfolded his arms and held one out to her in welcome, patting the mattress at his side with the other. 'Come,' he said.

Without thinking, she went to him, as obedient as a trained dog. Her own lack of resistance disgusted her. Had Montague schooled the last of the spirit from her? She buried the thought deep, so that it did not show on her face. It would not do to go frowning to her husband's bed.

As she drew near, he threw back the blankets

so that she might climb in beside him. She glanced down at the bare flank it revealed and then back up into his face, then sat down on the mattress, swung her legs up beside his and let him settle the covers over them.

His arm wrapped around her, holding her easily to his side. 'Is this as strange to you as it is to me?'

Stranger than he could possibly imagine. She sought a comfortable place to rest her own arms, settling them gently against his chest. 'It has been some time,' she said, trying to sound sympathetic.

'You, at least, remember who I am,' he pointed out.

'Will it really matter so much, once the lights are out?' she asked.

She had said something wrong. He leaned away from her, clearly shocked. Of course it should matter. If the man one loved could not remember, it should hurt. If he had cared enough to marry her, he should at least pretend that she was not just another warm body in his bed.

He cleared his throat. 'If it were simply a matter of desire, perhaps it would not matter. We share something more, do we not?' This last came with a leading, hopeful tone, as though he was still longing to remember what it was that had brought them to marry.

She had no answer, other than 'yes.' Then she snuggled closer to him and eased a leg over his, hoping that the discussion might be over for the night.

He did not move away. But neither did he tumble her on to her back so that they could begin. Instead, his other hand reached out to her. It hovered over her breasts for a moment. Then he ran a finger along the neckline of her rather chaste nightrail. 'Did you make this for yourself?'

'Of course.'

'And the lace here. What is it called?'

She shrugged, for it was no great achievement. 'A simple picot edging.'

'Do you make it with the pins and the cushion?'

She shook her head, surprised that he would be asking about her work now, of all times. 'I use a shuttle. It is called tatting. Very easy. I can make enough for the whole gown in an evening.'

He looked down at her body again, seemingly more interested in the simple dress than the body beneath it. 'Is this indicative of your other nightwear?'

'I have several identical to this,' she admitted.

'It is very practical,' he said, politely.

She had a sudden memory of lying with Montague, wearing the sheer lawn he preferred. And then there were the nights he expected her to come to him wearing nothing at all. She could not help the sudden shudder of revulsion.

He lifted the blanket and bunched it around her shoulders. 'As I told you before, old houses are cold. But you may trust that I will keep you warm when we are together like this.' With two fingers, he plucked the nightcap from her head and dropped it on the floor beside the bed. Then he blew a warm breath against her ear.

This made her shiver as well. But it was accompanied by a sigh of delight that surprised her and drew a satisfied nod from him. Then he spoke again. 'I am curious. You take the time to make masterpieces for your friends. They could talk of nothing else but the cleverness of your work. When I did not see lace trimming on your gown during the day, or at dinner, I assumed I would see some tonight.' He glanced down at the cap on the floor and shook his head in disappointment. 'Why do you not wear the finer stuff yourself?'

She had a sudden memory of the chest her mother had kept. It was as big as a wardrobe, the outside inlaid with intricate tracings of sulphur, the inside smelling of beeswax and cloves. *You will have it some day*, she had said. *For your trousseau.*

How long had it been since she'd thought of it? After Montague had come to her, she'd realised that marriage was a lost dream. That had been the day that she'd set the items she'd already made aside, so that Margot might have them.

Her husband was waiting for an answer.

'It is nice to see others happy,' she said.

'I would like to see you happy as well,' he replied. 'You would be most attractive in a gown trimmed with the lace you were making tonight.' He drew a finger across her bodice, as if to indicate where it might go.

She shivered. 'It would not be very modest. You would see…' She stopped. She could imagine her nipples, poking through the lace.

'I know,' he said, with a smile, his hand pausing dangerously near to one of them.

'If you wish, I will remove the gown,' she said, squirming under the covers to draw up the hem.

He covered her hand with his to stop her. 'You misunderstand me.'

Perhaps she did not. 'You do not wish to see my body?'

He gave a nervous laugh. 'I wish to. Very much. I am sure I enjoyed the sight of it before and I look forward to seeing it again. But there is no reason to rush.'

'Of course not,' she said, stretching beside him again and pressing a hand to the middle of his chest.

In response, he stroked her hair. 'It is quite embarrassing to admit this, but I do not know if I have the strength to perform. The day has been tiring and I am still weak as a kitten. I am likely to shame myself, should I attempt to be intimate with you.'

When she glanced down, his body said otherwise. She could see the beginnings of arousal growing beneath the bedsheet. 'We will do whatever you wish,' she said, surprised to feel disappointment.

He closed his eyes and sighed, as though it were a relief. Then he said, 'Then we will go where the mood takes us. And I do enjoy your being here, with me. The sound of your voice is soothing. I was told you read to me, while I was unconscious.'

'I did,' she said. 'Only novels. Nothing of substance.' She smiled. 'It seems we share an interest in them.' It had been a chance to indulge a guilty pleasure of her own, while pretending to help him.

'I do not remember the words,' he said. 'But I think I remember the sound of you. You must speak more often for I love to hear it. Your voice is like music.'

'Thank you,' she said.

He closed his eyes, and leaned back into the pillows. 'You have listened to me all night. Now you must speak. Tell me of yourself.'

Her hands froze on his chest and she hoped he did not feel her go rigid with panic. What could she say that might not trigger the very memories she did not want to awaken? 'What do you wish to know?'

'How did you become so clever with your hands? Did your mother teach you?'

She relaxed a little, for that topic was harmless enough. 'It was a skill of hers. But much of the work I taught myself. She was carrying my sister when my father died.' The words almost stuck in her throat and she hurried past them. 'After the birth, she was so very weak.' Memories of her mother were equally painful. 'When Father had been with us, she'd been young and happy. But without him, she'd go days without speaking, staring out of the window of our tiny apartment, her beauty fading a little each year, until the life was gone from her.'

Will must have recognised the fact, for his hand tightened on her shoulder, as if he could lead her away from the past. 'But you still have your sister.'

'Her name is Margot,' she said, relieved. 'She is in school.'

He opened one eye and glanced at her. 'At this time of year?'

'She spends summers and holidays there as well,' Justine said. 'I have no money to help her and must tend to my own work. It is better that she remain there, if there is nowhere for her to stay.'

He had opened both eyes to stare at her now. 'You have somewhere now,' he said, shaking his head in disappointment. 'You are mistress of a house that is more than large enough to hold a young woman, no matter how extravagant her needs might be. Tell me, how old is little Margot?'

'Nearly twenty,' she admitted.

'And still in school?' he said, surprised. 'Is she not out yet?'

'There was no money for a Season.'

'There is now.' He settled back into the pillows again, as though there would be no further discussion. 'She will stay with us until we can arrange for her come out. Let Penny settle everything. She might appear to be a wallflower at times, but she is quite good at organising things. And she is a duchess, after all.'

'Well...' she said, running through the list of reasons that such a trip would be impossible, to search for one that made sense.

Will was staring at her again. 'You want to see her, do you not? There is no estrangement between you?'

'I want to see her more than anything else in the world,' she admitted, feeling the tightness in her heart when she thought of her sister ease a little.

'Then you shall write to her first thing tomorrow and we will have her here, while the weather is still good.'

'Thank you.' She would find a way to change his mind in the morning.

But then it occurred to her that she didn't have to. She could summon Margot and have her in Wales before their guardian knew a thing about it. Once she was part of the duke's family, he could not threaten her or attempt to remove her without admitting who he was. If he attempted it, Justine would threaten to sacrifice herself and reveal what he had done. She did not know much of chess, but she suspected this was what players called a stalemate.

She looked at William Felkirk again, a smile spreading slowly across her face. He had that slightly puzzled expression she associated with men in the jewellery shop who had been surprised when a word or gesture held more significance than the gems they were offering. With one casual suggestion, the man in the bed beside her had the power to reorder her world. 'Thank you.' She said it with more feeling so he might know she was truly grateful. Then, to stop further conversation, she leaned forward and kissed him on the mouth.

She had been kissed often enough. It had been unavoidable. But had *she* ever kissed a man before? Certainly not like this. It was wet and open mouthed, as though her happiness could not be contained behind closed lips. His mouth was surprisingly sweet, as though the ice cream he had rejected was still on his lips. She tasted the flavour. She quite liked it and the feeling of his firm lips against the tip of her tongue.

She could tell her sudden boldness had surprised him. He was still at first. Then his hand settled into the small of her back, drawing her closer to him, pulling her body up on to his chest. Then, everything about him seemed to relax, his mouth falling open against hers, his tongue easing into her mouth to caress hers.

Such kisses had always seemed like an invasion. But this was very different. Will Felkirk's touch was gentle, as though he were learning her from the inside out. She probed gently in response. It was different to respond. She did not feel desire so much as curiosity. What harm would it do to indulge that, as long as it kept him from asking any more questions?

He tasted different. The shape of his mouth was different as well. She could feel the playfulness of his smile, the fullness of his lips and the smoothness of his cheekbone as she stroked it. She moved her hands lower, to his bare chest, which was no longer as sunken and hollow as it had felt while he slept. With a little sunlight and solid food, the health was coming back to him. His heart beat fast and strong under her fingers. She could feel it beating even faster as she touched him. And there, on his arm, was the strange smooth skin of the burn scar.

While she might admit that the duke was the more handsome of the two brothers, he was a trifle too perfect to look at. This man, with the crease in his skull and the scars on his body, was so much more real and she knew him almost too well.

He sighed at her touch and his kisses became a sudden opening and closing of his lips as though he was taking a bite of fruit. Then he sighed again, in satisfaction as if he needed her to feel complete, as one might need air or food.

She stilled for a moment, not sure she liked it. She understood being desired. She understood what it was to be used. She had understood his need when he was too helpless to care for himself. But now the feeling was different. She wanted him to be stronger for her help, not more dependant.

Suppose, when she finally managed to escape from this place, she left him feeling less than whole. She had expected to lose some of herself by this joining. But suppose she grew to depend on him? She could not afford such feelings, if she was ever in her life to be free.

Perhaps it was simply that it had been so long since lying with a man that she had forgotten how to behave. The trick was to disengage one's mind from the activity, so that it might be somewhere else, while the body acted. She tried it now and found it strangely ineffective. The feel of his skin under her hand, was too real to ignore. Instead of hiding from it, she wanted to lose more of herself to him, to be more deeply entwined. In a daring moment, she ran her hand down his chest, following the trail of hair on his belly until it slipped beneath the sheet to grip him.

He inhaled sharply at the touch, taking her tongue more deeply into his mouth.

This was interesting. She had never felt this sense of control before. She took advantage, running a fingertip lightly across the opening at the head of his member.

He pulled away, 'I do not think…' Though his member stirred at her touch, his body moved weakly under hers, a reminder that he was still not fully recovered.

She had but to release him, with an apology for her forwardness. She would be safe from intimacy for another night, or more. Perhaps he would even let her return to her room. Instead, she kissed his lips again and murmured, 'Let me.' Then she moved her hand on him.

As she watched, he settled back into the pillows, but did not relax. His eyes were shut tightly, his mouth shut so tightly that his lips went white. Did her touch hurt him? She thought not, for he made no move to stop her. His nostrils flared as he took a slow steady breath as though struggling to maintain control of his own body and prolong the climax.

Did she really affect him so? The idea that she could award or deny his happiness with a single touch was exhilarating. She gripped him tighter, stroking slowly from root to tip, and felt him growing under her fingers.

He was longer and thicker than she'd expected. Silky skin stretched tight over blood and muscle, growing slippery with the first drops of his seed. She wondered what it would be like when he entered her. Probably not as pleasant as she was imagining. In her experience, real life seldom lived up to imagination.

But the current moment was satisfying enough. As she moved her hand on him, his whole body seemed to tighten, tension building like a coiled spring. His eyes were open again, head had arched back so that he could stare at the ceiling and his lips worked, almost as though praying. In this moment, he was hers in a way that no man had ever been. It made her wish that she could keep him. Or, at least, that she could keep pretending for a lifetime.

She used his vulnerability to kiss his exposed throat, running teeth and tongue along the tendons until she heard the hitch in his breath. Then she released him, just for a second, to raise the hem of her nightdress, brushing him with the picot edging he had found so intriguing.

He shuddered at the contact. She changed her grip, wrapping him in the linen, and tightening her hand to finish him. Beneath her, his whole body jerked and his breath released in a moan. Then, as she had expected, he lost control and sagged helpless back on to the mattress.

She lay still against him, her palm flat against his chest, waiting until he had stopped trembling and his heartbeat began to slow again. Then she rubbed him gently with the linen, rolled away from him and stood to pull the soiled gown over her head and drop it on the floor beside her discarded nightcap.

She glanced at it with a frown. Should she summon a maid, or search in her own bureau for a replacement? She did not normally like sleeping bare. The vulnerability of it was so distressing that she could not rest easy. But tonight felt different. She stretched her arms above her head, noting the pull of muscle and skin, feeling stronger and more confident than before. She smoothed a hand over breast and belly, surprised at how warm they felt. Then she turned towards the connecting door between the rooms.

'Stay.'

She looked back at Will, surprised. How could she have forgotten that he was there, just behind her, watching this shameless display of her body?

But she had nothing to fear. There was no avarice

in his gaze. His look held more wonder than lust. He reached out a hand to her, as though to stop her departure. 'Come back to bed. We need do nothing more. But sleep here tonight, at my side.'

'Very well,' she said. She came back to the bed and climbed beneath the covers, letting him gather her close. In less than a sigh, he was asleep.

She lay awake beside him, surprised at how relaxing it was to share a bed with William Felkirk. She dreaded those nights that Montague expected it of her, for it invariably meant that she would be wakened at some point and required to service him.

But judging by the slight snore that escaped his parted lips, the man at her side now was not likely to wake. His arm wrapped loosely around her, his thigh brushing her leg. But the limbs were as relaxed and heavy as they had been as he'd lain in a coma.

This feeling of skin against skin was a new thing as well. She ought to be frightened, lying hip to hip with a stranger. But this was more decadent than disturbing. She yawned. Perhaps this was what it was like to be a courtesan, taking and discarding lovers without a second thought.

Or perhaps it was how she'd have felt, had she been a wife.

The thought was gone as quickly as it had come, for she was slipping away, into a dark and peaceful sleep.

Chapter Ten

When Will awoke the next morning, she was gone from his bed. Perhaps last night's release was what he had needed. It was the first real rest he'd had since waking from the coma. He'd slept so soundly that he had no idea whether she'd stayed as he asked.

He rather hoped she had. His dreams had been deliciously lurid, opium-drenched fantasies of some Turkish paradise where he reclined on a pillow while a nubile woman ministered to his every need.

He grinned. What he had thought of as a dream was very close to what had actually happened. She had seemed so prim when she came to him in her plain gown and cap. Then she had kissed him soundly and taken him to heaven with a single hand. After, she'd stripped naked at his bedside and stretched like a satisfied cat.

Was it any wonder that he had dreamed of paradise? When he closed his eyes he could still see her high, full breasts bobbing above a narrow waist and hips that made a man long to hold on to them. What had he been thinking, to invite her to bed so that they might simply talk? She had pleasured him to the point where it had not mattered in the slightest who she was or where she'd come from. His only concern had been that she continue until she had finished.

When he came down to breakfast, she was already there. He should not have been surprised. He thought himself an early riser, but she seemed to pride herself on being ahead of him. The post had come and she had kept a single letter for herself and arranged the rest at his place. Then she made sure that his plate and cup were prepared just as he would like it.

Today, instead of greeting her with a curt nod, he went to her side and kissed her lightly on the cheek. He glanced down at the paper in front of her.

He frowned. Despite what had happened between them, she still seemed to stiffen at the touch of his lips and shift nervously away as though fearing a blow. Her movement obscured the note, which had all but disappeared beneath her plate. Then she relaxed into the passive doll he had come to expect. 'Good morning, William,' she said dutifully.

'And good morning to you, my dear.' *And where have you gone?* It was not as if he expected her to arrive at the table like a slave in a harem, attired in nothing but scarves. But when he looked at her, he'd expected to find some sign of the change between them.

She glanced down at the paper peeping out from beneath her breakfast plate. 'If you are wondering about the letter, it is a note from a friend of my parents, congratulating me upon our marriage. I will answer it after breakfast.'

'Of course,' he said. It was not so unusual that she had friends, nor that they would correspond with her. But since she had not mentioned them before, he had flattered himself that he was her entire world. It did him no credit that he felt jealous of the person who wrote to her and the time she would spend on them. 'And you will write to your sister as we discussed?'

Her expression, which had been pensive, changed to a brief, radiant smile. Then it faded to the more sedate half-smile she usually wore. 'If you still wish me to, I would like that.'

It was as if the sun had come out from behind a cloud only to disappear again. He grinned at her, hoping to remind her of the previous night. 'Of course I still wish it. And if there is anything else that will make you smile as you have just done, you must ask immediately. On such a fine morning as this, I could deny you nothing.'

She glanced at the window, as though expecting to see a change in the weather. 'I thought it rather chill, when I was walking.' She looked back at him, giving no indication that she understood the reason for his happiness could be traced back to last night. She held out his cup, 'Coffee?'

He took his usual seat and accepted the cup.

'Thank you.' Perhaps it was an ordinary thing for her, or had been so before the accident. If that was true, then damn him for forgetting so much. He leaned closer to her, catching her eye and smiling. 'And thank you for last night as well.'

The delightful pink of her cheeks clashed with the reds in her hair. 'You are welcome.' She glanced down at the table. Toast?' She pushed the toast rack closer to his plate, as though appeasing one appetite would make him forget the other.

He ignored her offer of bread and continued on his original topic. 'I enjoyed what you did for me, very much,' he said, thinking the words oddly polite. But they seemed a match for her reserved response.

'I am glad,' she said, sending the marmalade pot after the toast with a nudge of her finger.

He ignored that as well. 'Did you enjoy it as well?'

To this, she gave him an odd look, as though it had not occurred to her to have an opinion about it. 'It makes me happy when you are happy.' Then the placid smile returned.

'That is not what I asked,' he said. 'I want to know if you enjoyed touching me.'

She glanced around her, as if to remind him that they were in the breakfast room, not the bedroom. She looked down at her plate as though trying to decide if it might be possible to pretend she had not heard. She took up her knife and fork and began slicing the sausage on it into ever smaller bites. Then, as if she'd noticed what she had done to the rather significantly shaped meat, she set down her utensils with a clatter and said, in a rush of words, 'Enjoyed it? Of course. Why should I not? You are my husband, after all, and it is my goal…'

'To make me happy,' he finished. 'That brings us back to where we began.' He pushed the toast rack out of the way and reached for one of her hands, holding it gently in his and noticing how cold the fingers were. 'It is not that I object to being happy. But I assume, when I married you, that I wanted you to be happy as well. Surely I said something of the kind.' He hoped that it was true. This morning, she was acting almost as if she was afraid of him.

She blinked at him, as though the details of their past were as murky to her as they were to him. Then she glanced down at their joined hands with an expression of such modesty and beauty that he wanted to capture it in oils. 'Of course, my love. It is just that I do not want to seem less than grateful for all you and your family have done for me. Your offer last night, to allow me to send for Margot…' She looked up hopefully, as though fearing he meant to retract it in the cold light of day.

'Grateful?' Was that why she had been so affectionate? It was oddly annoying to think that her treatment of him had been some sort of a reward for a perfectly normal offer of hospitality. 'You needn't be, over such a small thing. Where else would you sister stay, if not with us? If you pine for her company, then you shall have it.'

'I do. Very much so.' Her smile returned, and for a moment he was afraid that she might cry. Or stranger still, that she might repeat her behaviour of the previous evening and sink to her knees before him during breakfast. Exciting though the idea was, it was rather alarming to think of her putting a hand in his breeches each time she wanted a favour.

'Then it is what I wish as well,' he said carefully. 'For I want to see you happy, just as you wish to see me happy.'

She nodded, as though all was settled.

'But I wish that your happiness, last night and in nights to come, can be separate from the thought of your sister's visit. It is quite a different thing, you see.'

'Of course it is,' she said, nodding. But there was something in her tone that announced she had no idea what he was talking about. What kind of a selfish beast had he been, if he had not taught her that the bedroom was a place to seek mutual pleasure? This obtuse behaviour on her part was almost enough to set his mind to doubting again. It did not sound like him, at all.

At least, it did not sound like the sort of husband and lover he had wished to be. But how was he to know, really? His experience thus far had been limited to the sort of women who knew what they wanted in bed, even if it was only to pretend satisfaction in exchange for jewellery and rent.

Did gently bred virgins behave in the same way?

Were they taught to submit to their husbands and trade favour for favour like courtesans? Did no one speak to them of the pleasure of the act? Perhaps it was his job to teach that particular lesson. The prospect of that made him want to grin like an idiot. Instead, he smiled at her with as much kindness and gentleness as he could muster, then leaned forward to kiss her on the cheek again. 'Tonight, I shall demonstrate what I mean.'

'Oh.' It was but one word. But she said it in a tone that said, *oh, dear.* Or, worse yet, *oh dear, you needn't bother.* If he had not seen her on the previous evening, totally in control of both his body and her own nerves, he'd have thought she was frightened.

'For now, let us finish our breakfast,' he said, dismissing the subject until later. 'I will leave you alone so you might go to the morning room and write letters to your friend and to your sister.'

With that, the relieved smile returned to her face as though it had never left.

He expected something of her.

Justine was not sure what it was that he had wanted, but it seemed some display of happiness was in order. Clearly, he did not understand how difficult it was to appear pleasant and at ease when one was already holding a paper full of admonishments on how she must behave if she was to ferret out the Felkirk family secrets. In his note, Montague had approved of the move to this house, since it was most likely to hold what they were looking for.

But he had also hinted that he would expect a detailed accounting of her activities when next they met in the woods. She rather feared that was more than just a description of the rooms she had searched and what she might have uncovered in them. He would want to know exactly what had transpired in the bedroom with Will.

Of course, Will seemed to want to talk of that as well. What was wrong with men, that they could not put what happened in the bedroom firmly in the past, as she meant to do? His kisses were nice, of course. She especially liked the little ones he had given her in the breakfast room, as though it were a matter of course to remind her of his feelings throughout the day.

But she wished he would stop. Small kisses only made her think of other, more intimate ones and the feel of his skin under her hand. It felt nice, just as the kisses did. But it would all lead to the same place in the end, where he had all the control and she had none. Badgering her about her own happiness was unnecessary. Life was what it was. Even the difficult bits went more smoothly if one did not brood on one's feelings from moment to moment.

This morning, he meant to leave her alone, just as promised, to write her letters. Once the door was closed, she began with a thorough examination of the room. As she'd expected, she did not find a desk drawer full of loose stones, or a treasure map rolled up in a pigeon hole. Yesterday's tour of the house had convinced her that the library was the only room worth searching. It held the books and papers left behind when the previous duke had moved to the new house.

If there was nothing to be found, so be it. She assured Montague in the note she wrote him that she would follow his orders to the letter, but she had no real intention of rooting through Will Felkirk's mind for the truth. Why risk disturbing the conveniently forgotten past, on the slim hope of gain?

It was far better, in her opinion, to ensure Margot's safety through the rather ordinary method Will had suggested. If money was needed to make her situation permanent, she did not need stolen diamonds. Her husband was a most agreeable man. If he meant what he'd said at breakfast, she had but to smile and ask for it, and he would open his purse and give her whatever she needed. It would work for a time, at least. Justine would face the consequences if and when he remembered what had happened in Bath. With luck, Margot might be safely married before the truth came out.

But the first step towards that happy state was to invite her sister for a visit. Justine chewed on her pen, unsure of what to say. There was so much that had happened and so little that could be explained. Suppose someone at the school saw the letter, or enquired as to the reasons for Margot's sudden departure. Suppose Montague had spies to prevent Margot's escape from his power. She must not think of that. There was little she could do, other than to hope that Montague heard nothing until Margot was well under way.

In the end, she settled on a brief note, explaining that she had married and was eager for her sister's company. Margot was cautioned to tell no one of the wedding, as it had not been announced to the whole of William's family. Under no circumstances was she to communicate with Mr Montague, as it was a sudden elopement and Justine had yet to tell him of it. If anyone asked, she must simply say that she had been called home for a visit. Then she was to take the next carriage north. Once she was here, all would be explained.

She folded sufficient bank notes in the letter to allow for comfortable travel, sealed it up and summoned a footman to place it and the note to Montague in the outgoing post. Now she had but to hope that Margot appeared before her next visit with her guardian.

Will was secretly relieved that Justine had plans to occupy herself for the morning. If she had taken such care in nursing him to health, he doubted that she would approve of what he had planned for his day. If one wished to regain one's life, some risk must be taken. He had no plans to remain swaddled in cotton wool, simply to please his lady.

His lady. The idea was more appealing than it had

been, just a day ago. There were still problems, of course. But many of them involved coaxing his wife out of the shell she had built around herself.

His own problems would be dealt with as they arose. He meant to conquer the first one today. He walked out from the house, choosing a stouter walking stick than usual, in case he became unsteady. Though he tired easily, and had to rest once on his way, there were no instances of imbalance. While he did not feel as strong as a bull, he could almost forget that he had recently been an invalid.

His nose pricked at the scent of hay and horse, growing stronger with each step. Justine would laugh at him, should he tell her that the smell of manure was its own sort of cure. But it reminded him of how he felt in the saddle, riding a beast that was the epitome of strength and freedom. He paused at the doorway, offering a brief prayer, should anything remain of the spirit of his faithful Jupiter. If there was a heaven, Will's place there must have a stall for Jupe.

He paused again, staring into the barn and allowing his eyes to adjust to the dim light within. Then he ignored the sadness and carefully searched his heart for any signs of fear. He had been telling himself it was his own foolhardiness that had nearly killed him. A weaker man might have blamed the horse that failed him. Of course, a stronger man would have had the sense not to take a jump. Could he really trust his own mind at all?

'Hello, my lord,' the stable master said.

'Hello, Jenks.' Jenks was technically a servant of the duke's, but he had been with the family since Will and Adam were boys. The man had taught him to ride. Who better to understand the problems that might occur today? 'I suppose you heard of my accident?'

'Yes, my lord. We were all most concerned for you.'

'I cannot remember much of what happened.' It was a lie. But it was too painful to own the total blank of the incident. 'It seems I lost my mount as well.'

'A shame, my lord.' There was no censure in the voice, even though he deserved it. 'Are you planning a trip to Tattersall's?'

Will sighed. 'I do not know if I am ready to purchase another. But I must get a horse under me, sooner rather than later. If there is a problem with my judgement…' For instance, if he collapsed in terror before taking the saddle. He had known of a man so shaken after a little tumble that he had sold his hunter and now travelled in nothing more exciting than a barouche with full livery.

Jenks nodded again. 'It is widely said, sir, that when one falls, one must get right back on.'

'It is almost a cliché,' Will agreed, 'but very true. What do you have ready in the stalls for me? I fancy a gentle ride about the property.' He had emphasised the word gentle, but just the sound of it depressed him.

'If you wish a gentle ride, I have a mare right

here, ready to saddle.' Jenks patted the neck of a nearby grey and her head swung round slowly to look at them.

Will had expected fixed feelings, when the moment came to ride again. Perhaps he would not experience outright terror. At least there would be some trepidation at mounting. However, at the sight of the horse Jenks suggested, he felt nothing but scorn. 'You might as well put a saddle on Penny's pet terrier. It would have more spirit than this beast.'

There was a sparkle in Jenks's eye, as though he had meant the first choice as nothing more than a joke. He walked down the row of stalls, and stopped before a chestnut gelding. 'Perhaps Aries will suit you better. Sound legs. A good chest. Not prone to starts or skittishness. He is a fine horse, my lord.'

'True.' He could handle the beast easily. But somehow, the thought of riding did not excite him as it once did. He glanced down the row at the largest stall, a place of honour in the centre of the stable. 'Do you think my brother would mind if I borrowed Zeus?'

Jenks started in surprise. 'He would not mind, for the beast needs exercise. But do you think it wise?' Zeus was black as Satan and notoriously bad tempered. But he shared a sire with Jupiter and was as close as Will was likely to get to his old friend.

'It is probably not the best decision,' Will admitted. 'But I would like to try. Keeping control of him will teach me to be alert, when in the saddle.'

'Of course, my lord.' Jenks gave him a doubtful look, but set about saddling the horse. And, as Zeus was wont to do, he spat out the bit, blew out his stomach to fight the saddling and danced in the stall, making it as hard as possible to accomplish the task.

The sight should have worried him. If he had nearly split his head after a ride, shouldn't such a spirited animal worry him? Instead, when he looked at Zeus, he felt excited and eager to ride. It had been too long since he had felt a horse under him. When Jenks finally got control of the stallion and led him out of the stable, Will practically itched with the desire to mount.

It was not as easy as he'd hoped. His legs were still weak and he had to resort to a mounting block to get a foot into the stirrup. But once he was astride, the problems were minimal and he set out from the stable at a walk.

It was good to feel the wind in his face again and good to see the family lands from the accustomed combined height of man and animal. He glanced back at his house, hoping that Justine was not too near any of the windows, as he did not want to frighten her, then nudged the horse to a trot. There was still no sign of the fear he had expected to find in himself. Other than the strangeness of a new mount, there was nothing exceptionable about the ride.

He experimented with cantering, and even galloped for a short stretch with similar results. Zeus seemed more bothered by the outing than he, he recognised that the commands he was given were not from his true master and was still trying to decide whether he needed to obey them. But Will kept a firm hand on the reigns and tightened the grip of his thighs which, if truth be told, were still not strong enough to take too much more of this.

One last test and he would go back to the stables. He turned the horse towards a low fence at the bottom of the pasture. There was no risk in it. He had been jumping that particular obstacle since he was a boy and the horse was familiar with it as well. As they approached, he felt nothing but pleasant anticipation of both man and beast, for the moment of weightless flight as they passed over it. And they did, with ease.

It was then that Zeus chose his moment for rebellion, landing hard, dipping his head and digging in his feet to send Will over his neck and to the ground with a thump. His moment of triumph was immediately followed by the air being jarred out of his lungs and the warning snap of large sharp teeth beside his ear.

'You dirty bastard,' he wheezed, rolling out of the way.

'My lord!' Jenks was rushing to his side to take the reins and help him to his feet.

Will held up a hand to signify that all was well and managed a weak laugh. 'Nothing to worry about, Jenks. I have not cracked my pate, or damaged anything but my dignity.' Hardly even that. The fall had been tonic, just as the ride had been. He had not feared the jump or the fall. His riding clothes were stained with mud and he smelled of grass and dried leaves. But he had not shattered as he'd feared he might. His mistake had been in taking his brother's miserable horse out in the first place. But there was nothing particularly fragile about him that might prevent such rides in the future.

He thanked Jenks for his help and promised to visit again soon and choose a more manageable horse. Other than that, the day had been a success. Yet it did not fully content him. Would he never regain anything from the time before the accident?

It was sad that he could not remember his wife. But how near to death did one need to go to erase even the fear of falling from one's mind? He had been half-expecting that an innocent tumble would knock the memory back into him. He would see a flash of that time, on a different horse. Perhaps Jupe had startled at the sight of a rabbit, or stumbled on a hole. He had sent Will sailing through the air with the knowledge that the landing was likely to be a bad one, ending in pain and darkness.

Still, there was nothing. His mind was as smooth and as blank as a block of ice, with the things he wanted frozen for ever inside. He would find Justine and beg her for more information on the day of his accident. Perhaps she had seen something that might have indicated the reason for it, other than carelessness on his part. Had he been drunk, or in some other way completely unaware of what was about to happen to him?

When he returned to the house, she was nowhere to be found. The morning room was as tidy as if she had never occupied it at all. Her bedroom was equally empty, as was his. Only in the library did he see evidence of her presence. In the darkest corner of the room, a table was stacked with leather-bound journals his mother had kept while she still lived in the house. What she sought there, he was not sure, for his mother had been an indifferent correspondent at best.

Beside them, the family Bible was open to the page where his birth had been recorded, along with the significant events of his childhood. Was she really so eager to please him that she chose to research his past? What else could she be looking for but his mother's anecdotal record of his life and perhaps a few favourite recipes and menus?

He smiled. He'd have found the behaviour strange, had it been described to him. But there was so much about his new wife that was odd, it hardly surprised him. If she had a fault, it was her almost obsessive desire to make him happy. Tonight, she would be surprised to learn that to accomplish her goal she must take as much pleasure as she gave.

Chapter Eleven

Justine pulled a row of pins and undid the last few knots of the lace on her pillow, so that she might fix the mistakes she'd made when she'd lost concentration. Perhaps she should ask Will to read Walter Scott tonight, especially the bit about tangled webs and deception. Of course, a dishonest woman in that story had ended up walled alive in an abbey. In her current frame of mind, that story would not be light entertainment.

'You are sure there is nothing you can recall about the accident that might make things clearer.'

Since she was making the story up as she went, she doubted that she had the detail he was hoping for. 'I was not close enough to see. And it all happened too fast.' He had been questioning her all through dinner about the past. After nearly two hours, he was no closer to what he expected to hear, but she balanced on the edge of a knife.

He was silent for a moment and she took the opportunity to turn the tables on him. 'In my opinion, it is fortunate that you do not remember. Suppose it had come upon you suddenly and given you a turn. It was very dangerous to ride at all. What if something had happened and you had fallen again?'

Now he was the one who was uncomfortable, squirming in his seat like a guilty little boy.

She looked up from her work, too surprised to remember the role she was playing. 'You fell again, didn't you?'

'It was nothing,' he replied hurriedly. 'I was back on my feet as soon as I regained my wind. But it makes me all the more confused at what caused the earlier accident.'

'I do not know why I bothered to nurse you, if you use your recovery foolishly.' Was this real alarm she was feeling at the thought of him lying hurt again? It was always sad when a man so young and alive met with a tragic accident. But when had it begun to matter to her?

He was at her side now, full of apology. 'If it bothers you, I will take no more chances. Adam's horse is a brute. I will not take him out again.' He knelt in front of her now, until he was sure that he had caught her eye. 'Am I forgiven?'

'Of course,' she said, trying and failing for her usual calm smile.

'Very good,' he said, then stared down at the work in her lap. She resumed her knotting, and he watched, fascinated by the rhythmic click and switch of the bone bobbins, the exactitude of pins and the slow but steady increase in finished work. 'What are you making?' he asked at last, unable to contain his curiosity.

'I do not know, as of yet,' she said. 'A bit of trim for something. It is an old pattern and I do not have to think to work it. But it makes up very pretty.'

'If you do not know what it is for, then why are you doing it?'

'To keep my hands busy,' she said. 'Idle hands are the devil's playthings, after all.'

'Have you given thought to my suggestion of last night?'

She frowned, trying to remember what it was that he had said.

'When I told you to make something for yourself,' he said. 'A tucker for that bodice, perhaps.' He was staring at her breasts.

She placed a hand on her chest to hide them. 'I am sorry if the gown is too low. I will change, if you wish.'

He pulled her hand away, wrapping the fingers with his. 'There is nothing wrong with the dress, other than that it is rather plain. Not that you need to adorn yourself, to be more beautiful,' he added hurriedly. 'It simply surprises me that you do not treat yourself as you do others.'

She nodded, relieved that she had done nothing to offend. 'It is such a large amount of work, if it is only to go for me.'

He thought for a moment. 'Then you must make something for me,' he said.

At this, she let out one small laugh, before stifling the emotion so as not to seem disagreeable. 'Now you are being silly. Men do not wear lace such as this.'

He walked to her side and reached into her work basket, removing a particularly feminine scrap and draping it over his wrist. 'Perhaps I shall create a fashion for it. Can you not see me in a neckcloth trimmed in birds and butterflies?'

'I cannot,' she said, without looking up.

'Then you must make something for yourself, as a gift for me. I wish to see you adorned in lace, as I said last night.' Then he draped it over the bare skin of her shoulder, admiring the flesh through the holes in the cloth.

The gentle brush on her shoulder seemed to strike at the very heart of her. Her breath caught in her throat and the room seemed strangely warm. She shrugged to get free of it. 'I do not think it would suit me.'

'It is not as beautiful as you are,' he admitted. 'But it is lovely all the same.'

This time, it was his words that stopped her breath. He had complimented her before. Why did it matter now?

He trailed the lace up the length of her arm. 'When we married, did you not promise to obey?'

'Yes.' She almost whispered the word. Even for this man, would she ever have the courage to make such a promise, knowing what it might entail?

He smiled, triumphant. 'Then I should like to see you wear lace. Not all the time. But often enough to prove you understand your own worth. If you will not make it for yourself, I shall buy it for you. Yards and yards of it.'

'Now, that is certainly a waste,' she said, imagining what such foolishness was likely to cost, compared with the work she might do for the cost of thread, was she willing to take the time.

'It would be worth it to me,' he said, 'if it meant that I might see you dressed head to toe in nothing but that.'

If the idea had ever occurred to her before, she had set it aside as the kind of sinfully decadent thing a kept woman might do. That was reason enough to avoid it. It was less pleasant than one might expect to spend days parading about the shop in jewels like a mannequin brought to life. It was even worse to spend her evenings dressed as an object of desire.

But that had been when she was with Montague. Why was it strangely appealing when the man making the request was Will Felkirk? 'It would not be very practical,' she said at last. 'Too likely to tear.'

'I would remove it carefully,' he assured her.

Her heart was beating fast now and she could feel her skin flushing, as though she was already displayed before him in a transparent gown. 'It would take months to make a whole chemise,' she said, hoping that might settle the matter.

He pretended to frown at this. But she could see

the smile playing at the corner of his lips, as though her perfectly sensible response had amused him. Then he trailed the lace lightly across the back of her hand, up her arm and away, to hold it in front of her face. 'Perhaps you could make a veil.' He peered through it at her. 'Did you wear one at our wedding?'

'No,' she whispered.

He nodded, 'Because you had nothing to hide. But I can imagine it, all the same.' He dragged the lace across her face, covering her eyes like a mask. Then he lowered it to cover her mouth. 'Do you know there are cultures in the East where women hide their faces beneath veils from all but their husbands?' He raised his eyes above the edge and gave her an arch look.

'You would not expect that of me,' she said, surprised.

'It would be selfish of me to obscure such a face,' he said. 'Besides, you are almost too modest already, without my encouraging. You have no idea how arousing it is to see you so prim and proper, knowing what you keep concealed beneath your gown.' He sighed then and kissed her through the lace. It was worthy of the innocence of the decoration, a simple touch of lip to lip through the barrier that separated them. There was nothing dangerous or demanding about it.

But her reaction to it was a surprise. She pressed her mouth into the fabric in eager response, her tongue licking at it as though she expected it to dissolve like spun sugar. That was what she wanted.

A hint of sweetness, then a long, hot, meeting of mouths and tongues.

Did he share her feelings? Perhaps not. He lingered there, for a moment, then pressed a closed-mouthed kiss on to each of her closed eyes before dropping the lace back into the basket.

He smiled, as if he had discovered a secret. 'It is just as I thought. Your beauty does not need gilding, but a touch of your own handiwork makes you all the more alluring. Now promise me that the next thing you make will be a gift for yourself.'

'Yes,' she whispered. It was an answer to a question he had not asked.

'Very good,' he said and stood up again. Then he yawned as he had the previous evening. 'And now, if you don't mind, this conversation has put me in a mood to retire early.' Perhaps he had understood, for the smile he gave her was warm and so full of confidence that it made her blush. 'You may join me at your leisure.' When he turned to leave, he barely needed the support of his cane.

She waited until she was sure he had gained the stairs before beginning to pack up her work for the night. She would lie with him tonight, if he wished it. She could not play the role of wife to him without submitting to his desires. It was what he expected. Montague expected it as well. But what had she wanted, when she had first come here?

Nothing more than to be left alone. She wanted to be able to decide for herself what her future held. Instead, she had become an obedient servant to another man. He was kinder than the first. More handsome as well. They shared interests. And they understood each other, or would, if she allowed him to know more of her.

But if she allowed him to know all? Then whatever they shared would be over, as quickly as it had begun. His gentle seduction and caring ways would disappear once he realised that she was another man's cast off. Worse yet, that she was still that man's property, set in Will's house as a spy.

She set the needlework basket beneath her chair, where it would be ready for the next night. She took one last glance at the bit of lace that Will had held, before closing the top of the basket to hide it. It would be wise to shut her dreams away as well, for they would only lead to heartbreak in the end. She would lie with him tonight, as he expected. He deserved her obedience for what he was doing to help Margot, even if he did not understand the urgency of it. But there was no point in investing the act with hopes and plans that would all come to nothing.

Chapter Twelve

She went to her room and summoned the maid to prepare her for bed. She looked at the simple gown laid out for her and thought with distaste of the more daring garments she had left behind in Bath. It was something of that sort that Will expected to see. If this charade continued, she would purchase new ones that were free of memories of her old life.

She donned the gown and refused the nightcap, since he had expressed his dislike of it the previous evening, and requested only a loose braid in her hair. All things would be as he wished. Then she dismissed her maid and went through the door connecting their rooms, shutting it softly behind her.

Tonight, he was just as he had been the night before, leaning against the headboard and waiting for her. He smiled as she entered the room, and moved on the mattress to give her space. As she approached, he gave a single disappointed glance at the gown she was wearing.

Without a second thought, she removed it, draped it over the foot of the bed and climbed naked into the bed beside him. Then she very deliberately rubbed her bare leg against his in a way guaranteed to arouse him.

She felt him start and pull away. For a moment, it almost seemed that he would climb from the opposite side of the bed to get away from her.

She made to withdraw. 'If you do not want…'

'No,' he said. 'I mean, yes. Stay. Just like this.' He had relaxed again, drawing her closer, wrapping his arms about her so her breasts pressed into his side. 'It is just that, as I have told you before, there is no need to rush.'

'Oh,' she said, trying not to sound vexed. In her opinion, just the opposite was true. The sooner they were done, the sooner she could put aside the disquieting feelings he raised in her, and restore peace to her mind.

He took a breath. 'And I must be truthful. After last night, I am somewhat concerned about the way things might proceed this evening.'

'Did I do something to displease you?' she said, searching her brain for an answer.

'No,' he said hurriedly and touched her chin with a fingertip, tipping her head up to offer a long, slow kiss. When they parted, he spoke again. 'Perhaps I did not make myself clear this morning. Last night, you were all I could have hoped for. It is obvious that you know how to pleasure me.'

She nodded in agreement. She had taken a portion of the day to search his rooms for some clue to the diamonds. She had found nothing exceptional, other than a collection of rather risqué etchings in the table by the bedside, that might serve as instruction should she need to maintain his interest in her.

'I am ashamed for ever doubting you,' he said. 'Your beauty is unparallelled. Your devotion to me unwavering. And last night? Your touch was heaven. Though I cannot remember what was in our past, I have no trouble imagining our future together.'

'Then you have no reason for concern,' she said, trying to empty her mind of anything but the moment. Tempting as it was, she dare not think such things herself. If she stayed, disaster was almost inevitable. But there was something very unnerving about the way he reached to the core of her heart when he spoke.

'I do,' he insisted. 'While you know just what it is that I enjoy, I still cannot remember the details of our life together.'

'What do you wish to know?'

'For example, I do not know if you prefer the left side of the bed, or the right.'

'The left,' she said automatically. Then she remembered that it would have been better to allow him to choose.

'Which is where you are now,' he said, satisfied. 'Perhaps I do remember, for it feels very natural to have you here.'

He was probably confusing her with someone else who had shared his bed. The thought was strangely annoying. But if he was happy, then what did it matter?

'And last night,' he said cautiously. 'We have done that before, I assume.'

'Something similar,' she admitted, not wanting to think how she had gained her knowledge of the male anatomy.

'It has been some time since I have truly felt myself. You must forgive me if, for any reason, I am not the man I was.'

'It will not matter,' she said and then lied through her teeth. 'You are still my husband.'

'As your husband, I owe you what you have given to me,' he said firmly. 'I am sorry,' he said with a sad smile, 'that I cannot remember the details of it.'

The conversation was beginning to worry her. If their bed became a place for talk, and the sharing of secrets, she would soon make a slip that could not be explained away. Better to distract him with her body, as she had last night, and save conversation for breakfast, when she had her wits about her. 'The past does not matter,' she said. 'Only the present. And your happiness.' She gave him what she hoped was an encouraging kiss and ran a hand down his body to be sure he was ready. Then, she stretched out on her back, legs sprawled, waiting.

He remained, propped on his elbow, watching her. Then he cleared his throat. 'This is embarrassing to admit. But you will know soon enough, so I had best simply put it out there. I do not remember how to love you.' He had paused before he said it, sounding almost sincere in his apprehension.

She rolled on to her elbow to stare back at him.

'You have forgotten how to…' Was that even a thing that could be forgotten? How was she to describe it to him without resulting to crass gestures and words that no lady should know?

He laughed, relaxed on to the mattress and reached for her, rolling her so that her body was on top of his. The suddenness of it left her breathless. 'Clearly, I married you not for your extreme beauty, but for your sense of humour. I am not so damaged that I could forget that, Justine. And you should know by now that some parts of the act are autonomic.'

He meant the erection pressing into her belly as she moved on top of him. As she slid her bare leg against his it grew even harder. She felt a sudden, nervous swooping in the pit of her stomach, at the thought of it, sliding into her body. She wet her lips. 'I am aware of that.'

'My response to you is not at issue. You are a beautiful woman. If there is strength in my body to act at all, I will know how to take pleasure in you.'

She nodded. What man did not know how to take from a woman, without thinking?

He smiled and kissed her again, short and quick. 'What I do not remember is how to make love to you. As opposed to some other woman, I mean. I do not remember the things that are most important, the things that make you different from all others. I have forgotten how to give you pleasure.'

Help my sister. Give me the diamonds. Let me leave. Those things above all others would be the best way to make her happy. But that was not what he was wondering about. 'If you are pleased, then I shall be as well,' she said, straddling him and hoping that this would be enough to end the talking so that they might commence and be done with it, before she lost her nerve. She gave a nudge with her hips, then she set about clearing her mind, forcing herself to relax so that he might enter her easily. Better to think of nothing at all, during the act, than the disquieting thoughts he insisted on raising in her. She wanted to be in another world entirely: a garden, the sea. Anywhere but in a bed feeling lips and skin, and the loss of her own will.

Still, he did not move, other than to shift the thing growing between them to a more comfortable position. 'Anything I like?' he repeated, with a sigh. 'So you said, last night. And this morning as well. While what happened last night was very nice—'

She frowned. It had been better than nice. She had been sure of it.

'—tonight, I am seeking mutual pleasure.' He gave her a wicked grin. 'Ladies first, as they say. Now, where would you like me to start?'

She closed her eyes tight, not wanting to see his expectant look. He could not possibly understand what he was asking of her. It was taking all her skill to remain calm and not succumb to the things he wished from her. Did she truly have to explain to him that kisses and petting were unnecessary, once they had got to this stage? Did he mean to paw at her breasts, trying to arouse her before pushing himself into her and having his way? To feel pleasure from such a thing, when one had no choice in partners, was the definition of defeat.

'My elbow,' she said, hoping that the sarcasm would put a stop to the questions.

'Your elbow.' Without hesitation, he reached for her arm.

She pulled it away. 'The left one. Not the right.'

He laughed. 'I do not know how I could have forgotten.' He cupped it in his palm and yanked her forward, so she was stretched the length of his body. Then he pulled her bent arm to his lips.

'What are you doing?' she said, unsure whether to laugh or scream. But it was obvious what he was doing. His tongue was circling the little round knob of bone now, as his whole mouth closed over it, sucking and laving as though it were her nipple.

'Exactly what you asked,' he said, blowing on the skin. 'Although it hardly seems fair to ignore your other arm.' His fingers were toying with that, giving a sharp pinch before running the nail lightly back and forth along the skin.

It was too ridiculous to be angry with him. And to her surprise, it was rather pleasant. When he pressed in a certain way, there was an occasional tingle of the nerves beneath that made her breasts tighten as they rubbed against the hair on his chest.

He paused. 'Was that what you meant? Or perhaps you meant the inside of your arm,' He turned his head and buried it in the crook of her arm.

Now this was something quite different. The deep, open-mouthed contact reminded her of something. One of the pictures in the etching book had held her attention for some time. A man's head rested between a woman's legs. He could not be emulating that, could he?

But he was the one who had the book. And he was nipping at the skin of her arm as though trying to take a pinch of it between his teeth. Now his tongue was working, probing, hard against soft, as though he meant to lose himself in her flesh…

'Oh, God.' Had she actually said that and in such a gasping, desperate voice? Because at the thought of his tongue, and what it could do, she was as wet between her legs as if he had licked her. His member rested between her thighs and she squirmed against it, not sure if she was trying to resist or encourage. 'I was not serious,' she whispered, wishing he would stop, but fearing it as well.

He paused for a moment, looking up at her with a smile. 'I know. But a woman who teases will be teased in return. It is fair, is it not?' He rested a thumb where his mouth had been and turned to her right arm.

She moaned in response and circled her hips, rubbing against him to spread the moisture and the sensations that came with it. It was not supposed to be like this. She was sure of it. The detachment she needed to maintain her sanity was melting like spring snow.

She was losing her mind over nothing at all. The only contact between the most intimate parts of their bodies was the result of her urging. And urge she did, wanting desperately to break his resolve as she had last night.

He paused again, dropping a brief kiss on to the skin of her forearm. 'My memory returns, I think. You like this as well, do you not?' Suddenly, he dropped his hands to her legs and pulled them up, until her body spread over his. Then he ran his fingers slowly over the skin at the back of her bent knees.

She gripped the pillow on either side of his head with clenched fists. Of their own volition, her hips bucked against his. His touch should be harmless, but her body was on fire, burning up with the need to be filled. And still he did not advance.

She forgot her need to be passive, the importance of compliance and the need to keep herself apart and safe. She released the pillow and tangled her fingers in his hair, pulling his mouth to hers. But he continued to tease her, running the tip of his tongue along the edge of her teeth and going no further. His fingers played at the back of her legs, stroking at the crease in the skin until all she could think of was his hand between her legs.

She rubbed her body against his, needing the contact, the touch of his tip against the nub of pleasure hidden in the folds of her body. And suddenly she was as far away from her fears as she had ever longed to be. There was no peace here, no separation from the needs of her body. There was only the wildest kind of pleasure, pounding blood, beating heart and the trembling of each ecstatic muscle. Somewhere, in a very distant place, she was begging for more, calling him her beloved, Will, William, Will.

When he was slow to respond, she pushed away from him, reached down, gripped his manhood and impaled herself on it, soaring even higher as he thrust within her. She held him close with arms and legs and the very centre of her being.

When had she ever felt like this before? It was if her body was one with his, feeling that rush of release that men seemed to crave above all things. He was already spent when she came back to earth again, sinking slowly down the length with a sigh, too weak to move.

He took the opportunity to roll her to the left side of the bed again, the one she preferred. Then he followed her, burying his face against her breasts and taking the nipples into his mouth, licking and sucking. His fingertips played over her body with featherlight touches, stroking her shoulders, her calves, and slipping between her legs. Before she could protest, she was flying again, not as high as she had, but flying all the same, then settling gently back down to see Will's smiling face, close to hers.

'Justine,' he whispered. 'Justine. If you were not already mine, I would have to make you so, after this night. How could I have lived, before I met you? And how could I go on without you?'

'You will not have to,' she whispered. 'I am yours, for now, and for ever.' It was good, for a change, to be speaking the truth to him, for that was what this was. She knew not how, but she would make it so. Diamonds or no diamonds, she would be William Felkirk's wife.

Will stared at the ceiling through half-closed eyes. How good it was to feel this way again, exhausted from lovemaking, half-sleeping, half-waking, with a beautiful woman in his arms. Justine lay curled beside him, sweet and soft as a kitten, her face pressed against his shoulder as if she had fallen asleep in the middle of a kiss.

He was struck, once again, by how unexpected she was. If he'd had to envision the woman he would take as his wife, she would not have been it. He rather thought he'd have ended up with one of the giggling chits at Almack's. Though empty headed, they seemed the most logical choice. He would choose the least annoying of the bunch and marry her. They would be seen around London together, travelling in a smart set, going to parties, dinners, musicals and balls. Eventually, there would be children.

But this girl? Empty headed was the last thing he'd have thought to call her. There was a sense that something was going on, running deep, like the proverbial still waters. But on the surface, there was the quiet of an undisturbed pond. Did she like parties, games and dancing? If so, she did not say.

She liked marmalade and novels. And him. He smiled. In her company, he found an unexpected joy in quiet. The sight of her in his sitting room, in her plain cap, bent over her needlework was a study in contrast. It made him want to uncover the beauty beneath the simple gown and peel back the linen covering her hair, so that he might kiss it.

To find her so willing in his bed, and so bold… He felt another rush of emotion. Desire. Possessiveness. Was it too soon to claim this as love? Had he known her for months, or less than a week?

Or had he known her for ever and spent his life waiting for the moment they might be together? Common sense told him he could not feel love after so short a time in her company. But his heart announced that, in this case, common sense was wrong. There was nothing common about the sensations he felt, when with her. And after tonight, he knew she felt the same when she was with him.

He laid a hand on her hip, smoothing over the curve. As he watched her, she twitched in his arms, went rigid, shuddered, then was still for a moment before going rigid again. Was it a dream? Apparently so, for she did not open her eyes as she tossed her head from side to side as though trying to escape from something or someone. To comfort her, he held her tighter. She jerked away and said, quite plainly, 'Don't touch me. Never again.' Then she sat up, suddenly awake. She gasped for air as though she had been running and looked wildly around her for a moment.

He carefully withdrew his hand from her body. Did his touch frighten her? She had not been bothered by it a few hours before. 'You are safe, Justine. It was only a dream.'

She looked at him for a moment, unable to recognise him. She shrank away from him, wrapping her arms around her body, looking smaller and more helpless than he had seen her.

'It was a dream,' he repeated.

'Only a dream,' she repeated. Then her eyes focused on him and she smiled in relief.

'Do you wish to tell me about it? Sometimes it helps to take away the fear.'

'No!' She shuddered again, then carefully composed herself to show him the usual, placid smile. But it was only an illusion, for her hair still hung damp with sweat on her face and her limbs trembled with suppressed energy.

'Very well,' he said, in a soft calming voice. 'But know that you needn't be afraid, as long as I am here.'

'Of course not,' she said, although she did not sound convinced. Was it nothing more than fantasy? Or was there something in her past that gave her a reason to fear? Life was not always kind to women who were poor and alone. Men could be predatory and a weak girl would not be able to protect herself. Whatever it was, it was clearly no fault of hers, for when he looked at her in the candlelight he could not imagine a more innocent creature. He patted the mattress.' Lay back down beside me. Let me hold you. I will make everything better.'

She did as he bade her, relaxing into his arms as the tension drained from her body. He smoothed her hair away from her face and kissed her temples. 'There, see? Nothing to be afraid of.'

She sighed. 'This feels so good.' She wrapped her arms around him and buried her face in his shoulder again. 'I could sleep here and never wake.'

'Do not say that,' he said, tipping her chin up so he could look in her eyes. 'Do not even think it. Now that I have found you, I do not want to lose you so soon.'

She blinked slowly and, for a moment, he thought that she might be about to cry. But when she spoke, there was no trace of a sob in her voice. 'I am sorry if I frighten you. But in my life, until now, there has not been such happiness. Some of the things in my past, before I met you…were very difficult.'

Difficult. It was said in her quiet, unassuming way, as though she might not truly understand the meaning of the word. Where she might say difficult, another might speak of horror and bear scars greater than the one on his arm that she was now stroking.

Do not touch me? They were the words of someone who had been beaten, or violated. All the more reason for him to be gentle with her and treat her like the treasure she was.

'Are you not the one who taught me it is only the future that matters?' He kissed her again. 'That future will be as sweet as I can make it for you.'

'And for you as well.' She stroked his arm again, running her fingers lightly over the smooth, red patch, where the skin had been ruined by the fire. 'Does it hurt, when I touch you here?'

He shrugged, embarrassed that he could not feel her touch through the thickness of the scar. 'It did at one time. But now I feel nothing.'

'It is the same for me,' she said. 'Sometimes, it is better not to feel anything at all.'

'But you can feel my touch, I hope,' he said sleepily, stroking her arm again.

'Yes,' she said.

'And my scar does not frighten you?' It had been a fearsome thing at one time. Even he had cringed when looking at it.

'I like it,' she whispered back. 'You are like your house. Not too perfect. Just right.'

His throat tightened with a strange rush of emotion, as he remembered her reaction as she had stared up at house and proclaimed it a castle, when most others would have called it a ruin. The touch of her hand on his numb skin made him feel like the battle-scarred king of the keep who had married a princess.

She rolled to face him, her head resting on his damaged shoulder. 'In the dark, when I am by your side, I have but to touch your scar and I will know who you are. I do not even have to open my eyes.'

Strange. 'I am a fortunate man to have a woman love me for my imperfections and not in spite of them.'

His face clouded, for a moment. 'Would you do the same for me, I wonder?'

He smiled back at her, kissing her hair. 'We shall never know, dear. You are perfection. I shall not believe otherwise, no matter what you might say.'

She frowned, as though ready to correct him. So he kissed her once, softly. 'Now, go back to sleep. No more bad dreams.' He touched the tip of her nose with his fingertip.

'Yes, William,' she said with a happy sigh and curled up beside him again, closing her eyes.

Chapter Thirteen

Will rode out to meet his brother that morning, still full of the strangeness of his new life. The horse beneath him was the chestnut gelding. It was a better choice than his foolish attempt to ride Zeus. But while full of spirit, it simply was not Jupiter.

It still hurt to think that he had been the cause of the old horse's death. His father had cautioned him, practically from the cradle, that the Bellston family was known for its hot blood and rash actions. He had taken the advice to heart and been cautious and circumspect in all things. Because of this, his life had been well ordered and scandal-free.

At some point in the last year, his training had failed him. He had lost an old friend and his memory as well. But he'd gained the most precious gift a man could earn: the love of a woman who he could love in return. There was probably something to be learned about the need for balance in all things and the danger of being too punctilious for one's own good, but he could not quite grasp it.

He could remember the feelings of unease, before the christening. He'd had the nagging feeling that his formerly feckless brother was somehow leaving him behind and that his own youth was slipping away unspent. Since then, he had allowed himself to be driven by passion to foolishness.

Not that passion was such a bad thing, when in its rightful place. Most times, Justine was as moderate and sensible as the old William might have wished. But last night, she had proven to be as wild and tempestuous as an adventurous man might have longed for.

They had woken at the dawn and made love again. Her bad dream was forgotten. Each time he'd touched her, she'd laughed. It was a joyous, abandoned sound, as though she'd never laughed before in her life, keeping the happiness bottled inside her until he had come to release it. Her climaxes had been much the same, giddy with desire and overcome with love for him. Her eagerness to please was no longer mechanical and worrisome. It was just her half of a shared gift.

When they were finished, she had thrown herself back into the pillows again, pulling him with her to share kisses and drowse until it was time to rise. When he had left the room for breakfast, she was still there, the covers pulled over her face to reveal nothing but a tangle of red-gold hair. The thought made him smile in a satisfaction deeper than he could ever remember.

Adam cantered up to him on the path leading

away from the house and noticed the change almost immediately. 'Enjoying the summer weather, Will? Or is there some other reason for this total transformation in you?'

'Transformation?'

'Just now, you were grinning like an idiot.'

Will grinned all the harder in response. 'It would be ungentlemanly to say more than that I am a happily married man.'

Adam raised his eyebrows. 'You have rediscovered the reason for your sudden union?'

'Some of it, at least.' If he'd had even a taste of this before they'd married, the need for an immediate elopement was now clear to him. 'Let us say, I am pleased to find her as devoted to me and my happiness as I am to her and hers.'

Adam laughed. 'I would have said something similarly vague after only a short time with Penny. As I remember, you doubted our compatibility.'

'I could not have been more wrong about that,' Will admitted. 'And I am pleased to admit that I have been wrong about Justine. I do not remember what first drew me to her. Perhaps I never will. But I no longer question the rightness of it.' If that much was true, did he really need more? He pushed his previous thoughts aside. 'I think I will not brood over-long about the absence of memory. The present is more than enough to keep me happy.'

'And your wife is settling into her place in your home?'

'She seems to be managing well,' he said. Then added, 'But it will be difficult to know for certain. She really is quite shy. I doubt she would complain if things were difficult.' He thought of her fear in the night, and wondered if he should press her about it. She would deny all, he was sure, and smile until he was convinced that there was no reason to question her.

He gave his brother a worried look. 'She is not likely to request help, even if she needs it. It is as if she does not think herself worthy.'

Adam frowned. 'We noticed similar behaviour when she came to us. I think she is unaccustomed to having family on whom to rely. Perhaps her life was more difficult than she lets on. I am sure, in time, she will come to be more comfortable with you.'

'I should certainly hope so.' Will frowned as well. 'But I should hate to think that I contributed to her isolation in any way. Her sister is some distance from here, boarding in a school in the south.

'You are sending for her, I assume?'

'Of course.' He frowned. 'But why did I part them at all? It was most unkind of me. Justine has no wedding ring on her finger. Did I not bother with that, either?' Nor had he written his family to expect her. 'What if I'd died from this injury, without making provision for her happiness?'

'She arrived with your own ring, worn on a chain around her neck. She said that all was done in a hurry and you had promised to take care of it when you arrived home. In the meanwhile, she has been content to do without and never once complained of it. Do not be so hard on yourself,' Adam finished, with a slight shake of the head. 'A newly married man can be allowed a moment of selfish pleasure.'

So, it had been selfish of him. Even Adam had noticed. And it had been more than a moment. If he understood the situation, he had seduced her without promise of marriage, then kept their union a secret for some weeks. It sounded almost as if he was ashamed of his actions.

Things would change, from this moment on. 'She is always doing without, even when there is no need of it. I will not allow that in the future. I will find some way to bring her out of herself. She is delightful company, when I can get her to speak.'

'So I told you,' Adam said, smiling. 'And she does enjoy her morning stroll.' He pointed ahead of them, on the path. The woman they had been discussing was walking through the wood, pale and quiet as a ghost. She had stopped at the darkest part of the little copse of trees, the dull gold of her gown and spencer blending with the dying leaves. Will had always felt there was a certain air of mystery about it. But today, it was as if they had interrupted a fairy in some mystic rite. 'Justine!' he called. 'What are you doing here, darling?'

Her response to his voice was surprising. Rather than greeting him with pleasure, she started like a rabbit, turning this way and that, as though searching for concealment. Only when she realised the hopelessness of escape did she straighten her shoulders and turn to them. She smiled timidly, offering a curtsy. 'Your Grace. My lor—' She stopped herself in mid-word and said, 'Will', as though just remembering their relationship.

If Adam thought her behaviour odd, he did not remark on it. They dismounted and walked their horses towards her. 'You should have told me that you wished to visit the grounds,' Will said, being careful to keep any censure out of his voice. 'We might have ridden out together.'

'I did not think to, until after you had gone,' she said, eyes downcast. 'And I prefer to walk.'

'You must find her a horse,' Adam remarked. 'Even for an indifferent rider, the skill can be useful in such remote holdings as ours.'

'You are right, of course,' Will said, thinking of the placid mare in the stables. He did not wish to see her cooped up in his house, afraid to ask the servants to harness the carriage horses. 'If you do not wish to ride, I will teach you to handle a pony and cart.' When she looked at him with trepidation, he added, 'Then you might take your sister for rides to the village, whenever you want.'

That was the trick, he suspected. At the mention of her sister, her mood changed instantly. 'Whenever I want,' she repeated, with a marvelling smile.

'But today, I hope you are enjoying your morning.' He leaned forward to kiss her lightly on a cheek which was warm with the flush of embarrassment. 'The trees are lovely this time of year, don't you think?'

'It is most glorious,' she agreed.

'The gardens are nice as well. I am surprised to find you here and not touring them.' Nice as it was, this was hardly the most interesting spot on the property.

She paused for a moment, then admitted, 'I was reading something, and it put me in a mood to explore.'

'Really?' He remembered the stack of old books that had been set out in the library and the probable contents of his mother's diary. Then a thought struck him and he smiled. 'Are you chasing ghost stories, my dear? For certainly, if there is a place on the property that is haunted, it must be here, where the murder occurred.'

Perhaps that had not been what she meant. At the mention of death, her face went white as a sheet. 'Here?' she said in a breathless squeak.

'A murder here?' Now it was his brother who was surprised. 'I do not recall any such thing.'

'You were away at school that year,' Will said. 'I was kept home. It was the year I had the fever. Mother told me later that she did not write to you for several months. They were dreadfully worried that, if you guessed how sick I was, you would want to come home and they would lose us all.'

'Ah, yes,' Adam said, remembering. 'You could not have been more than eight at the time.' He looked to Justine, filling in the details of the family history. 'You are lucky to have your husband. I did not learn until much later that he was near death several times that year. We lost our baby sister as well. The details of that will be found in the family Bible, should you be interested.'

'I looked,' she admitted, as though it were some guilty secret. 'But there was no mention of the other man. The murdered one, I mean.' Then she added in a strangely cool voice, 'I should have thought such a thing was worthy of more notice.'

'The household was far too distraught to deal with the situation as it should have,' Will admitted. 'And our mother was an excellent woman, but scatter-brained in such things as record keeping and correspondence. I am not surprised that she did not tell Adam at all.'

'But you knew of it,' she said. 'Even though you were sick.' She was looking from one to the other of them intently. 'I gather the robber was not caught.'

'Robber?' he said. He could not remember if he had mentioned the circumstances.

She glanced around her. 'In a place such as this, the motive must have been robbery.'

'Yes. Of course.' After so much pretended apathy, it was a surprise that such a gruesome tale drew her interest. Or perhaps it was not so surprising. Will had to admit, this particular story was a mystery to him as well. There was something about it, itching and scratching at the back of his mind. Perhaps it was the effort of looking so far into the past that gave him a pain in his head. 'I do not remember many of the details either,' he admitted. 'I heard only bits and pieces of the story myself and was far too sick to care for most of it.' Then he smiled, for he was sure this would interest her. 'But I will tell you one thing that I am sure the family did not write down. I was the one who found the body. I do not remember very clearly.' He glanced at the others in apology. 'That seems to be my excuse for so many things lately. But I was near to lost in the fever, the night the crime occurred. My nurse had fallen asleep and I wandered from bed, looking for something to cool me. The doctor had forbidden that I have ice in my water.' He shook his head, trying to remember. 'I went through the kitchen, down the hill towards the ice house to get some. It is lucky I did not fall into the river and drown myself, for we are very near to it now.'

'And you found a dead man?' Now Justine's eyes were wide with shock.

'Or near dead. I seem to remember him speaking to me.' Will frowned again. 'Although I cannot remember what it was he said. That was probably part of the delirium. He was quite cold when they found him. It took some time for me to get back to the house, and to persuade the family that there was, indeed, something to find here.' He glanced around him, pacing off the space. 'No. Here. Almost exactly. I remember standing beneath this tree and seeing a raven on the branch above me.'

'A raven,' Adam said sceptically.

Will shrugged. 'It was probably another symptom of the fever. The raven screamed and dropped a crown at my feet, then it flew away.' There was that moment of blankness again, where he felt that there was something important that he should remember, but could not.

Then Adam laughed, 'You saw King Arthur? In our wood?'

Will looked to his wife again, who was watching him with round eyes, totally confused. 'Wales is the land of Arthur, my love. If you like fanciful tales, I will read to you of him some night. But there is a legend that he was transformed when he died, and became a raven.'

'Or was buried in a cave. Or taken to Avalon,' Adam supplied unhelpfully. 'There are many stories about what happened to him. But I think we can guess what my little brother was reading, on the night he went wandering in the woods.'

At this, Will laughed himself, then offered up a moment of silence for the poor lost man. 'And here I am, twenty years later, with a head full of nonsense. But that is all I know of the story.

'If you are worried, you needn't be. Adam's lands are quite safe. Even in my father's time, such a crime was the exception, not the rule. This is the only instance I can recall where the perpetrator was not captured and dealt with.'

'You can recall?' she repeated. For a moment, the look of doubt in her eyes was replaced with a sceptical glint.

It was so out of character with her usual passive nature that he laughed. 'We both know how well I can trust my memory. But you can trust me when I tell you that you may walk these paths in safety, day or night, and you will have nothing to fear. Now let me take you up into the saddle and I will give you a ride back to the house, so you do not ruin your slippers in the mud, or misstep and slip down the bank and into the pond. The water on this side is clear as glass and very deep. Perfect for swimming in summer, if you enter on the opposite bank, near Adam's house. But here, it is better for cutting ice. At Christmastime, we will come with skates and you shall see.'

Then he mounted his horse again and scooped his wife up to ride in front of him, so he might point out other, less morbid landmarks of her new home.

Back in her room, Justine glanced down at the mess she had made of her day dress and slippers scuffling around in the leaves of the forest. She had been a fool to go out before ascertaining the location of her husband and the duke. But in his note, Montague had advised that he would meet her near the oak at the head of the village path, should there be news. Until she was sure that Margot was safe, she must at least pretend to obey and make a daily visit to the spot.

Did he know he was directing her to the very place were the murder had occurred? She shivered again. This had been the first morning in ages where her father's death had not been her waking thought. To lie in Will's bed, for even a few minutes, thinking of nothing but the night before was an unimaginable liberty. It could not last, of course. After breakfast, she was back to playing Montague's spy.

She had made her way to the rendezvous point with the hope that she would soon be free of him. Then, out of nowhere, the past had come to remind her of her duty. She must go there again and search more thoroughly.

It had been years, of course. No trace of evidence could have remained. If there were truly diamonds to be discovered, they would not be stuck in a hollow tree where anyone might see them. But she knew she would return to the place, even so. She would not be able to help herself.

It had been even more foolhardy to encourage Will to remember. He might just as well have said, 'Of course. How could I forget Hans be Bryun, the diamond merchant? And you are his daughter, the woman that stood and watched as I was nearly murdered in Bath.' Despite what had happened on the previous evening, she'd have been in custody before she could explain herself.

But she could not have resisted the temptation to ask. It was fortunate that William Felkirk's amnesia was as impervious as ever. Her hopes had risen when he'd admitted to being there the night of the murder. But even then, he could not remember anything helpful. Nothing but useless details about birds and crowns, while her father had lain bleeding in the oak leaves at his feet.

She must remember that he had been but a child and very sick. If there had been a death in the family, and illness, she now knew why the old duke had been far too preoccupied with their own family to give any thought to hers.

But still, to have learned her father's last words after all this time would have been as valuable as diamonds. She let out a sigh and with it she released the last of her bitterness towards the Felkirk family. While her life had been unfair, she must admit that it was no real fault of theirs. Having walked the path where the crime occurred, she had no reason to believe it was not as safe as William claimed. She had always imaged some lawless wilderness where a merchant might fear to tread after dark. But she was sure that there was not so much as a poacher on the land, much less a highwayman. No one could have predicted that his cries for help would be delayed by worries over a sick child. His death was not accidental. But the circumstances around it were much easier to understand then they had been.

It did nothing to ease the hurt of her past. But if

she had thought to get revenge, as Montague had, she could find no logical justification for it. The duke, his wife and her William were quite blameless in what had happened to her father, and to her.

But if they were not at fault, then who was? If the path was not particularly dangerous, how had someone discovered her father on it? He would not have announced, when passing through the local inn, that he carried a bag of valuable stones in his pocket. Yet, someone must have known of his plans and waited on the path for him.

'I have something for you.'

She started again and looked up to see Will standing in the doorway that connected their bedrooms. She must learn not to jump at the sound of her husband's voice. It should be as familiar to her as her own. And after last night, sleeping in his arms, she had to admit that it was a pleasure to hear. At the memory, she remembered to greet him with a smile. 'A gift? I am sure, whatever it is…'

'Is not necessary? On the contrary, the thing I bring is yours already. You should have had it for some time. Giving it to you was one more thing that I had forgotten.' He held out a closed fist to her. 'Close your eyes and open your hand.'

She did as he wished, trying to stifle the feeling of excitement. He might be simply be rewarding her for her behaviour in bed with him. She had received such gifts before and felt the disappointment and shame that came with them. Could not the pleasure be enough to satisfy them both?

Then, she felt the slim, cool band of metal resting on her palm. She had an illogical desire to yank her hand away before she opened her eyes and saw what she knew must lie there.

'I must have promised you this, I am sure,' Will said, in the voice he used when trying to manufacture memories to fill the void of the last six months. 'It belonged to my mother and was set aside, waiting for my marriage.' He shuffled his feet, as though embarrassed that he could not offer her more. 'It is not so grand as the duchess ring, of course. Although I doubt Penny would mind giving it up to you, should you want it. She says it is far too heavy to be practical. All of the best pieces are already in her jewel box. But they are entailed. This is mine. And now, it is yours.'

He withdrew his hand to show the delicate gold setting with a single rose-cut diamond at the centre of it. She could not help her instincts. What her father had not bred into her, Montague had taught, so that she might be his partner in the shop. She held the stone up to the light, searching for flaws.

It did not shine as a brilliant cut might, but the stone was perfect, a testament to elegance. The setting was etched with vines and made it look even more like the flower it was meant to represent. The colour was a clear blue-white, the weight, if she subtracted the gold, was slightly over a carat.

It was not worth as much as the stones her father had lost. But should she sell it, she would have several thousand pounds. It was more than enough to launch both herself and her sister on a new life, free of the interference of Mr Montague.

'Don't you like it?' Will was still standing before her, hand outstretched, ready to place it on her finger. Instead of responding with gratitude, she was calculating the value of a lover's gift.

She closed her eyes for a moment. When she opened them, she spoke from her heart. 'It does not matter to me what Penny has. This is the most beautiful ring I have ever seen. I would not trade it for the world.'

'That is what I hoped to hear,' Will said, with a satisfied smile.

It was true. She wanted this ring as she had no other. She'd no jewellery of her own, other than the string of pearls she had been given on her sixteenth birthday. They had been her mother's and had been less a present than an inheritance. For all the other pieces that passed through her hands, she had never been more than a model. A pretty neck to hang things on so that Montague might sell them. She had long since stopped coveting them.

The more she looked at this ring, the more she wanted it and all it symbolised. She burned to have it and to have the man that held it. It meant safety, peace and an unbroken circle of union.

'Let me help you.' He meant with the ring, of course. He wanted to put it on her finger. But something in his voice was coaxing her to tell him how much help she really needed.

She let herself be wooed and closed her eyes again. He slipped it on and whispered, 'With this ring, I thee wed. With my body, I thee worship. With all my worldly goods I thee endow.' Then he warmed the finger with a kiss. She opened her eyes to see him looking up into hers. 'That is right, isn't it? Were they the words I spoke to you, when we married?'

She did not know, nor did she care. They were the words he'd spoken to her, right at this instant, and she could feel that he meant them. 'They are perfect,' she whispered back.

As was the ring. The fit was comfortable. The weight was not awkward. It added elegance to the hand. It made her want to gesture, casually, so that others might notice and envy what her husband had given to her. She could not stop looking at it. And she could not stop smiling.

He gave a sigh of relief. 'You do like it. Sometimes, I wonder. You are so quiet and too easily pleased. I cannot always tell your mood. As I have told you before, you must not do things just to please me.'

'Of course I like it,' she said. 'And…' She stopped, frozen. Then she said what she was thinking. 'And I love the man who has given it to me.' Unlike so many other things she said, it was truth. An inconvenient truth, perhaps. She still did not know how to free herself from Montague, or what might happen if Will remembered Bath. But even if there could be no future for them, she had to share her feelings.

Things were not as bad as she feared. Or perhaps they were worse. He wanted to help her. Soon, she would ask him for aid and see if he was as good as his word. If she truly loved him, she would have to tell him the truth. But not today. The moment was too perfect to risk ruining it with talking.

So she threw her arms around his neck and kissed him. This was truth as well. She liked kissing him. She liked being kissed by him. She liked the way it felt to touch him and to have him touch her.

'You love me,' he said, when their lips had parted. It would have been better had he declared his feelings for her. It was unfair of her to expect that. No matter what she had been telling him, he had known her but a few days.

But she had been watching over him for weeks, and in that time she had found nothing that was not admirable. She knew him now, better than she knew herself. Though it was not real, it was just the sort of marriage she could have wished for. 'I love you,' she repeated. 'And, if you are not too busy, or too tired, I should like to go to your room now.' She smiled into his chest, letting her ringed finger play with the buttons on his waistcoat.

He laughed. 'I cannot imagine a better response to this gift, or a better way to celebrate it.' He kissed the top of her head. 'In the days before the accident, did I tell you what a delight you are, my beautiful Justine?'

'I do not recall,' she said. 'But you might say it all again, if it is true.'

'Later,' he said. 'At the moment, I have a much more physical demonstration of my feelings.'

Chapter Fourteen

It was nearly a week since they had moved to the old manor and life could not have been better. Justine had grown so used to behaving as a wife to Will that it no longer felt like play acting. She loved the shared meals and the quiet evenings with lacework and novels. She especially loved what happened after, when she retired to her husband's room. Even if they did nothing more than sleep in each other's arms, there was a warmth more cosy than the fire in the drawing room and a peace stronger than she'd ever known.

All the same, Justine tempered her excitement at the arrival of her sister with a very real fear. Suppose Mr Montague learned of her plan and put a stop to it? She had been able to avoid him thus far. Three days' steady rain had made walks in the woods impossible. She had persuaded Will to send a carriage to meet the coach in Cardiff, thus avoiding a chance meeting between Margot and their guardian at the local inn. But there were still so many things that might go wrong.

Suppose, once she arrived, Margot blurted out the truth, or asked embarrassing questions that could not be answered. She had shielded the poor girl from her sordid relationship with their guardian. Margot thought of him as nothing more than a rather silly older man. As such, she did not know why she needed protection. There was nothing more dangerous than not knowing of the risk.

Now that the day of Margot's arrival had come, Justine was pacing the floor of the morning room, staring out the window for the approaching carriage.

'You need not worry,' Will said, taking her hands in his and kissing them. 'I have persuaded Adam to send the barouche. The ride will be comfortable and the driver will take utmost care.'

Justine smiled at the thought. Margot must have started in disbelief at the sight of the Bellston crest on the door and the liveried servants calling her Miss de Bryun with a bow, eager to be of service. Even if it was only an illusion, it would be a memory that she could share with her children, should she have any. The chances she might marry and have those children would increase once she was safely out of the clutches of Montague.

At last, she heard the distant jingle of harnesses through the open window, and the approach of the carriage, the calls of the coachman and the butler at the door, ready to welcome the new guest. She hurried to the hall and pushed past him so she could be at the foot of the carriage steps when her sister alighted.

For a moment, Margot was framed in the open door of the carriage above her. Then she took the few steps to the ground as if in a daze, staring up at the house in front of her. Before she could say a word, Justine rushed forward and enfolded her in her arms.

For a moment, she forgot everything but how good it was to see Margot again. It had been too long since they had been together and even longer since they had been able to speak freely. Before they could do that, it would be longer still. But for now, it felt as if their troubles were over. She whispered in hurried French in the girl's ear, 'Guard your tongue, Margot. The situation is complicated. I will explain everything soon. For now, all you must know is that I am Lord Felkirk's wife and this is my home.'

'For now?' Her sister whispered the two words back, then let it pass, allowing Justine to take her arm and lead her into the house. She stared up at the high ceiling and wide stone stairs that had been part of the original castle. 'Your home? *C'est magnifique.*'

'It is,' agreed Justine, in a whisper.

'It is your home as well, my dear.' William had arrived in the hall in just in time to hear the compliment to the house he held so dear. He stepped forward to offer his hand to her. 'Introductions are in order, I think.' He looked expectantly at Justine and flashed a disarming smile to show that his formality was little more than a jest.

It gave her a strange thrill of pride to see Margot's reaction to her dear William. At his worst, when he'd been wasting away in the sickbed, Justine had thought him tragically handsome. But today, he must have requested Stewart to take extra care with his dressing so that he might make a good impression on their guest. He was turned out in a coat of midnight-blue superfine and the snowy-white cravat made his hair look as dark as a raven's wing in comparison. The walking stick he had chosen was not the common wood staff he'd been using around the house, but ebony chased with silver and topped with a polished ivory knob. She was sure that she had never seen him look better. In fact, she doubted there was a more handsome man in all of London. And by the dazzled look in Margot's eyes, her sister thought the same. 'Lord William Felkirk, may I present my sister, Miss Margot de Bryun,' she said, smiling back at him.

Will made a very proper bow in response to Margot's awed curtsy. Then he gestured into the house. 'No need to linger in the doorway, my dear. Come in and be comfortable. Would you care for refreshment? Are you in need of rest? There is a room prepared for you. There will be one in our London home as well. Once you are settled, we will send for the rest of your things.'

'My things?' Apparently, it had not occurred to her that the visit might be permanent. 'I must go back to school,' she said to Justine in a half-whisper. 'Mr—'

Justine rushed to cut off mention of their guardian and his wishes on the matter. 'Now that I am married, I would prefer that you stayed here with us.'

'At the very least, you must consider a school nearer to us,' Will added. 'Your sister pines for you, when you are not nearby. And I would not see her unhappy, even for a moment.' Then he gave his most winning smile, using his good looks to charm the girl into agreement.

It appeared he had made a conquest, for Margot's eyes widened in surprise, and gave a confused nod of assent, Mr Montague all but forgotten. 'You are too kind, my lord.'

'William, please,' he said. 'Or Will. You are my family now, just as Justine is. She will show you your room and give you a tour of the house. Then, perhaps, we shall have tea in the garden. Tonight we will dine with the duke and duchess, who are most eager to meet you.'

Justine needn't have worried about the girl blurting secrets. Margot was already stunned nearly to silence. But the casual announcement that they would be dining with a peer reduced her to mute shock.

'Come, Margot,' Justine said, tugging on her hand to propel her towards the stairs. 'Let me show you to your room. We have much to talk about, for it has been ages since last we saw each other.'

'We certainly do,' Margot agreed, staring back over her shoulder at her new brother-in-law, as they mounted the stairs.

Once they were alone in her room, Margot sat down on the bed, giving one satisfied bounce on the soft mattress before looking at her with curiosity, waiting for her to speak.

Justine sank down beside her, unsure of where to begin.

Margot held out her hands as though expecting the explanation to drop into them. 'Do you mean to tell me the meaning of this, or do you leave me to guess? And do not think you can lie to me over this, Justine. At least not any more than you already have.'

Justine recoiled in shock from the accusation. 'When have I ever lied to you?'

'When have you ever told me the truth?' Margot answered. 'You hardly speak to me at all, if speaking is what I can call the sparse letters you send to me in Canterbury.'

'The shop has been busy,' she said, trying to evade the truth. 'There has not been time to write much.'

'If it is busy, then I should be there with you, helping,' Margot replied. 'And then we might speak whenever we wished.'

'A shop is no place for an impressionable young woman,' Justine said firmly.

Margot scoffed. 'It is a jewellery shop, not an alehouse. And you have been working in it since you were two years younger than I am now.'

Justine felt a moment's revulsion at the true nature of her duties. At seventeen, she had been more naïve than Margot was now, and fallen easily into the trap Montague had set for her. Then repeated what she said each time Margot argued for a return to Bath. 'Perhaps, when you have completed your education...'

'I have more than enough education to take my place in a family business,' her sister said. 'I am older than most of the girls at the school and have learned all that they can teach me. Everyone remarks on the way I remain there between terms, as if I have no family at all.' The girl's face clouded and she appeared on the verge of tears. 'Whatever I have done to earn this rejection from you, I am sorry for it. I will prove I have learned my lesson, if you will but let me come home.'

'Do not think that,' Justine said hurriedly, putting an arm around the girl. 'It is nothing you have done. I have done what I have done to protect you.'

'But why do I need protection? Why must I remain in school, so far away from you? Can you not at least tell me that?'

At this, she hugged Margot close and felt tears wetting the shoulder of her gown. She had hidden so much, in an attempt to keep her sister pure. What could she reveal now that would calm her fears? 'Do not cry, little one. Our separation is at an end. You will live here, now, with Lord Felkirk and myself. It was never my desire that we be apart. The situation in Bath was...complicated.'

Margot lifted her head and rolled her eyes. 'If this is over you and Mr Montague, I know of it already.'

Justine shrank back, horrified.

Margot smiled at her. 'I have seen the way he looks at you, Justine. And I have seen him kiss you, when you both think I am not nearby.'

'You know?' She could not understand the whole truth, or she would not speak so casually of her sister's disgrace.

'Of course. It is quite plain that he has a *tendre* for you. He must wish to wed you, even though that is not at all proper for a guardian.' She frowned. 'Since you have been of age for years, and I have heard no announcement of engagement, I assumed that you were not similarly interested. But that does not explain why you married another so suddenly. And why did you not tell me of it immediately?' Margot's tears had dried. But it was clear that she was still deeply hurt by the sudden turn of fortune.

Justine smoothed her sister's hair and kissed her lightly on the cheek. 'I am sorry I did not tell you immediately. But my dear, the situation is so much more complicated than you think.'

The ever-pragmatic Margot pulled away and cocked her head to the side, as though considering. 'I fail to see why. I assume you kept me in the dark because you have not told Mr Montague of the marriage. Since you are of age already, you can do what you wish without his permission. Do not mind his tender heart, if your happiness lies with another. Simply demand your inheritance and go. If you wish, I will return to Bath and explain for you.'

'No,' Justine said hurriedly. 'You must not. I have not told you before because I am not actually married to Will.'

Margot's jaw dropped. 'You are his mistress?'

'No. That is not it either.' And how was she to explain the rest of it? 'There was an accident,' she said. 'Lord Felkirk was injured and I was responsible. He remembers nothing of our meeting, or what happened after. I brought him here and told his family we were married.'

At this, Margot laughed. 'How did you come to meet the man in the first place, much less cause an accident?'

'This next will be difficult to explain. When Father died…' Justine took her sister's hand '…he was here, Margot. On the road that runs just past this house. Lord Felkirk was the one who found him. He sought me out in Bath, claiming that he found the diamonds. But then…there was an accident.'

Margot withdrew her hand. 'And you are only pretending to be married to him so that you can find the stones.'

'They are ours, Margot. We have but to find them. If we sell them, we shall have more than enough money to last a lifetime. We need not go back to Bath at all.'

The girl looked more disappointed by this revelation than she had at any of the others. 'We have more than enough money now, Justine. Is not half the jewellery shop rightly ours?'

'Well, yes,' she admitted. 'But it is not the same as money in the purse. Mr Montague—'

'Mr Montague has managed both halves for years,' Margot interrupted. 'As long as it is profitable, I see no reason he cannot continue to do so. You may not approve of it, dear sister, but when I am old enough, I mean to help him there. You might tell me that it is improper to do so, but I know just as much about gems as you and am ever so much better at maths than I am at lacemaking.'

It was a future that Justine had not bothered to imagine. Once Margot was safely of age, Montague might cease to threaten the girl's innocence and allow her to marry. But if she insisted on returning to her old home, she would be walking into a trap. The only way to escape him would be to sell the business and start again.

'If Father knew what had become of us, he would not wish us to remain in partnership with Mr Montague,' she said, as gently as possible. 'He would want us to find the diamonds and take them as our real inheritance. Or perhaps appeal to the Duke of Bellston for help. If he wished you to continue in business, Father would rather have seen you with a shop of your own than beholden to Mr Montague.'

Her sister sighed and took her hand. 'Justine, it has been twenty years. You still talk of finding justice for Father and regaining what was once ours. It has earned you nothing but trouble. This wild scheme of pretending to be Lord Felkirk's wife is proof of that.'

'I had my reasons,' Justine said, trying not to let her frustration show.

Margot shook her head. 'I cannot understand what they could possibly be. But I know you must let go of this quest for lost family treasure. Perhaps it is because you can remember Father and our old life in Belgium. But I cannot. He was dead before I was born, Justine. Mother died when I was still young. I have known nothing but England and school, and Mr Montague. And difficult though he is, he is not such a bad man.'

'He is evil, Margot,' Justine said, unable to contain the truth. 'I cannot go back to him. And I will not allow you to do so, either.'

'I fail to see how you can stop me,' Margot said, in a reasonable tone. 'In a year, I will be old enough to make my own decisions on the matter. My own mistakes as well.' She gave her sister an arch look. 'But whatever I do, I suspect it will not end with me in a false marriage to a stranger. How you can manage to stay out of the man's bed is beyond me.' She paused and then said in a worried voice, 'Lord Felkirk is a most handsome man, of course. And kind as well. But I trust that you have not stooped so low as to give up your honour to convince him that you are his wife. If Mother were alive, she'd have told you that virtue is more precious than the diamonds you are searching for.'

'Lord Felkirk has been ill. He is still very weak.' Hopefully, this was enough of an answer to set Margot's suspicions to rest. But it left Justine sickened by her own lies.

'Good,' her sister said with a relieved sigh. 'I would not want to know if you thought so little of yourself that you would seek a man's protection for expediency's sake. All the same, it is obvious that the man dotes on you. Tell him the truth as quickly as possible. It is likely he will forgive all and marry you, then you will have nothing to worry about.' She smiled and added, 'Only then will I come to live with you, at least until I am of age. It is much nicer here than at school.' She gave another little bounce on the mattress and ran her hand over the painted silk of the coverlet.

'I will do as you wish, when I am able,' Justine said, with a sigh. 'But it is not time for the whole truth. At least, not just yet. Until then, you must keep my secret. Can you do that?'

Margot sighed and fell back on to the bed, staring up at the ceiling, as though she'd had quite enough of her sister, her worries and her complicated problems. 'Of course I will. But do not wait too long, sister. For Lord Felkirk's sake, you must be honest.'

That night, a dinner was held to honour the visitor at the duke's manor. If Margot had been impressed by the luxury of Will's house, she was truly dazzled by an invitation from the handsome duke and his plainspoken, bespectacled duchess. Justine hoped that they were not imposing in some way. Bellston was quiet this evening, offering a warm greeting to his brother and a somewhat more reserved welcome to both Margot and Justine.

But Penny was as gracious and affectionate as ever, anxious to make Miss de Bryun feel welcome. She complimented her on her education, quizzing her in Greek and Latin, and declaring her quite proficient for a girl of such few years.

At this, Daphne Colton rolled her eyes. 'Such skills will leave you permanently on the shelf, if you display them in London, Miss de Bryun. But since you are as perfect as your sister, we will take care not to let that happen.' She reached down the table to touch the girl's cheek and turning her head from side to side, admiring her profile. 'If you were turned out in the latest fashion, there would be none to compare to you. We must take you shopping.'

Penny laughed. 'Even I know that there are no suitable shops within miles of here.'

'There are in London,' Daphne said. 'It is quiet there, now. But surely Bond Street would welcome commerce.' She glanced at Justine. 'Have plans been made for a Season for her? She is very nearly of age, is she not? It is rather old to be making a come out, but if she is sponsored by a duchess, I should not think it too late. Now that Will is doing so much better, we might all go south for a week or two.'

Margot shot a surprised look in her direction, unsure how to respond to such a generous offer.

London was the last place Justine wanted to be.

It would be dangerous to call attention to the fact that Margot was not in Canterbury, as Montague expected her to be. 'I do not think that would be possible. The expense…'

Daphne gave a wave of her hand. 'It is miniscule, compared to what she will gain by a good marriage. Will has the blunt for it, I am sure. It would be a shame for such a pretty girl to remain a spinster, don't you think, Penn?'

'I do not think we are entitled to an opinion on the matter, without speaking to Miss de Bryun,' the duchess said with a smile, turning to the girl. 'Perhaps she has more important goals.'

Margot blinked, still surprised that the conversation had turned to her. 'I do not think I should mind being married,' she said cautiously, 'if the gentleman is as kind as Lord Felkirk.' She shot a quick glance at her sister that made Justine feel, had she been close enough to reach, she would have received a sisterly kick on the shin. 'But my plan for some time has been to manage a jewellery shop.'

Justine stopped her fork, halfway to her mouth. Of all the subjects she had warned Margot to avoid, had she remembered that this one was most important?

'Sometimes, I think my wife would like that as well,' Tim Colton replied with a sigh. 'She would have me buy out the jewellers, on each trip to town. What she means to do with it all, I am not sure. She has but one neck, after all.'

Margot opened her mouth, ready to correct the

misunderstanding. But before she could say more, Daphne let out a short, merry laugh. 'Then we must make sure that your husband is both kind and willing to spoil you as mine does.'

As she spoke, Justine at last caught her sister's eyes, and gave her a desperate look that warned her to silence. Then she gave a flourish of her own hand, to indicate the ring Will had given her. 'A single, perfect gift is more than enough to please me.' She gave a nod to her smiling husband and accepted the approving comments of the ladies at the table that it was, indeed, a most lovely ring.

Only the duke was silent, his eyes speculative, his lips set in a straight, inflexible line.

It was nearly midnight when Will called for the carriage. He'd have been happy to stay some hours more, partnering his sister-in-law at whist, while Justine sat in the corner with Penny and her lacework. But it was clear that Miss de Bryun was close to dozing over her cards, probably tired from the long journey to Wales.

When he went into the hall to find the butler, his brother followed him. The duke's steps on the marble tile were sharp, almost military in cadence as he hurried to catch him. 'A moment, Will. I need a word before you go.'

Will turned and waited. His brother had been behaving strangely all evening. Perhaps now he would learn the reason for it.

Adam glanced back at the open door to the salon where Justine and her sister were taking leave of their hostess. Then he said, *sotto voce*, 'There has been a discovery that concerns the time you were missing from us. Tomorrow I will come for you, in the carriage. Tell any who ask…' He paused as though searching his mind for a likely lie. 'Tell them we are going to purchase a horse. But until tomorrow, be cautious.'

'In what way?' What risk could there be in a short ride to his own home and a night in bed?

The ladies were coming into the hall to join them and Adam gave no answer but a warning shake of his head. Then he turned to his guests. To an outsider, there would be nothing unusual in his behaviour. His Grace, the Duke of Bellston, was ever a genial host.

But Will had known him for a lifetime and recognised the mood for what it was. Adam was playing a role, just as he did when playing politics in London. His true feelings, whatever they might be, were buried so deep that Will would not know them until the morning.

Chapter Fifteen

'Are you going to explain the purpose of this trip? Or do you mean to leave me guessing?'

Will's question was met by silence from his brother, who sat in the opposite seat of the coach, staring out of the window as though he had not heard.

After Adam's warning, Will had half-expected that there would be an attack on his person as he rode home. But the remainder of the night had been uneventful. Young Margot had chattered all the way home, amazed at the manor, the food and the hospitality of the duke and duchess.

Justine had smiled behind her hand and did her best to calm the girl, assuring her that she had made an excellent impression on them. Once they had sent their guest off to bed, they had gone to bed themselves. And once again, Justine proved what a lucky man he was, to have married so well.

Will smiled at his brother and waved a hand before his face to get his attention. 'You said this was about my lack of memory. If you are carting me off to prison for something, the least you could have done is let me say a proper goodbye to my wife.'

Adam shook his head. 'It was nothing you did. At least, I do not think so.'

'What the devil does that mean?' Other than that the situation had changed from annoying to alarming.

'It means that I do not know what to say, until I have seen for myself the thing that Jenks described to me and your reaction to it. If we are wrong, as I pray we are, then it will be better that I had not spoken at all.'

'Very well, then.' Will gave an expansive gesture. 'Continue to be mysterious. But you might at least tell me where we are going.' They had been on the road for nearly an hour and he was beginning to fear that the whole of the day would be wasted.

'It is not much longer,' his brother allowed. 'There is an inn a little up the way. The Fox and Hare. We do not stop there often. The ale is watered and the food is mediocre at best. But yesterday, while transporting Miss de Bryun, there was some problem with a carriage wheel and a stop needed to be made. Jenks saw something of interest in the stables and wished our opinion of it.'

'You want me to see a horse?' he said. He'd thought last night's comment had been nothing more than a ruse. 'I do not wish to buy one, if that is what you have been told. I am not ready to make such a purchase today, at any rate.'

Adam shook his head again. 'This horse will interest you, I think. But we must go see for ourselves.'

They pulled into the coach yard a short time later and followed Jenks and the driver directly to the place where the horses were kept. The coachman was shifting uneasily, foot to foot. 'I thought you would want to know, my lord. I am sure you will think it foolish of us and see the obvious difference.'

'There is no difference,' Jenks said flatly. 'It is what we think it is. But only Lord Felkirk can tell us so.'

'Can tell you what?' Will said, his patience growing thin. 'I still have no idea what you are on about.'

From a stall halfway down the row there came the thump of hooves hitting boards.

'Careful with that one,' a stable boy called. 'We can barely handle him.'

'I am sure we are up to the task,' Will said, taking a firmer grip on his stick.

They were standing in front of the animal in question now. At the sound of his voice, there came a frantic whinny.

He knew that sound.

It was impossible. But he could not doubt his own ears. He pushed past the stable boy, dropped his stick and put a hand on the neck of the horse, reaching for his tossing head.

'Now tell them they are fools and that all black horses look alike.' His brother's voice had a plaintive quality to it, as though wishing could give him the answer he wanted.

But to say that would have been foolish. All black horses did not look the same, any more than all blonde women looked like Justine. This black horse looked exactly like Jupiter, because it was Jupiter. He ran a hand on over the horse's shoulder and felt the height, just as he remembered it.

The spirited horse calmed instantly. It was not because he had any gift for animals, but because the horse recognised his touch, just as it had known his voice.

'Hello, old fellow. It has been some time, has it not? Did you miss me?' He turned the face so that he might look into the eyes and the gigantic head gave a nod as if to say, 'Yes.'

Will stroked the soft, black nose and got another nod of approval and a nudge at his pocket, where the sugar should be.

This was impossible. Many men kept a treat of some kind in their pinks. This was no indication of recognition, just a learned behaviour. As for the rest, he was only seeing what he wished to see and hearing what he wished to hear. It could not be Jupe. Jupiter had died because of the same fall that injured him.

Will walked to the back of the stall, trailing his hands along the smooth back. There was the barely noticeable pattern of white hairs on the flank. He felt under them and found the fine line of the scar from the time they had taken a fall, going over a fence in a hunt. How he had worried over that, walking the young horse home, and fussing over him until the scratch had healed. But there should be other scars, should there not?

Perhaps Justine had been misled about the extent of the injury. The fall in Bath that had laid him low must have done some damage to the horse. He stroked down the back, the withers and the legs, all the way to the hooves, and could find none. Jupe was as sound as the day he'd ridden out on his way to Bath, to see Mr Montague.

Montague.

The scrap of memory appeared, as though it had always been there. He had found the bag in his nursery dresser, searching for a gift for Billy. Just a scrap of silk and velvet that he'd used to hold pretty rocks. But more properly, it was meant to hold loose stones. A jeweller's bag. And where had he got it?

In the woods.

He gripped Jupe's neck, now, letting the horse support him as he searched his mind for the rest of the story.

'My lord?' Jenks was leaning close now, fearing that his behaviour was a sign of weakness.

Will waved him away. Standing on his own feet again. 'You were right. This is Jupiter.'

'You know what this means, don't you?' Adam was speaking now and his voice was surprisingly bitter.

How was he to answer? Did he know what it meant? In truth, he did not. More than Adam knew, perhaps. He knew the facts. He had found a jeweller's bag in the nursery and pieced together the story of the murder by questioning the oldest servants. A diamond merchant had died and the stones had been stolen. No one could remember more than that.

He had traced the origin of the bag through the monogram on the silk: the entwined M and B of Montague and de Bryun set in an embroidered gold crown. He had gone to Bath, seeking information about the bag's missing contents.

The woman in the main salon of the store had been too beautiful to be an ordinary shop girl. Her satin gown was too bright for day, and too low, revealing a pale throat hung with emeralds. Her hair swept high on her head, to show ears hung with matching drops. Her fingers were heavy with rings, her wrists circled with bracelets. It was as if a statue had been decorated and come to life as a walking advertisement for the store.

Her face had been just as impassive as a statue's as well. In her eyes, he had seen far too much knowledge for one so young. The smile she wore was too polite and distant to be anything but ironic.

Montague had come into the room and looked at her, eyes flicking from gem to gem as though counting his possessions. The final intimate sweep of his eyes indicated that his ownership did not end with the jewellery she wore. When he turned to look at

Will, there was a faint warning in his expression. One might look at the merchandise, and the woman beneath it, but one must never touch.

And then, to Will's shock, he had introduced her as de Bryun's own daughter.

Montague himself had been strangely familiar. He had seen the face before, he was sure of it. But he could not think where. The man had escorted him into a parlour at the back of the shop, where they might talk in private. But he had quickly become irrational over what were simple and innocent questions.

It was clear that Will would learn nothing more than what he already knew. As he turned to go, he saw the woman, standing before him, blocking the door.

And then, pain. The last thing he could remember, before darkness closed over him was those knowing green eyes.

He knew what had happened. But that still did not explain how it had come to this.

'I said, do you know what this means?' Adam was shaking his shoulder. 'She lied to us, Will. I took her into my home. I treated her as family. I encouraged you to trust her.'

If he'd not still been in shock himself, he'd have found it funny. The Duke of Bellston was ranting over his injured dignity and abused hospitality. As if that was worse than surviving a murder attempt, only to fall in love with one of your attackers. How she must have laughed, to find him so easily manipulated.

'Who knows if there is any truth at all in what she said? But fear not. I will call out the watch and we will take her into custody immediately. Then we shall have the real story out of her. Her sister as well. The girl is likely an accomplice to whatever happened.'

'You will not.' At last he had found his voice. With a final pat, he turned away from the horse and silenced his brother with a look. 'You will get in the carriage, ride home and say nothing to anyone.' Then he looked at Jenks. 'Find out what you can of the man who left the horse. If he is still here, set someone to watch him. Follow him, if necessary. But do nothing until I give you direction.'

'And what do you mean to do, while this is going on?' Adam was still angry and using a warning tone to remind him that a man who was both a peer and one's older brother should be given the respect he had earned.

'I mean to saddle my horse and ride home.' He held up a hand to silence objections. 'And I will tolerate no nonsense about my being too weak to ride. It is not as if I am likely to fall off of Jupiter, now is it?'

His sarcasm shocked the two other men to silence. But the horse answered with a soft nicker of amusement.

He turned back to Jupiter, stroking his face. 'Do not laugh at me. I thought you dead. I grieved over your loss. And all the while you were eating oats and snapping at stable boys.' He looked up to see the other two, still staring at him, as though trying to decide if his current behaviour was a sign that the recent injury had driven him mad.

'Go,' he said, more softly to his brother. 'Please, keep what you have learned to yourself for a time. A day or two, at most. I need time to think. And to speak with…Justine.'

He had almost said *my wife*. And what a bitter lie that was. He put it aside and continued. 'I will send word when I have decided how best to proceed. You needn't worry. Now that I am aware of the situation, there is no risk.'

No risk at all, now that he knew not to turn his back on Justine de Bryun or her lover.

Chapter Sixteen

'I don't know why you bother attempting to teach me this,' Margot said, looking at the mass of knots that was her first attempt at lacemaking. 'Of all the skills I might wish to develop to honour our family, this is not one of them.'

Justine bit her lip in frustration. Margot was still talking of the shop and her desire to return to Bath as soon as Mr Montague allowed it. While her younger sister might deny any allegiance to a father she had never met, she seemed to have inherited that man's business acumen. 'It is better that you cultivate virtues that might attract a husband. With Lady Colton's offer of a Season and the sponsorship of the Duchess of Bellston…'

Margot laughed. 'It is a lovely dream, of course. But no gentleman will want to marry the daughter of a merchant.'

'You would also be a member of the Felkirk family,' Justine reminded her.

Her sister responded with a surprised look. 'You know that I am not. Have you forgotten what you told me, just yesterday? You are not truly married to Lord Felkirk.'

For a moment, she had forgotten. The truth was becoming increasingly clouded by what happened each night, when she was alone with Will. Today, all she could remember was the sweet kiss he had given her in parting. Then he had gone off with his brother in the carriage, saying something about the possibility of purchasing a horse.

That would be good for him, she was sure. He still pined for the one he had lost. While no other animal was likely to take the place of Jupiter, it was better that certain, unexplainable parts of his past be put aside.

She was thinking like a wife, again. It left her unsure whether to smile or frown. If love were all that was necessary to make a marriage, she would be his true wife. 'For the moment, you are right,' she admitted to Margot. 'I am not Will's wife. But you were also right when you said that I must find a way to explain to him. For I do so wish…' She bit her lip again. She wished that their meeting had occurred, just as she had imagined it. For how could she ever tell him the truth?

'You love him?' Margot said, softly.

'Very much,' Justine admitted. 'I cannot imagine life without him. And I am so afraid, when he learns what I have done…'

Her sister rose and put an arm about her shoulders. 'Do not distress yourself. I am sure you will find a way through this. Once you have told him the truth, he will forgive you for the ruse and all will be well again.'

'You cannot know that,' Justine said.

'Nonsense. It is clear that he adores you,' Margot said. 'But it will not change my opinion on the matter of a marriage for myself, or my plans for the future. With you married and living here, someone must go back to Bath and be the second half of Montague and de Bryun.'

'That will not be possible,' Justine said, in a tone she hoped would brook no argument. After all she had sacrificed to keep the girl safe, she seemed intent on throwing herself from the frying pan into the fire.

'Sometimes, I think you are simply jealous of my interest,' Margot said. 'If you did not enjoy your place there, it was unfair of you to exile me, so that you need not share our birthright.'

Justine set her lace aside and turned to take her sister's hand. 'It is not from jealousy that I keep you away. I do not want the place that I have, Margot. I would be quite happy if I were never to see Mr Montague or that horrible store again. If you were to know the whole of it, you would not want it either.'

'Then tell me the whole of it, and let me decide.'

For a moment, she was tempted to tell all. What would it feel like, to finally be free of the worst secrets of her life in Bath? Then, silently, she shook her head.

Margot gave a short, frustrated sigh, glanced out the window and smiled. 'Then perhaps I shall ask Mr Montague what problem lies between you. I believe that is him coming up the drive right now.'

Justine had not thought of this possibility, when she had ceased going to the wood to wait for him. The last three days, there had been letters from Mr Smith in the morning post. She had thrown them away unopened, not wanting to read the demands for information, and the threats of punishment for disobedience. Once Margot was safe with her, what could the man do? She was sure he would not dare to come to the house and risk being seen by Will.

But Will was gone, travelling in a carriage past the very spot that Montague would have waited for her. He knew she was alone and unprotected. Thus, he had come to the house, knowing that she could not avoid him without raising suspicions.

'Margot, go to your room.' At the very least, she could prevent him from seeing or threatening her sister.

She had not counted on her sister having an opinion. 'Certainly not,' Margot said, settling herself in her chair to prove she had no intention of moving.

'It is not wise that you remain,' Justine said, firm but gentle. 'We did not get his permission for this trip. It is quite likely he will be angry.'

'Angry at you, more likely,' Margot answered

with a wicked smile. 'Your crimes are far worse than mine, misleading this poor family and luring me away from school.'

'It is not that way at all,' Justine said, in a desperate whisper. The enemy was so close he might hear their argument through the half-open window of the morning room.

Margot gestured towards that same window. 'It is he who deserves the explanation, not me. Since you have been trying to dissuade me from my goals all morning, I am not in a mood to help you out of this by hiding under my bed.'

She could hear the knocking on the front door, the butler opening and the approach of the footman to announce a guest. 'Margot. Please. You do not understand.'

'That is about to change, I think. We will all understand much more, if we speak to each other honestly. Now give permission to admit our guardian, or I shall call out to him that I am being held against my will.'

What was she to do? Justine gripped the edge of her lace pillow, twisting the velvet in her hands. Even the best servants were prone to gossip. To create a scene would make it all so much worse. When the footman announced Mr Montague, she gave the smallest of nods. And now the villain was in the room with them, his eyebrows arched in surprise at the presence of Margot.

He flashed a look in the direction of the servant, not wanting to speak until they were alone.

How much protection could the poor footman offer to them, should they need him? The boy was barely thirteen and Montague outweighed him by several stone. With another, helpless nod of her head, Justine dismissed him and instructed that the door be closed.

The moment it was, Montague dropped into a chair opposite them. His insolent slouch was meant to remind her how complete his mastery was over them and the situation they were in. 'Well played, Justine. I see now why you have been ignoring my instructions to meet.'

'I suspect she had been too busy, what with my arrival yesterday,' Margot responded for her, fancying herself the diplomat between two warring states.

'Silence, child.' Montague did not even glance in her direction, making it clear that she was a point of contention rather than a part of the discussion.

'I was ignoring your instructions because I did not wish to meet with you. In fact, I do not wish to see you, ever again. If you continue to threaten me, or my sister—'

'Justine!' The sharp rebuke came from Margot, who must think she was being overly dramatic.

'—I will tell Lord Felkirk all I know and accept the consequences for it.' She spoke louder, to be sure she could be heard over the protests of her sister.

'That would be extremely unwise,' Montague said, staring at her as though expecting he could shatter her resistance with a single icy stare.

'It is the only choice I have,' she said. 'I am but a weak woman, unable to settle my disputes with violence, as some do. Nor can I survive any longer on a diet of lies and deceptions.' To speak thus was the boldest thing she had done in her life.

She was rewarded with a flash of cold fury in his eyes and a momentary pause that told her he had no easy answer to this. It had never occurred to him that some day she might rise up and fight.

'Honesty is the best way to deal, in life or in business,' Margot said softly from her side, as though hoping her agreement would in some way bind the other two together.

'Yes,' responded Montague, seizing upon the words. 'If we are all to tell the truth, it is time for your sister to be honest with you and tell you what she has been willing to do to secure her place beside me in the shop. There is much you do not know, I think.' He looked to Justine then, in challenge. 'Is honesty still so attractive to you, I wonder?'

'We do not need to involve her in a thing which is just between the two of us,' Justine said. Surely he would not reveal the sordid nature of their relationship. It would reflect just as poorly on him as it did on her.

'If it involves the shop, it involves me as well,' Margot interrupted. She looked at Montague pleadingly. 'You have always promised me in your letters that I would help you there. I should have done so, long before now.'

'I gave your sister the power over that decision and she has refused to allow it,' Montague answered without hesitation.

She could not call him a liar, for the statement was at least a partial truth. 'His offer is not as it appears,' Justine said.

'You will not allow me?' Margot looked more than disappointed. She was furious. To her, it must appear as if Justine had no care for her wishes at all. 'You tell me time and time again that you do not want the shop. You do not like Bath.'

'Yet, she was willing to trade her virtue to keep her place there,' Montague announced, then feigned sorrow at the sudden revelation. 'You were always better suited to work at my side. But your sister would hear none of it. She used her beauty as a weapon against me. I knew what we were doing was wrong, but I could not resist.'

'That is not true,' Margot said. She was very still now, waiting for her sister to explain that it was all some horrible lie.

'That is not the way it happened,' Justine said. And it was not. She'd had no choice in the matter. To pick between her freedom or Margot's had been no choice at all. 'He forced me…'

'As I forced you to come here?' Montague countered. He turned to her sister again. 'You know she is pretending to be married to Felkirk, pretending to love him, engaging in Lord knows what vice. And all because she wants the diamonds.'

'Justine?' Justine watched as her sister's expression changed from doubt to horror. She believed him. How could she not? There was more than enough truth in what Montague was saying and it matched very closely to what she had told her sister.

But he had omitted one important detail. 'Montague struck him. With a poker. If I had not brought him home to heal, he'd have died on the floor of your precious shop and we would both have been hanged for murder.'

It was plain that the facts made the story no better. Margot stuffed a fist into her mouth, as though she could not decide whether to scream or be sick, but desperately wished to avoid either. Her hand muffled the sob that matched the tears starting in her eyes. Then she was up and gone, probably to her room, where she'd have been all along had she followed Justine's first order.

The door shut and silence fell in the room again, as though Montague expected her to speak first. Justine reflected that the wait for words could be prolonged, since she had no idea what to say next. Even if she managed to get him to leave again, it would take some time to calm her sister and to explain things in such a way that did not make her seem like a conniving whore.

Perhaps that was what she was, after all. She had thought herself the victim. But Montague's version of the truth seemed equally plausible. In either case, it was possible that her bond with her sister was irretrievably broken. Margot would never again look with trust upon either Justine or their guardian. Who did that leave to support and encourage her?

'What have you to say for yourself?' Montague said at last, as though dealing with a recalcitrant child. 'You see all the trouble you have caused, trying to get around me and disobeying my wishes? Next, I suppose you will tell me that you've learned nothing of the stones and the whole trip has been for naught.'

'Not for naught at all,' she said with a sigh. She sounded as tired as she felt. 'I have not had to endure your touch for several months. In my opinion, that is almost as good as a holiday.'

'Then your holiday is at an end,' he said, rising from the chair and standing over her. 'You will be coming away with me, today, while Felkirk is away and cannot ask questions. Tell your sister to pack as well. We are all going back to Bath.' There was something in his voice that made her wonder if that was their destination at all. Perhaps he meant to take them only part way. There was likely a cliff or a crag somewhere between there and here, where three might walk out and only one would return. He would be safe and there would be no more troublesome women, threatening unfortunate revelations.

'No,' she said, feeling rather proud of herself. 'I do not mean to stir a step from here. When Will comes back, I will tell him all and he can decide what is to be done with me.' She looked up at Montague, trying to raise some real defiance to disguise the apathy she felt creeping over her, now that all was lost. 'Since you cannot carry me bodily from the house, you might as well go away.'

'I will take your sister, then,' he said.

'She will be nearly as difficult to move as I am,' Justine said, with a slight smile. 'I suspect she is having hysterics in her room after what she has just heard from the pair of us. Better that you should go alone. You can travel faster that way and be far from here before my husband and the duke return.'

'Your husband?' Montague laughed at her.

It had been a stupid mistake. She must learn not to believe her own lies. 'Lord William Felkirk,' she corrected. 'The man you attacked. Perhaps he will not even seek you out, if I am here to take the blame for the crime.'

Montague considered for a moment and shook his head. 'You think you shall persuade him to forgive you, with your sad eyes, your bowed head and your gentle manners.' He reached out then and plucked the cap from her head, running his fingers through the curls and then pulling sharply back on them so that she was forced to meet his gaze. 'You will bind him with lust and pity, until he is as trapped by you as I have been. Then you will send him to find me and I will be the one who hangs.'

'Then I suggest you run as far and as fast as you can,' she said in a calm voice. She could feel the skin of her scalp pulled tight in his grip and the muscles in her neck straining against the force of his hands.

It did not matter. After today, she had likely lost the love of her sister. She would lose Will as well and the respect of everyone else she had met here. There was little left that Montague could do that would hurt her.

'I am not going anywhere,' Montague said with a smile. 'Unless it is back to the woods to await the return of your precious Felkirk.' He released her, pushing her roughly back into the cushions of the chair, and withdrew a pistol from his coat pocket. When he was sure she had seen, he dropped it back to where it had been hidden. 'How hard would it be, do you think, to finish him with a single shot?'

'Harder than you think,' she said breathlessly. 'He is with his brother the duke. There will be coachmen, outriders, livery. You cannot have so many bullets as that in your little gun.'

'Perhaps I shall wait until he rides out alone,' Montague replied. 'He is still weak, is he not? And probably just as careless as he was the day he turned his back on me.'

'You would not dare,' she said, suddenly quite sure he would.

'I would not act, unless you gave me reason. If you were to stay here, to blather the story to him, for example. Or if you plan on raising the alarm against me.' He paused, reaching for her again and running his thumb down her cheek. 'I would have no reason for it if you came away with me. Things will be as they were between us. Then, if it pleases me, we will discuss your freedom and that of your sister.'

Her heart sank. He would win, just as he always did. She would go with him, if only to lure him away from Will and Margot. If she did not, he would wait and watch, and eventually he would strike.

He could feel her weakening. It made him smile. 'Very good. I knew you would come to see things as I do. You of all people should understand what might happen to a man alone on that path. There are places that are shadowed, even in daylight. At night, when the moon is new as it was when your father died…'

'How did you…?'

'He thought he was too clever for me, just as you did,' Montague said. 'He hid the diamonds and carried nothing but an empty pouch. In the end, he gained nothing and lost his life. I got the insurance money, of course. But I wanted the stones as well.' His voice trailed off, as he thought back to the incident, his face marked by a childlike disappointment.

'You.' She felt no surprise. It was as if she had known, all along, but it had been too awful to contemplate, so she had refused to think too closely about it.

'Me,' he said, with a proud smile. Then he gripped her by her shoulders, pulling her to her feet. 'There is no point in resisting. I have been the architect of your fate for most of your life and I do not mean to change that now. In a few moments you will get your shawl and come away with me. You will leave this place and have no more contact with sweet William and his family. If you do anything to warn him, seek help of any kind, or reveal secrets that have been hidden for years, then things will be far worse than the lesson I mean to teach you now.' He kissed her, if such an open-mouthed punishment could be called a kiss. She fought, but the contact was relentless, his tongue pushed deep into her mouth until she was near to gagging on it and had ceased her struggles. Only then did he release her, following it with a slap that sent her reeling on to the sofa.

It was happening again. And as usual, she could think of no way to stop it. To cry out would mean discovery and an end to the assault. But it would also require explanations and the story would eventually get back to Will and then to his brother. The servants would not conceal an attack on their mistress from the very people who might punish the perpetrator.

There would be questions, so many questions. Why would she welcome such a man into the house? Why had she not called out sooner? And the question she asked herself most often: Why had she not found a way to stop this, years ago?

As usual, she had no answer. And as usual, she closed her eyes and imagined she was somewhere else.

Chapter Seventeen

Will needed only a moment to decide the route and speed for his return trip to the manor. Keeping a sedate pace on the road beside the carriage would give him time to think. He did not need to do that. He had spent too much time in the last weeks trying to understand the circumstances of his new life. But when one was basing one's cogitation on a horribly flawed series of supposed facts, one had nothing but nonsense at the end of it.

What he needed now was action, not thought. He set off cross country at a full gallop, through pastures and fields, scattering sheep and taking fences as a series of easy jumps. He had nothing to fear, after all. Jupiter was not dead. He had not fallen from a horse. And the injury he'd suffered was no accident.

He would arrive home much sooner than expected and surprise Justine de Bryun. The thought made him smile, but it was with none of the foolish, misplaced joy he'd been feeling lately. This was the kind of cold, grim satisfaction that thief takers must feel when they had their man dead to rights and heading towards the gallows.

He would arrive home and he would shake the truth out of her. He would ignore the huge, sad eyes and wistful smile, toss the lace into the fire and follow it with the ridiculous, prim cap she was likely wearing. A whore did not belong in modest gowns, nor did she bother to cover her head like a housewife. That she would sit with ladies under a scroll of virginal lace was an affront to him and his entire family.

She was a liar, nothing more than that. Below stairs, above stairs, and all the places in between. An image arose in his mind of the sweet, seemingly innocent face that had looked up at him as he'd touched her in their shared bed. Then he imagined that same face, smiling in a much more knowing way at Montague as they plotted against him. The beautiful body that had twined with his had writhed under another man, as she moaned with pleasure.

She was a liar and he had been a fool. Now it was not just her and Montague, but her sister he had to contend with. Lord knew if the girl was in any way involved in this. But was it really his problem, if she was not? He supposed she might be as big a victim as he was. All the same, it did not entitle her to much more than a ticket back to the school she supposedly attended.

The house was in sight now and he bore down on it, gaining speed, rather than slowing. After so long abandoned in a stall, Jupiter relished the speed, just as he did. But now he was eager to return to his own pasture and to be curried and cosseted by familiar hands. He stopped, still dancing with excitement, at the front door.

Will dismounted, handing the reins to a footman who could only manage an awed, 'My, lord', at the sight of the familiar, black stallion. Then Will pushed past him, into the house, to find his wife.

Not his wife, he reminded himself. No more weakness, no more foolishness. She was a madman's plaything, nothing more than that. Soon she would be gone. She and her lover would be in the hands of the law and life would return to normal.

When he opened the door of the morning room, the scene before him left his mind as blank as it had been when he'd first awoken. Justine was sprawled upon the couch, eyes shut tight from fear or pain, or both. Her face was dead pale, except for a red mark on one cheek, where a man's hand had slapped life into her complexion. Montague stood over her, radiating menace.

For a moment, Will could not think of anything, other than how wrong it was that such a thing should happen. Men did not hit women and they certainly did not do it while under his roof. That such a beautiful creature as his wife should have to fear anything, ever, was all the more wrong. Had he not promised her, over and over, that she would be safe with him?

He was halfway across the room, his hand already

raised to strike before he even remembered how satisfying it would be to hit this particular man, who had stolen six months of his life and ruined the one good thing that had come of it: his sweet and innocent Justine.

'No!' The word seemed to come, not from his mouth, but the very depths of his soul. With one hand, he gripped Montague by the shoulder and spun him. With the other, he struck. It was a full-armed cuff to the side of the head that sent Montague crashing to the floor.

'Will.' Justine's eyes were open now and he watched their expression change quickly from shock to relief, then change again to sorrow. Then she whispered, 'He has a gun. It is in his coat pocket.'

In response, he gave her a curt nod and focused on the man at his feet.

'If you stand, I will knock you down again. If you move for a weapon, I will break your hand with my boot. And do not think that I will turn my back on you, even for an instant. There will be no more chances to strike me from behind.'

Montague seemed barely bothered by this revelation. 'You finally remember, do you?' His lack of fear was unnerving.

'I remember it all, down to the last detail. You were a fool to bring my horse back to Wales, you know. It was bound to be discovered.'

Montague shrugged at this. 'Of all the things that would be my undoing, I did not think that would be the one. Do you mean to call the magistrate? It is your brother, is it not? He will arrest me and my mistress, and you will be free of us. I am sure it will be a terrible scandal and very embarrassing to all concerned. People will wonder that Bellston would be so easily fooled as to take a whore into the bosom of the family.'

Though Montague was mocking him, calling down the law would be the sensible thing to do. But now that justice was at hand, it felt strangely unsatisfying. There was something missing. Will resisted the urge to look back at the woman on the couch. If she was carted away to be punished for her crimes, he might never understand why she had gone to such lengths to trick him.

Instead, he stared down at Montague. 'You will hang, of course. Stealing my horse would be reason enough. But your list of crimes is longer than that. Attempted murder, fraud…'

'It is Justine who is guilty of fraud,' Montague supplied, as though trying to be helpful. 'It was her idea to come here, to masquerade as your wife, and to try to steal the diamonds you claimed to have found. If I hang, then she must as well.'

'He killed my father.' Justine spoke at last, her voice barely a whisper. 'Let justice be done.' If he turned to her, he would likely see that same, resigned, annoyingly obedient woman who had sat at his bedside and later come to his bed. Now she meant to go uncomplaining to the gallows.

Surely an innocent woman would have spirit enough to defend herself. Did she not understand that it would take only a word of entreaty and he would face down the devil himself to protect her?

But Montague was another matter entirely. Will glared down at him in disgust. 'I would much prefer that we settle this like gentlemen, if that is even possible. I know you prefer to strike men from behind and threaten women. If you can find someone foolish enough to stand with you, I will meet you at dawn.'

Montague laughed at this, as though the very idea of a duel was beyond him. 'And if not?'

'Then you will go to the gallows, just as you wish. Do not think to run. You will not cross the borders of my brother's land unnoticed.'

'That is not much of a choice,' Montague responded.

'It is the only one I am prepared to offer. With one, you stand a small chance of success and I can have my vengeance. If not, I shall turn you both over to the law and not think of it again. Although I would most like to be responsible for your death, I can live without the chance.'

'Then of course we shall duel,' Montague replied. 'And since Justine tells me you are weakened since the accident, I will choose swords. They are a weapon of a man with finesse. Very hard to handle when one's hand still shakes.'

'They are also more difficult to handle than a

fireplace poker,' Will said, pleased to see Montague flinch as the shot hit home.

By the time he answered, he had regained his aplomb. 'Very well, then. Swords at dawn. Send word of the location to the inn. Now, if you will excuse us?'

Will gave a slight tip of the head.

Montague stood and gestured to Justine. 'There is no need of a spy in your house, now that you are aware of her. Come, Justine.'

'The girl stays.' Will did not want to look at her, afraid of what he might see. Even now, she might be stirring on the couch, ready to return to her master.

Montague dropped his hand and shrugged. 'If you wish to keep her, she is yours. Until tomorrow, of course. Then I shall kill you and she will return to me. She will have no choice. Send word to the inn where you wish to meet and I shall see you at sunrise.' And then he was gone.

With the departure of Montague, a terrible stillness fell over the room. As if there was anything Justine could say that would explain or justify what had happened. Instead, she said the first words that came to her mind. 'How long have you known?'

'Just today,' Will said, still looking at the closed door. 'The coachmen found Jupiter yesterday, while bringing your sister to you.'

'And your memory came back?'

'All of it,' he said, turning to her with a grim

smile. 'Including the memory of you doing nothing to stop him, as he struck me down.'

That must be how it appeared to him. He would never believe her true feelings for him, if he remembered her from that day in Bath. Her future was destroyed. But perhaps there was a way that some good would come from this whole sordid mess. 'Margot had no part in any of it. She did not even know of my…intimate association with Mr Montague.'

'Is that all you have to say to me?' he said, with an ironic lift of his eyebrow. He took a seat on the opposite side of the room from her, as though he would keep as much distance from her as was possible. When he looked at her it was with the same, cynical appraisal he had used on the day they had met, in the shop in Bath, so many months ago.

She stared back at him, although not nearly as boldly. 'I have many things to say,' she admitted. 'But I can think of none that is more important than the welfare of my sister. What good would an apology do? There is no way to say I am sorry for the deception I have perpetrated. Mr Montague's assault on your person was so sudden that I did not know how to prevent it. To stop him from striking the second blow to finish you, I suggested that it would be better to bring you home so that I might steal the diamonds you claimed to have found.'

'And if you had found them?' he asked. 'Would you have gone back to him?'

'I meant to steal from him as well,' she said. 'To

take them and escape with Margot, to a place where he could not find us.'

'And the rest of it?' he said. 'Our elopement? My tragic accident?' He was sneering now, as though the very idea of a past with her disgusted him.

'I could think of no other way to explain myself.'

'And so you lied.'

'I lied,' she admitted.

'I suppose the things that happened when we were alone together were lies as well.'

'Would you believe me if I said they weren't?'

'Probably not,' he admitted.

Had she been hoping for a different answer? If so, her time here had made her foolish and overly optimistic. Perhaps it had been her imagination that his voice had softened, just for a moment, as though he, too, wished there could be a different end to this.

'Then all I can say to you is that I am sorry,' she said, at last. 'For hurting you and for tricking myself into believing my own lies. I should have admitted all, the day you awakened. I knew, from that moment, that this day would come. The longer I waited, the easier it became to pretend that there was a chance for happiness here. And now you hate me. I do not blame you.'

He said nothing in response and, in her mind, she cursed herself for wishing that he would offer some sop, to tell her she was wrong about his feelings. 'Now that we are at an end, I have but two requests.'

'You are not in a position to bargain with me over anything,' he said, emotionless.

'I know that. I deserve nothing, just as I have told you from the first moment we met. But I know you to be a good man, a kind man, a man of honour. As I said before, my sister had nothing to do with any of this. What I have done, from the first, I did for her.' She bowed her head. 'Do what you will with me, but do not punish Margot. At the very least, do not let her fall to the same unfortunate depths I have.'

He stared at her, without answering. Then he said, 'Your second request?'

'Do not duel with Montague.'

Will gave an incredulous laugh. 'You wish me to spare his life?'

'I wish you to protect your own.'

He made another disgusted noise. 'You have no faith in my abilities to defend myself.'

'On the contrary, I have infinite faith in Mr Montague's ability to turn a situation to his advantage. He will find a way to cheat. And then he will kill you.' She rose from the chair and sank to her knees before him. 'I would not see that happen for all the world. Have him arrested and be done with this.'

'They would take you as well,' he said. 'Do not think that I can protect you from this, for I do not know if that is possible.'

'Then let them take me,' she said, taking his hand in hers. When she squeezed it, she felt an answering grip. But there was no sign in his face that it was anything other than a reflex. 'Since I've been with you, I've had a lifetime of happiness. But that is over now. I must be punished for what I have done to you and your family. Let me go.'

It seemed he might not want to, for the grip on her hand was even stronger than it had been. Still, when he spoke, there was no sign of it in his voice. 'No matter what you might wish, I cannot go back on my word to Montague. If I could offer a challenge, and then take him unawares tonight, I would be no better than he is.'

'If you mean to throw your life away, then what was the point of saving you?' she said, pulling her hand away to wipe away a tear. 'If I had not stopped him, he'd have killed you in Bath and I would truly have been a murderer. Now you will be dead and I will have to go on, knowing I am to blame.'

'I am sorry to have inconvenienced you,' he said. He stood up and stepped around her. 'I am going to my room. I need to think. I will write to my brother and try to explain any of this.' He gave a vague gesture, as though it might be possible to draw a sensible version of events out of the air in front of him. Then he added, 'And I suppose I must think of something to do with your sister. At the very least, I can arrange to send her back to where she came from.'

It was such a small thing, yet it was more than she could have hoped for. 'Thank you,' she said, softly. 'In return, what do you wish me to do?'

'I have no idea. Nor do I care.' He gave a half-bow, as though he had rendered her a service of some kind. 'I am locking the door between our rooms, if that is what you are hinting at. Knowing what I do, I will not sleep easy if it is open. For the rest?' He shrugged. 'You are your own woman, Miss de Bryun. You are free of Montague and I no longer want you. What you do now is totally up to you.'

Chapter Eighteen

Will stared out of his bedroom watching the sun set through the first of the autumn leaves. It had been a lovely day. That it might be his last was a disappointment. But it could not be helped.

The righteous anger that had sped his journey home had disappeared like fog in sunlight, at the sight of Justine sprawled helpless before the angry Montague. In that moment, all he could remember was that she was his and she was in danger. Perhaps, tomorrow, she would laugh over his bleeding body and ride away with his killer. Today, in this house, he could only see the pale, beautiful woman who had watched over him as he suffered and came to his bed as though it was the only place she found happiness.

He should have called the servants, then called Adam and trusted it all to the law. Instead, he had informed his brother, in a terse note that his services would be needed in the morning, as a second. Since he had got no outraged response, he assumed that Adam had not yet returned from the inn.

Perhaps it was for the best. If Montague was left unwatched, he might decide to cut his losses and run. It would leave only Justine and her sister to deal with. That had best be done at a distance, with lawyers and bank drafts. One look into her beautiful green eyes and he would lose what was left of the common sense he had been so proud of and believe that they had actually been in love.

He stared at the door connecting their rooms. Despite what he had threatened, he had not locked it against her. Now he was possessed with the thought that she stood on the other side, ready to test the handle. If it opened, he would welcome her to his bed, just as he had every day that they'd lived here. Knowing what he did, it would be bittersweet to have her in his arms. But better that than the empty flavourless existence of a life without her. If she would just open that door and allow him some tattered scrap of pride, he could forgive anything and they would be together again.

There was a sharp rap upon his door, but it came from the hall and not her room. There was a moment of silence, then another knock, as though the person in the hallway had no time to waste. It was far too bold for a servant, but who else would it be?

When he opened it, he was surprised to see the younger Miss de Bryun staring up at him. Though nearly as lovely as her sister, Margot's looks were spoiled by a certain stubborn set of the mouth that promised continual strife to the man who did not let her have her way.

Without a word, she pushed past him, and sat upon the end of his bed. 'I need to speak with you, Lord Felkirk,' she said, swinging her feet impatiently.

'Then it would be far better that we do it in a public room,' he replied, standing by the open door. Did no one in Justine's family have an understanding of basic manners? Or was this another seductive trap?

'You are not in a public room,' she reminded him. 'You have not come out of this one all day. When I asked after you, the servants told me you were not to be disturbed.'

'It is plain you did not listen to them,' he said, closing the door and leaning against it.

'I cannot get Justine to talk to me, either,' Margot said with a frown. 'She is locked in her bedroom, weeping and writing what I expect is a tragic confession of her imagined sins. And no one will explain to me what is going on.' She glared at Will as though it was all somehow his fault. 'I am tired of listening to people who do not really say anything.'

'Perhaps they do not speak to you because what is happening is none of your business,' he said with a pointed look.

Margot's lips pursed with a stubbornness that almost diminished her loveliness. 'How would you know if it was my business or not? You hardly know me at all. I have no family but Justine and Mr Montague. Since they are two out of three of the persons involved in this problem, that is a clear majority.'

'Montague?' he said in surprise. 'You claim him as kin?'

'He is our guardian,' she said, with a frustrated huff. 'Surely you realised that.'

Will had nothing to say to this that did not indicate supreme ignorance, so he remained silent.

Margot continued to glare at him. 'He was my father's partner. When Mother died, he all but inherited us, along with the store.'

If that was true, his dear Justine's past was even more sordid than he'd suspected. 'That is no concern of mine,' he said, doing his best to contain his emotions. 'I do not know what your sister has told you, but I am not really her husband.'

'Of course she told me,' Margot said, speaking clearly as though she thought him slow of wit. 'I am her sister. She is not an open book. Until recently, I did not understand the depth of her troubles. But it is obvious that the two of you are well suited and very much in love. I urged her to explain everything to you immediately, so that you might be properly married.'

His mouth opened to deny her claim. But the only thought in his mind was a desire to question her further on the subject. What had her sister told her? Did Justine actually have feelings for him, or was that just another part of the lie?

Margot ignored his silence. 'I thought I understood the situation in Bath. But after what Montague said this afternoon, it is plain that too many secrets have been kept from me. And now you mean to keep secrets as well.'

'You spoke to Montague?' he said, surprised.

'I was there when he arrived,' she replied. 'Since my dear sister has denied me the truth, I blundered through the conversation, thinking he was nothing worse than a foolish old man with an unreturned penchant for Justine.'

'And what persuaded you otherwise?'

'When he announced that she had seduced him in an effort to keep me from returning to take my place in the business.' The girl shuddered in disgust. 'As if his word would be enough to turn me against one who has been like a mother to me since my birth.'

'You do not trust Montague?' he said.

'I did not distrust him,' she said cautiously, 'until today, at least. All I knew was that I was packed off to school as soon as it was deemed proper to send me, and I have hardly been home since.' She frowned again. 'I had hoped that there would at least be useful lessons, like bookkeeping. But instead, they attempted to teach me needlework, which I have no skill for, and French, which I already knew. It was an enormous waste of my time.'

Will ignored the girl's almost masculine views of education and turned the conversation back to the subject that interested him. 'If you were not home, you cannot possibly know what was going on between the two of them.'

At this she sighed. 'I know because, despite how everyone has been treating me, I am not some naïve child.'

'You are very young,' he argued.

Now she was looking at him as though he was the innocent in the room. 'You are fortunate, Lord Felkirk, that you were not born female. It is even worse to be born a pretty one, if you have no family to keep you safe. Our father died before I was born. And Mother was...' She paused again. 'She was not right. I remember a pale woman who did not speak and who died when I was almost ten, because she could find no reason to live. But through it all, I remember Justine, putting her needs aside and caring for me as a mother should care for a daughter. She warned me that men who talk loudest of chivalry will throw it aside in a heartbeat, if they see an opportunity to satisfy their desires without repercussion.'

'You have a very dark view of mankind, Miss de Bryun,' he answered.

'That is the fault of mankind, Lord Felkirk, for proving my sister right. I have known of Mr Montague's unwholesome interest in my sister for quite some time. But I had no idea that he would be so villainous as to act on it. If she wanted me to stay at school, she was likely ashamed...' For a moment, the girl's rather brusque manner faltered and she seemed on the edge of tears. Then she swallowed and went on. 'I had no idea that her warnings spoke from experience. If she refused to let me return home, it was because she feared for my safety there. And if she remained with Montague...'

The girl did cry now, pulling an already-damp handkerchief from her sleeve and wiping at her eyes. 'She would never have given herself to him willingly. And she would not have stayed with him had she not feared something even worse would happen should she leave. She should have let me come home. I'd have helped her.'

Will sat beside her and gave her a gentle pat on the arm, pressing his own dry handkerchief into her hand. Even in tears, she was pretty. In a few years, she would be as beautiful as her sister. But until she was of age, she had no choice but to accede to the wishes of her guardian, just as Justine had done. 'You needn't think that. After all, what could you have done?'

'I'd have killed him,' she said, vehemently. 'I'd have struck him down with the same poker he used on you, before I let him touch me. And I would not have let him hurt Justine, ever again. But she would not tell me the truth. She is not like me. She thinks of no one but herself, she never complains and she will not ask for help, no matter how much she needs it. She thinks she must be the strong one.'

He remembered her, in this very room, stroking his arm in the dark, kissing the scar as though the brand he bore was a mark of honour. It had been after the strange dream where she had demanded to be left alone. She had all but admitted the truth to him, talking of her difficult life.

At the time, he had been full of sympathy for her. He had vowed that he would keep her safe. But today, when she needed him, he had walked away as though she did not matter to him. Even after she had announced that she was willing to go to the gallows if it might spare him the risk of a duel, he had refused to trust her.

He took Margot by the hand and pulled her up from the mattress, walking her towards the door. 'Do not fear, little one. That time is over. From now on, I will be her strength.'

'Fine words,' she said, almost spitting them back at him. 'I have heard similarly vague promises from Mr Montague himself. But know, Lord Felkirk, that I will not allow you to treat my sister as he has done. She is not some pretty bauble to be used and discarded when you are bored with her.'

'That was never my intention,' he said softly.

'Intentions mean nothing,' she said, with a dismissive wave, 'if they are undone by one's actions. You claimed to love her. And yet, at the first sign of real trouble, you mean to cast her out.' She turned to glare at him. 'You will forgive me if I think my sister has suffered enough at the hands of men. In short, my lord, if you do not want her, do not think you can send her back to Montague with a clear conscience. It would be better to have her arrested and let her take her chances with the courts than to return her to the suffering she has endured from that monster.' And with that, she was gone, slamming the door so hard that even the stone walls seemed to shake.

Chapter Nineteen

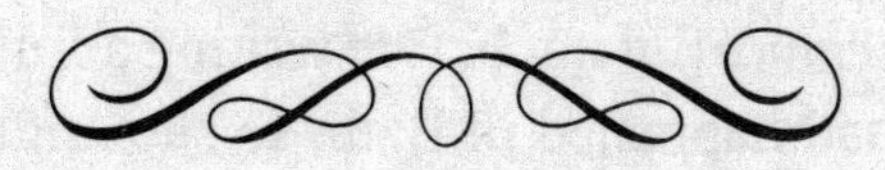

'Justine.'

She woke with a start to find Will standing over her bed, a dim outline in the darkness. For a moment, she hoped that he had changed his mind and would gather her in his arms to assure her that it had all been a horrible dream. When he did not speak, the hope changed to fear. As she did with Montague, she lay perfectly still, feigning sleep and hoping that he would pass her by, just once.

'There is no point in pretending any more. I know you are awake,' he said, taking a taper from the bedside and lighting it with the last coals of the fire. 'Dress and come with me. There is something I must show you, before tomorrow.' Then he removed himself from her room, as though allowing the privacy to prepare herself.

Come back, she wanted to whisper. *Come back to me.* There was no need to be so distant. What had they not shared with each other, these last weeks?

Could they not have one last hour together? Even if he did nothing but sit silently in a chair while she dressed, it would be better than being alone.

But their time to be together had passed and the distance between them was more than just the space between their rooms. She had cried herself to sleep worrying about what was likely to happen when morning came. But not before writing a full account of what had happened in Bath, so she might give it to the duke. If Will brought a second, there would be no other man he might choose. Perhaps, if she delivered a full confession before the fight began, Bellston might call a halt to it and save Will's life.

She pulled on a gown and found stockings and shoes, wishing she had asked what it was that was expected. When she had seen him just now, he'd been fully dressed. But since it was the same coat he had worn in the afternoon, she suspected he had not gone to bed.

He should be resting. If he meant to carry out his foolish plan, dawn would come soon enough and he must be ready for it. Perhaps the duel was worrying him more than he let on. Perhaps he meant to run away with her. That was too much to hope for. There was something funereal in his demeanour that was far more frightening than his anger had been.

When she was finished dressing, she found him waiting in the hall for her, a candle in his hand to light their way. He preceded her down the steps and through the servant-less corridors to the main floor. The house was still asleep. The hall clock chimed three as they passed it, on their way to the back of the house.

From there, they went to the servants' stairs, down again, through the kitchens and beyond, down another flight of steps to a part of the house she had never seen. She could feel the cool air rising from the brick walls and see the racks upon racks of bottles. The wine cellar? 'Where are we going?' she finally raised the nerve to ask.

'To get you what you wanted, from the first moment you arrived here.'

For a moment, she could not think what that might be. Then she remembered.

The diamonds.

He had told the truth, in Bath, when he had claimed to know where they were. Their location had come back to him, with the rest of his memories. Then it would have been better had they stayed lost. 'It does not matter,' she said.

'Does it not?' He stared back at her. 'The stones I very nearly lost my life for have no value to you. I should think, given the things you were willing to do for them…'

'Stop!' If this was the last time she would be alone with him, she did not want to be reminded of what had happed. 'You know it has been more than that, for some time,' she said. There was no bitterness in her comment. It was too late for that.

If he knew, he did not want to admit it. There was a ghost of his old smile on his face, as though it had all been a huge joke. But the joke was over now, the memory fading. 'Well, in any case, if I have guessed rightly in their location, you shall have them.' His expression changed, yet again, to something different, solemn but peaceful. 'Should something happen this morning…to me, I mean…I want to make sure that you have what you have wanted from the first: your freedom. If there is trouble, you are to take them and your sister, and go.'

He turned back to focus on the way they were taking, turning left, then right between the racks to go deeper into the room. Justine followed in silence, her mind racing. At one time, what he'd offered would have been more than enough to satisfy her. She would not be punished for what had happened in Bath. She would not have to return to Montague. Her sister would be safe.

But the preface that had come before it was unbearable. He meant for her to have the jewels if he died. She could have said the same of her father, she supposed. It was likely his wife and daughters he had thought of, as he hid them from Montague. She was to have them at last. But if they cost her lover his life, it was far too high a price to pay for them.

They had come to a corner, to a heavy wooden door with an iron ring for a handle. He turned back to her, explaining. 'This part of the house is very old, hundreds of years, in fact. At that time, the place was more of a fortress than a home.' He pulled on the ring and the door, which looked so solid, swung easily open, revealing an arched stone hallway, stretching forward further than the light from the candle could reach. But from what she could see of it, it was swept clean and free of cobwebs. The gentle breeze coming from it was cold and fresh.

'This is the one thing that my mother wished she could have taken with her, when they built Bellston Court,' Will said, with a proud smile. 'After all this time, it is still dead useful. But not practical to replicate.' He led the way down the corridor and they walked for some minutes, until she was sure that they must have passed beyond the walls of the house. Not a corridor, then. It was a tunnel under the yard and it led in the direction of the woods.

'Adam and I played here, as children.' Will smiled at the memory. 'We were looking for Arthur, under his mountain. We were sure he must be here.'

'The raven,' she said, remembering the story he had told in the woods.

He nodded. 'It was a fever dream. But I was so very hot. I heard the maids crying over how I must surely die. I did not want to. I wanted to be cool again and I wanted Merlin's magic, so that I might live.'

'It is cool here,' she admitted, 'Even in the heat of the day, I'm sure.'

'And magical,' he insisted. They had come to the end of the tunnel, to another wooden door as large and heavy as the first one. He pushed it open and she saw starlight through tree branches, smelled the mossy scent of pine and loam and heard the low slap of water on rock.

'Be careful,' he said. 'Go left and there is a steep path, down to the pond. But right and up the hill…'

'The path through the trees,' she said.

'I opened the door and looked up. And I saw a man, tall and gaunt, with a black coat.'

'Your raven,' she said.

'Montague,' he answered. 'I must have surprised him, for he dropped this.' He reached into his pocket and pressed a scrap of velvet and silk into her hand.

She did not need light to know it for what it was. She'd handled hundreds of them, over the course of her time in the shop, bagging up loose stones in the little sacks, pulling the gold drawstrings tight so that all stayed clean and safe. She ran her fingers over the stitching, not needing the candlelight to see the ornate M and B intertwined and the tiny gold crown embroidered above it.

'I did not understand what it meant. I did not even find it in my pocket for another year. When I did, I told no one, because it was too late to do anything. They burned most of my playthings at the end of the summer, fearing that they were contaminated by my illness. I did not want to tell anyone of this for fear it would be taken from me and thrown into the fire. So I hid it in the nursery. And then I forgot.'

'I did not look in the nursery,' she said, surprised by her careless assumptions.

'Why would you? I had not been there in years

and I live in the house. But I was searching for a christening gift for Bill. And there it was.'

'And Montague dropped it,' she said, imagining the scene.

'He threw it, more like. As if he was angry. And then he saw me and was gone.' Will gave a low laugh. 'He must have thought he'd escaped unnoticed. Then, twenty years later, the little boy from Wales appears in his shop, holding the very same bag. No wonder he split my skull. He must have been very near to panic.'

'If he was angry because the bag was empty...' Justine said, trying not to be excited by the story.

'Then what happened to the diamonds?' Will was smiling broadly now, pleased that she was following his reasoning. 'If your father stumbled off the path and came upon this door, he might have gone inside.' Then he turned back into the tunnel, shining his candle along the wall to reveal another door, this one of metal. 'And he'd have found this.'

When he opened it, a blast of cold air struck her, causing her to pull the shawl tighter around her shoulders. 'The ice house?'

Will held his candle high, until he spotted a lantern set into a niche in the wall. He lit it, setting his candle beside it, to make as much light as he could. 'What better place to hide diamonds? It is so dark here that a robber would not find them unless he was led to the spot.'

'He hid them in the ice,' she said, wondering how they were to find them if that was true. The room was still a quarter full of huge blocks, layered with sawdust and hay. The flickering lantern light on the smooth wet surfaces cast weird blue shadows around the room. They seemed to dance in time to the soft, musical drip and trickle of melting ice.

'Most likely he tucked them into a crack in the wall, or dropped them on the floor. If he had put them in the ice, I suspect we'd have found a loose stone in the bottom of the ice-cream bucket by now.' He pulled a penknife from his pocket and searched through the ice-working tools on the hooks and shelves by the door to find something for her. He pressed an ice pick into her cold fingers. 'I could not look in spring, when I first had the idea. Winter had just passed and the room was full to the doorway. But it is very near to the time of year when your father died. The same spaces are exposed.' Then he turned her gently to face into the room. 'Now, you must imagine that you are your own father. You have only a few moments to conceal something of value. Where would you put it?'

He lifted the lantern high over his head, so she could see the details of the room. While the tunnel leading to it was mortared stone, this space had been carved directly into the rock under the hillock. The walls were marked with the fissures and cracks of the excavation, any one of which could hide the jewels. Under her feet, the layer of damp sawdust that had frozen to the ground was thick enough to conceal any manner of things. If they had not been discovered for all this time, then what chance had she?

Then she remembered Will's words. She must think like her father. She had no trouble picturing him walking the path above. She had done it before. But now she imagined it not bright with morning sunshine, but gathering gloom. She was being stalked. She could feel the eyes on the back of her neck. But the silence of the approach told her the identity of the assailant. Montague meant to betray her. She felt her quickening pulse and the overwhelming desire to run.

If she did, he would catch her easily and take what he wanted, just as he always did. She must not give way to panic. Her father had kept a cool head, even when death was imminent. He might have lost his life, but he had denied Montague what he'd most wanted. The thought made her smile. It gave her strength.

She looked around the room again. 'It would have been dark. There was no time to light a candle. And he did not want to be discovered.' She closed her eyes tight, to shut out the lantern light, and reached out a hand. Ice in front of her. It was shockingly cold and she drew back quickly, until her shoulders were against the wall behind her. Her hand bumped against a shelf.

That would be far too obvious.

She worked her way along the wall, trailing hands against it, following it around the corner until she had worked herself into what little space there was between the stacked ice blocks and the wall. Then she felt for a likely hiding place. There was nothing here. She could not find a notch to hide a single stone, much less a handful.

And then she remembered her father. When she had last seen him, he'd seemed huge to her, like a great blond bear. She had been but five. But it had been more than imagination. He had been a large man who could not have wedged himself so deeply into this space. She moved back towards the door again, until there was barely enough space for a large man. Then she ran her hands over the bumps and crevices in the wall. That was when she found the crack. It was large at the top and even larger near the floor. But in the middle, at a place about equal with the height of her shoulders, it narrowed. While much of the wall was rimed with frost, the ice in this particular place was hard and smooth. She opened her eyes, but it was too dark to see much more than what she had discovered with her touch. 'Here,' she said, tapping the ice with the pick in her hand. 'Bring the lantern.'

Will crowded close behind her, holding the light so it shone over her shoulder.

Without thinking, she leaned back into him, trying to steal some warmth from his body to fight the growing chill of being so close to the ice.

Had he forgotten that he hated her? It almost seemed so. He did not draw away from her, but pulled her closer to shield her from the cold as she worked.

Her hand trembled as she jabbed the pick into the ice, only to feel it slide away without leaving so much as a chip. She struck harder the next time. And harder still after that. The ice in this spot was solid, as if it had rested there until it was as hard as the rock around it. Compared to all the other problems that had come between her and her goals, it was a very small thing. But it was very annoying. She struck harder, again and again.

And then she gasped. Just for a moment, she thought she had seen a glittering that was brighter than frozen water. She took her lover's hand and directed it, to form a cup at the base of the crack. She struck one last time, prying outwards to lever out the last of the ice. And what looked, at first glance, like a trickle of water, split into a multitude of tiny sparkles.

She heard Will's laugh of satisfaction as the gems poured into his hand. She poked about for a moment longer to be sure that nothing remained hidden between the rocks. Then she ran a fingertip through the shavings of frost and felt the sharp edges of faceted stones. If she got her jeweller's loupe and looked closer, she was sure she would recognise her father's work in the cuts, just as she could when she looked at the stock from Montague's safe.

She glanced down at the little velvet pouch, still dangling from her left wrist like a reticule, and opened it so that Will might tip his hand and pour the stones inside. Then she tightened the drawstring and offered him the bag.

He shook his head. 'Now that you have them, they are back where they belong.'

'Not quite,' said a voice behind them.

Chapter Twenty

'Montague.' Will let out a curse under his breath at the sight of the man and the pistol he held pointed at them. 'How did you find us?'

Justine berated herself for being so foolish as to lower her guard, even as she'd imagined his silent approach. She had warned Will that the man would find a way to cheat. But what was the point of winning the duel if he left Wales without the diamonds? 'He waited in the woods and saw us when you opened the tunnel door.'

Montague gave a slight bow of acknowledgement, as though proud of his cleverness. 'When you said you remembered all, I knew you would get the stones before it was too late. I had but to wait where the murder occurred to see if you would come and lead me to them.'

'I should have remembered to lock the door behind me,' Will said with a scowl. 'You have already proven that you are a coward who will creep along behind, waiting for a chance to take from the unwary.'

Montague shrugged. 'Not as noble as your family would be. But my method has proven effective so far. Now give me the diamonds and we will be almost finished here.'

'Almost?' Will said, watching the pistol in his hand.

'There is still the matter of your threats of prosecution and the impending duel.' Montague smiled. 'While the odds are in my favour, I would not like to leave killing you to chance.'

She and Will had turned as a couple and she still stood slightly in front of him. Now he was taking her by the shoulders, trying to move her behind him, out of the line of fire.

That would not do. If she moved, her guardian would have a clear shot. She planted her feet and refused to budge. 'Have you forgotten that you have but one bullet in your little gun?' she said.

'I need but one,' Montague said. 'Once William Felkirk is dead, the duke will want justice. And no tale of lost diamonds and evil strangers will save you from the hangman's noose. It does not matter to me if you stay or come away with me, Justine. But leaving Wales might be the more sensible choice.'

Will gripped her firmly by the shoulders again, still trying to move her behind him. 'Perhaps we could continue this conversation in a place where the lady is not trapped between us.'

'The lady?' At this, Montague laughed. 'You poor deluded fool, that you should still call her that now that you remember what she was to me. Justine will move of her own accord, soon enough. Once she has worked out, with her tiny, feminine brain, how hopeless her situation is, she will come back to me and leave you to die. Like all women of her type, she cares for no one but herself.'

After killing her father, forcing her into a life she did not want, and threatening the only two people she loved, was that really what he thought of her? The idea that she would come tamely to his side and resume her old life was a sign of madness. Or perhaps it was only stupidity. Margot was safe, no matter what had happened. Will had promised her that, even when he was so angry he could hardly look at her. But without Will, she would have nothing left to lose. When one did not care about the future, there were far better alternatives than sharing a bed with a man she despised.

Justine watched as Montague's gun hand twitched ever so slightly, as though trying to decide if it were possible to shoot past her and hit his target. She was too small to be an adequate shield for him, especially when Will seemed intent on being the protector, not the protected. He was still tugging at her arm, trying to ease her out of the line of fire.

She spread her arms wide, trying to cover as much of him as she could, staring at the hand that held the gun, watching for the telltale tightening of tendon and muscle. Her own hands clenched in response. The slight movement set the bag that held the diamonds swinging slowly on her wrist. It was too light to be a weapon. But perhaps…

She extended her arm suddenly and twisted her wrist. The drawstring slipped down her hand and the bag fly off her arm, arching through the air to land behind Montague. 'Here are your diamonds. Take them and go.'

He was not distracted, as he should have been. Instead, the movement had startled him. He raised the gun, finger on the trigger.

He was going to shoot and it was her fault. Without thinking, she threw herself forward, as though it might be possible to stop what was surely to occur. Then she remembered the ice pick, still clutched in her right hand, and fell forward, holding it in front of her.

There was a noise, very close and very loud. Then Montague's body weighed heavy against hers, as they fell to the wet ground. The warm, wet ground. That could not be right. An ice house should not be warm. Will was standing over her, the lantern swinging wildly in his hand, casting shadows against walls and ceiling, and over his very white face. He was so very pale. But at least he was still alive. He was moving his lips, but she could not seem to hear what he was saying. It was easier, just to close her eyes and think of something else.

Chapter Twenty-One

'Justine! Oh, my God. Justine!' He had been hatching a plan to get clear of her and wrestle the gun from Montague. He had not been paying attention to her. That had been Montague's problem as well, he was sure. Neither of them had given her enough credit. Nor had they expected her to spring like a tiger for the throat of the man who had persecuted her.

God help him, there had been a shot. His head was still ringing with it. The foolish girl had given no thought to her own safety, throwing herself at an armed man. She might have been injured, even killed. If she had been lost because of his slow reflexes…

He was at her side in an instant, rolling Montague's inert body to the side so that he might tend to her. 'My darling, are you all right?' Was she his darling? He hadn't thought so, this afternoon. But why else would she risk her life to protect him? 'Justine?'

She stared blankly up at him without answering.

Had she been shot? There was a prodigious quantity of blood, but it did not seem to be hers. He ran his hands carefully over her body, looking for tears in her garments, or the flinch and cry as his fingers accidentally probed a wound. But she could not seem to feel them at all. Her flesh was impassive at his touch, cold, but whole.

'Justine.' Then he remembered the shot, so near to her ear. 'I think you have been deafened by the gunshot, love. Do not fear. It will be better soon.'

Perhaps she had heard that, for she closed her eyes, as if to shut out the scene.

It was just as well. If she was not already aware of it, he did not want her seeing what she had done. Now that Will had moved him, Montague lay on his back, eyes wide and sightless, the blood pooling behind him, the ice pick buried to the handle in his chest.

He must warn the servants, before some maid wandered down to fill an ice bucket and frightened herself witless. And a man must come to take care of the corpse in the ice house. Although, until he could be buried, this was the best place for him.

And, of course, someone must be sent to the big house to get the duke so that he might swear a statement, or whatever one did when a crime occurred. There would be no question of self-defence, for the gun Montague had threatened them with was still clutched in one lifeless hand.

The little bag that held the loose stones lay just at the edge of the spreading pool of blood. Will scooped it up and dropped it in his pocket. Then he gathered up the real treasure: the body of his precious Justine. She was limp in his arms and so very cold. Was that the fault of the ice around them, or was it shock?

It was no trouble getting her back down the tunnel, through the kitchen and back up the stairs to her room. Once there, he did not bother with the maid, but stripped the bloody gown over her head and threw it into the fireplace, shifting the coals and poking it until he was sure it would catch and burn.

From behind him, he heard her soft voice. 'You oughtn't to have done that. It is probably evidence of some kind.'

He turned to see her staring into the fire. Her expression was still frighteningly blank, as though she could not quite understand what she was seeing. But he was relieved to see some colour returning to her face. 'My word to my brother will be evidence enough, I am sure. You will not be forced to sit like Lady Macbeth, covered in gore.'

'I do not think the blood on her hands was real,' she said, staring down in puzzlement at her own hands, which were quite literally stained.

Will filled the basin and brought it to her along with a towel, that she might wash. When she made no move to do it, he helped her, wiping away every last trace of what had happened. He took the basin away again, dumping it in the yard so there would be no trace of the pink-tinged water. Then he brought a dressing gown, wrapping her tight so that she would not take a chill, and a glass of brandy from a decanter he kept in his room. He added a few drops of the laudanum the doctor had left for his headaches and swirled the liquor in the glass. While he normally did not believe in the need for soporifics, his head wound was nothing compared to what she must have suffered in the last day. He pushed the glass into her limp hand, wrapping the fingers around the stem, and said, 'Drink.'

She refused at first. But he would not release her until she took it and coughed it down. 'You do not have to wait upon me, hand and foot,' she said, rising as if to prove it and sinking weakly back on to the bed.

'And you did not have to save my life,' he said. 'All the same, I am glad you did.' He lifted her legs to swing them up on to the bed and covered her, fluffing the pillows behind her head. 'Rest.'

'But I must speak to someone, to explain… And I need to tell you…' Her brow creased as though she could not think what it was that she meant to say.

'You will do that in the morning,' he assured her. 'For now, I will call Margot to sit with you, in case you need company in the night.' He kissed her lightly on the cheek. 'And then you will go to sleep, Justine. No arguments.'

'Yes, Will,' she said softly and closed her eyes.

Justine woke the next morning, her mind woolly, her thoughts confused. Most notably, she was surprised to be waking, for it meant that she had managed to fall asleep. As Will had carried her into the room, she had half-feared that she would never be able to close her eyes again, much less free her mind long enough to get any rest.

Perhaps he had put something in the brandy he had given her. Or perhaps it was the sight and sound of her sister, sitting beside the bed and struggling with the thread and bobbins in the dim candlelight, as though attempting to prove that she had any interest in the skills Justine had been trying to teach her.

'You needn't bother,' Justine had told her, gently.

'I know that,' Margot had answered, frowning down at the lace in a way that would have seemed very bad tempered of her, had Justine not seen the expression on her face almost since birth.

'The things Mr Montague said about my trying to keep you from your place in the shop…'

Margot had looked up at her with the same direct, no-nonsense expression she often wore. 'Mr Montague was a villain. He is gone now and we needn't worry ourselves about what he did or did not say. In fact, I recommend we do not think of him at all.' Then she smiled more softly. 'It is just the two of us, Justine, as it has always been. The two of us and your Lord Felkirk, of course.'

'Of course,' Justine said, dutifully, thinking that it remained to be seen whether she had a Lord Felkirk or not. Will had been very gentle with her, as he had put her to bed. He could just as easily have left her in the ice house and called for the duke. Perhaps he was merely grateful for the action she had taken to defend him.

As he'd carried her, she had felt the tear in the shoulder of his jacket that the bullet had made as it had flown past his head. Only a few inches down, or to the left, and it would have struck him. It did not matter what happened to her now, as long as she knew he was safe and Montague could not hurt him again.

It would be nice if he had forgiven her, even in a small way, for concealing the truth from him. But there was a limit to how much a man could forget, especially one who had been trying for weeks to remember the past.

She had done an awful thing to Mr Montague. But perhaps it was mitigated since she had prevented him from doing something even worse. And though murder was by far the most serious of crimes, she had done many horrible things already. No matter how hard she had tried, she simply was not a very good person. She was a murderer, a schemer and a fallen woman. All the good behaviour from this moment on would not erase any of it.

It shocked her even more to know that she did not regret what had happened with her guardian in the ice house. If she had been the sort of proper woman that Will deserved, she would have been distraught over what she had done. It had been awful. But every moment she'd spent with Montague had been nearly as terrible. There was a strange peace in knowing that, having done the worst thing possible, she would not see him, ever again.

With no particular plan, she got up and woke Margot, who was dozing in a chair beside the bed, a trail of tangled silk threads trailing from the pillow in her lap, the lace pins scattered on the carpet at her feet. Justine kissed her lightly on the cheek and sent her back to her own room to get some rest. Then she called for the maid and dressed with care in her simplest of muslin gowns, a pale yellow patterned with tiny oak leaves. The maid finished by pinning her hair up beneath a plain linen cap.

Justine looked at herself in the cheval glass. She declared the look suitable for a morning walk to either the wood, or to prison. Was there a prison within walking distance, or would she be driven there? She imagined herself in the back of a cart, driven down the high street of the village, displayed before all as a criminal.

She smiled and turned away. With such a dramatic imagination, she should be writing novels of her own. This one sounded like the sort where the fallen woman died in jail, after writing lengthy apologies to God and man for crimes which were caused by the actions of others. Family and friends, and the handsome hero all mourned her loss, though none of them had done a thing to help her when she was alive and with them.

While she had no objection to confession, she would offer no more apologies. Had she been forced to live her life again, it would most likely have gone much the same. Many of the choices had been forced upon her. Others, like the decision to come to Wales and give herself to Will Felkirk… No matter how wrong it had gone in the end, she could not bring herself to regret it. She reached up and plucked the cap from her head, dropping it to the floor beside the bed. Then she left her room and went down to meet her fate, head unbowed and uncovered.

She found Will and the duke in the study, a light breakfast on the desk between them. The diamond pouch lay there as well, leaning casually against the sugar box as though loose diamonds were but one more thing that the aristocracy sprinkled into their tea.

At her entrance, both men rose and Will said, 'Will you join us, Miss de Bryun? And close the door behind you,' he added, glancing towards the hall to make sure no one had heard.

Miss de Bryun. That was her name. But she could not think when she had heard it pronounced in that particular tone. Perhaps this was what she'd have heard in that imaginary meeting between herself and a pleasant young man in a shop in Bath.

'My lord,' she said, closed the door and curtsied. 'Your Grace.' She had done that wrong. She should probably have acknowledged the duke before his brother. But there had been no duke in her fairy-tale meetings. Nor had she needed to plead before one for life and liberty.

Will got a chair and pulled it up to a corner of the desk, then seated her and passed a third plate and the toast rack. There was a third teacup as well. They had expected her and had not wanted to disturb the conversation with the comings and goings of servants.

'My brother has given his version of the morning's events,' the duke said, sipping his tea with no sign of anxiety. 'Since I trust him, we will spare you the repeating of what must have been a most traumatic event. For the purpose of the inquest, I will say that an intruder threatened you both and met with an unfortunate end. Since he was also responsible for a murder on the property some years ago, and an earlier attack on my brother, we have been saved the price of the rope needed to hang him.' He gave her a pointed look. 'And that is all that will be said about that.'

'Thank you, your Grace.' Was it really to be so easy as that? She deserved some sort of punishment for taking Mr Montague from the world, even though it was a great relief to think that she would never see him, or hear his voice again.

'Did the man have family?' Bellston asked. 'Was there any that we need notify?'

'None but my sister and myself. He was our guardian, when our mother died, and in charge of our affairs.'

'Your guardian,' the duke repeated, clearly appalled.

'He was not just my father's partner, but his oldest

and dearest friend. In Father's will, he was charged with the keeping of the business and of our family. And when my mother died…' She swallowed. 'We went to him, hoping he would be like a father to us. That was not the case.'

Beside her, Will cursed beneath his breath.

'When you came of age,' the duke said, regaining his composure, 'why did you not leave?'

Will gave a warning growl in the direction of his brother. Clearly, he did not like the line of questioning. The duke held up a hand. 'Silence, William. I have other questions about recent events involving Miss de Bryun. I mean to have them answered to my satisfaction.'

Justine gave them both an encouraging nod. It had all been very polite and rational so far and not the barrage of shouted accusations she had imagined. 'When I came of age, there was still my sister to consider. Until she came of age as well…' She busied herself with the marmalade pot, trying not to think of all the horrible things that might have occurred '…I could not leave her alone in his care.'

'And when you came to my home under false pretences and lied to Penelope and I, pretending to be my brother's wife?'

'Lord Felkirk was bleeding and near death. But he had not yet expired and I did not wish to be an accessory to his murder. If he could be healed, I would attempt it. But if he was to die, it would be better that he did it in the presence of his family.

Lying about our relationship was a bad idea, but on the journey here I could not manage to think of a better one.'

The duke sat quite still for a moment, thinking. 'Nor can I,' he said. 'Considering all the evidence, I have no real desire to prosecute you. Saving my brother's life on at least two occasions tips the balance in your favour. As to some of the more unsavoury parts of this story, I will leave them to you to explain or conceal from my wife and friends, as you see fit.'

'Thank you, your Grace,' she said, rising as he rose and curtsying again.

Now that business was done, Bellston seemed to relax again into the more brotherly figure she had grown accustomed to seeing. 'I will leave you and Miss de Bryun alone now, Will. I am sure you have much to talk about.'

'We do, indeed,' Will said and rose to walk him to the door.

Once they were both gone from the room, Justine relaxed back into her chair, surprised to find her hands trembling as they raised her teacup. She had avoided prosecution. At one time, it was all she had hoped for. But who knew there would be so much to lose?

Will returned to the room and took his chair beside her again, putting his hands on his knees and sighing in satisfaction. 'That went well, I think,'

'Better than I'd hoped,' she said, setting down the

cup, careful that it did not rattle against the saucer as she did so.

'Now that Montague is gone, you and your sister are free to do as you like.'

Free. Justine rather liked the sound of the word. But it bothered her that he could be so cavalier about her freedom. Had her dependence on him been such a burden?

'My brother has agreed to help with any legal matters concerning the transfer of the shop to your full ownership. He will take the guardianship of your sister upon himself, until she is of age. The diamonds are yours, as well,' he added, sliding the pouch across the desk to her.

'Mine.' This was what she had wanted from the first. Why, now that she had achieved her goal, did it seem valueless?

'Well, in truth, they likely belong to the insurance company. Montague would not have gone to the trouble of trying to take them if he had not meant to file a claim. But even after they are reimbursed, you may see a considerable profit from their increased value.' Will was talking quite sensibly of things that would have interested Margot far more than they did her. The details of the transfer were probably important. Perhaps focusing on them would relieve the feelings of panic at being alone with the man whom she had tricked.

'What am I to do with a jewellery shop?' she said, baffled. 'I know how to purchase and grade the stones, of course, but Montague was the designer and goldsmith. And there are the books to be kept, employees to pay, customers to please…' There was so very much work. And it was all a very long way from Wales.

'You could always sell it,' he suggested. 'Or hire a manager until your sister is ready to take control.'

'I suppose it is too much to hope that she will forget her plan and find a husband,' Justine said, staring into the bottom of her empty cup.

'She seems very set on the idea of keeping it. In any case, you may settle it between the two of you,' Will said softly. 'It is your decision, and yours alone. But I suspect, what with a successful business and a safe full of jewellery, that you are now a wealthy woman, Miss de Bryun.' He cleared his throat. 'You shall have your pick of young men, should you wish to marry.'

'Marry.' Did he really need to remind her of the fact that they were not attached? Each time he called her Miss de Bryun, it was as if he hammered nails into her heart. What good would it be to finally have control over one's own life, when one could still not have what one truly desired? 'I will not marry,' she said softly. After Will, she could not bear the thought.

'It would be a shame if you did not,' he said.

'Now that you know my past, you must understand that it would not be possible.'

'I am part of that past,' he reminded her.

He was. But if he was the past, then what point was there in finding a future?

He cleared his throat and shifted uneasily in his chair. 'No matter what you choose, I do not wish the events of the last few weeks to weigh too heavily on you. You are free, just as I said before.'

Was this what freedom was? To be alone and heavy hearted? If so, then she did not want it after all.

'If a child results, of course I will claim it.' He was talking quickly, as though wanting to get through all the difficult words that would separate them, before she could raise an objection. 'For my part, I would be willing to forget the whole affair. No word of it shall ever pass my lips.'

'You mean to forget me?' Perhaps it was all the talk of freedom going to her head. She had expected a dismissal. She had even been prepared for it. But now that it was here, she could not manage to go meekly. 'How convenient for you, William Felkirk, that you have such a porous memory. If you insist on forgetting anything, why could it not be everything that had happened before the last two weeks?'

'You misunderstand me,' he said hurriedly.

She ignored his interruptions. 'You were quite happy to lie with me when you could not remember how we had met. But now that you know of my past, which was no fault of mine, you would forget me, as though I was never here. I was a fool to allow myself to believe, even for a moment, that a wonderful man like you might love me, in spite of what had happened. I—'

Suddenly, he pulled her out of her chair and into his lap. Warm, strong lips on hers cut off any desire to argue. As it had been for some days, during their kisses, they were in total agreement with each other. One of his hands cupped her bottom and the other plucked at the pins that still held her hair, eager to touch it now that there was no cap in the way.

He pulled back and shook his head in wonder at how out of hand things could get with a single kiss. 'It was so much easier, when I thought you were my wife. Then I simply assumed that you would obey me and commanded that you come to bed. But now I have no right to hold you.' To her surprise, his face was suffused with a schoolboy's blush. 'When I look into your eyes, I can barely find the words…' He smiled. 'Now that I have your attention, may I be allowed to speak in my defence?'

She nodded cautiously, afraid that if she moved too much, he would come to his senses and return her to her own chair.

'As I have been trying to tell you, the decision is yours, just as it should have been from the first. You did not come willingly to my house or my bed. I will not force you to stay here, if you would prefer to be elsewhere. And I am hesitant to even offer this, for it is quite possible, when the accounts are totalled, that you will be worth more than I am. I would not want to be thought a fortune hunter. Nor would I press my advantage to force you into a union that might disgust you…'

She kissed him back to prove that she was most definitely not disgusted. In fact, his words were so sweet she was trembling in his arms. Or else she was finally giving in to the terror she had felt over the last twenty-four hours, when she was sure she would lose him.

In answer, his hands became less demanding and wrapped loosely around her, offering protection and support, as his kisses soothed her brow. 'It is all right,' he whispered. 'You are safe now. If you stay with me, I promise you need never worry again.'

'My past.'

'You have none. Nor do I.' He buried his face in her throat, pressing his lips to her skin. 'My life began when I opened my eyes and saw you leaning over my bed.'

'Suppose we met, just as I imagined,' she said dreamily. 'Quite innocently, in a shop in Bath?'

He smiled. 'I would have been struck mute by your beauty and would probably have embarrassed myself by talking nonsense as I did just now.'

'I'd have thought it charming,' she said.

'But you'd have been too proper to respond,' he replied. 'From what I have seen, you are a very reserved young lady, with your prim dresses and your silly caps.'

'I would not have been wearing a cap,' she reminded him. 'They are for married ladies. It is why I no longer wear one.'

He stroked her head. 'Then I am glad that you are unmarried, for I do love to touch your hair.'

'I would not wear one, if my husband wished otherwise,' she said. 'You must realise by now what an agreeable wife I would be.'

'Wife,' he said, purring the word into the skin of her neck. 'That is what I wish you to be. I had grand plans to court you slowly and properly, so you might come to me by your own choice. But it seems I am just as impulsive as you made me out to be, when you invented our elopement. Come away with me, Justine. We will go to Scotland this very day and marry over the anvil. We will bring our families this time to witness it. Other than that, it will be just as you imagined it.'

She would be married, just as she had dreamed. And it would be to the man she loved, more than life itself. 'Almost as I imagined it,' she reminded him. 'In my story, we were forced to marry because you could not contain your desire and seduced me.'

He smiled and she felt the hand on her hip tighten, ever so slightly. 'I had forgotten,' he said, pushing her from his lap so that he could stand. And then, before she could protest, he has scooped her up in his arms and was carrying her towards the door. 'Let us retire to my chamber, Miss de Bryun, and I will show you just how it happened.'

* * * * *

A RING FROM A MARQUESS

To Melanie Hilton, for some fabulous information about Bath.
Bowing, as always, to your superior knowledge.

Chapter One

Margot de Bryun ran a professional eye over the private salon that had once been the back room of Montague and de Bryun Fine Jewellery, then paused to plump the velvet pillows on the *chaise*. The old shop had been a rather stuffy place. But now that she was in charge and the late and unlamented Mr Montague's name had been scrubbed from the gilt on the windows, she felt that the design was cheerfully elegant. The walls were white and the columns on either side of the door were mirrored. In the main room, the gold and gems lay on fields of white velvet and carefully ruched blue silk, in cases of the cleanest, clearest glass.

Once she was sure the stock was in order, she checked each shop clerk to make sure their uniforms were spotless. The female employees wore pale-blue gowns and the gentlemen a not-too-sombre midnight blue. She inspected them each morning, to be sure that no bow was crooked, no button unpolished, and no pin in a pinafore out of line. She required nothing less than perfection.

She took great care with her own appearance as well, making sure that it did not distract from the wares on display. It was vain of her to dote on it, but she shared her sister's fine looks. Until her recent marriage, Justine's beauty had brought her nothing but misery and Margot wanted no share of that. Better to dress simply than to attract the attention of alleged gentlemen who thought a slip on the shoulder would be preferable to an honest living in trade.

But neither did she want to appear dowdy. She avoided bright gowns and excessive jewellery in favour of the same simplicity that decorated the shop. Today's gown was a muslin as white as the walls with a gold ribbon at the waist to match the amber cross worn on a thin gold chain around her neck.

Such aloof elegance inspired awe from the customers and not the discomfort gentlemen sometimes felt in surroundings they deemed overly feminine. They left de Bryun's Fine Jewellery convinced that they had gone no further than the anteroom of the female realm to seek advice on those strange creatures from an oracle. They trusted that the luminous Miss de Bryun would know better than any other jeweller in Bath what their wives, daughters, and even their ladybirds might want in way of a gift. And it amused Margot to be treated as a high priestess of human ornament.

It was good for business as well. When she had taken over the shop she had not been able to make head or tail of the books that Mr Montague had kept. She suspected that the profits had been meagre. The majority of them must have gone into his own pockets, for she and Justine had gained little more than modest allowances when he had been in charge.

But now that the business was totally in control of the de Bryun sisters, the figures in the ledger showed a careful line of sales adding to a tidy profit. Her sister, who had sworn that there were nothing but bad memories in it for her, could not help but smile at the success Margot had made of their father's business. Justine might not need the fat cheque Margot sent her each quarter, but it was concrete proof that her little sister was more than capable of handing the place on her own,

Once she was sure all was in order, Margot gave a nod of approval to the head clerk, Jasper, who unlocked the door and turned the sign in the window to indicate they were open for business. Only a few minutes passed before the brass bell on the door jingled and one of her best customers crossed the threshold.

And, as it always did when the Marquess of Fanworth entered her shop, Margot's breath caught in her throat. He was probably going to make another purchase for one of his many mistresses. There must be several Cyprians fawning over him. What single woman could wear as much jewellery as he seemed to buy? Since arriving in Bath, he'd visited her shop at least once a week. Sometimes, it was twice or more.

When such a smart gentleman took a liking to her humble business, it brought other patrons with equally full pockets. That was the main reason she took such care to treat him well and stay in his favour. He was good for business.

Or so she told herself.

Who could blame her heart for fluttering, at least a little, upon his arrival? Lord Fanworth was a most handsome man. In her opinion, he was the handsomest man in Bath, perhaps in all of England. His chestnut hair gleamed in the morning sunlight, even as his broad shoulders blocked the beams that came to her from the open door.

But it was so much more than his looks or his patronage that made him her favourite customer. He did not buy a *bijou* and hurry away. He lingered over each transaction, sipping wine and chatting with her in the private salon reserved for her most important customers.

When they talked, it was as if there was no difference in their ranks. To speak with him made her feel as important as one of the great ladies who sometimes frequented the shop, dithering over the baubles in the glass cases that lined the walls of the main room. In truth, she felt even more important than that. They might speak briefly with Lord Fanworth in the crush of the pump room or the assembly rooms. But each time he visited de Bryun's she had his full attention for an hour, or sometimes more. He treated her like a friend. And she had far too few of those.

Today, his emerald-green eyes lit when they fell upon her, standing behind the main counter. 'Margot,' he greeted her with a bow and a broad smile. 'You are looking lovely this morning, as always.'

'Thank you, Mr Standish.' That was how he had introduced himself, on the first day he had come to her. Not with a title, but with his surname, as though he was an ordinary man. Did he truly think his noble birth was so easy to disguise? Everyone in town knew of him, whispered about him and pointed behind their fans as he walked down the street.

But if he wished to be anonymous, who was she to enquire his reason? Nor would she demand formality from him. Her heart beat all the harder whenever he said her Christian name. He pronounced it with the softest of Gs, ending in a sigh. It made him sound like a Frenchman. Or a lover.

That thought made it difficult to look him in the eye. She dropped her gaze as she curtsied, to compose herself before returning his smile. 'What may I help you with today?'

'Nothing important. I have come to find a trinket.' He pinched his fingers together to indicate how insignificant it was likely to be. 'For my cousin.'

In her experience, the smaller he made the purchase sound, the more money he was about to spend. 'Another cousin, Mr Standish?' she said with a sly smile. 'And I assume, as always, it is a female cousin?'

He sighed theatrically. 'The b-burdens of a large family, Margot.'

After one such visit, she had taken the time to check Debrett's and discovered that his family was exceptionally tiny and, other than his mother and one sister, exclusively male. 'Such a large family and so many of them undecorated females,' she said playfully. 'Do you not have a single piece of family jewellery to offer them?'

'Not a stone,' he said with a solemn shake of his head.

She gestured towards the door that led to the salon. 'Well, we must help you with this immediately. Come. Sit. Take a glass of wine with me. We have something to suit, I am sure.' She touched the arm of the nearest shop girl and whispered the selections she wished brought from the safe and the show-cases. The work she had just finished for him must be delivered as well. She had been waiting all week to see his reaction to it.

Then she held aside the gauzy white curtain that separated the private salon from the rest of the shop so that he might enter. There was already a decanter of claret waiting on a low table beside the white-velvet divan.

As she passed the doorway to the workroom, she caught a glimpse of Mr Pratchet shifting nervously in his seat at the workbench. He did not like the special attention she paid to the marquess. She frowned at him. What Mr Pratchet liked or did not like was of no concern. She had hired him as a goldsmith, but he sometimes got above himself in thinking that he was a partner here and not just another of Margot's employees. To take orders from a woman, and a young woman at that, must be quite difficult for him.

But he would have to learn to do so, she thought, with a grim smile to herself. If he harboured illusions that his talent with metals made him indispensable, he was quite wrong. Nor did she intend to marry him so that control of the shop might fall to him. Mr Pratchet was the third man to occupy the workbench since she had taken over the business. The last two had found themselves without a position at the first suggestion that their place at de Bryun's would be anything more than back-room craftsman.

Before she could step through the curtain to follow the marquess, Pratchet came to the doorway and whispered, 'It is not wise for you to be alone with a gentleman in a private room. People will surely talk.'

'If they did not speak of what went on here, when Mr Montague was alive, I doubt they will have anything to say about me,' Margot said firmly. The whole town had turned a blind eye to Montague's mistreatment of Justine, ignoring the fact that she was more a prisoner than an owner of half the shop. No one had offered to help her. Nor had Montague's unsavoury behaviour halted custom. Why should her innocent interaction with a member of the nobility be a cause for talk?

'Lord Fanworth is a perfect gentleman,' she added, glancing wistfully towards the salon. Almost too perfect, if she was to be honest.

'He is a rake,' Mr Pratchet corrected. 'A gentleman would not lie about his identity.'

'Who are we to question the ways of the gentry?' she said with a smile. 'If he wishes anonymity when visiting my humble stop, then I am the last person who will deny it. Especially not while he is such an excellent customer. And since the curtain that separates us from the main room is practically transparent, I am hardly secluded with him.' She passed a hand behind the cotton to demonstrate. It had been a particularly clever addition of hers, she was sure. It gave privacy to the more important clients, while giving the less important ones a glimpse into the dealings of the *ton*-weary aristocrats. If they should happen to gossip that Lord Fanworth had been seen at de Bryun's today, there would be all the more customers tomorrow, hoping to catch a glimpse of him.

But there would be no customers at all if her employees scolded her instead of working. 'Please tend to your job, Mr Pratchet. There is a necklace with a clasp that needs mending and I wish to see the setting for my most recent design by this afternoon at the latest. You had best hurry for you have not even carved the wax for it.'

Pratchet looked as if he wished to correct her, then thought the better of it and went back to his station without another word.

Only then did Margot sweep through the curtain, letting it whisper shut behind her. Before approaching the marquess, she resisted the urge to check her appearance in one of the many mirrors on the shop walls. But a single glimpse wouldn't hurt. It was only to be sure that she was showing the proper, professional smile that such a good customer deserved.

And a professional relationship was all this was. Mr Pratchet was right in part. Lord Fanworth was a rake and a very handsome one. For the sake of her reputation, she'd never have dared speak to him outside of de Bryun's.

But Mr Standish made her smile. And it was no polite, ladylike raise of the lips. It was far too close to a grin. When he realised that he could make her laugh, he went out of his way to do so. His visits were the highlight of her day.

But it was more than that, she was sure. He acted as if it was also the best part of his day to sit in the salon with her, drinking wine and spending his money. Today, his features lit into a dazzling smile at the sight of her. Then, he leaned forward, eager for her company.

Without his asking, she poured the wine into a crystal glass and offered it to him, pulling up a cushioned stool to sit beside him, as he drank. 'And what may I show you today, sir?'

He gave her a low, hot look. 'There are any number of things I would like to see. But let us limit ourselves to jewellery, Margot. We are in a p-public place, after all.'

She pretended to be shocked. And for a moment, he looked sincerely alarmed to have offended her. Then she laughed, for there was never any real harm in him. And it was clear by his returned smile that she knew he was not laughing at the stammer that sometimes appeared when he said certain words.

They both smiled in silence for a moment, enjoying the easy camaraderie. Then she said, 'Jewellery is all you are likely to be shown. It is all you will get from me, at any rate.'

That had been foolish of her. If she wanted the world to believe that these visits were innocent, she must learn not to encourage the man when he flirted. But it was too tempting not to play along with his little game.

He grinned back at her. 'I must hope, when I find a wife as lovely as you, she will be more agreeable.'

'Oh, I seriously doubt so, Mr Standish. You seem like the sort of man who will be back in my showroom the day after the wedding, buying gifts for your many cousins. I would advise any wife of yours to bar the door against you, until you promise some modicum of fidelity.'

'If you were my wife, I would bar the door myself, with us both inside.' She was sure that he meant it in jest. The idea of him taking her as his wife was quite ridiculous. It was only her overwrought imagination that made the words sound like a sincere offer.

But that did not keep her from dwelling on the scene. The thought of the two of them, locked together in a secluded room gave her a strange, nervous feeling, somewhere between anticipation and fear. She ignored it and gave him a wide-eyed innocent look, as though she could not possibly understand what he meant by such a suggestion. 'But if you locked me up, how would I get to the shop?'

'You would not need to be in this showroom, to show me all the treasure I wished to see,' he pointed out, quite reasonably.

'All the more reason not to marry you then,' she said triumphantly. 'The shop belonged to my father and now it belongs to me. It would be like denying my first love for another, were I to marry you.'

He was still smiling. But it was clear, by his expression, that he did not understand why she would not choose him over her work. She had not really expected him to. It hardly mattered, really. Even if he had been joking about marriage, he assumed it was the ultimate goal of any woman, no matter her station.

All the same, she was quite serious in her love for the shop. It would have been nice had he been the least bit serious about his feelings. But if marriage required that she sacrifice everything she had worked so hard to achieve, it was better that they remain friends.

As it sometimes did, at moments like this, the other likelihood occurred to her. Some day he would suggest an arrangement that had nothing to do with marriage. Late at night when she was lying alone in bed, in the little apartment above the shop, she wondered what her answer to such a question would be. But thinking about the Marquess of Fanworth at bedtime led to the sort of complicated, confusing feelings that had no place in the simple elegance of de Bryun's. Especially not when he was sitting right in front of her and all he wanted was to buy some jewellery.

Now, he gave a theatrical sigh to assure her that the day's flirting was at an end. 'You torment me, Margot, with your unattainable beauty. You do not b-blame a man for trying, I hope.'

'Of course not, Mr Standish. I presume wine and proposals are not the only thing on your mind this morning. Do you wish to look at bracelets? Earrings? Or have you come for the necklace you ordered last week?'

'It is not finished so soon,' he said, amazed. 'The thing you sketched for me was wondrously complicated.'

It had been. All the same, she had refined the design immediately on his leaving the shop and encouraged Mr Pratchet to rush the execution of it. She had set the stones in their places herself, so that she might make sure that there was not even the slightest deviation from her plans. It had been a tricky business. The largest of the stones had a small occlusion which kept it from true perfection. She had considered recutting it, or trying to find a replacement. But the gem had been so perfect in colour and form that she could not resist. Instead, she had chosen to frame the flaw with a tiny cluster of pearls. Now, it was like the beauty spot on the face of an attractive woman. The tiny mark accented the perfection of the rest. The result had been, in her opinion, a masterwork. She was eager for him to see it.

'For you, sir, there must be no waiting.' She gave a gesture and the shop girl at the door stepped forward with the velvet-lined case, placing it into Margot's hands so she might present it with sufficient ceremony. She undid the latches and offered the open box to her friend with a slight bow of her head. Inside, the red stones glowed with the heat of a beating heart.

His breath caught in anticipation as he took it from her. 'It is more marvellous than I imagined.' He lifted the necklace carefully to the light and it sparkled like frozen fire. 'So clever. So modern in its execution. And yet, respectful of the rank and beauty of the wearer.'

'Pearls are a much more refreshing look than the diamonds you suggested,' she said. 'No one will have a necklace like this.'

'I have never seen one like it,' he admitted. 'And

I am sure the lady will be as impressed as I. She has been pining for rubies. Her unhappiness will be quite forgotten, when she sees this.'

Why a woman would have any right to be unhappy when she had the attention of such a man was a mystery to Margot, but she nodded in approval.

There was an awkward pause for a moment, as he smiled at her over the necklace. Then he spoke again. 'You really are an amazing talent, Margot de-de B-Bryun.'

There was another of the slight hesitations in his words that appeared when he was being particularly candid with her. She ignored it, sure that such a great man would have been appalled to demonstrate vulnerability. Tonight, when she remembered the conversation in her mind, she would think of that tiny fault with fondness, or perhaps something even warmer. He was like the ruby at the centre of the necklace he admired, all the more interesting for being slightly less than perfect.

It gave her pause. She was already planning the time before sleep to include thoughts of the Marquess of Fanworth. It was unwise to have such fantasies, even in the privacy of one's own room. Perhaps Mr Pratchet was right. She was encouraging a rake and courting ruin.

When she answered, she made sure that her tone held no significant meaning, other than that of a craftsperson gratified at the recognition of her skill. 'Thank you, sir. It is a great compliment, coming from one who needs as much jewellery as you seem to.'

'I mean it,' he said softly, and with even more conviction. 'Not many jewellers would be able to improve on the original…original idea, that is. You seem to know instinctively what is needed.'

She bowed her head. 'It pleases me that you think I have inherited some small measure of my father's talent.'

'It is more than that, I am sure. You said your father died before you were born.'

'Unfortunately, yes, sir. In a robbery.'

'Then you have taught yourself the skills necessary to honour him.' The marquess nodded in approval. 'It shows a keen mind and an excellent understanding of current styles.' Then he frowned. 'But there was a robbery, you say?' He glanced around him, as though measuring the security of the vault doors against threat.

She smiled and shook her head. 'Not in the shop. He was set upon in the country while delivering stones to a client.'

'You would never take such risks yourself, I hope.'

Since that threat had come from the dead man whose name she had taken such care to remove from the shop window, she was sure that she would not. From now on, there would be no other name on the shop but de Bryun, therefore no risk of villainous partners. 'I take a great deal of care to be sure I am not put in the same situation as my poor father.'

He smiled again. 'That is good to know. But if you find yourself in need of p-protection…' He stopped when he realised how the offer might sound, 'I mean, in need of a strong arm to d-defend you, you must call upon me immediately and I will come to your aid.'

Suddenly, the poised rake who liked to flirt with

her seemed totally out of his depth. She understood the feeling. At his offer, her heart had given another inappropriate flutter and she had very nearly sighed aloud. For a moment, it seemed they were both utterly lost in the confusion and hopelessness of their situation. The attraction between them was strong, but she dared not call it love. When a rich and powerful man became infatuated with a woman so far beneath him, the future was inevitable, and far more like this accidental offer of protection than the earlier offers of marriage.

She gathered her poise and smiled to put him at his ease, again. 'If I am in difficulty, of course I shall seek you out, Mr Standish.' From the outer room, there was the distant ring of a bell and the sound of female voices. Her sister, and her friend Lady Daphne Collingsworth, were enquiring after her, in the main shop.

If they caught her spending too much time with the marquess, they would bother her over it just as Mr Pratchet did. It would be even worse should they suspect how she truly felt. She must bring today's meeting to a premature and unwelcome end before she became so foolish as to reveal herself.

She rose, to signify that she had other customers to attend to. 'Thank you so much for your kindness. But as I said, there will be no more robberies. I am perfectly safe.' She held the case out to him and he replaced the necklace. 'Would you like this wrapped? Or perhaps we might deliver it to you.'

He rose as well. 'No need. I will take it now, just as it is. You shall be receiving the balance we agreed upon from my bank, later in the day. When I come again tomorrow morning, you will be here to greet me and will sell me some earrings to match this necklace.'

'You may be sure of it, Mr Standish.' She held open the gauze curtain, so he might exit the salon.

As he passed Justine and Daphne in the main room, his demeanour changed, just as it sometimes seemed to when others were present. His smile was cool and distant and he offered the briefest bow of acknowledgement. He did not so much as look at Margot as she escorted him to the door, signalling a clerk to hold it open as he approached. It was as if their conversation had never taken place. Then he was gone.

Once the shop door closed, Daphne reached out to clutch her arm. 'Fanworth, again?'

'Mr Standish,' Margot said firmly. 'I respect his desire for anonymity.'

Justine looked worriedly out the shop window at the man's retreating back. 'These frequent visits are becoming worrisome, Margot.'

'But the frequent purchases are not,' Margot said in response. 'He is one of my best customers. If he tells others the source of the piece he has just commissioned from me, I expect a sharp uptake in trade.'

'No amount of money will make up for a lost reputation,' Justine said, in a dire tone.

It certainly had in Justine's case. Margot bit back the response. It was horrible and unfair to her poor sister, who had suffered much before finding a man who adored her, despite her unfortunate past.

Instead, she took a deep breath and said, 'I am taking no risks with my reputation. We are in a public place in full view of half-a-dozen people. He comes here to buy jewellery. Nothing more than that.' There was no reason to mention the private jokes, the innuendos, and worst of all, the florid proposals he offered her on an almost daily basis.

'No one needs as much jewellery as he buys,' Justine said, stating the obvious. 'He is a marquess. And you are not just the daughter of a shopkeeper. You are a woman in trade.' Though she had been just that a few short months ago, Justine spoke as if it was something shameful. 'There can be nothing more between you than commerce, Margot. Nothing honourable, at least.'

'I am fully aware of that,' Margot said, in a tired voice. It was a painful truth, but she did not wish to think of it any more.

Justine was staring at her, her gaze holding and searching, as she had when Margot was a child and caught pinching sweets from the kitchen. 'See that you do not forget it. Because I would not wish to see you succumb when he finally makes the offer he is likely to.'

'He would never...' Margot said, trying to sound more sure than she felt.

'Such men are all the same, when it comes to women beneath their class,' Justine answered, just as resolute. 'Though you claim the marquess is amiable and kind, his reputation in the *ton* is quite different. He is the proudest member of an already proud family. His blood is as cold as it is blue and he holds all of society in disdain. He has hardly a word to say to his equals, much less his inferiors.'

'That is not how he acts when he is with me,' she said, wondering what it meant.

'If he behaves differently when he is with you, it is a ruse to weaken your resistance. When he is done toying with you, he will attempt to collect you, just as he has the pretty baubles he comes here to purchase.'

It was more than that. She was sure. Perhaps he did want something more than jewellery. But it had risen out of genuine affection. She was sure when he finally made his offer, it would be more than just a conquest to him. But Justine would not have believed that, had she been witness to his behaviour, only moments ago. He had angled after her shamelessly. And she had allowed it.

She had allowed him to be too forward. If so, he would think less of her. Perhaps he assumed that she was as free with others as she was with him. If that was so, things would end exactly as her sister predicted. He would use her and discard her. She would be lucky if the only damage left in his wake was her broken heart.

For now, she would give the answer her sister wanted to hear. 'I will be on my guard,' Margot said, avoiding her sister's gaze. For if Justine looked at her, and into her soul, she would see the truth that Margot was unable to hide.

She had fallen in love with a man no more attainable than the moon.

Chapter Two

Damn and hell.

If you need pruh-pruh-protection...

What had he been thinking? To use those words made it sound as if he intended a dishonourable offer. Since the lady in question laughed at his offers of marriage, the last thing he needed was for her to think there was some darker, ulterior motive for these visits. And even worse, he had stumbled over the word, making it sound as if he was afraid to say them.

Stammering idiot.

He'd been called that often enough, as a youth. At times like this, he still had to remind himself that it was not accurate. Stammering and idiocy had no link. One could be the first without being the second. One could even control the first, with practice and care.

Stephen Standish, Marquess of Fanworth, strolled through the gauze curtain and back into the regular shop. As always, it was like stepping from a dream of paradise into the harsh light of reality. At the counter stood Miss de Bryun's sister, giving him a disapproving look. The woman was almost an equal in looks to his own dear Margot. More importantly, she was a sister-in-law to the Duke of Bellston.

He returned a look of equal coldness which prevented the need for speech, but offered a barely respectful bow to show he knew of her family connections. To the others in the shop, he offered nothing more than a sweeping, disdainful glance. He felt them shrink ever so slightly in response.

It was not as if any here were likely to address him. They would not dare. But he had grown so used to avoiding conversation of any sort that the attitude came as second nature. Better to let the world assume that you could not be bothered with them, than to call you a fool should your tongue tangle during an unplanned sentence.

He walked down the street, away from the shop, holding his scowl and aloof stare like a shield before him. He was the heir to a dukedom. There was nothing his father or the rest of the world could do about it. That alone was enough to keep him safe and untouched by the opinions of those around him.

But if one refused to speak for fear of embarrassment, one walked alone. It made him miss, all the more, his time in the shop with Margot de Bryun. Who could have guessed a chance encounter with a shopkeeper would have altered his world and his future?

A month ago, he had come into her shop meaning to purchase a trinket for an actress he was planning to seduce. He'd left two hours later with an emerald bracelet in his pocket and the target of his affections totally forgotten.

At first glance, it was the beauty of the woman waiting upon him that had given him reason to pause. Red-gold hair, playful green eyes, and a figure far too perfect to be hidden behind a shop counter. But it was her smile that most affected him. He could not have been more dazzled had he stood on the street and stared directly into the sun.

'May I help you?' she'd said. It might as well have been a choir of angels, for all he heard.

It had made him careless. He'd attempted to be glib.

'Miss de Bryun, I presume?' At least, that was what he'd meant to say. And as usual, when presented with a combination of Bs and Ds and Ps, his speech had failed him altogether. In a moment of profound cowardice, he'd dispensed with his title and given her his surname, hoping that it might still be possible to slink away, unnoticed.

She had not been like some people, when presented with such a disaster. She had not tried to help him by finishing the sentence. Nor had she looked at him with pity. Her smile had not dimmed an iota. Instead, she had waited patiently for her turn. And then she'd purred, 'If you please, Mr Standish. A gentleman who is about to spend as much as you are must call me Margot. Now come into the inner salon and I will pour us a glass of wine. Then you will tell me what it is you desire.'

What did he desire? Her. For ever. From that moment on. It took no great skill to bed a woman, but had it ever been so easy to talk to one? She had questioned him about the taste of the woman he wished to impress and about his own. She did not so much as blink at the pauses in his speech when he struggled for a word. And then she had presented him with a bracelet which she assured him was worthy of the temptress he described.

It was formed as a serpent. Each linked section had been studded with emerald scales. Moonstones were set for eyes. It had been so flexible it had seemed to slither as he held it, almost as if it were alive. The little jaws opened to clamp the tail and hold it closed.

When he'd realised she was the artist responsible for the design, he had questioned her for more than an hour until she'd explained each joint and hinge, and showed him sketches for other works. She had promised to show him the workroom, should he come again. And of course, he had returned, again and again. He had met the craftsman, learned the names of all the tools and expressed such curiosity about all elements of the business that she'd joked he was well on his way to managing the shop himself.

While he had learned much about jewellery making, Margot de Bryun was still a mystery to him. He knew she had a sister, but little more than that. Since she clung adamantly to the de Bryun surname, he doubted that there was a husband waiting in the rooms she occupied above the shop. But might there be a lover, or perhaps a fiancé, ready to greet her when the shop closed?

It did not matter. He might want her to be as sweet

and innocent as she appeared on the day he finally found the right words to make her consider his proposal. But even if she was not, he would marry her the moment she agreed.

And if she refused marriage? Then he would dispense with propriety, dazzle her with his rank and wealth, and seduce her, right there on the white velvet of the divan. When she had been loved near to insensibility, she would be much more agreeable to a permanent union. He would wear down her objections and he would have her and keep her.

Generations of breeding informed him everything that was wrong with the situation at hand. He supposed it was the same for Margot, since she treated his advances as little more than playful banter. But common sense informed him, even louder, all the things that were right about such a marriage. He could talk to her. For when would he ever find another woman so perfect?

Society could go hang. She made him happy. And by the smile that lit her face each time he walked in her door, the feeling was mutual. They were in love. They would marry. The rest was not important.

His family was a concern, of course. But he cared no more for the duke's opinion than he did for society. The plan was already in place that would win his mother to his side. Once they had married, and Margot had given up the shop to be his marchioness, her past would be forgotten.

He returned to his apartments with his head full of dreams, only to be dragged back to earth by his butler's announcement. 'Lord Arthur Standish is waiting for you in the drawing room, my lord.'

'Thank you.' Stephen's first impulse had been to curse in response. His brother was quite good company, in the evenings when they were both the worse for drink. But in broad daylight, it was all too easy to see his flaws. To see him now would tarnish all the pleasure of his visit with Margot.

As expected, he entered the drawing room to find Arthur sprawled in the best chair by the window, a large glass of brandy already to his lips. At the sight of his host, he paused to raise his drink in salute. 'Hail the conquering hero, returned from Montague and de Bryun.'

'Not Montague, any more,' Stephen corrected, moving the brandy decanter to the other side of the room. 'What do you know of my visits there?'

'All of Bath knows of it by now, I am sure.'

'And why is that?' Stephen could guess the answer. He reached past his brother and opened the curtains wide to let in the morning sun.

Arthur groaned at the sudden brightness, grabbed up a decorative pillow from the divan and disappeared behind it. 'How does Bath know of you and the shop girl? I make sure to remark upon it whenever I have a chance.' The empty brandy glass appeared from behind the cushion, waving as if a refill was expected.

Stephen grabbed the pillow and tossed it across the room to fall beside the brandy bottle. 'It is a wonder that anyone listens to you. You are so often in your cups that you are hardly a reliable witness.'

The shaft of light that hit the younger man caused a shudder and a squint. 'I only tell the story to those similarly inflicted.' Then he grinned. 'On holiday, it is not difficult to find people who overindulge in the evenings and then drink their weight in the pump room the next morning hoping for a cure.'

Stephen grunted in response. He was on the verge of losing his temper, and with the excitement would come the stuttering. He fixed his brother with a warning glare.

Arthur paid no attention to it, walking across the room towards the brandy. 'But enough of my flaws. Let us discuss yours.'

Stephen ignored both the drinking and the comment, but redoubled the intensity of his glare.

'How is Miss de Bryun today? As beautiful as always, I assume?'

'It is no concern of yours.'

Arthur pursed his lips and gave a small nod, as if the statement was a confirmation of his suspicions. 'Have you made her your mistress yet? Or does the rest of Bath still stand a chance with her?'

'I have no intention of making her my mistress,' Stephen said, though his body hummed softly at the suggestion. 'And, no, to the second question as well. The lady is virtuous.' He spoke the next slowly, so that Arthur might hear the warning. 'You would do well to remember the fact yourself.'

'All women begin as virgins,' Arthur reminded him. 'But it is easy enough to rectify. Perhaps I shall pay her a visit and discuss the matter.'

This was quite enough. Stephen kept his tone low and menacing, then let each word drop slowly from his mouth, each clear and in the proper order. 'You will regret it. I assure you.'

'Threatening me?' Arthur laughed.

Stephen responded with a grim smile and silence. It was usually enough to set his opponent out of sorts and rendering a hasty apology. But when the man in question was Arthur, there were no guarantees.

'If our father cannot scare me into behaving, then you stand no chance at all. Now, to the matter at hand. You are far too concerned with this girl, Stephen. I quite understand the attraction. She is a beauty. But if you do not have an understanding with her, to be so possessive of her makes no sense. It is not as if you can marry her, after all.'

His impending marriage was not Arthur's business. The comment was not worthy of a response. But silence no longer served to smooth the conversational road. The lack of denial gave away far too much of his future plan.

Arthur noticed it and very nearly dropped his glass in surprise. 'That is not what you intend, is it? You mean to marry her? His Grace will never approve.'

'His Grace can be damned,' Stephen said. Those words, though inappropriate for the scion of the family, never came with difficulty.

'Well, think of the rest of us then,' Arthur said, looking mildly horrified. 'It will embarrass the entire family if you run off and marry a shop girl. You cannot make someone like that the next Duchess of Larchmont.'

'She is not a shop girl,' Stephen said, a little too sharply. 'She owns the establishment. A different class from us, certainly, but hardly a menial. And once we are married, she will not have a need to keep shop.' He had more than enough money to keep her in jewellery of her own. 'Her sister married a Felkirk,' he added. Once the shop was closed, they would play up the connection to the Duke of Bellston and the marriage would not seem so remarkable.

But Arthur was still so shocked that he put down his glass and gave his full attention to the conversation. 'You truly are serious.' His brother was shaking his head in disbelief. 'You really mean to do it? I understand that you do not listen to Father. The pair of you loathe each other. And what am I but to be ignored? But think of our sister. Her reputation will suffer for this.'

'Her father is Larchmont,' Stephen said, frowning at the mention of their father. 'If she survives that, what harm will my marriage do her?'

'What of Mother? You will break her heart over this.'

'I most certainly will not,' Stephen said. 'Louisa and Margot will be like sisters, once I've introduced them. And I have just the thing to placate Mother.' He reached into his pocket for the jewellery box.

Arthur looked even more shocked. 'You got the duchess a gift from your ladybird's shop?'

'She is not my ladybird,' Stephen said, struggling to maintain his patience. 'And this is not some idle trinket.' He opened the box and produced the necklace.

'It is a replacement for the Larchmont rubies. And it is one of Margot's own creations.' He offered it to his brother, still quite pleased with the result. 'If you do not tell me the thing is magnificent, then you are a liar and I have no time for you. Margot is amazingly talented. I will not hear otherwise.'

Arthur was silent for a moment, then nodded in agreement. 'It is a beautiful thing, to be sure. I am sure Mother would appreciate it.'

'Would?' This doubtful answer sounded almost like his brother meant to add a 'but' to the sentence.

Arthur did not speak for a moment, but took the necklace to the window, squinting again in the brightness, before his eyes adjusted. 'How familiar were you with the necklace that was stolen?'

'Enough to have this made,' Stephen replied. 'It is not as if I spent my youth fishing in Mother's jewel casket, as Louisa did.' He glanced at the necklace in his brother's hands. 'It is close enough, is it not? The stones seem about the right weight. The pearls are new, of course. And the setting is lighter. Still, it is as impressive as the original.'

Arthur gave him a worried look. 'That is not what I mean. I saw the insurance report. It had a description of the stones. There is a flaw in the main one, right near the corner.' He held the necklace up to the light again and the sunlight cast a blood-red shadow through the ruby and on to the floor. 'And this has one as well.' He looked back at Stephen again, sombre this time. 'This is not a close match, Brother. This is the same stone.'

'The one that was stolen?' The necklace in question had been gone for almost two months. It was his mother's sadness at the loss that had brought this idea into his head.

'Taken from the house in Derbyshire,' his brother agreed. 'Strangely enough, the stones found their way into the hands of your Miss de Bryun. If I were a suspicious man, I would think that you had given them to her.'

'Of all the cheek.' Family connections did not give Arthur the right to hurl insults about over something that had to be an innocent mistake.

His brother held up a hand in apology. 'I know that it was not you. Someone sold them to her. If she is responsible for the buying and selling in that shop, she must know the source and, therefore, the thief. It is quite a coincidence that she sells them back to the very family that lost them, is it not?'

'Only that, I am sure.' If Arthur was right about the origin of the stones, it was beyond strange. Margot claimed to choose her stock with care. There was nothing in her manner to suggest that she might be guilty of trading in stolen goods. And that the family's own jewels should find their way home without some comment from her… 'She knows nothing of my family,' he said, relieved to have found the flaw in Arthur's logic.

His brother responded to this with sceptical silence. 'Do you really suppose that is true? Many people in Bath know who you are, Stephen. You cannot think that a marquess travels unnoticed by society.'

'I make no effort to trade upon the title.' But neither did he act like an ordinary gentleman. When he was not speaking directly with Margot, he behaved just as his father did: as though the rest of the world was far beneath his dignity.

'Surely someone must have remarked upon seeing you there,' his brother said quite reasonably. 'You said yourself that her sister is connected to Bellston.'

He had seen the sister more than once and she had acknowledged him as if she knew perfectly well who he was. Had he expected her to remain mum on the identity of the man visiting her shop? She must have told her sister. 'Even if she knows who I am…'

'Then it is still an amazing coincidence that she put these very stones back into your hands. How much did she charge you for them, I wonder?'

A small fortune. But considering the reason for the necklace, he had not thought twice. 'I was the one who requested rubies,' he said. But a clever criminal might have led him to the idea before he'd even noticed.

'I suspect she had a good laugh about it, once you were gone from the shop,' his brother replied gently, placing one hand on his shoulder and returning the necklace to him with the other.

'She would not.' She would not dare. If he did not allow the Duke of Larchmont to make sport at his expense, he certainly would not take it from a Bath shopkeeper.

Or there might be an explanation. There had to be. If not, he had been behaving like a mooncalf over a heartless jade. And all because she had not laughed in his face when he spoke.

Arthur continued, unaware of his darkening mood. 'Well, in any case, thank God we discovered the ruse before you had given this to Mother. She would have recognised the stones immediately, I am sure. And Father...'

He did not need to finish. They both knew what would have happened. His father would have proclaimed that his heir was an idiot, just as he did every time they met. It was why they no longer spoke.

'If what you say is true, Larchmont will never hear of it.' If Margot de Bryun proved false, he would see that she was punished, as she deserved. Then he would distract himself with any number of females who were too awed by his rank and temper to comment upon his flaws. The whole mess would be buried and forgotten before his parents arrived later in the month so that the duke could take the waters for his gout.

'Let me handle this,' Arthur said, his voice still soft with understanding. 'We will show the stones to an enquiry agent. If I am right, than he can go to the shop and take her into custody.'

'Certainly not.' Perhaps the girl had made a fool of him. Or perhaps there was still some perfectly innocent explanation for the reappearance of the stones. But if there was a decision to be made, he would do it himself. His heart was not so tender that it needed coddling. Nor would he endure, for another moment, the pitying look his wastrel brother was giving him now.

He glared back at Arthur until he felt his brother yield, as a dog might when it saw a wolf. Then he spoke. 'I will take the stones to your enquiry agent, so they might be identified. Then I will deal with the shopkeeper.'

Chapter Three

Margot stared out the window of the shop, leaning her elbows on the glass case in front of her. She would never have allowed such slack behaviour from the people in her employ. But they were not as dejected as she was, after another day alone in the shop.

Lord Fanworth had not come yesterday, as he had promised when their conversation had been interrupted. She'd hoped he'd at least visit long enough to tell her how the necklace had been received. She liked to be told that her designs made others happy.

Of course, if the happiness meant that her Stephen Standish was currently entwined in the arms of some ruby-bedazzled Cyprian, she was not so sure she wanted to know. It was foolish of her to be so obsessed with a man who spent so much of his time buying jewellery for his lovers. But to her, the time they spent together, just talking, was more valuable than anything he had purchased at her shop. Surely he must realise that true affection could not be bought with rubies.

Once again, the worrisome thought occurred to her. Her sister and Mr Pratchet were right. He had seduced her mind, convincing her that she was more important to him than the other women he courted. On the day he finally asked for her body, she would give herself freely, without a second thought. It would be the death of her reputation, if they were not very discreet. But to refuse would mean that she would never know his touch. To imagine such a future was intolerable.

Of course, it might be the only alternative available. He had not come yesterday. Today was almost through and there had been no sign of him, either. One more day and it would be longer than any interruption since the first day he had found her. How long could one stay in bed? It was another question she did not want an answer to. If he gave even a hint of what he had been doing, it would surely make her cross. Assuming he came back at all.

Perhaps these visits meant nothing to him. Or perhaps their interaction was becoming too expensive. The ruby necklace had been very dear. Even the pockets of a marquess must have some limit to their depth. But he must realise he did not need to make a purchase to command her attention. She would have happily poured out the wine and invited him to sit and rest himself. Anything to have him here, for even a few minutes, to lighten her spirit and ease the passing of the day.

It was not as if she did not enjoy her shop. But at some point in the last month, she had come to think of the marquess as a part of her day. His absence was like coming to the tea tray and finding the pot empty.

Not quite. At least one knew that there would be more hot water and a few leaves left in the bottom of the tin. But suppose India ceased to exist and there were to be no more tea ever? Or, worse yet, that the tea had simply gone back to London, or to somewhere even further?

Or to someone else?

It was all the more troublesome that she could not share her fears with those around her. Her sister would remark that it served her right for growing accustomed to those unnatural visits. Mr Pratchet would inform her that it was for the best. Even now, she could sense him lingering in the doorway of the workroom, trying to catch her attention.

She turned and caught him squarely in her gaze. 'Is there something I might help you with, Mr Pratchet?'

'If you are not too busy.' He glanced behind him, as if to indicate that their discussion was better unheard by the small group of customers already in the shop.

She sighed and walked towards him into the back room, shutting the door behind her.

When he was sure that he could not be heard, he announced, 'The Marquess of Fanworth has not visited in almost a week.'

'Only two days,' she said, without thinking.

His eyebrows rose. 'It is a great relief to me that he seems to be losing interest. If he returns, you must not encourage him. People will talk.'

'I must not encourage him?' Margot laughed. 'He is a customer, Mr Pratchet. I certainly hope people talk about his presence here. If people of a certain class notice that we get regular trade from the son of the duke, they will come here as well.' And if, just once, he should give one of her pieces to a member of his family, rather than wasting them on opera dancers, there was no telling how much trade might result.

'I do not like it, all the same.' There was something in Pratchet's tone that was more than concern for a vulnerable young woman. This sounded rather like jealousy.

Oh dear.

It was happening again, just as it had with Mr Perkins and Mr Jonas. He was becoming too familiar. He was acting as if he had any right to control her personal behaviour, as if she were just some woman and not the person who paid his salary. If it was not nipped in the bud immediately, she would be placing an ad for a new goldsmith within the week. 'I fail to see what your opinion has to do with the workings of this shop,' she said, using a voice that should remind him of his place.

Rather than take the tone as the warning it was meant to be, Mr Pratchet ruffled his feathers. 'It need have nothing to do with the shop at all. I will not see you damage your reputation for base profit. You are a lady and must take care.'

'I am your employer,' she said and waited for him to realise his mistake.

'One does not preclude the other,' he said, still oblivious. 'If we are to have an understanding—'

'Clearly, we do not understand each other at all,' she said, cutting him off. 'Not if you think you have a right to dictate to me.'

He seemed surprised at the interruption, 'You would be wise to listen to me.' It was as if he was scolding an unruly child. 'You could not manage the shop alone. You have some talent for design, I'll admit…'

'Thank you,' she said in a way that should have put him on his guard.

'But you know nothing of working in metal.'

'I know enough to appraise the talent in a goldsmith. It was why I hired you,' she said. 'And why I pay you handsomely for your skill.'

'But if we are to enter into a more enduring partnership, for example a marriage…'

'Marriage?' she said, glacial.

He blundered on. 'You mentioned, when you brought me on, that there might be a chance to be a partner in the shop. What better way to establish such a partnership then with the most permanent alliance?'

'What better way?' She laughed out loud at this. 'Why, with lawyers, of course. And an exchange of money, from you to me. At such time as I consider taking on a partner…a junior partner,' she corrected, 'there will need to be contracts and negotiations on both sides. I will expect you to buy a share of the business, just as you would if I were a man.'

'But you are not a man,' he said, as though she might need to be reminded.

'I do not intend to marry you, simply to secure a partner for my business. With the current matrimonial laws in this country, that would be little better than handing you the keys to the front door and walking away.'

'There is nothing wrong with the law,' he said. 'It is just as God intended.' By the long steady look he gave her, it was clear that he thought any problems lay not with the state, but with the woman in front of him.

'I will discuss the matter with God, when I meet him,' she said. 'But that will not be for a good many years. And when he greets me, he will still be calling me Miss de Bryun.'

The pronouncement was probably blasphemy. But it was clear by Mr Pratchet's shocked silence that he finally believed she was in earnest.

She continued. 'You have been labouring under a misapprehension about your future here. I hope I have corrected it. If I have not? As your employer, I am well within my rights to let you go, no matter how good your work might be. But one thing I am most assuredly not going to do is marry you, Mr Pratchet.'

'Yes, Miss de Bryun.' The answer was respectful, but there was something in his expression that did not match the agreeable tone. He seemed to be recalculating, like a chess player who had found another path to mate. When he spoke again, it was in a more humble voice, though there was no apology in his words. 'All the same, I stand by my warning to you about the Marquess of Fanworth. Do not trust him, or his family. I am sure what he intends for you is more than a simple transaction. If he is no longer coming to the shop, then you are lucky to be rid of him. And now, if you will excuse me, there is work to attend to.' He turned and walked away.

As Margot went back to the main salon, she realised that she had just been dismissed from her own workshop. She sighed. It did no good to become preoccupied over the mysterious marquess, if it meant that she was not paying attention to more important matters. The erosion of her authority over Mr Pratchet should be foremost in her mind. One more such unusual outburst and she would have to let him go, for both their sakes. She would give him a letter of reference, of course. He did excellent work. In a shop run by a man, he would be no trouble at all.

But she had no intention of allying herself to a man who thought he could choose who she did or did not talk to, or who thought that a marriage was the next logical step after a position as an underling.

The idea left her in such a mood she barely remembered to smile in welcome as a customer came into the shop. He waved away the assistance of the nearest clerk, but remained at the front counter, staring thoughtfully down at a tray of inexpensive rings. Then he removed a pair of spectacles from his pocket and consulted a small notebook, nodding to himself and making notes with the stub of pencil that was tied to the binding.

Margot paused to assess him. Something was wrong about his demeanour. She could tell by the cut of his coat that he could afford something much better than the work he was admiring. But the style of his garments was simplistic to the point of anonymity. She almost expected to see a clerical collar flopping over the lapels and not an ordinary neckcloth.

To a seller of fine jewellery, he was disappointingly unornamented. There was no chain or fob on his waistcoat, no stickpin in coat or cravat, and his buttons were polished ebony to match the fabric of the coat. His only vanity was a gold ring worn on the left hand.

How strange. With no sign of a signet or stone, it looked almost like a wedding ring. She had never seen one on a man before. But one look at it and she was sure that it was a gift from a woman. A fellow who chose to wear such a thing must be a romantic. If so, he should show his devotion to the lady with a purchase of some kind.

'May I help you, sir?' Margot stepped forward with her most brilliant smile.

'You might if you are Miss Margot de Bryun,' he said, giving her an equally charming of smile. There was something behind it that was quite different from the expressions of the men who were usually trying to capture her attention. He gave the impression that he knew more than he was likely to tell.

Her own smile never faltered. 'I am she. But I am sure any of the staff can help you, if you wish to make a purchase.'

'Oh, I am quite sure that they cannot.' His smile grew even more secretive as he reached into his pocket and produced a neatly lettered card.

E. A. Smith
Problems solved. Objects found.
Private enquiries handled with discretion.

She looked at him again, losing the last of her shopkeeper's courtesy. 'What sort of problems do you solve, Mr Smith?'

'If I told you, I would hardly claim to handle my enquiries with discretion.'

'But you can tell me what brings you here to seek out me, specifically.'

He nodded. 'In this case, the problem is missing jewellery. The owner would like the item returned and the person who took it remanded to the authorities.'

'You are a thief taker?'

He shrugged. 'Sometimes. In this case, you must tell me.' He reached into his pocket and removed a carefully folded piece of paper. 'I am searching for a particular necklace. It belongs to the Duchess of Larchmont.'

She stifled a gasp. The mother of the Marquess of Fanworth. Her Mr Standish had spoken of a woman who missed her rubies. Had he been asking her to design a necklace for a duchess? She struggled to compose herself and examined the drawing. 'It is lovely, but I have nothing of the sort here in this shop.'

Mr Smith looked at her carefully, as though he had some reason to doubt the story. 'It is quite possible that the stones were removed from the setting and sold separately. Perhaps they have already been reset.'

She risked a nod. When ridding oneself of such a distinctive piece, it would be the most sensible thing to do. She waited for Mr Smith to explain himself.

He was looking at her with an equally curious expression. 'Do you deal in rubies, Miss de Bryun?'

His continual questions were growing tiresome. 'We deal in many stones, sir. Rubies are among them. But we do not deal in stolen merchandise, if that is what you are asserting.'

'Perhaps, if you were to look more closely at the stones, you might be able to help me find them. I have a list of their weights and qualities.' He pushed the paper across the counter towards her.

She felt a cold chill on her neck, before even looking at the sheet. The man was so calm, so assured, and so carefully avoiding any hint of accusation that his visit seemed all the more ominous.

The sketch was followed with a detailed description of the stones: their carat weight, colour and grade. Two stones, emerald cut, one half-carat each, perfect. Two more at a carat, pear-shaped, also perfect. And the largest centre stone, almost two carats by itself, with a little flaw at the corner.

All her previous denials were for nothing. She knew these stones. She'd reset them herself and given them to Stephen Standish. But how had they come to be in her possession? And what was to happen to her now? Most importantly, how was she to explain to Stephen that she had sold his family's gems back to him?

Unless he already knew.

Once the thought had entered her head, it pushed out all others. The stones had been in his family for generations. Surely he had recognised them from the first. Why had he said nothing to her? Had he been the one to send this man? To what purpose?

She was doing him an injustice by doubting him. He might be as innocent of this as she was. Or he might be in some trouble over this that she did not fully understand. Until she had spoken to him about the necklace, she would not be sure.

If she blurted what little she did know to this stranger, she might make matters worse for him and not better. What good would it do to declare her innocence, only to shift the blame and the disgrace on to the man she loved?

She stared down at the description of the rubies, doing her best to keep her face impassive. 'I have no such stones at this time.'

'Should we look in your locked room? Perhaps you might have forgotten.'

'I am not likely to forget stones of this size. But if you insist.' She led him to the room at the back of the shop, taking the key from the chain around her neck. Once inside, she removed the velvet-lined trays that held the loose stones to show him that they were indeed devoid of the things he was looking for.

He did not seem as surprised as he should have, if he'd truly expected to find them there. 'You are sure you have not seen these stones before?'

It was a cleverly phrased question and one that she could not lie through so easily. It hinted that he knew exactly where the stones were and was awaiting her confession. 'Do you doubt my word?'

By the flash of triumph in his eyes, she had given him the answer he expected. 'I only know what I have learned from others. The name of your shop was mentioned in relation to the disappearance of the stones. It is why I have come to ask you about them.'

Her shop? Maybe Stephen had nothing to do with it. Her mind raced. Perhaps it had happened while Mr Montague was still alive. If he had been in the habit of buying stolen property, there was no telling how much of her current stock was compromised. How many such mistakes might she have to apologise for? And would all the people involved be as understanding as Mr Smith seemed?

Perhaps it was not so dire as that. But she would not know until she had searched the records and learned what she could about the rubies. But for Stephen's sake, and her own, it would be wise to wait until she had learned all she could on the subject, before speaking to Mr Smith. 'I know nothing of stolen necklaces,' she said. 'Nor do I understand why anyone would accuse me of such a thing.'

'Let me explain the situation to you.' Mr Smith gave her a sad, almost understanding smile. 'You asked me earlier if I was a thief taker. I must tell you, in some cases, I would most prefer not to be. There are times when one has been led astray, or misinformed, or trusted those that were unworthy. Though they had no intention of breaking the law, those people find themselves in a great deal of trouble. They might be imprisoned, or even hung for a single mistake. But all it would take to avoid the difficulty is to admit the whole truth and return the stones to their rightful owner.'

'If I had the stones, I should most certainly return them,' she said, for that was perfectly true. Then she followed it with half a lie. 'If I see them in the future, I will contact you immediately.'

'That would be wise,' he agreed. 'I will give you a few days to think on the matter. Then I will return to see if you have anything to tell me.'

'Of course, Mr Smith.' She gave him her most co-operative smile. If the Duke of Larchmont wished to see her hang, innocence would not be enough to protect her. But she could swallow her pride and go to Justine with the story. The Felkirk family was more than strong enough to shield her from Mr Smith and his threats. 'If I discover anything, I shall most assuredly tell you.'

'Until then, good day, Miss de Bryun.' He gave a slight respectful bow and exited the shop.

For a moment, Margot was frozen in place, unsure of what to do next. Then she glanced around her to be sure that the other customers in the shop had been too preoccupied to hear any of the exchange between herself and the thief taker. When she was sure that not even the nearest clerk had eavesdropped, she hurried to the little office she kept at the back of the workroom.

Once there, she brought down the account books, tracing her fingers down lines of sales until she found the records of shipments taken in. And there was a purchase of loose stones large enough to hide the Larchmont rubies.

Had the merchant passed the stones on to her? The man was a gypsy, but well connected, and the natural son of an earl. She'd never had reason to be suspicious of him before. But then, she'd never been accused of dealing in stolen merchandise.

She went to the files and found the detailed inventory of the purchase. It had been checked in by Mr Pratchet, the description of the gems written in his tidy hand. They were mostly opals, this time, and a nice selection of emeralds. It appeared that she'd had the best of a shipment from the Americas: Brazil, perhaps. And there, at the bottom of the list, were the rubies. Their description was identical to the one that Mr Smith had just shown her.

The pure red of those stones could only have come from Burma. What were they doing with Brazilian emeralds? Mr Pratchet had paid out more than she'd expected to spend on that order. But the amount listed for the rubies was less than a tenth of their actual value. The ink on the line did not seem to match the rest, as though the last item had been added as an afterthought. The total below it had been carefully altered to include the amount paid out for the stolen stones.

She stared at the books for what seemed like hours, trying to understand how she had not noticed before. But hadn't Pratchet just demonstrated how careless she had become while fawning over the Marquess of Fanworth?

When the senior clerk, Jasper, came to her for permission to shut the shop, she gave an absent nod. The sun was near to setting. The other clerks had already gone home to their tea and the building had grown dark and quiet. She followed the boy out into the shop and locked the door the minute he was thorough it. Then she hurried back to the workroom.

If there was an explanation to any of this, it would lay with Pratchet. She went straight to the desk he used as a workbench and searched the drawers, not sure what she expected to find. More stolen gems? Thank

God, there were none. Perhaps he was not responsible, after all. He might have been gulled, just as she had been, when presented with a fine bunch of loose stones and a price too good to resist.

But then she turned to the box of scrap gold on the floor beside the table, waiting to be melted and recast. It took only a few moments' prodding to find the setting for the duchess's rubies lying twisted and empty at the bottom.

'What are you doing there?' Mr Pratchet was standing in the doorway, watching as she rifled his workspace.

'What are you still doing here?' she said. For a moment, irrational instinct took her and her eyes darted around the room, searching for a defensive weapon.

'I forgot to take my coat...' As he stared at the broken necklace in her hand, his voice trailed away, reminding her that such fear was overblown. He might be a thief, but he was an unprepossessing specimen who would not further risk his livelihood by attacking her.

'You know what I am doing.' She held the setting out in front of her, so that there could be no denying. 'Explain this.'

'You will not like what I have to tell you,' he said, stepping forward, unthreatening but unafraid.

'There is no doubt of that,' she said. 'You used me and my shop to trade in stolen materials.'

'Only once,' he replied, as though it should matter.

'And the one time you were caught in it. An enquiry agent has been here today, searching for the necklace. What am I to tell him?'

'I warned you of the dangers in dealing with the marquess,' Pratchet said, as though it were somehow her fault that they had come to this.

'What has he to do with it?' she asked, afraid of the answer. 'Other than that he came to the shop looking for rubies, only to have me sell him his own gems. And how am I to explain that?'

'You won't need to explain it,' Pratchet said. 'He already knows.'

'He does not.' Her heart sank. He had not so much as batted an eye on taking the stones back. But then, her sister had always warned her that attractive men were often the most skilled liars.

'You are naïve, Margot,' said Pratchet, in a voice he probably thought was kind. In truth, it was no less patronising than the tone he had used to discuss marriage. 'Have you not wondered how I came by the stones?'

'I assume the thief sold them to you.'

'But why did the thief choose this shop and not some London Lombard merchant? And why did I succumb so easily to the temptation?'

'I have no idea what your motives might be. Perhaps he knew you to be a habitual criminal.' She wanted that to be true. But he had said that this was an isolated occurrence and she believed him. Even now that he was caught, there was nothing in his nature that seemed suspicious.

His face was as bland as it ever was, offering no sign of subterfuge. In fact, he was looking at her with pity. 'I took the stones because I feared giving offence to the man who held them. I had no idea he would report them as stolen, or that his family would send the law to this shop to harass you over them.'

'Are you claiming that the marquess himself gave them to you?'

'I gave my word as a gentleman to say nothing of the truth to anyone,' he said. 'But I did the best to warn you that such a close association with a man like Fanworth was unwise. You cannot understand the motives of the nobles in their great houses. Perhaps it is all an attempt to gain the insurance money while keeping the stones for themselves.'

There was a perverse logic in it. To have a new necklace made would be one way to hide beloved heirlooms in plain sight.

'The fact that he involves you in his schemes is particularly worrying,' Pratchet continued, although she had not asked for his opinion on the matter. 'Since you are young, lovely and unprotected by marriage, I think we can draw the obvious conclusion as to his real motives.'

He made it sound as if those qualities rendered her one step from stupidity. Or perhaps that was what he thought of all women. 'Until I have spoken to Lord Fanworth on the subject, I will not know what to think.' But she did not wish to speak to him, ever again. The truth was likely to ruin everything.

Mr Pratchet let out an incredulous laugh. 'You mean to speak to him? It is clear that the family does not want to admit their part in the disappearance. To call attention to it will only anger them. And to admit that you held the stones...' Pratchet shook his head. 'If you go to him over this, he will have you arrested. Or he will make the unsavoury offer he has been planning all along.'

'I refuse to believe that.' But she could not manage to sound as sure as she had been. Hadn't her sister offered the same warning? But she had been too flattered by Fanworth's visits to heed.

Mr Pratchet gave her another pitying look. 'When you are proven wrong, come to me. Perhaps, if you are married, he will leave you alone. Together we might find a way out of the mess you have created for yourself.' He went to the corner, collected the forgotten coat and went out into the street.

The mess she had created? It was true. She had convinced herself that the Marquess of Fanworth would stoop to be interested in a shopkeeper. Now, she would need to go to Justine and beg her to solve a problem created by her own vanity.

But she would not forget Pratchet's part in this disaster. He had bought the stones and kept the truth from her. If anyone deserved to be gaoled, it was him. But despite his protests of a gentleman's agreement, he could prove in court that she'd had no knowledge of the provenance of the rubies she'd sold. She would pretend to overlook his crime, for the moment, at least. If she sacked him as he deserved, he might disappear just when he was needed to swear to her innocence.

She stared down at the twisted metal still in her hand that had once held such magnificent stones. It was a sad end to see it thrown away as scrap. But it would be even worse if she lost her livelihood over a piece of jewellery.

In the front room, the bell of the shop door rang. Pratchet had not locked it when he'd gone. Without thinking, she stepped to the doorway and called, 'I am sorry, the shop is closed for the evening.'

'Not to me.' The voice was familiar, and yet not so. While she had heard him speak a hundred times, he had always been kind. Never before had she heard him use so cold a tone. Nor would she have thought it possible that three words could be imbued with such calculating, deliberate threat.

Framed in the entrance was the Marquess of Fanworth. And he was staring at the gold in her hand.

Chapter Four

Even as the evidence mounted, Stephen could not help wishing that it was a simple, easily explained mistake.

The enquiry agent had positively identified the stones. There was no question of their identity. Stephen had written to his mother to assure her that the rubies were safe in the family again and would be returned to her when she came to Bath at the end of the month.

But that did not explain what Margot de Bryun had to do with any of it. Arthur claimed that the answer was obvious. Meaning, Stephen supposed, that he was as big an idiot as Father had always claimed. He had been duped by a pretty face and refused to believe the truth even when he could hold the evidence in his hand.

Stephen had stared, frowning at his brother, until the speculation had stopped. Arthur was always willing to see the worst in people, for he was the most cynical creature alive.

Then, he had sent the enquiry agent to speak to

Margot directly. Mr Smith returned to say that Miss de Bryun had denied all knowledge of the gems. But there was no chance she would not have recognised them by the description he had given to her. In his opinion, feigned ignorance was little better than a lie and a sign of culpability on her part. A professional opinion from Smith was far more worrisome than Arthur's accusations.

But damn it all, Stephen knew Margot de Bryun and was willing to swear that there was not a calculating bone in her body. And a luscious body it was. He would go to her himself and settle this small misunderstanding about the rubies. If she was innocent, then things would go back to the way they had been.

And if she was guilty?

He hoped, for her sake, that she was not.

Stephen would not know until he saw evidence with his own eyes, and not just assumptions and suppositions. He'd waited, all afternoon, hoping that she would come forward and explain herself, after Smith's visit. But there had been so sign of her.

Perhaps she truly did not know his name or direction. Or perhaps she was avoiding him. If he wanted the truth, he must go to her and get it.

Dusk was falling as he was walked down Milsom Street towards de Bryun's. It was later than he'd ever visited. It must be closed, or nearly so. But it would give them a chance to speak in private. He was sure she would be the last one out of the door in the evening, for she had but to climb the stairs and be home. When he arrived at the shop, the front room was dark and the sign turned to read 'Closed'. But there was still a glow of light coming from the doorway of the workroom.

On an impulse, he tried the door and felt the handle turn. Not totally closed, then. The bell that rang as he opened was unnaturally loud in the silence of the empty room. When night fell, the cheerful elegance was replaced with a ghostly hush, made even more eerie by the gauze-framed doorways.

Margot de Bryun stepped through the sheer curtains, uttering the standard apology to a customer that had come too late. Then she recognised him and froze, framed in the doorway.

His beautiful Margot, in her simple white gown, was surrounded in a halo of candlelight and holding the empty setting that had once held the Larchmont rubies.

'My Lord Fanworth.' She dropped into a curtsy, as humble and submissive as any shop clerk that had ever waited upon the son of a duke.

The sight turned his stomach.

Idiot. Dolt. Worthless fool.

The words echoed in his mind as they had since he had been old enough to understand their meanings. But this time they were true. Damn his feeble wits. He had trusted her as if she'd been a part of his own body. Now he saw the truth. She knew him. She knew the rubies. Yet she'd said nothing. She'd let him stammer and flirt. She had pretended to laugh with him. But all the while he had been the butt of the joke. The whole time, she had been waiting for the right moment to spring the trap and prove him for the fool he was.

He ignored her beauty, staring through her as if it

would be possible to see the black heart beating in that admirable bosom. From this moment on, she would see no more weakness in him. He would see her punished for what she had done. And then he would see her no more. 'How long have you known my title?'

'Since the first,' she said, in a whisper.

'Yet you said nothing.'

She shook head, bracing herself against the doorframe as though she needed support to hide the trembling in her body. 'It was not my place to question you.'

'Neither should you have sold me my own mother's stolen rubies.'

'I swear, I did not know.' Her eyes were round, luminous coins in the firelight. If he was not careful, the soft side of him that had allowed her to lead him by the nose would be believing this story as well. She had lied once. She would do it again.

He stepped forward and snatched the twisted gold from her hand. Arthur might fault him for not recognising the stones, but on this part of the necklace he had no doubt. The prongs that had held the gems canted at weird angles where they'd been pried away. A few of the surrounding diamonds still remained, but most were like so many empty eye sockets staring back from around the gaping wounds that had contained rubies.

'Do you wish the money back? I will get it for you this instant.' Her voice was weird, distant. But he was lost in all the times he had seen the necklace on his mother. How happy it had made her. How devastated would she be to see it now?

'I need no money.'

'Then I will reset the stones, as they were. Simply bring them back and—'

'You will not touch them again!'

He heard the gasp, as the words hit her like a whiplash. It was exactly what she deserved for ruining something so beautiful, treating it as nothing more than scrap.

'Then what do you wish of me?' she said, taking a deep breath to steady herself as she waited for his response.

What did he want from her? If the stones were reset, there would still be the memory of what had happened to them and how he had behaved, in this very room, mooning over her like a lovesick boy even as she had tricked him. No amount of money would erase such a thing.

'Your Mr Smith was here today, threatening me with gaol or worse,' she said, softly. 'I beg you, my lord, there is no need. You have the stones. You have the setting. Keep the new setting as well. If you will not take it from me, I will return the money you paid for it to your bank, the minute it opens in the morning.'

It was not enough. Reparation would not make him feel any less a fool. Nor would it bring back the time he had spent with her, or the feeling of easy conversation that he'd imagined could go on for ever.

But sending her to gaol would be like throwing roses on a dung heap. It was wasteful. Even now, the thought of her youth and beauty fading in a lightless cell made him feel guilty, not triumphant. God had not designed such a perfect creature to be hidden away and allowed to rot.

'Please,' she said urgently. 'There must be something. If you will not consider my reputation, think of the people who work under me. If you send me away, they will lose their livelihoods. They are totally innocent in this.'

They were innocent. Which meant, he supposed, that she was not.

'What can I do to make this right?' she said, her voice turning desperate. 'Name the thing and you shall have it.'

Without thinking, he stepped closer to her.

She backed away.

It was hardly a surprise. The days of easy camaraderie were over. Stephen Standish might have missed it, but the Marquess of Fanworth felt a grim pleasure to see her shrink before him. She had just offered him anything he wanted. It had been stupid of him to love her. But the very real, very physical desire he felt for her had not changed.

He had thought she was sweet and innocent. But of course, she lied. He continued to advance on her, feeling the flutter of chiffon as they passed into the back salon where they had spent so much time chatting together. It was even darker than the front room had been. The faint haze from the workroom candle cast little more than an eerie glow.

'Anything?' He reached out and touched her face with the tip of her finger. Let her offer, then. She was just as beautiful as ever. Though he might be no smarter, he was not blind. He could stop wanting her. Even if he closed his eyes, he would see her, all the more desirable because he should not have her. The lust rose in his heart, dark and thick as treacle.

At his touch, she was still. She neither shuddered nor flinched. When she spoke, her voice was as cool and businesslike as any whore. 'If I do what you are most likely suggesting, do you promise that I will be safe from gaol, safe from the gallows? That I will keep my reputation…'

'For all that is worth,' he said with a sneer.

She ignored the insult. 'And my shop and the people who work here will be safe from persecution?'

'I care not for them, or the shop. My quarrel is with you.' He stroked her face, letting his fingertips linger on her cheek before settling under her chin, touching her throat. She was as soft and smooth as he had imagined she'd be. When he withdrew, a whiff of bergamot seemed to follow his hand, as though trying to draw him back.

'How many times?'

For a moment, he did not understand. And then, he did and the answer was stunned out of him. The sweet creature he had chatted with in daylight was haggling over the use of her body, now that the sun was down. How could she be so cold and fearless, so masculine, when faced with the loss of her alleged virtue? Perhaps her virtue was not as valuable to her as the shop he sought to protect.

'How many times, my lord?' she repeated. 'How many times must I lie with you to be free of this?' Her eyes narrowed.

'Five,' he said, pulling a number out of the air. 'Once for each stone.'

'Four,' she countered. 'My maidenhead should be worth twice as much, since I have but one to barter with.'

He barked with laughter, even though there was nothing the least bit funny about it. 'Four, then.'

'Four times,' she said, staring coldly back at him. 'After that, swear that I need never see or hear from you or your family, ever again. Swear on your honour as a gentleman. For all that is worth,' she added, throwing his own insult back at him.

Never to see her again. For a moment, something stirred in him, like an eel in deep water. He'd had such hope for their future. But that had been lost the moment he'd walked into this shop and seen her holding what was left of the pride of the Larchmonts. The sweet girl he'd wanted was an illusion, just as his easy speeches to her had been. 'I swear,' he said, 'you will never see me again.'

He reached for the gold setting in her hand, took it and slipped it into his pocket. Then, he reached for her. Women were all alike. Four times would be enough to rid himself of this madness. She was as beautiful in candlelight as she was in daylight. He had lain with beauties before and their company became tiresome after the excitement of courtship was through.

But those women had not been as dangerous as this one. It would be safer to sleep with a viper than to be with a woman capable of such duplicity. The risk held its own sort of excitement.

He was standing so close to her now that his skin tingled in awareness of their first kiss. She stared back at him, defiant. Good. He did not want a weeping virgin trying to make him guilty for a reparation that was far gentler than the punishment she deserved.

He closed the last inch between them and their lips met. The kiss was exquisite. Not cherries or strawberries. They were both too sweet. Blackcurrant, perhaps. Tart, complex as wine, her lips closed around his tongue, her teeth grazed it as if she wished to bite.

His balls tightened in his breeches.

How long had he been dreaming of taking her, right here on the white-velvet divan? His fantasies had been innocent compared to this. He had not imagined this helpless feeling of abandon as her body touched his. She fit perfectly against him, the curve of her hip in his hand, her belly cradling his erection. He ran his hand over the bare skin of her shoulder, circling to the back of her neck so that he might press her mouth to his. Such a delicate nape, fringed with the soft hair he had longed to stroke. He rubbed it with his knuckle and her lips opened even wider, eager for him.

One kiss, and she was driving him mad. He wanted to ravish her with his mouth, mark her with his kisses, to claim her body as his own.

If he felt so about an innocent touch, how would he survive a more intimate one? He experimented, sliding a fingertip inside her bodice to seek her nipple. Finding, pinching, kneading the whole breast, a match for his cupped palm.

Her throat arched and her breath caught, and she whimpered like a hungry kitten. She wanted more.

The response flashed through him like heat lightning. He'd been mistaken. Four times would not be enough. Not four hundred, or four thousand. What she had done did not matter, compared to the need he felt for her after a few simple touches. He kissed his way down her throat, making her arch backward in his arms, easing her to the couch so he might kiss his way down the graceful hollows of her neck and shoulders.

Her legs spread wide. One rested on the floor, the other bent at the knee, foot resting on the upholstery. He knelt between them, pushing her skirt up and out of the way. He leaned over her, his mouth suckling an exposed breast, his hand on her calf. Smooth curves, a seemingly endless expanse of silk-encased flesh. He was an explorer on his way to an undiscovered country.

'No.' Suddenly she shuddered under him, pushed away, and rolled off on to the floor, scrambling to be free of him.

It was the most wonderful mistake she had ever made.

When she had seen him, staring at her from the front of the shop, she had known their innocent flirtation was at an end. All that was left was the reckoning that had been predicted by everyone around her.

Had he ever felt anything for her, other than lust?

It did not seem so, tonight. In return, she would feel nothing.

She refused to feel fear, if that was what he wanted from her. And hatred was too much like passion. She felt nothing. And she spoke from the emptiness, with her offer.

It amused him. He responded. She negotiated. He accepted.

Then he approached.

If what he was doing with her was a punishment, then perhaps she was one of those poor souls who thrived on abuse. His touch had been like a feather stroke, awakening her appetite.

But cravings could be resisted. She would yield her body, but not her mind. And not her heart.

Then his lips touched hers.

A taste was not enough. She was starving for him, desperate for the kiss. To feel nothing was impossible, with his lips on hers. Anger, then. Hatred. But the rage fed the flames and she raked his tongue with her teeth.

His finger played at the top of her gown.

She pushed her breast into his hand and was rewarded for her boldness. Her dress was open, his hands on her breasts, and then his lips. He was possessing her, making her body his own.

And she wanted him to do it. She was on her back, spreading her legs to make it easier as he gripped her ankle and raised her skirt. Her nipples grew between his teeth. Her legs were wet. And everything inside her ached and trembled, begging for him to hurry, to finish, to take her.

Justine had explained the process of joining with a man, like some kind of unpleasant warning. There would be blood and pain. But God help her, why did she want to be hurt?

Justine had been wrong. It would be different with Fanworth than it had been for Justine. She had been forced into a liaison, with Mr Montague in this very shop.

'No!' She pushed him away, scrambling for safety. She had changed the look of the room, but she could not change the past. And at the thought of her poor, helpless sister, she wanted to be sick.

'No?' She could not look at him. But the frustration and anger were plain in his voice. 'You agreed.'

'Not here,' she said, breathing deeply until her stomach settled. Then she gave a hasty swipe at the tears on her cheeks. When she looked up at him, her gaze was every bit as unwavering as it had been when she'd bargained away her honour. 'It cannot be here. I cannot explain it to you. I will abide by our agreement. Anywhere but here.'

He pulled himself to a sitting position and stared at her. At the feel of his eyes on her body, she tugged the bodice of her gown up to cover breasts still wet from his kisses.

'Not here, then,' he said, without emotion.

The brief passion that had flashed between them was a pale imitation of the easy communion she thought they'd shared. It had been an illusion. He was as distant now as when he spoke to her sister. 'Tomorrow. In my rooms. And then, no running. No more excuses, or I will send for Mr Smith.'

She responded with a single nod.

He nodded back, as though he could no longer trust his voice. He stood, turning away from her and running a shaky hand through his chestnut hair. Then he was gone, the front door of the shop slamming behind him.

Chapter Five

'You are sure there will be no difficulty?' It was the third time Mr Pratchet had asked about the necklace that day.

For the third time, Margot answered with a quelling glance and a single word. 'None.'

'Perhaps it would be better if you allowed me…'

'No. I have spoken to Lord Fanworth. The matter is settled.' She ignored the leap her insides gave when she thought of the marquess. Pratchet had been right all along. It had all been nothing more than an elaborate seduction.

She would give Fanworth what he had wanted from the first. But she had done her best to minimise the damage through smart negotiation. If such a man was capable of keeping his word, then the matter would be settled in no time. She would not have to go to Justine about the necklace, or admit what had almost happened in the private salon.

But, for now, she had to endure Pratchet's curiosity. And if that was not bad enough, she was watched by the marquess as well. He'd passed by the shop in the early afternoon and glanced though the window at her, pausing just long enough to tip his hat and give her an ironic smile.

She had not been able to breathe until she was sure he was gone from view.

Thank God, he had agreed to leave when she'd begged him to on the previous evening. Once he had touched her, things had all happened too fast to understand. But the longer she had to think, the angrier she became. She was angry that he could pretend to blame her for the theft of the necklace. Angry that he had the nerve to be angry with her. And most angry of all that he had been so false to her for so long, acting as though he loved her and pretending that they shared some secret bond.

The least he could have done was stated his desires honestly, from the first. To make her believe that he cared for anything but her body had been unfair. If he had come to her some evening, after any one of those conversations, and suggested something they might do that would make that bond even deeper? She might have been seduced by smiles and soft words, opened her arms and gone freely. Instead, he had used blackmail. And though it disgusted her to admit it, the price was surprisingly low.

If last night had been an indication, the act of physical intimacy would not be as unpleasant as her sister had described. When he had come into the shop to claim her, Fanworth had been frightening, infuriating and intimidating. But at no point had he been repellent.

And while some might say he was threatening her with a fate worse than death, those people had never contemplated an earned place in a hangman's noose. Nor had they considered the other alternative: months or years wasting away in prison.

She could avoid punishment, if she went to her sister for help. But that would likely end with Justine insisting that she close the shop to prevent further such problems. If that happened, she would lose all she had sought to build. She would be encouraged to move in with Justine and Will, to live off their charity until such time as she made a proper marriage.

If she valued her independence, a few nights in the bed of a rich and handsome nobleman was hardly suffering. And if that man touched her as if she was made of porcelain and kissed like a fallen angel…

Apparently, when it came to the physical act of love, the pleasure varied with the participants. Though Justine sometimes blanched at the unpleasant memories of the jewellery shop, she was all smiles when she spoke of her husband.

She had shamelessly enjoyed the beginning of their first encounter. Perhaps, if she could manage to think of Stephen Standish while making love to Fanworth, it would be even better. But she had no intention of waiting meekly for him to take her. If she had her way, he would never be allowed over the threshold again. It had taken nearly a year to exorcise the demons from these rooms. Whether the result of her bargain with the marquess was good or bad, memories of it would not be allowed to taint the place where she meant to spend the rest of her life.

Tonight, she would go to him. She would be the aggressor, not the victim. It would set the tone for their blessedly brief relationship and allow her to escape with her dignity, even if she could not keep her virtue. She would like or dislike the act, as fancy took her. But she would perform it the four promised times. Then she would return here, never to think of it again.

She waited until the last customer had gone, shooed the clerks and shop girls out and gave Mr Pratchet another stern look to discourage his lingering. Then she took only a moment to straighten her hair before putting on a bonnet and shawl and exiting from the back of the shop into the street.

She did not want to be seen or questioned about this solitary journey. There was still enough light left in the sky to be easily seen and a woman walking alone on the Circus gave entirely the wrong impression.

Or perhaps it was the right one. She was most definitely up to no good. Her stomach twisted at the idea of going brazenly to the front door of the marquess's residence and demanding admittance. The fashionable street on which he lived was all too public and still full of holiday visitors on their way to various nightly balls and entertainments.

She stopped a street short of the building she knew to contain his residence, searching for the mews or alley that would lead her to the kitchens and the servants' entrance. Then she tipped the bonnet forward to shield her face, trying to disappear behind the scrap of veil that decorated its brim.

She counted down the row of doors until she came to the correct one and knocked quietly on the panel.

A scullery maid opened for her, wiping her wet hands against her apron.

For a moment, Margot's voice faltered. Then she whispered, 'Lord Fanworth?'

'If you have business with him, then go 'round the front,' the girl said, her suspicious glance sweeping Margot from head to toe.

'It's a private matter,' Margot said, even more quietly, glancing over her shoulder at the other servants working in the room. 'If you could show me how to get to his bedchamber…'

The girl let out a hiss of disapproval and held up a finger, indicating that she stay where she was. Then she turned from the door and went across the room to a woman sitting at one of the long wooden tables in the kitchen. Judging by the severe cut of her gown, and her equally severe expression, it was the housekeeper. There was a whispered conversation between the two and many sharp and disapproving glances cast in her direction.

Before a reason could be found to put her off, Margot stepped into the kitchen and shut the door behind her. Then she walked forward into the room to speak to the housekeeper directly. The woman did not rise as she approached, but watched her in silence.

'I have come to see Lord Fanworth,' she said, meeting the woman's gaze without flinching. 'He expects me.'

'Then it is surprising he is not here to greet you,' the woman responded, with a sour smile.

'If I could wait for him…'

'In his bedchamber,' the woman finished. By the look in her eyes, it was clear that she knew exactly why Margot had come. And she did not approve.

Margot could not blame her. She was not proud of her own actions, either. But pride and approval were not necessary. All that mattered was that she fulfil her part of the bargain so her life might return to normal.

She squared her shoulders and stared the woman down. 'Yes. I wish to wait for him in his bedchamber. No doubt he told you he would have a guest this evening. Unless you do not know what goes on in the house you manage.'

The woman opened her mouth as if to retort, then snapped it shut again. Without a word, she led the way to the servants' stairs and they climbed to the first floor in silence. The housekeeper opened the door and pointed down the hall. 'The third door is his suite of rooms. If the valet is there, it is up to you to explain yourself. I will not help you further.' Then she disappeared.

Margot swallowed the response that help was not necessary. If she did not want to appear helpless, then why was she shaking in her shoes? She took a moment to steady her knees and her nerves. Then she walked briskly down to the indicated door, opened it, entered and shut it behind her.

She stood in a pleasant but unremarkable sitting

room. It certainly did not seem like the stronghold of an evil seducer. It looked more suitable to the man she thought she'd known.

It was also blissfully empty, as was the dressing room that connected to it and the bedroom that connected to that. As with the sitting room, there was nothing about the place Fanworth slept that made her think of a seraglio. It was rather a relief. If lying with him turned out to be unpleasant, she would rather it be devoid of erotic nonsense that would make her feel more awkward than she did already.

There was no sign of him as yet. But it would be better to be prepared for his arrival. With a sigh, she pulled off her shawl and bonnet and slipped out of her shoes, wiggling her toes in the thick rug before undoing her gown and pulling it over her head. She draped it over a chair beside the bed and removed petticoat, stays, shift and stockings, folding her clothing and piling it neatly on the seat.

She stood for a moment, naked at his bedside. She felt both free and rather ridiculous, standing about in her skin and making no move to dress. As an afterthought, she picked up the man's dressing gown spread at the end of the bed and slipped into it, knotting the sash loosely at her waist. She was more than covered now, lost in yards of silk. The sleeves fell to cover her hands and the hem trailed inches past her feet, pooling on floor around her.

It smelled of him. Because she could stop herself, she inhaled deeply and felt her knees go watery again. She wrapped her arms around her body to steady herself, but this only served to press the fabric of the gown against her bare skin and remind her of his arms the previous night. She sat down on the edge of the bed, suddenly dizzy. If he did not come soon, she would lose her nerve, dress and leave.

But it was already too late to escape. There was a commotion somewhere in the house. Slamming, shouting, and stomping about on the lower floor. Was he always like this when at home? It certainly seemed in keeping with the sort of man who would go to such lengths to trick a humble shopkeeper out of her innocence.

She heard him shouting to a servant, as he approached his rooms. 'I d-d-d-do not need your help. You cannot g-g-get me anything I need, unless you can haul a certain woman to j-j-justice by her p-p-pretty guh-g-gold hair. I will call for Smith tomorrow and p-p-p-p…' The stutter ended in a clear exclamation of 'Bloody hell!' and a deep breath. 'God's teeth. I will bring the law down upon her. I…'

He stood in the doorway between the dressing room and the bedroom, tearing at his own cravat as a worried valet danced at his side, trying to catch the abused linen.

'You are here,' he said, frozen to the spot. The shouting was gone, replaced by quiet and confusion.

'As I promised, last night,' she said.

'I went to the shop,' he said.

That explained his anger. He thought she had gone back on their bargain. He was staring at her now, puzzlement clear in his eyes. But he did not speak, probably because asking how she had found his residence would result in another bout of stuttering.

She spared him. 'I knew your direction from before. When I realised who you were, I enquired after it.' She had made it a point to learn everything she could about the Marquess of Fanworth. Such curiosity was unladylike and all too embarrassing.

'Oh.' He was staring at her, obviously mollified, but still struggling with her sudden appearance in his rooms.

To remind him of the reason for it, she glanced in the direction of the valet and down at the dressing gown she wore.

He glanced at the valet as well and uttered a single word, 'Out.'

'Yes, my lord.' The servant evaporated with nothing more than a soft click of the sitting-room door.

Fanworth continued to stare at her, then said, 'Have you taken supper?'

'I am not hungry,' she said, sure that so much as a bite would make her ill. Then, before she could lose her nerve, she stood, untied the sash and dropped the gown to the floor.

He continued to stare. At first, there was no change in his expression at all. Then, very deliberately, he looked into her eyes and gave a final tug on his cravat, letting it flutter to the floor. There was another pause, lasting several seconds, before he began to undo the buttons of his waistcoat.

Was it her imagination, or did his fingers tremble, just a little? Perhaps a more experienced woman would have helped him with his garments. It would have at least hurried the process of disrobing. He seemed to be taking unnecessary time with it.

The part of her that wanted this over as soon as possible warred with the part of her that wanted to grab her own clothes, turn and run before things progressed any further.

But if she was honest, there was a small portion of her soul loyal to neither of those sides. This one was fascinated by the deliberate pace he took and the patch of skin that had appeared at his neck, as he'd removed the neckcloth. As her eyes followed his hands down the line of undone buttons, she got occasional glimpses of bare chest through the gap in his shirt front.

He slipped coat and waistcoat off in one motion and hung them over the back of the chair that held her dress. Then he stripped his shirt over his head and tossed it carelessly in the direction of the wardrobe.

She swallowed, performing an unwilling inventory. He looked rather like one of the Townley marbles at the British Museum. But those had been frozen in place. Back, shoulders, arms, chest and stomach were all more beautiful when seen in motion. He turned away from her for a moment as he bent to remove his boots and hose, and she could not help but imagine him rising up with a discus in his hand, like a Greek athlete brought to life.

But there was more to be seen. In a few moments, he would be as naked as she was. Now he turned to face her and she found herself holding her breath, as the breeches fell.

At the proper boarding school her sister had forced her to attend, there had been a teacher who had actually been to Italy, and to France, before the war. It had been that woman's job to educate them in art and to train them to make even poorer copies of the sad sketches she had done of the art she had seen in the museums on her tour. That woman's well-thumbed sketchbook had contained a rather large collection of male nudes.

Had that poor woman been trying to minimise the male organ, to prevent shock to her students? Or was the marquess in some way deformed? He made Michelangelo's David look quite puny.

With barely a glance, the very real Adonis in front of her walked to his bed, threw back the covers and reclined. Then he patted the mattress at his side.

They were playing a game. She was quite sure of it. Her plan had been to startle him with her presence and her nakedness. His had been to come for her, to win her with kisses and touches, tricking her into last night's eager response.

In the end, that might have been easier. Now, he was daring her to prove her bravery and make the next move. Since she had set the tone for the evening, he meant to test her nerve.

Very well, then. Standing by the bed, gaping at him was accomplishing nothing. Though her feet seemed to be rooted to the floor, she would be here all night if she could not bring herself to move. She took three very deliberate steps towards the mattress, then knelt upon it. And then, with one deep breath, she swung a leg over the glorious male torso in front of her and straddled him.

From Justine's rather blunt explanation of biology, a good portion of it was an autonomic process. Once begun, it did not require thinking. And soon after that, it would be over. But how to get to that state? Clearly, one part did not leap to meet the other like a spawning trout. Fanworth lay beneath her, his arms folded behind his head and a sly smile upon his lips, enjoying her discomfort.

She closed her eyes and reached out and held the organ in front of her, which seemed even larger with proximity. For a moment, she lost her nerve again. Smooth. Or was it ridged? Soft. No, hard. Could a thing be both? What she was feeling was full of interesting contradictions. It was growing slippery. She tilted it towards her own body, tipping her hips trying to discover some way that two could become one.

'Stop.'

She froze, looking up at him. Fanworth was staring at her with a most odd expression. 'Am I hurting you?'

'No,' he admitted with a sigh. 'You are more likely to hurt yourself. Let me.' He reached forward, detached her grip and pulled her down to lay on top of him. Then he stroked her hair and kissed her. First, lightly, on the side of the head. His tongue traced her an ear, nuzzling her jaw line.

Her breathing was shallow, shaky. 'I do not need this. Just finish.'

'No,' he said softly and found her lips.

It was like it had been in the shop, when she had

felt her reserve slip, and her will leave her. Only this time, it was better.

No, worse.

No. Better. Their mouths were sealed together, sharing life and breath. And while he might find speech difficult, his tongue was more than clever enough for kissing. He licked. He thrust. He teased. She would give him anything he asked, just for another kiss like this.

Her breasts were touching his chest. It felt good. Now, his hands were touching them, and it felt amazing. It was even better than it had been last night, when the gown had been in the way. Now she was free of her clothing, he could do whatever he liked to her. First he stroked, with just a fingertip. But then he pinched. The rougher he was with her, the more she wanted his touch. After a few moments of play, she slid up his body.

Slid.

She was growing wet, as he had. Her body was melting, longing to be one with him. She slid up his body and rested on her elbows, thrusting her bosom towards his mouth until he realised what she wanted and took the nipples, one after the other, between his lips, circling them with his tongue.

It was glorious.

And positioned thus, a most intimate part of her body was resting on top of his. He had been right. It had been too soon, before. Now, it was as if her body wanted to open like a mouth and swallow him whole. Yes. His hand had found the spot. Fingers inside her.

Stretching. Good. But not enough. More. She wanted more. She needed more. And then, his hands were on her bottom, and…

It hurt. Why did it have to hurt? And why, even though it hurt, did she still want more? His hand was back between them again, touching somewhere close to where they joined. He was moving in her, groaning. Had he called her name? The sound was distant, as if he'd shouted into a storm. A few gentle, soothing strokes of his thumb had struck the core of her body like lightning. She shook, trembling not with cold but with heat. And he did as well, inside her, in a wet shuddering release.

It was over. And to her surprise, she wanted to remain in his arms, still joined to him, holding the moment for ever, hoping that the future might never come.

Chapter Six

Three.

It was the first thought in his head, on waking. And decidedly odd. It could not have been the chiming of the clock, for it was full daylight. He was quite sure he'd heard ten bells.

Then he remembered the night before and threw an arm to his side, searching for the body that should be lying next to his. He was alone in bed and the fine linen sheets were cold. He had fallen into an exhausted sleep after their love making, not so much from strenuous activity as the release of a month's eager anticipation, in one orgasmic rush.

As he'd drifted away, he'd imagined a lazy morning tempting her with morsels from his own breakfast plate and a bath scented with rose and lavender to ease any aches she had from the previous evening. He would scrub her back, rub her shoulders and comb out her hair. Perhaps she would end wrapped in his dressing gown, as he had discovered her the night before.

Apparently, she'd had no such plans. She had escaped while he'd slept. He could see the smear of blood on the bed beside him, a source of pride and anguish. No matter what sins she might be guilty of, she had not deceived him about her innocence.

Of course, that innocence was gone now. He had taken it.

Three.

He had promised her four nights only. One of those was already spent. If their first encounter was indicative of the rest, he had been a fool to agree to her bargain. Three was not nearly enough.

When he had not found her waiting penitent in her closed shop, he had been positive she'd betrayed him. He had been thinking in anger, wishing to punish. And then, she had been there, waiting for him, trying to turn the tables and control a situation she had not the least experience with.

It was shock enough to see her, in full naked glory, without any kind of preparation. The anger in him had evaporated, leaving the awe he'd felt when he'd first looked in her shop window and seen her smiling back at him. And when she had sat upon him and taken him in her inexpert hands…

What had he been thinking to suggest this at all?

But he had not been the one to suggest it. He might have implied, of course. She was the one who had made the offer of her body and set the boundaries of their association. It was he who was being tortured over this. He was to be given a taste of heaven and then yanked viciously back to earth in three more nights.

Assuming she allowed him that. She was a thief and not to be trusted. She had likely used the same skills that got her the necklace to creep past his defences and conceal herself in his own room. But that had not mattered, once they had gone to bed.

It was even less important, this morning. The theft of the rubies was settled to his satisfaction. He had the necklace back again and the setting. The money spent on the replacement was back in his bank. He had found the culprit and she was far too pretty to be turned over to the rough hands of justice. To send her to the gallows would have been like smashing a priceless artwork.

But he would not go so far as to forgive her for making a fool of him. If was probably for the best that she had overreached herself by selling him the rubies. Otherwise, he might have married her and ruined the rest of his life. Now, she would be what she should have been from the first: a temporary amusement.

Three times more.

Or longer, if he wished it. Why did he need to honour the agreement that he'd made to such a person?

He sighed. Because he was a gentleman. He had given his word. How stupid had that been? He would lose her long before he had tired of her, unless he could convince her to extend the arrangement. Until he discovered what he might offer to convince her, he must be miserly with the time he was promised.

He leapt from the bed and hurried naked to the writing desk to scribble a note. Then he rang for a footman.

Thank you for a delightful evening.
Since you left so soon after, you are likely fatigued. Wait a week's time before coming again, that we might renew our acquaintance when you are fully recovered.
Yours,
Fanworth

Damn him.

Margot crumpled the note, then noted the alarmed but curious look from the nearest shop girl and smoothed it again, folded it and tucked it into her bodice. It burned against her skin like a shameful kiss.

Yours, indeed. He was not hers, and she wouldn't have wanted him if he was. He did not like her. He did not trust her. He had tricked her into his bed. Now he meant to draw the agreement out.

She had hoped to be free and clear of him, with her peace of mind returned, in less than a week. With too much time to brood on what had already occurred between them, she might never have a calm thought again. She glanced into the mirror kept on the counter, so that customers might admire the wares that they modelled. Did she look as changed as she felt?

She was tired, of course. She had left his room before the sun was fully up, taking the servants' stairs, as she had when she'd arrived. From there, it was home to wash, grab a few hours' sleep and be back downstairs in time to open the shop for the first customers.

She was hungry as well. She had missed supper, being too nervous to eat. Breakfast had been a hurried affair of cold tea and toast. Now she was coveting the Bath bun that Jasper was munching in the back room.

And she ached in strange places.

She yawned and caught another surprised glance from the girl polishing the class of the showcase.

Could she see something more than just fatigue? Worse yet, did Mr Pratchet suspect? Today, he kept looking at her with a vaguely disappointed glare, as though he had any right to concern himself over what she did after the shop closed.

Suppose that worldly poise she had admired in her older sister was actually the result of knowledge? The same light shining in the eyes of Eve as she had held out the apple to her husband.

She'd have preferred age-old wisdom to this feeling of smug satisfaction and the irrational desire to smile for no reason. She could not shake the feeling that there was something about her behaviour that signalled to the people around her what she had done.

Perhaps Fanworth was right. She would not have been able to stand another night like the previous one. If the first morning left her smiling, the next might make her laugh. By the fourth time, she would greet the dawn crowing like a rooster.

Oh, no, she would not. She shook her head to reinforce the thought, drawing a surprised look from the girl at the opposite counter. If she took to nodding and talking to herself, the employees would think she'd gone mad.

But that would be better than if they suspected the truth. She had lost her innocence. It was a disaster, not a cause for celebration. It was a good thing she had no desire to marry, for what man would want her now?

There was one, of course. Nothing about last night, made her think that Fanworth's desire was abating. And even after learning his true character, she still wanted him, as well. Lord Fanworth was most decidedly not the man of her dreams. But he still had the face and body of her beloved Mr Standish. He might have tricked her into his bed, but once there his touch had been as sweet and gentle as she'd dreamt it would be.

The girl next to her was staring again and Margot frowned at her, then gave her a quick scold to send her across the room to dust the rings and polish the bracelets.

Her effort to contain herself came not a moment too soon. As soon as she was gone, Pratchet took the girls' place. He leaned towards her, far too close to be proper, so that he might speak in a whisper. 'I know what you have done.'

'I beg your pardon.' She managed the proper level of confused outrage, but was sure it was spoiled by the crimson flush that must be spilling across her hot cheeks.

He went on, as though she had confirmed his suspicions with a full confession. 'I warned you, from the first, that the Marquess of Fanworth was a dangerous man. Now he has confirmed it with his actions.'

'A receiver of stolen goods has no right to speak to me of honour,' she said, hoping that it did not sound too much like a confession. 'If you no longer like the working conditions here, I suggest you take your things and leave.'

'And abandon you in the busiest season, with so much unfinished work on the bench?' He glanced back towards his table which was heaped with orders. 'It is almost as unwise for you to threaten me as it was to become involved with the marquess.'

His recriminations were almost as annoying as the amount of truth in them. She would have been better off had she never met Lord Fanworth. Not any happier, certainly. But her life would be far less complicated. She gave Pratchet a pointed stare. 'While I know that you are capable of mending a broken watch, I have yet to see you successfully turn back time. Without that particular skill, what good can further conversation on the subject do either of us?'

He cleared his throat and straightened as though it were possible to present himself in a more impressive way. 'I come to you as a friend, Miss de Bryun. I am not trying to censure you, no matter how it might sound. I understand and sympathise. Although you have run this shop successfully, it was inevitable that you would be bound by the limitations of your gender. The same qualities which are the virtues of the female sex, your softness and sweet nature, make you easily led.'

'Do they, now?' she said, in a tone that should have given him warning, had he known her as well as he claimed to.

'You have fallen into the clutches of a devious and evil man. When it goes wrong, as it most assuredly will, you must come to me.'

'And exactly what will you do to help?' She tried to imagine Pratchet facing her seducer on the field of honour, only to be cut down like the weed he was.

'I could give an unexpected child my name,' he said, glancing around to be sure that no one was near enough to hear. 'You and your family are far too well known in Bath to pretend that there was a legitimate marriage and a husband lost to sea or war.'

She had not thought of this. There must be ways to prevent pregnancy, or her sister would have fallen into that unfortunate state long before she had found a husband. But who did she dare ask about them?

Mr Pratchet continued to stare at her with an earnest, fatherly expression. 'You mock me. You think me old and foolish. I know you do. But surely a hasty marriage to a man who will care for you would be better than facing the disgrace of mothering a bastard.'

And here they were, back to her losing control of her own life to a man who knew what was best for her. When it had happened with Fanworth, at least there had been some pleasure gained in her mistake. But to enter into an empty marriage with a man she barely respected, for the sake of her reputation, was a punishment she did not deserve.

She turned to him then, giving him her most firm, professional smile. 'We have already discussed the matter of marriage and I have no intention of entering into that state with you or anyone else. As for the rest of it?' She gave a vague wave of her hand meant to encompass her loss of innocence and any child that might have resulted from her carelessness on the previous evening. 'I have no idea what you are hinting at, Mr Pratchet. And I do not wish to be enlightened. I fear you are suggesting something that would be a grave insult to my character. Now, as you say, there is a considerable pile of work that you must attend to. I suggest you apply yourself in the way you were hired to do.'

The man gave her one last disapproving look, before returning to his work station.

Margot closed her eyes for a moment, struggling to regain her calm. Even if it was already too late, she was not yet ready to brood upon the worst possible outcome of her current course of action. She needed food and rest before she could even consider what she would do if there was a child. And if there was not, she must find a way to take precautions in the future.

But it seemed she was to have no peace at all today. At the door were Justine and Daphne, doing up their parasols and smiling at her.

Margot smiled back, adjusting the position of the note in her bodice with a tug at the neckline of her gown.

Justine froze, staring back at her in shock. Her big sister knew her too well. With a single glance, she had uncovered every last secret. Then she relaxed, choosing to pretend that she had not. Her manner was all blissful ignorance as she said, 'Tea, Sister? Or have you no time for us today?'

'There is always time.' Margot gestured to the private salon. 'I am most unexpectedly hungry and could eat a plate of Sally Lunns all by myself.'

'I see,' Justine said. And now Daphne was looking at her with the same, overly curious expression.

'Or not,' Margot amended, trying to decide what was so shocking about wanting a bun with her tea. 'They would not be good for me, after all.'

'Indulging one's sweet tooth never is,' Daphne said. 'It leads to a thickening waist.'

Justine glared at her with such vehemence that Daphne took a large bit of the first bun offered, giving her reason to remain silent.

Justine glanced around her again. 'No visit from the marquess this morning?'

'No,' Margot said, relieved to be able to answer truthfully. 'He has not been to the shop in almost a week.' Not in daylight, at least. She tried not to think about what they had been doing, on this very spot, two nights ago.

Justine gave an audible sigh of relief. 'That is good to know. You might have considered him a friend, love. But the true motives of such a man are often hard to predict. There is a rumour that he has taken up some new scandalous affair…'

'Really?' Margot said, taking a very deliberate sip of her tea. 'What concern is that of ours?'

'Simply that I would not want you to be hurt by his actions. Since you are fond of him—'

'Not really,' Margot inserted.

'That is good,' her sister said, doubtfully, setting aside her cup and reaching out to touch her sister's hand. 'Because there is no guarantee as to the permanence of his affections towards you or anyone else.'

Margot took another sip of tea. Any illusions she'd had about his motives had died with the discovery of the necklace. Strange how long ago that seemed and how little it seemed to matter. 'Do not worry about me, dear. I shall be fine. And I most assuredly will not allow myself to be hurt by the Marquess of Fanworth.'

Justine allowed herself to be comforted by the words. And then the three of them chatted of ordinary things for nearly an hour, before the two guests rose to leave.

Margot escorted them as far as the front door, only to see them step into the path of a gentleman walking by the shop. He was near enough so Margot could hear the polite greeting, 'Ladies', which was accompanied by a bow and a gesture permitting them to pass.

And through the glass of the shop window, she saw the shocked look on her sister's face as the Marquess of Fanworth looked into the shop directly at her and gave her a knowing smile.

Chapter Seven

With a week to prepare for it, Stephen took special care to set the scene for their next tryst. There was a dinner ready in the main dining room, should she wish to sup with him. If not, there was a selection of dainties arranged in the sitting room of his bedchamber. Oysters, prawns, strawberries and chilled champagne.

Perhaps it was too obvious that he had chosen foods that might inflame desire. Or perhaps not. She had known little enough about the act a week ago. Still, if there was a simple way to increase her ardour to the point where she might forget their ridiculous agreement and remain with him, he was not above resorting to it. He had no intention of letting her escape him after only three more nights. But such a strong-willed woman would wish to think the decision to stay had been hers.

He had sent her another note, earlier in the day, reminding her of their engagement and informing her that there would be a carriage waiting for her when the shop closed that would take her directly to his door with curtains drawn for her privacy. She might still refuse and find her own way here, but he would not be so stupid as to leave his bedchamber to search for her, only to be surprised on his return. This time, he would claim the battleground for his own.

For a moment, he considered greeting her as she had him, wearing nothing but his dressing gown. He rejected it, almost immediately. She would likely think it was vulgar. And he would feel more than a little ridiculous lounging about his rooms nearly naked. Instead, he took the time to change into his best tailored, dark coat and trimmed the lapel with a gold stickpin he had purchased in her shop.

Then he had nothing to do but to wait. When, at last, he heard the sound of the footman escorting her down the hall, he did his best to gain control of what could only be described as boyish enthusiasm.

That emotion was the parlance of Stephen Standish, the besotted fool who had fallen under the spell of the bewitching Margot de Bryun. The Marquess of Fanworth knew better. It was he who turned to face the door with a cool smile, as his lady entered.

Once again, he faltered.

He had not seen her in a week, other than brief glimpses through the shop window. No matter what he had promised, he could not manage to stay totally away from her. He savoured those walks along the street, pretending that he took them for his health. But if that was true, he must admit that a brief glimpse of her each day had become as necessary to his well-being as respiration.

The glass of the front window and blinding whiteness of the shop's interior must have dulled his perception, for he had noticed nothing unusual as he had glanced in at her. Could one week really so alter a person?

To say she was pale was an understatement. Her normally luminous skin was as grey as moonstone and there were dark circles under her eyes. If he were to guess, he would say she had not slept since she'd dozed in his arms almost a week before. Her perfect brow was creased with worry. He had never seen her timid, but her step tonight was hesitant. She reminded him of one of the true invalids that came to take waters, hoping for miracle cure.

'Sit.' He came forward to her, taking her arm and leading her to a chair in the sitting room.

She resisted. 'I would prefer that we finish what I have come for.'

'And I would…' *Prefer.* He could feel the P tremble in his throat, 'I would rather we sit.' He poured the wine for her, wrapping her fingers around the stem of the glass.

She downed it in one swallow. Then she looked over the rim of the glass. 'Satisfied? May we begin, now?'

He refilled her glass. 'No.' He pushed the tray of oysters towards her.

She glanced down at them and shuddered. 'They are out of season. I will likely end even more ill than I am already.'

'Ill?'

She gave him a wan smile and drank the second

glass of wine. 'Yes. Perhaps it is the prospect of lying with you that makes me so.'

'The first time is always...' *painful, difficult* '...awkward. Tonight will be...' *different, better* '...more enjoyable.'

She laughed. 'For you, perhaps. But tomorrow, I will still be surrounded by people who know exactly what I have done and split their time between scolding me and worrying over me. I've had a week of that, while you grinned in the shop window at me like a dog at the butcher's shop.'

'Who knows?' Damn them all. He had promised discretion.

'My sister. Her friend. The rumours of your new lover were all about town before I'd even climbed from your bed. My employees guessed, just by looking at me. But they, at least, are too afraid to comment on it. Except for Mr Pratchet.'

'He can be damned.' Some words came easier than others and the curse flew unhindered. When he had visited the shop, he had seen Pratchet watching her just as she accused him of doing, as though she was the juiciest chop on the platter.

She gave Stephen a false smile and held out her glass for more champagne. 'You should not say such things about the man who is likely to be the father of your natural son.'

'I b-beg your p-p-pardon?' The suggestion shocked him out of his sang-froid.

'He has promised to marry me, should a pregnancy

result from my indiscretions. For all I know, I am pregnant now. I feel like death warmed over.'

'You are simply overwrought,' he said. But if she was not? A mixture of terror and elation ran through him at the prospect that she might be carrying his child.

'Perhaps I am,' she said, then sprawled on the couch before him, almost spilling what wine was left in her glass. 'Or perhaps it will happen tonight, when you take me. And then I will end by marrying Pratchet to salvage my reputation and give the child a name.'

'That is nonsense,' he said, without a second thought. 'I would…'

'You would what?' she said with a bitter laugh. 'Give me money? I have more than enough to raise a bastard, I assure you.' She laughed again. 'You must have realised that yourself. I assume that is why you tricked me into dishonour, instead of making the simple monetary offer my friends and family warned me about.'

'I tricked you?' He had done no such thing. She had no right to act the innocent in this.

'Did you think Pratchet would keep your secret?' She gave a sorry shake of her head. 'He wants the shop for himself, you know. He was only too happy to buy the necklace when you brought it to him. In the end, he knew I would be the one to face the consequences.'

'When I sold the necklace…' he repeated. There was only one place she could have got such a ridiculous idea. Pratchet had misled her, probably hoping to leverage the lie into a quick marriage to a helpless, panicking female. It served the goldsmith right that the revelation had driven Margot straight into his bed. If he thought that Stephen would let her go again, he was sadly mistaken.

He looked at her, on the couch beside him, exhausted, but still beautiful. It was as if, for the first time in days, he could see her clearly. She was his beloved, not the conniving female his brother had…

Arthur.

It was all coming clear now. He had been tricked, right enough. And his offended honour had led him to punish an innocent.

She went on with her story, not noticing his silence. 'You could not have picked a better ally in Pratchet. How neatly the spoils are divided between you. You took my virtue and, when you are through with me, he will take my shop.' She reached for the bottle on her own this time, filling her glass to the brim and drinking deep. 'I thought you were my friend. Or, perhaps, something more than that.'

'I was. I am.' He reached out to stroke her hair.

She gave no indication she had heard his words. But instinctively, she leaned into the pressure of his palm, as though seeking comfort. 'Everyone warned me. They told me that you were dangerous and wanted to bed me. But I refused to believe.'

'They were right.' Though he could not have helped himself, it had been careless of him to love her. The world had assumed the worst.

'Then you needn't have bothered with trickery,' she said, in a small, hopeless voice. 'You were so handsome, so charming.' She let out a shaking breath, half-sigh, half-sob. 'There was no reason to steal the rubies or to threaten my business. If you needed money, I'd have given it to you. And if you wanted me, you had but to ask.'

His hand tightened on her shoulder, hiding his feelings of elation in a caress. She'd loved him, just as he'd hoped. 'I want you,' he said softly.

'Then take me. Do what you wish with me, so I may go home and rest. For I am so tired.' The defiance he had seen in her a week ago was gone now. She was too exhausted to resist him.

Which meant she was also too weak to accept. He removed his hand from her shoulder and stood. 'Eat.'

'I told you I could not.'

'I have no wish to make love to a corpse.' He pushed the tray to her, turning it so she might reach quail eggs, strawberries and cream. 'If you wish something else, then ring.'

She gave him a militant look.

He glared back at her to hide his smile. 'When you are through?' He pointed at the bed. 'Wait for me there.'

'And where will you be?'

'Out,' he said. There were things he needed to think about and the thought of Margot de Bryun in his bed left him deliciously unclear. If he was not firm in his resolve, he would be back with her, before he had done anything to earn a place at her side. He walked quickly to the door and through, shutting and locking it behind him.

* * *

The next morning, despite an uneasy night spent on the couch of his sitting room, the Marquess of Fanworth was nearly as resplendent as he had been while waiting to greet his lover. When he had returned to his rooms an hour after ejecting himself, Margot lay huddled under the covers, asleep in the middle of his great, soft bed. She looked tiny and helpless, curled in upon herself as a protection against God knew what indignity.

How could he have thought this innocent child was a devious jewel thief, entrapping him with her feminine wiles? Not a child at all, even if she looked like one in sleep. Her clothing was piled neatly on a chair, as it had been on their last evening together. He tried not to think of the naked flesh beneath the sheet, as he examined the empty wine bottle and the few bites of food missing from the tray. She would have a foul head in the morning, but at least she would sleep uninterrupted. If her colour was not better after some rest, he would call for a physician.

And it seemed exhaustion had been her problem. When he left the house at eight, she was still sleeping.

Stephen didn't bother calling for a carriage. There were times when it was better to walk. The exercise cleared his head, though it did not lessen his anger one bit. When he arrived at de Bryun's, his hand hit the door hard, causing it to spring open and bang against the wall. The little bell at the top that usually tinkled, lett out a rattling clank at the assault.

The shop girls and clerks looked up, alarmed at his entrance, but none had the nerve to approach him. It was strange to go to her shop, knowing full well that she was not there to meet him. But better that the world assume he did not know where she was than that she was asleep in his bed.

He went to the nearest clerk, a gawky boy with red hair and ears like jug handles, and favoured him with his most terrifying frown. 'Where is she?'

The boy was quaking in his shoes, but did not desert his post. 'Miss de Bryun is not here, my lord.' No attempt at pretending he was not titled, then. Had his ruse really been so thin as to be transparent?

He glared towards the back room and gave a dismissive gesture. 'Then…' Pratchet was nearly as hard to say as de Bryun. 'What's his name…?' He snapped his fingers, as if trying to remember.

The polite thing to do would have been to excuse himself and get the man. But in the absence of his mistress, the ginger clerk had reached the end of his nerve. 'Mr Pratchet!' The call came not as an answer, but a plaintive, rabbit's bleat for mercy.

The goldsmith appeared in the curtained doorway. His annoyance disappeared when he realised the reason for the disturbance. At the sight of the marquess, his face went a shade of white that rivalled the walls. 'Lord Fanworth.'

Stephen contained his glee at finding someone so obviously at fault and so worthy of his anger. He redoubled his glare, raised a finger, dire as death, and spoke the single word. 'You.'

As Stephen advanced, Pratchet shrank back, out of his reach, until they had passed through the doorway and were standing in the middle of the workroom. There would be privacy, in theory, at least. If half the shop clerks were not listening in at the doorway, he would be most disappointed in their lack of curiosity.

He backed Pratchet up until his arse hit the edge of his work table, sending a shower of loose gold chain-links scattering on the floor.

'I can explain, my lord.'

Stephen stared down at the man who had caused him to ruin his own future. 'Really?' He let his frown deepen, staring with even more intensity at the little man before him.

'When I was given the rubies, I did not know they were yours.'

'Liar.' Stephen swept an arm across the desk beside him, spilling its contents on the floor and tipping over the spirit lamp that Pratchet had been using to melt casting wax.

The goldsmith rushed to douse the flame, beating it out with the wool mat he had been working on, looking up frantically at Stephen. 'All right. I knew they were the Larchmont rubies. But I was too afraid to refuse.'

'You told her they came from me,' he said and watched the man squirm beneath his wrath.

'Not in so many words,' he argued. 'Is it my fault if she misunderstood?'

'It was your intention, all along.' Stephen continued to stare. When, at last, he spoke, he did so slowly and deliberately. It guaranteed the clarity of his consonants and had the added advantage of making each word sound as if it was to be the last thing Pratchet might hear. 'Who. Was. It?'

'Lord Arthur!' he blurted the expected answer, backing away from the table. 'Your brother brought them here. Who was I to refuse them? I went to the day's receipts and gave him everything we had. Then I hid the stones in the safe and made the transaction disappear.'

'You lied to her.'

'I did not. I said your family could not be trusted. I said I was frightened for her,' the man said, gathering what nerve he could, and spilling a torrent of words. 'It is clearly the truth. Your own actions prove that you do not care for her. Nor does she understand her place. She is getting above herself by running the shop at all. She needs the aid of a strong husband to protect and advise her, or it will all end in ruin.'

He had thought such a thing himself, two weeks ago. But he'd not been thinking of Pratchet as a font of wisdom.

'Aid from you?' He snorted. 'For your help, she might have been hanged as a thief.'

'You would not have let it come to that,' Pratchet said, still sounding surprisingly confident. 'If she was dead, you'd not have got what you truly wanted from her.'

That had been true, of course. But he had never considered that their affair would leave her vulnerable to a loveless marriage with this worm. 'So you spread rumours about her?'

'Her sister deserved to know the truth.' The man raised his chin, as if Margot's humiliation had been a righteous act and not despicable.

But it proved that what she'd said last night was true. All around her had known of their bargain and berated her with it until she could neither eat nor sleep. This man deserved whipping. Or at least he would have, if so much of what had happened had not been the result of Stephen's own unchecked pride.

But some punishment was definitely in order and it must suit the criminal. Stephen smiled. 'Since you are fond of truth telling, my agent, Smith, must hear some as well. I will explain that Margot is not at fault. It was you.'

'You would not dare,' Pratchet said, ruffling his feathers like a cockerel who did not know he was a capon. 'Your brother is equally guilty.'

'My brother is Larchmont's son. And you?' He snapped his fingers. 'Are no one.' Then he smiled with satisfaction at the thought of Pratchet squirming on the dock. It would likely not come to that. The man would run like a rabbit the moment he turned his back. But he would be seeking employment without reference and lie down at night in fear that the law might take him before dawn.

It was very similar to the ruined reputation and perpetual fear he had sought for Margot. In Stephen's mind, it seemed quite appropriate. He turned and walked away, to show that the interview was at an end, calling over his shoulder, 'Until we meet again, Mr...Ratchet.'

As he left the room, he heard the beginning of correction. But the goldsmith got as far as 'Pra…' before he realised that if the powerful, and likely vengeful Fanworth could not remember his name, it was probably for the best.

He turned back to give the man a final glare and exited the shop with a slam of the door that was almost as violent as his entrance had been.

Arthur had rooms in a hotel on the Circus. It was there that Stephen went next. He entered as he had at the jewellery shop, with much noise and no words. He pushed past the valet, going directly to where Arthur sat, nursing his usual morning hangover. Then, he grabbed his brother by the lapels and lifted him out of the chair, until his feet dangled, barely touching the floor. 'Explain.'

Arthur laughed with much more confidence than Pratchet had been able to manage. 'I suppose this is about the rubies.'

'You suppose?' Stephen punctuated the words with a little shake.

Arthur did his best, in his constrained position, to shrug. 'I needed money. Gambling debts, old boy. I could hardly ask his Grace. And I knew Mother would cry if she was forced to defend me, yet again. Better that she weep for her lost necklace than for her useless son.'

'You could have come to me,' Stephen reminded him. It would not have been the first time that he'd needed to rescue his younger brother from his own folly.

'Perhaps I should have,' Arthur admitted. 'Poor little Pratchet did not pay nearly so much as I'd hoped to get.'

'Then why take them there?'

'Two birds, Fanworth.' Arthur smiled. 'I was not the only one who needed rescuing. You were far too involved with the de Bryun woman. Something had to be done, before Larchmont got wind. I knew if Mother's rubies turned up missing, sooner or later, you would go to her, seeking a replacement.'

'Really.' Arthur had approved of the idea when Stephen had suggested it. Since his younger brother's judgement was notoriously bad, he should have seen it as an ill omen.

'I thought you'd recognise the stones from the first. But you had them reset, ready to give back to Mother.' Arthur laughed again. 'It really is rather amusing, when you think about it.'

'It. Is. Not.'

'But it has given you a reason to put Margot de Bryun in her proper place, on her back and in your bed. I assume, after a week with her, your lust-addled mind is clearing and you are no longer talking nonsense about making her a member of the family.'

At this, Stephen released his brother's coat, letting him drop to the floor. It was a relief to see Arthur waver on his feet, for a moment, then remain standing. What Stephen intended would hardly have been sporting had he collapsed.

He punched his brother, once, hard enough to break his aristocratic nose, and turned and left. It proved, yet again, that one did not need words, when one had actions.

Chapter Eight

When Margot finally woke, it was to daylight streaming through the curtains of the room and an aching head. There had been wine. Too much wine. And too little food, although it was not as if he hadn't offered.

Fanworth.

She sat up, gathering the covers about her for modesty. She was alone in the room save for a breakfast tray, set for one, and growing cold beside the bed.

She glanced around again to be absolutely sure that there was no servant lurking about, ready to help her. Then she climbed out of bed to get her clothes, grabbing a piece of burned toast as she did so. She did not remember lying with him on the previous evening. But then, she did not remember much of anything, other than the wine. Had he truly left her untouched? And if so, why? Perhaps she had done something to render herself repellent to him. Dear lord, she hoped she had not been sick. That would be even more embarrassing than waking naked in a strange bed.

But his disgust and her humiliation might be the easiest way out of the situation. If he had already tired of her, she could go home and sin no more, and pretend that none of this had ever happened. Assuming, of course, that he did not call down the law upon her because of the necklace.

But what should have been a relief left her vaguely sad. Was what he had felt for her really so shallow that it could be satisfied in a single night? It put paid to the fantasies she'd had that her dear Mr Standish would confess his title and his love, and offer some deep and lasting connection.

She'd have had to refuse, of course. Such a match would have been unworkable for both of them. But still, she could live a lifetime alone, sustained on an offer and perhaps a few chaste kisses…

Passionate kisses, she corrected, rewriting the fantasy to include experience. Or perhaps the thing that had actually occurred between them. To have been loved once and well, as he had done the previous week, would be a bittersweet memory to balance a lifetime as a spinster. It would have been even better if he had been the honourable man she had fallen in love with and not a base villain who must be laughing at her naïveté.

She dressed hurriedly and downed the chocolate that had gone cold in the pot waiting for her to wake. The wine-induced headache eased somewhat with the food and a splash of cold water from the basin. Now, she must rush to the shop, for the clock on the mantel showed half past ten. Her arrival in yesterday's gown would be a fresh embarrassment. It was far too late to sneak back to her rooms before the business opened for the day. But the sleep had done her good. In spite of the humiliation, she was better rested than at any time since she'd discovered the truth about the rubies.

She reached the door to the hall, only to find it locked. She cursed once, softly, in French, then she rang for a servant. And rang again when the footman who came refused to allow her to pass without the master's permission.

The second summons brought the same housekeeper she had met on her first visit. Mrs Sims stared at her with a knowing glance that informed her she was no better than she should be, if she was on the wrong side of a man's door in the middle of the morning. A single, disapproving nod added that it was exactly what she has suspected would happen when Margot had turned up on the kitchen doorstep. After this protracted, silent judgement, she said, 'Lord Fanworth told me nothing about what to do with you, miss, other than to feed you. Which I did.'

'Thank you for that,' Margot said, attempting a friendly smile that had no effect on the scowling servant. 'It was delicious.'

By the surprised look on the housekeeper's face, Margot suspected that the tray had been served cold as a message from the kitchen.

'Now that breakfast is over, I must be going,' she said, giving another encouraging smile.

'Lord Fanworth said nothing about that, miss,' said Mrs Sims, not moving from the doorway. Though she had wished to bar entrance on the first visit, for the second, Mrs Sims meant to guard the exit.

'Is Lord Fanworth in the habit of imprisoning women in his bedchambers against their will?' She'd meant it to sound sarcastic. But given the circumstances, it was a legitimate question.

The footman and the housekeeper looked at each other for a moment, trying to decide if an answer was expected. Then Mrs Sims said, 'It will take some time before the carriage can be prepared.'

'Then I shall walk,' Margot announced and pushed past them into the hall.

'I will summon a maid to accompany you,' Mrs Simms said with a sigh that implied that would take almost as long as the carriage. Clearly, she was stalling until Lord Fanworth could return.

'A maid will not be necessary,' Margot said and headed towards the servants' stairs.

The housekeeper cleaned her throat. 'The door is this way, miss.' Apparently paying the wages of sin involved exiting through the front door in broad daylight.

'Very well, then.' Margot straightened her bonnet and walked, head held high, down the stairs, out the front door and into the street. Her willingness to walk alone probably cemented her impropriety in the eyes of the housekeeper. But in Margot's opinion, it would be worse to be seen with a member of Fanworth's staff than to walk alone. She had no wish to add to the rumours already spreading about her improper relationship with the marquess.

Once she was on her way, she walked quickly to discourage conversation, should she meet someone she knew. If someone saw her walking on the wrong side of the street and noticed her attire was not immaculately starched perfection, there was little that could be said in argument.

Once she arrived at the building that housed her shop, she had hoped to slip up the side stairs to her rooms, largely unnoticed. It should have been easy for the main salon was already crowded with customers.

But at the first sight of her, Jasper seized her hand and pulled her to the back room. 'Miss de Bryun, we were terribly worried about you. You were not here to unlock the door. And so much has occurred…'

'Calm yourself.' She detached his hand from her arm and glanced around the room. 'Where is Mr Pratchet? He should be helping in the main room, with the shop as busy as this.'

'That is the problem, miss. Mr Pratchet is gone.'

For a moment, all she felt was relief. Then she remembered the trouble it was likely to cause. 'Where did he go?' she said, puzzled. It was too early for a trip to the bank. And she could think of no other reason he might leave his post.

'We have no idea,' Jasper said. 'He did not say. But I do not think he is coming back. After the marquess spoke to him, he took his tools and—'

'The marquess was here?' she said, both surprised and annoyed. 'What did he want?'

Jasper looked even more nervous at this. 'He did not say, either. He asked after you, of course.'

'Or course,' she said drily.

'When he was told you were not here, he went into the workroom and spoke to Mr Pratchet, in private.'

'Do not pretend that none of you was eavesdropping,' she said in frustration. She had told the staff never to gossip about clients. But it would be most annoying if they took this instance, above all others, to follow a rule that they broke with regularity.

'He barely spoke,' Jasper admitted. 'And when he did, it was too quiet to hear. But he seemed angry. He nearly set the workbench on fire. The minute he left, Mr Pratchet gathered his tools and fled.'

What had she said the previous evening, to bring about such a visit? Perhaps it had been her mention of the man's offer that had set him off. The marquess might have taken exception to it and decided to dispense with a rival. It was madness. Was he really so possessive as to allow her no male friends? She had not really intended to wed Pratchet. Nothing short of total catastrophe would convince her to marry a man who was so shamelessly scheming for her hand.

Perhaps he was angry that Pratchet had revealed his part in the deception. If so, she was not sure she minded that he had faced the wrath of the marquess. Why should all the punishment for this situation fall on her shoulders? The loss of a goldsmith would be an inconvenience. But she'd have fired him herself, eventually, just to stop the proposals. The more she thought of it, the better she felt that he was gone.

'I think I understand what has happened,' she said, with a sigh. 'You are right. We will not be seeing Mr Pratchet again. Which means we are without a goldsmith.' She pinched the bridge of her nose, trying to focus her thoughts. 'We will manage as best we can, today. If someone comes, seeking repairs, we will send them to Mr Fairweather in Bristol. Tomorrow, I shall put the ad back in the London papers to replace Mr Pratchet.'

'Very good, miss.'

'I will check the workbench to see what he has done. Hopefully, Mrs Harkness will not come for her necklace. I did not think he had finished mending it yesterday.'

Jasper looked nervous for a moment. 'Miss Ross dealt with that this morning, miss.'

'Did she now?' Margot glanced around the room to see the youngest of the shop girls peering at her from the back room.

With a twitch of her skirt and a bowed head, Miss Ross stepped forward. 'It was only a single weak link, Miss de Bryun. And I have watched Mr Pratchet work, when the shop was not busy. A twist of the pliers, boric acid to prevent discolouration, a bit of flux, a bit of polish…' She gave another curtsy. 'I was very careful not to heat the rest of the chain.'

'It sounds as if you learned well,' Margot said, doubtfully. 'But I would still have preferred that you had waited until I returned, so I could see the finished work before it left the shop.'

'I sized a ring, as well,' the girl said shyly. 'It is still here.'

'Show it me.' Margot felt a strange thrill, half-apprehension, half-excitement. Could the recurring problem of overreaching goldsmiths be solved as easily as this?

The girl retreated into the back and returned with a plain gold band. 'It was only half a size,' she said modestly. 'And up is easier than down. But really, down is nothing more than fixing a very big chain link.'

Margot took the ring and slipped it on to the sizing tool, noting the perfect roundness and the tidy way it rested, just on the size that the client had wished. Then she took up a jeweller's loupe, examining each fraction of the curve for imperfection or weakness. When she looked up again, she smiled. 'You do nice work, Miss Ross. Very tidy. I am sure, if this is a sample, that the chain was fine as well. Are there other repairs that you feel capable of attempting?'

They brought out the list and examined each item. The girl felt confident with all but two of the current requests.

'Perhaps we can find something similar in the shop that you might use to practise those skills,' Margot suggested. 'We could break an existing piece and let you mend it.'

'Ruin good work?' the girl said, shocked.

'They are my pieces. There is no reason we cannot do as we wish with them,' Margot said reasonably. 'If it means that I do not have to place an ad for goldsmith, it is worth the risk.' Even better if it meant that she would not have to put up with the inconvenience of a gentleman developing a penchant for her, or her shop.

'From now on, I wish you to spend as much time as possible at the workbench, attempting these repairs in order of difficulty. If that goes well, we can discuss wax casting.'

The girl's eyes lit up. 'I watched him at that, as well. He sometimes let me work the little bellows and pour moulds. It would be ever so exciting.'

'Very good, then.' Margot thought for a moment. 'And it is hardly fair for me to employ you at the rate of a junior clerk if you are taking on more work. As of this moment, you will see a rise in salary to reflect your new duties.'

The girl's eyes were as round as the ring in her hand. 'Thank you, miss.'

She felt a ripple of jealousy throughout the room. It was hardly warranted. Other than Jasper, her staff had done little more than gossip and panic. 'As for the rest,' she said, loud enough to be heard, 'we must see how we do without Mr Pratchet to help with the customers. It is quite possible that there might be more for all, if one less person is employed here.'

There was an awed whispering amongst the other clerks. And for the first time in a week it was not about Miss de Bryun's recent strange behaviour.

All went well, for the rest of the day, except for one incident.

The shop was near to closing and the room quiet. The two well-dressed ladies who were her final customers had refused her help more than once. Yet they continued to glance in her direction as they pretended to stare down into a case of diamond ear bobs.

Margot moved closer to them, hoping that they would be encouraged to either make a purchase or leave. It was near to eight o'clock and despite the good night's sleep she'd got, she was eager to return to her own rooms.

Before they realised she was near, she caught two dire words of their whispered conversation.

'Fanworth's mistress.'

Chapter Nine

'A gentleman to see you, my lord.'

Stephen looked up from the writing desk in his private sitting room and waited for the footman to explain himself.

'Lord William Felkirk,' the man supplied.

'I will be there shortly.' He had been expecting such a visit since the last time he'd seen Margot de Bryun.

She deserved an apology, of course. Once she had forgiven him, he could make the offer he'd intended from the first. She'd been an innocent dupe in the matter of the necklace and would never have been involved at all, had he not taken an interest in her. That had been the thing to draw his brother's negative attention. Then, Stephen had made everything worse by jumping to conclusions. But how could he ever set things right if she refused to so much as look him in the eye?

Conversation had been so easy between them, just a fortnight ago. She'd looked up and smiled each time he passed by the shop, as if she'd been searching each face that passed by her window, hoping to see him. In turn, he had been able to talk for hours without having to plot out each sentence to avoid embarrassment.

Now, when he paused each day in his walk past her shop, she gave him a Medusa stare, as if she would strike him dead should he cross the threshold. In response, his tongue felt like leather in his mouth. Even if he could have managed speech, when they had their agreement, he had given his word not to return to the shop. He could not very well hold private words of apology up on a card from the other side of the front window.

It was some consolation to see that when she was angry, her colour was slightly improved. But he missed the carefree happiness that had drawn him to her in the first place. He must find a way to return it to her, if only to put things back the way he'd found them before he had entered her shop and ruined her life.

Since he could not manage to speak to her, he'd thought a letter might do. He attempted one on several occasions, his left hand smudging and crabbing the letters, forming them even worse than usual. Carefully phrased sentences, which spoke of 'mistakes' and 'misunderstandings' were feeble and inadequate for the situation at hand. After hours of painstaking composition, he'd managed a worthy attempt. He'd taken full responsibility for what had happened. He offered marriage if she would have it. At the very least, he would give her so much money that she might close the shop and move to a place where no one had ever heard of her, or her association with him.

It was returned unopened.

Apparently, she feared another request for a tryst and had decided that their association was at an end. He could not blame her. By now, even he had heard the rumours that the Marquess of Fanworth had taken up with the jeweller. When he entered an assembly room, pushed his way through a rout, or attended a musicale, ladies whispered about it and gentlemen congratulated him on his excellent taste.

He glared at all of them until they went silent. But as soon as he was out of earshot, the conversation began again. Avoiding her did not stop the gossip. But going to her would only make it worse.

Something must be done. This visit from Felkirk came as a relief. She might choose to shun Stephen. It was wise to do so, he had earned her scorn. But in her brother-in-law, Stephen would have an intermediary who could not be ignored.

'Felkirk,' he greeted the man with his most formal bow, silently thanking God that it had not been the Duke of Buh-Buh-Belston he'd needed to greet. The man come to deal with him was the duke's brother. In precedence, he was beneath Stephen and owed him respect. But his demeanour was of a disapproving schoolmaster, about to administer a whipping.

Felkirk took the chair he offered, but refused refreshment with a look that said he would rather sup from a pig's trough than share a drink with the person he'd come to visit. 'I understand that you have entered into a relationship with Miss Margot de Bryun?'

'If I had, I would not speak of it,' Stephen replied, narrowing his eyes to seem equally disapproving.

'The lady in question is my wife's sister.'

'I know.' When he'd imagined a union between them, he'd hung much on this relationship. The older sister had married well. If Margot was also elevated, would it really come as such a surprise?

'Our connection is not widely known,' Felkirk admitted. 'That has less to do with any reticence on the part of my family than it does with the single-minded independence of Miss de Bryun. Margot did not wish to trade on the family name to make her success.'

'She would not have to,' he replied with no hesitation. 'Her work is the finest I have seen in England.'

By the shocked look on Felkirk's face, a two-sentence reply from the notoriously silent Fanworth must have seemed like a flood of words. That it came in praise of a woman he refused to acknowledge was even more interesting.

Felkirk gave a brief nod. 'I will inform her sister of the fact. It will be a great comfort to her. But other matters are not.' He gave Stephen a searching look, allowing him to draw his own conclusions.

When Stephen did not immediately answer, Felkirk continued. 'My wife and her sister are very close. They are similar in appearance as well.'

'Then you are fortunate to have a married a lovely woman,' Stephen said, again surprising the man again with his honesty.

'I am aware of that. But I am also aware of the sort

of attention such beauty can draw when one appears to be alone and unprotected—'

'Her looks are not Margot's only virtue,' Stephen interrupted, feeling suddenly eloquent when presented with his favourite subject. 'She is an intelligent young woman with an excellent sense of humour.'

If Felkirk had been surprised before, now he looked positively shocked by this quick admission. 'Since we can agree on her many excellent qualities, you must also understand how troubling it is to hear that she is entering into a liaison not likely to end in marriage.'

'I fail to see how it can end any other way,' Stephen said. Then he fixed Felkirk with a look that implied he was the one to put a dishonourable intent on their rather unorthodox courtship.

'You mean to…' It was like watching air leak from a billowing sail. Felkirk had not been prepared to win so easily.

'Marry her,' Stephen finished.

Felkirk responded to this with stunned silence.

The man expected him to explain himself. Not bloody likely, since any attempt to describe the current circumstances would end in a stammering mess. Stephen continued to stare, waiting for the man to speak.

He saw Felkirk's eyes narrowing again, as he tried to decide what to make of this sudden and complete victory. 'Margot would not tell us the reason that she went to you.'

'Nor will I,' Stephen replied and continued to stare at him.

'A marriage is necessary, of course, and the sooner

the better. The rumours flow faster than the water at the pump room.' Felkirk stated the obvious, but in a doubtful tone as though suddenly unsure of his mission.

'A special licence then. I will set off for London immediately.'

'Immediately,' Felkirk repeated. 'Without speaking to the lady you are to marry?'

Stephen sighed. Perhaps, with some other girl, the matter could be easily settled between gentlemen. But his Margot was not the sort to let her future be decided by others. 'I suppose I shall have to.'

'You do not wish to speak to her?' Felkirk was clearly offended.

'She will not speak to me,' Stephen clarified.

'Despite the circumstances, I will not force her to wed you, if she does not wish to,' Felkirk said.

'She wishes it,' Stephen said. 'She is not yet aware of the fact. But she wants to marry.'

'Then, how…?'

It was an excellent, if unfinished question. And then a plan occurred to him. 'You must offer her an urgent reason to wed,' Stephen said with a smile. 'For example, if there were threat of a…' He took a deep breath and forced the word out. 'A duel…'

'You wish me to call you out over this?' Felkirk said with an incredulous snort.

'If you would be so kind,' Stephen said, relaxing.

'I had hoped it would not come to that.'

'It is not for my sake,' Stephen reminded him. 'It is for hers.'

'But suppose she wishes me to fight you?'

'If I know Margot,' Stephen said, surprised by his own confidence, 'she will not. She would think it foolish.' His Margot was far too sensible to demand that men fight for her honour.

'Then what good can it do?' Felkirk asked.

'Your wife will not take it so lightly. Suppose I am not the one injured?'

Felkirk gave him a speculative look. 'Think you can best me, do you?'

Actually, he did. Fencing had been an excellent way to channel the rage he felt at his impediment. Those who had seen him with a blade deemed him a master. But now, he shrugged. 'For the sake of argument, you must make her think I might. Though it may appear so, Margot will not risk the happiness of her sister to see me suffer.' If such a strong-willed creature as his Margot had wanted to see him bleed, she'd want to stab him herself. Since he was as yet unmarked, he had hope.

Stephen favoured his future in-law with an expression that was positively benign. 'Surely, accepting my name and title is not too much of a hardship, if it assures your safety.'

Felkirk held up a hand, as if to stem the rising tide of confusing arguments. 'Am I to understand you? You are willing to marry my sister-in-law, if she would accept you?'

If he could not explain the whole story to Felkirk, he could at least give the man one small bit of truth. 'It would make me the happiest man in England to take Margot de Bryun as my wife.' He spoke slowly, to add clarity as well as gravitas. And he was relieved that there was not a tremor or a slur over the name of his beloved.

There was another significant pause before Felkirk said, 'Will your family say the same?'

In such moments, there was no point in giving ground. 'I assume you mean Larchmont. If you ask the question, you know the answer.'

'Your father is notorious for his strong opinions,' Felkirk said, as diplomatically as possible.

'His opinions do not concern me,' Stephen replied. 'I would be more interested to know the opinion of your family. Since you are married to the woman's sister, I assume I will be welcome in your house. And your brother married a cit's daughter.'

'The circumstances in both cases were unusual,' Felkirk said, but did not elaborate.

'In this case, they are not. I wish to marry Margot for love. The rest is immaterial.'

'Other than her unwillingness to see or to speak to you, of course,' Felkirk added. 'Or to tell any of us what is the matter so that we might know whether we do greater harm than good by yoking her to a man she despises.'

She had loved him once. That he had managed to ruin that…

Idiot. Dullard.

And that was his father speaking again. He would stand squarely against such a marriage—that was all the more reason to press onwards. 'I have no wish to make her unhappy by forcing this union. I simply wish for her to realise that she will be happy, should she marry me.'

'And to bring her to this realisation, you wish to trick her into accepting you?' Felkirk said with a frown.

It was not a trick, precisely. He merely wished to nudge her in the direction she secretly wished to go.

'The choice is still hers,' he said. But he knew her well enough to be predict her reaction. She would marry him. After they were together, he would find a way to make her believe that he had nothing to do with the necklace. Once she realised that they were both victims of a hoax, it would be as it had been and they would be happy.

For now, he smiled at Felkirk as though eager to meet his doom. 'At least, we will see, soon enough, if she cares whether I am living or dead.'

'But surely, you must see that this is best for all of us.' Justine was using the tone she had taken throughout their childhood to bring her difficult sister into line.

Margot gritted her teeth to resist responding. What she had hoped would be a quiet Sunday visit with her sister and brother-in-law was turning into a lecture on what she must do to salvage her reputation. Now that Margot was fully of age, Justine had no right to make such demands. Her life was her own. She could ruin it if she wished.

That was an especially petty argument and another reason to remain silent. She had not wanted ruin. But neither did she want to wed Fanworth.

Justine tried again. 'If he can be persuaded to behave honourably, we can end this quietly. Your good name will be restored and you will have married into one of the most respected families in England.'

'If I can be persuaded to take him, more like,' Margot said. She doubted she would have to make such a decision. If the plan hinged on Fanworth behaving honourably, there was no need to bother with it.

'If he can be made to offer, of course you will say yes.'

'Do you mean to answer for me, as well?' Justine had taken far too much on herself already. 'I did not ask you to send Will to him, angling after a proposal.'

'You did not have to ask,' Justine said. 'He did it for my sake.' She reached out to take her sister's hand. 'I cannot stand by to see you destroyed over this foolish shop, just as it very nearly destroyed me.'

'It was not the shop,' Margot argued. 'Mr Montague was at fault for what happened to you.'

'But if you had been here, to see the looks polite women gave me, as I walked down the street…' Justine's voice broke. 'I will not live to see the same thing happen to you. You will marry the marquess and retire to his home in Derbyshire. That is even further away than Wales. No one will know of the scandal and you might start anew.'

'And what would become of the business?' Margot said. Justine seemed to be ignoring the practicalities.

'We will close this place and never think about it again. It has brought nothing but bad luck to our family and we will do well to be rid of it.'

As always, Justine was blaming the building and its contents for any and all of their troubles over the last twenty years. It was nonsense, of course. But better that she fault the shop than take any part of the blame on herself, for things she had no control over.

'If only I had refused, when you told me of your plan of taking over de Bryun's,' Justine said, the first tear trickling down her cheek, 'I might have kept you safe.'

Now they were returning to Margot's least-favourite subject, the need for her older sister to control everything and make any and all sacrifices necessary to save the family. But it was unusual to see her so upset that she resorted to tears.

Gently but firmly, she withdrew her hand from Justine's, then returned it to cover her sister's hands to console her. 'You cannot fix everything, you know. You certainly cannot fix this, just by marrying me off to Fanworth and selling the shop. Especially since I am of age now and unwilling to do either of those things. I will stay away from him and be sure that he stays away from me. By next summer, all will be forgotten.'

Unless, of course, the marquess had her arrested for the theft of the Larchmont rubies. She must hope that the week's silence since their last meeting was a sign he deemed it better to forget certain details than to risk her blurting ugly truths about his character as part of a Newgate broadside.

Justine was readying her next argument when they heard the sound of footsteps in the hall and her husband appeared in the doorway. At the sight of his tearful wife, Will Felkirk gave Margot a grim, disapproving look, as if to blame her for Justine's distress. Then he came and sat at her side, close enough so their thighs touched and extricated her hands from Margot's so he might hold them himself.

His wife stared up at him with watery eyes. 'You have spoken to him?'

Will paused a moment, then glanced at Margot and nodded. 'The matter is settled.'

Margot breathed a sigh of relief. 'Good. The sooner we can all put this nonsense behind us, the better.'

'I put it to him quite simply. He will marry you, or I will meet him at dawn.'

'A duel?' At this, the normally stoic Justine dissolved into sobs.

'It will not come to that,' Margot insisted, alarmed at her sister's extreme reaction.

'You will marry him, then, if he offers?' Will said, clearly relieved.

'Not if he was the last man on earth,' she replied, not bothering to think.

'He is not the last man on earth. He is a marquess,' Justine snapped, tears still streaming down her face. 'Now stop acting like an honourable match with the son of a peer is a fate worse than death.'

'I cannot stand to be in the same room with him, ever again.'

'If you do not like him, you need not live with him after the ceremony. But you will not draw my husband into fighting him, to protect the reputation you were careless with.'

'I did not ask him to be involved in this,' Margot snapped back.

'And I did. Because I had no idea you would be such a ninny about it. It was quite clear, a few weeks ago, that you doted on the man. You would not leave him alone when I warned you what would happen. And now, because of your stubbornness, my Will could be injured, or even killed.'

'There, there,' Will said, gathering her close.

'It will not come to that,' Margot repeated. 'Do not allow yourself to become overwrought over nothing.'

'I will if I wish to,' Justine said, with another shower of tears. 'If you have no care for yourself, think of the child that will be born fatherless…'

This was too much. 'I am not increasing,' Margot insisted. She had been more than a little relieved to discover that herself.

'I was not talking about you. What about my child?' This was followed by more tears from Justine and a glare from Will.

'You?' Of course. It had to be true. Justine had been making sly admissions of morning illness, of tiredness, of a desire to start a family and of the readying of the nursery at the old Bellston manor. But had her shy sister ever said in so many words that a birth was imminent? Or had Margot been too busy with the shop, and with Fanworth, to notice?

'And now Will might have to risk himself because you are unwilling to listen to reason,' Justine said, sniffling into the handkerchief that her husband offered her.

He leaned close to her, whispering into her ear and kissing the side of her face. Whatever he had said seemed to calm her, for she turned back and pressed her face into his hair, smothering his lips with her own.

If possible, an awkward situation was becoming even worse. She had missed the obvious clues to her sister's pregnancy. Though she refused to believe that she had put him at risk of his life, she had managed to involve Will in her problems. And now they had all but forgotten she was here.

When Will managed to disengage his wife from himself, he looked over her head, glaring again at Margot. 'As you can see, Justine is distressed by recent events.'

'But I cannot simply marry him,' she said. Even when things had been going well, she had known that was impossible.

Now he was looking at her with disgust as though she were the most selfish creature on Earth. 'Either I will put the announcement of your betrothal in tomorrow's paper, or we will fight on Tuesday morning. One of us will be injured, or perhaps killed. I hope you are satisfied with that prospect, for there is no third alternative.'

At this, Justine let out a wail. 'There will be no fighting. I will go to him, myself, if that is needed. I will throw myself on my knees and beg him to do what is right for our family.' She raised a hand to her temple in a gesture that Margot would have called melodramatic, if her sister had ever been guilty of such a thing. 'Do not worry, Margot, I will take care of everything. Just as I always have.'

'No!' Margot's shout of frustration was every bit as loud and dramatic as the behaviour of the other two people in the room. But it brought an instantaneous halt to their emoting. 'I will go myself, immediately. And I will go alone. I will be back in time for supper, to tell you what we have decided.'

Whatever happened, it would not involve a pregnant Justine, on her knees, begging Fanworth for anything. She might think that it was her job to sacrifice for all and for ever. But, by the Blessed Virgin, Margot had caused this problem and she would solve it herself with no help from her older sister.

Chapter Ten

For the third time in as many weeks, Margot was arriving unescorted at the house of the Marquess of Fanworth. This time, she gave up even pretending that it was possible to move unnoticed and greeted any acquaintances she passed with the cheery wave of an unrepentant harlot. Let them think what they would. She was fairly sure that, no matter what happened today, it would end in a story that would give the whole town something to gossip about. For all she cared, they could choke on their tongues.

Mrs Sims admitted her without a raised eyebrow. Then she glanced at the steps towards the bedrooms, as though expecting Margot intended to show herself up. The insult was subtle, but it was there, all the same.

For all she knew, this woman was the one who had set the town buzzing about her disgraceful behaviour and brought Justine and Will down upon her like hounds on a hare. If so, she had best hope that Margot was not about to become Lady Fanworth, for there would be hell to pay.

'I wish to speak to Lord Fanworth. In the drawing room, please. Or wherever it is he receives guests,' Margot said, offering an equally aloof expression.

The housekeeper let out a dismissive sniff to remind her that they both knew why she was not familiar with the proper, public rooms of my lord's apartments. Then she took Margot down a short hall to the salon, not bothering with an offer of refreshments before she shut the door.

A short time later it opened again, and Fanworth appeared. He did not bother to bow. 'Margot?' He greeted her with that strange, soft pronunciation that went right under her skin and made her shiver, even on a warm summer day. But it was not dread she felt. It was anticipation.

Damn him. Even as she knew the truth about him, she could not help wanting him more than a little. She did not bother answering. Suppose there was an unexpected softness in her own voice as she spoke his name in return? 'I have just been speaking with my sister and brother-in-law.'

'Lord William,' he responded with a nod.

'And I have been informed that I must either wring a proposal out of you, or it is pistols at dawn.'

He thought for a moment. 'Easy enough.' He went down on one knee. 'Would you do me the honour of accepting my offer of marriage?' He delivered the proposal with such unemotional precision that, for a moment, she did not even understand the words. Then, just for a moment, she thought she saw a twitch at the corner of his lip. Behind that frosty façade, he was laughing at her. So she laughed in response, aloud and without kindness.

He looked up at her in surprise. 'I amuse you?'

'Because you can't be serious,' she said, sure that it was so.

'I am,' he said, just as sombre. 'Unless you wish to see me fight Felkirk.'

'Of course I do not,' she said. 'We will explain to William that there is no reason for that. What I did, I…I did of my own free will. It is over now. The less said about it, the better.'

'Technically, it is not,' he said, still sombre. 'We agreed on four. Once is not four.'

'Twice,' she said.

'Nothing happened that night,' he said. 'It is not fair of you to count it.'

'I have no idea what happened,' she replied. 'Because I was inebriated. You should know that. You were the one plying me with spirits.'

'Champagne is hardly a spirit.'

'Even worse. It is an aphrodisiac,' she argued.

'Not an effective one,' he countered. 'Nothing happened.'

'Then I am glad of it. I would rather go to gaol than to lay with you again,' she said in frustration. 'Look at the trouble a single time has caused me.'

'A marriage will stop the tattle. The rest…' He paused, as though he had suddenly lost his train of thought. Then he gave a helpless shrug. '…can be settled after the wedding.'

'But I do not want to marry you,' she said.

'Then I must fight Felkirk,' he said with a sigh and stood up, brushing the dust from the knees of his breaches.

'The devil you will,' she said, at the end of her patience. 'I will not risk you shooting my sister's husband because of me.' Or being shot himself. Though she loathed the man, she could raise no pleasure at the thought of him bleeding on the ground.

'It is a matter of honour. Such a challenge cannot be ignored.'

'Your honour, or mine?' she said. 'And what does William have to do with any of it?'

'B-B…' He took a breath. 'Yours and mine. Felkirk's as well. You are of his family…'

'A distant part, surely.'

'Near enough to matter.'

'Well, do not shoot him. I will give you whatever you want.'

'I was thinking swords,' he said, ignoring her offer. 'As the one who was challenged, I choose the weapon. There is an advantage to fighting with the left hand.' He gave an experimental lunge.

She tried not to notice his tight calves and the rippling of muscle beneath his coat.

'You bastard,' she said in a low breath.

'Unfortunately, I am legitimate,' he replied, rising and sheathing an imaginary sword.

'If you had not run Mr Pratchet off, I could have married him,' she said.

He looked surprised. 'You want him instead?'

'He was concerned for me.' And the shop, of course. That had been his real concern all along. But if she'd have married him, she'd have had to share his bed. Even now, the thought sent a chill through her. 'Marrying Mr Pratchet would have been the logical thing to do.'

'And you are a shining example of feminine logic,' said Fanworth, expressionless.

'I thought I had no choice.'

'You could have married me,' he suggested.

'You had not asked,' she reminded him.

'I have now. I await your answer.'

He was being sarcastic to goad her. She responded in kind. 'Why would you want to marry the thief who stole your mother's necklace? Is the punishment we agreed on no longer enough?'

'You did not take the necklace,' he said. 'I am sorry for having accused you.'

Now she had found the flaw in his logic. 'You knew that all along. Because you were the one to take it.'

'I am innocent as well.'

'You? Innocent? I cannot think of a less accurate word to describe you,'

He shrugged. 'In this case, it is accurate.'

'I do not believe you. It is but another lie. You have told many of those, since I met you, I cannot keep track of them.'

'Think as you will. Today I speak true.'

She sighed, wishing it were true. Then it might still be possible to trust him. 'It makes no difference now, whether you are lying or not. What's been done cannot be undone.'

'Then why not turn it to your advantage?'

'By marrying you?'

'Yes.'

It did not sound like help at all. It sounded like the world would think her a title hunter, instead of just a whore. 'I would be the only marchioness with a jewellery shop of her own,' she finished glumly.

'Eventually you would be a d-duchess,' he added, displaying more vulnerability than she had seen in ages.

'That would make it worse.'

Just for a moment, she saw another flicker of his old smile, as if the man she had always wanted was still there, hiding beneath the surface. Had this not been her fantasy, when he'd first visited the shop? That he would see past the difference in their different stations and want to wed her?

That had been nothing more than a dream. This was real, and nothing at all like she'd imagined. How could she explain to Justine that the reality was not what she wanted?

There were no words that would help. Her sister saw no further than her own miserable past and would be ecstatic at the prospect of such a marriage.

And the Marquess of Fanworth was still standing before her, awaiting her answer.

'What will your father say?' she said, grasping at straws.

His response was little more than the slightest twitch of an eyelid and a brief statement. 'It does not signify.' He might not care. He was annoyed that she had asked. But the silence accompanying it spoke loud enough. His family would not like it.

She closed her eyes and pinched the bridge of her nose, praying that when she opened them again, she would see some other solution to the situation at hand. 'You are adamant, then. We marry, or you duel.'

'Yes.'

'And you are willing to marry me.'

'Yes.'

'Then the only thing preventing a resolution to your argument with Will...'

'To Felkirk's argument with me,' he corrected.

'The only thing preventing a resolution...' she repeated.

'Is you.' His response was so gentle that, with her eyes closed, she could swear it was Stephen Standish who had spoken.

But then she opened her eyes and saw the cool, aloof Marquess of Fanworth, staring back at her as though he could see the chair behind her. Of course he would marry her. It meant that she would be back in his bed without the inconvenience of clandestine meetings and gossiping staff.

He had tricked her. Again.

She glared at him. 'Very well, then. Since I have no choice in the matter, I will accept. Send word through

Lord William when you have the licence and we will put an end to this nonsense. Until then, I do not wish to see you or speak to you, or receive notes, letters, gifts or anything else. And for God's sake, stop wandering past my shop, gaping in the windows at me. It is distracting to me and to my customers. And now, good day.'

It had not gone as he'd hoped.

Of course, Stephen had hoped, when down on his knees before the woman he loved, he'd have been able to come up with words a little more stirring than a brief proposal. At least he could have managed a better apology for his mistreatment of her.

I did not mean to dishonour you. I promised there would be no gossip. I did not give the necklace to Pratchet. It was my brother...

There were other ways to say those things, he was sure. But when he opened his mouth to tell her, his mind was awash with impossible consonants. And as it always did, his tongue glued itself to the roof of his mouth until he could say practically nothing.

Then he smiled. It had gone wrong. But all the same, she had agreed to wed him. He would get the licence, reserve the Abbey and make all things ready. Then, once they were properly joined in matrimony, he would take her back to his bed and demonstrate the sincerity of his affection in a physical way that did not become muddled when he most needed it to be clear.

When she had been properly loved and realised that he could buy her the contents of a dozen jewellery shops, she would see his side of things. There would be no more nonsense about the inconvenience of having a title. She would take her proper place in society. And all of London would take one look at her and fall at her dainty feet.

Once she realised that she was happy, she would smile at him again. He would be able to speak freely to her, just as he used to. They would declare their love. And their life together would be as he'd imagined it, from the first moment he'd met her. Perfection.

Chapter Eleven

'My lord, his Grace is waiting for you in the salon.' The butler in Fanworth's London town house announced the visitor with the barest trace of sympathy, for he knew of the strained relations between peer and heir. Stephen had hoped that his visit to the city to get a special licence would pass unnoticed. Obviously, this was not the case.

Usually, he made it a point to avoid any city where Larchmont was staying. The duke remained in London long past the point when fashionable people had quit it for summer. So of course, Stephen spent early summer in Bath. By the time Larchmont arrived to take the water and bathe his gout, Stephen would be on his way to Derbyshire again. If the duke came home for Christmas, Stephen went to London. So passed the year.

Because of his impending marriage, a temporary intersection of their schedules was inevitable. But Stephen had hoped that it would be postponed until after the ceremony when there was less the duke could do to influence matters. Still, if it occurred now, his bride might be spared the meeting with her father-in-law until the man had grown used to the idea. 'Thank, you,' he answered to the butler. Then he braced himself for battle as the servant opened the door to the receiving room.

Larchmont had aged. But who had not? It had been nearly five years since their last meeting. His hair was more grey than brown and the lines on his face had deepened. Five years ago, the ebony walking stick he always carried had been little more than a vanity. But as the door opened, he was using it for support. When he realised he had been caught in a show of weakness, the duke straightened and twirled it in his hand as if to prove that it had been nothing more than momentary fatigue.

Stephen did not bother with a greeting. He had learned long ago that to speak was to open himself to ridicule. As a child, he'd had no choice in the matter. But now that he was a grown man, he did not have to put up with it in his own house. He stood before the duke and offered a respectful, but silent bow.

His father dispensed with cordiality as well and went immediately to the matter at hand. 'I suppose you know why I am here.'

'No idea,' Stephen replied, with an insolent shrug.

'The word is all over London that you have gone to Doctors' Commons for a special licence. You mean to be married. To some shop girl in Bath.'

The temptation was there to offer correction about

Margot's position. Shopkeeper would have been a more accurate term. Since it would not have changed his father's opinion, Stephen held his tongue.

'I forbid it.'

'I am of age,' Stephen said, without raising his tone.

'It does not matter. You should act in regard to my wishes, since you continue to spend the money I send you.'

How like his father, to bring up the stipend he was awarded each month. The money was largely symbolic. He had long ago learned to invest his inheritance in such a way that a supplement was not needed. 'I will manage without,' he said.

'Do you mean to give back the house as well? You live quite comfortably on my estate in Derbyshire. Perhaps it would be better if I put it up for rent.'

It would be dashed inconvenient. Stephen had grown quite fond of that house and the properties around it. Though the income generated went into his father's pocket, he had been acting as landlord since his majority and considered it almost his own.

But he would relinquish it if he must. He chose the counter-attack most likely to madden his *pater familias*. 'Then I shall have to live off my wife's money. She owns her shop. It is quite successful.'

His father gave a growl, part-frustration, and part-anguish. 'No Standish has ever needed to marry for money.'

As far as Stephen could tell, none had married for love either. 'I shall be the first,' he said, answering both conditions.

'You bring shame upon our good name,' his father said, in disgust,

'So you always tell me,' Stephen replied.

'I should have drowned you like a puppy, the minute I realised you were foolish. Instead, I endured years of your squalling and yammering and stuh-stuh-stuttering. When I think of the heir I could have had...'

Which meant Arthur, he supposed. He was the son that Larchmont deserved: drunken, dishonest and disrespectful. But at least he had a silver tongue to talk his way out of the trouble he caused. 'It was not my request to be spawned by you. Nor to be first. Though I share your regret, I cannot change it.'

'But you could modify your behaviour,' the duke suggested. 'As you did your abominable penmanship.'

If he was not careful to wear gloves in summer, the sun still brought out the white scar across his knuckles that marked the reason Stephen had finally learned to use his right hand to make his letters. God knew what his father intended to break to improve his taste in women. 'I am satisfied with the way things are,' he said, with a calm that was sure to annoy Larchmont.

'Because you are an idiot. And like all idiots, you cannot control your lust. Tear up the licence, give this girl a bank draft and send her away. Then, perhaps we can find someone from a decent family who is thick-witted enough to have you.'

Stephen could think of a myriad of responses to this, involving his marks at Oxford, the shrewdness of his investments and the circumspection he employed when navigating the slew of marriage-minded young ladies who were more than willing to overlook his speech impediment for a chance to be the next Duchess of Larchmont. And then, of course, there was the genuine feeling he had for the woman his father wished him to cast off.

But as it always did, after a few minutes arguing with his father he could feel his tongue tiring. It was ready to slur or stick on even the simplest words, as it had done when he was a child. So he remained silent.

His father held a hand to his ear. 'What's that, boy? I did not hear your answer.'

So he gave the only one necessary. 'No.'

The old man glared at him in shock. 'I beg your pardon? I do not get your meaning.'

At this, Stephen laughed. 'And you call me idiot. Even I understand a word of one syllable.' It would feel good to say it again, so he did. 'No.'

'You seriously mean to defy me in this?' his father said, as always surprised that the world did not turn at his pleasure.

'Yes.' The fight was grinding to a halt, as it always did, when he had run out of words. Though the duke sometimes made up for the silence with one last, protracted rant, Stephen was down to monosyllables and weighty silence. He stared at the old man, barely blinking, with the same look of disdain he used on the rest of England. It was an expression that said that the person before him had nothing more of interest to contribute. The unfortunate presence would be borne with as little patience as was necessary, until the interloper withdrew.

The look was one of the least painful lessons he had received from his father. He had been on the receiving end of it since he'd said his first, malformed words. He had learned to ignore it. While a glare might frighten, it did not hurt nearly as much as a stout cane across the knuckles. But he had learned to use it as well. Now, he was every bit as skilled at hauteur as his father.

The duke was not impressed. 'Do not think to turn stubborn on me now. Call off this wedding or I will see that you and your bride are banned from society.'

What hardship would that be? he wondered. He had no use for society and Margot had not yet been introduced to the people who might snub her. 'As you will.' Then he continued to fix his father with the direct stare that informed him that the conversation was at an end.

The duke stared back at him, in a silent battle of wills.

This was a new tactic. It was doomed to failure, Stephen was sure. Silence was his oldest friend. He could remain wrapped in it indefinitely, quiet as a rock, still as an open grave. But Larchmont was an orator, an arguer, a speechifier. He could not *not* talk any more than he could hold his breath and wait to grow gills.

A minute passed. And then another. It was an eye blink for Stephen and an eternity for his father. And then, the duke erupted in a stream of curses, elegant and un-repetitive. He damned his son, his shop girl, resulting children, grandchildren and great-grandchildren. He damned the whole Larchmont line from Stephen until the end of time and then, with a final shake of his cane, he turned and stormed off, trailing invective like a stable boot trailed muck, all the way down the hall and out into the street.

It was the middle of a workday and Margot was trapped, against her will, two roads down from Milsom Street. While the sign on the shop insisted, in delicate gold letters, that it was a *beau jour*, she found nothing particularly *beau* about it. She had a new goldsmith to train and shrinking receipts from a sudden lack of custom. She did not have time to shop.

She swatted at the hands of the seamstress, trying to coax her into yet another style fresh from London, and glared at her sister. 'I told you, this trip is unnecessary. I have gowns enough. Any of them will do.'

'You would wear an old gown to your wedding?' Justine looked at her in amazement. 'Surely that is bad luck.'

Fine words from a woman who had eloped to Scotland after several months of pretending marriage to the man she eventually wed. Justine had been too much in love to care what she wore to the brief ceremony. And Will Felkirk had been so bewitched, he'd have declared her radiant though she had been wrapped in a grain sack.

Of course, Lord Fanworth was not similarly blinded by love. Someone of his rank probably expected that she would dress for the nuptials. It made her want this even less. 'The situation is unlucky enough already. I doubt my choice of gown will make it worse.'

'Nonsense,' Justine said, turning her sister and unfastening the current unsatisfactory choice. She had all but dragged Margot by the hair to get her to the modiste's. Perhaps she sought to make up for her own lack of a wedding gown by choosing her sister's. 'You got on fine with Fanworth before. Whatever problems you are having now will pass as quickly as they've arisen.'

For a moment, Margot felt that fleeting hope as well. It had been so good, when they had just sat together and talked. Of course, that was before she had seen the man he really was. Now, they seemed to get on best when the lights were out and no talking was necessary. But what was she to do with him, when the sun was up? Were they destined for a lifetime of sitting across the breakfast table from each other in uncomfortable silence?

'At least I will not have to sit in his house, day in, day out, pretending that I am content. I will still have the shop.' Not really, of course. Once they married, it was his. But surely, he could allow her this one small thing, after casually disrupting her entire life.

'You are not planning on continuing with this.' Justine's expression was incredulous, as though the possibility had never occurred to her.

'Have I said anything, at any time, about a wish to give it up?' Surely she had sacrificed enough since meeting Fanworth. She had given him her innocence. She had tarnished her reputation. And now she was marrying him to keep the peace. But she had no intention of moulding herself into a new person, just to gain approval from him or society. It was simply too much to ask.

Justine opened her mouth to argue, then smiled. 'That is something you must discuss with your husband, not with me. I am only here to find something suitable for a future marchioness to wear to her wedding.'

'Discuss it with Fanworth? What a ridiculous notion. Once he got what he wanted from me, he no longer had a reason to speak. If there is to be a discussion over my future, I will have both sides of it, while he stands in the corner and glares.'

Her frank admission that there had been something more than polite courting involved in the match caused the seamstress to drop her pins in shock. Then she scooped them up, slipped a few between her lips and pinched them shut in a tight, disapproving line.

And now, if she did not spend according to her new station, there would be more gossip. Margot sighed and pointed to several of the most expensive gowns in the catalogue and requested they be made in equally expensive fabrics.

Justine and the modiste gave mutual sighs of satisfaction, both convinced that they had won the battle of wills.

Perhaps they had. When she did not focus on the reason for the purchase, she was rather enjoying the attention. It had been ages since she'd spent time or money on herself. Since she could afford the purchase, what harm would it do her to look nice?

And she had to admit, if Justine was an indication of this woman's skill, this shop would be an excellent place to start. Her sister's gown was neither as gaudy as Mr Montague had encouraged, or as overly simple as she'd chosen for herself. Since she had married, Justine favoured styles that were well cut and elegant, often trimmed with the lace she made with her own hands.

Now that Margot looked at it, the frock they had all but forced her into was really quite charming. A bit of colour in her wardrobe would not be a bad thing. The pale blue of this silk suited her well, though it could have used some sort of ornament on the bodice.

As if she had guessed what Margot was thinking, Justine removed a small parcel from her reticule and set it on the counter in front of them. 'And you will do me the honour of wearing this as well,' she said. Then she unwrapped the tissue to reveal the most splendid lace fichu Margot had ever seen. 'I made it for your wedding day.'

'But when did you find the time?' There had to be many hours of work in the little triangle, for the threads that made up the knots were as fine as cobweb.

'I have been making things for you for years.' Justine gave an eager smile. 'Mother's old trunk is full of them.'

Margot did not like to think of the hundreds of hours her sister must have spent, preparing for a day that she had been doing her best to avoid. It was clear that Justine had pinned all her hopes on a favourable match for her little sister, ending in a proper, church wedding. Despite her misgivings, Margot owed it to her to at least attempt the part of happy bride.

It would be interesting to see Fanworth's reaction should she appear, for once, smartly turned out. He had only seen her dressed for work.

And naked, of course.

'Would the *mademoiselle* like a glass of lemonade? Or water, perhaps. She is quite flushed.'

'Thank you,' Margot said, trying to find an explanation for her sudden blush. 'The stays are just a bit too tight for me.'

'Of course.' The woman loosened the lacing and paused in the fitting to bring the promised refreshment.

Margot took a sip, but it did nothing to cool the heat as she thought of the marquess, gazing at her in surprise. Perhaps he would be moved to comment on how well she was looking. Even if he did not respond with the effusive compliments he had paid her in the past, it would be nice to see him smile again.

Or perhaps he would give her the same cold stare he had used lately, as though he could not quite remember what had moved him to speak in the first place.

She dragged her mind back to her sister, who had draped the lace around her shoulders and was tucking it into the neckline of the gown. Margot ran her finger along the picot edge of the scarf. 'It is too beautiful. With all the trouble I have caused, I am not worthy of such a gift.'

'You must accept it, for I have made you an entire trousseau,' Justine said, with a happy sigh. 'I cannot tell you what a relief it is that you are getting married. I have been planning for this day for as long as I can remember. When I had no hope for my own future, I dreamed of yours. And I made sure that you would have all the things I would not. It gave me hope.'

'Oh. Thank you.' Margot took another sip from the crystal glass of lemonade, which seemed overly sweet compared to the bitter taste in her mouth. She'd had only one wish for her own future: a successful jewellery shop where she could design and sell pretty things she had not even planned to wear for herself. That dream had come true, through her own hard work and stubbornness.

And through Justine's sacrifices, of course. She had been the one to endure the advances of the repellent Mr Montague while Margot had stayed safe at school, oblivious to what was happening. Even after she had learned the truth, she had been no help in rescuing Justine from her predicament. All that Justine asked in return was that she be happy.

And married.

'I am sure your current nightgowns are very sensible.' Her sister was still talking, Margot's lack of enthusiasm ignored. 'But I have made things for you, Margot. For your wedding night.' Justine gave a sly smile. 'Soft fabrics. Lace as delicate as a moth wing. You will look beautiful. And I am sure the marquess will find them very flattering.'

'The marquess,' Margot repeated. At least she knew what to expect from him, on their wedding night. Perhaps he was not the kind, friendly man who had visited her shop. But neither was he the odious Mr Montague, or pompous Mr Pratchet.

Fanworth was young, handsome and virile. Would

a man like that find a lace nightrail flattering? Like the wolf in the fairy story, he would lick his lips and swallow her whole. And it was a shock to realise what a willing victim she would be. She could already imagine his hot breath on her skin.

Her sister pushed against her arm to wake her from the daydream. 'You are so busy thinking about your husband to be that you cannot see him right before your eyes. He is walking on the street, opposite.'

And so he was. She had not seen him since the curious day of his proposal. But then, she had not really expected to. Will had mentioned that he would be gone for at least a week, since he must go to London for the licence. When he had returned, he'd abided by her request for privacy, sending the date and time of the ceremony in a message to her brother-in-law.

If he were to break his vow and walk past her shop, this was his usual time to do so. But instead, he was several streets away and walking in the wrong direction. And he was not alone.

He walked arm in arm with a lady she had not seen before. She was a dark-haired beauty, nearly his equal in height, and moving with the grace and poise of the finest society ladies.

Stephen was absorbed in conversation with her, totally unaware that his future wife watched from a dress-shop window. But then, why would he expect her here, in the middle of a workday? She should be in her shop, nearly a quarter of a mile away from where he talked with this beautiful stranger.

The easy flow of his words was something she had

not seen in weeks. While she watched, he tipped his head skyward and laughed out loud at something the woman said to him. It was not the usual behaviour of the Marquess of Fanworth, who had no time or desire to speak or be spoken to.

What she was witnessing today was annoyingly familiar. From her concealment, she watched Stephen Standish, at his most charming. And he was using that charm on his next conquest.

Chapter Twelve

Stephen was a nervous bridegroom.

That was all right, he supposed. According to the cliché, such nerves were expected. He had always assumed that they were in some way pre-coital.

He had no concerns in that matter. Even if they had not dispensed with the first intimacy some weeks ago, he had the utmost confidence in his abilities once the lights were out and the conversation was over.

But, the actual wedding required speaking, on cue and without hesitation. That was another matter entirely.

Since the moment he had been sure of her acceptance, he had got out the lectionary and begun to practise his part. The servants were used to the sound of him droning to himself before events such as this. On the rare times he had to speak in a crowd, he practised incessantly until the words came as second nature.

That a few short phrases should be so difficult was annoying. He supposed it was the gravity of the situation that caused the trouble. That such an important word should begin with a D made it all the worse.

And now, he was pacing in the nave, muttering softly to himself while awaiting the appearance of his bride. 'To love and to cherish, until d-d-duh...' He punched his fist into his twitching left hand. 'Damn it to hell!'

The curse echoed through the high ceiling of the Abbey, bringing a shocked gasp from the bishop.

Stephen smiled to put the man at ease, then went back to his practising. At least he would not have trouble with the bit at the beginning. He took a deep breath to relax and let the two words flow from his lips. 'I will.'

'You will what?'

He turned to see his bride, standing in the doorway with her sister and Felkirk. She had heard him practising. But the empathy that had drawn him to her on their first meeting was gone. Today, she was annoyed.

'Nothing,' he said hurriedly, glancing down at his watch as though obsessing over a prompt start to the ceremony.

'Fanworth?' Felkirk was at his side now, offering a frown of disapproval and a shallow bow. The man was still not sure whether his sympathies lay with the bride, the groom, or neither of the above.

'Felkirk.' Stephen bowed in response.

'Are we ready to begin?'

Stephen nodded.

Felkirk glanced about him and gave a nod of acknowledgement to the Coltons, who had accompanied his future wife and her sister. They were the only guests. 'I do not see your family here to witness the event.'

It was because Stephen had not bothered to inform them of the date. It would have been nice to see his mother again, so that she might meet the woman who would be the next duchess. But if Mother came, so would the duke. The interview with his father had been difficult enough without encouraging him to come and spoil the wedding.

And God forbid either of them brought Arthur. It would be a disaster.

He had told his sister, of course. She was the last person in the world he wished to offend. But she could not come alone. As a sop to Louisa, he had taken her to the jewellery shop, hoping that a violation of his promise to avoid his bride would be forgiven, so that he might make this very important introduction. But on that day, of all the days in the year, Miss de Bryun had elected to go shopping rather than man the counter of her shop.

Perhaps it was a sign that she might be ready to forgo the place in favour of married life. It would make things easier if she were just a bit more like other women of his acquaintance. Of course, none of those women had fascinated him in the way this one did.

At the moment, the object of his affections was having a whispered argument with her sister who was straightening the very attractive lace collar that adorned Margot's ordinary work frock.

'I thought we agreed, the blue was more becoming.'

'And I told you that such purchases were not necessary. Your gift suits this just as well.'

'But it is so plain,' her sister was practically wailing at her.

'Hush.'

It was true, he supposed. She was hardly dressed for a wedding. But it was very similar to the dress she had been wearing the first time he'd seen her. That was a day worthy of commemoration. He saw no reason to complain.

The frown upon her face now did not bode well for their future. She swept a glance over the empty church, then back at him, accusing. 'Are we waiting for other guests?' It was clear from her expression that she knew they were not. 'Or might we get this over with?'

He tried to smother his annoyance. Perhaps things had not gone as either of them had hoped. But was marrying into one of the noblest families in England really such a hardship?

Then he thought of his family and gave her credit for an accurate understanding of her future as a Standish. He signalled the bishop that they were ready to begin.

Once the ceremony was underway, he breathed a silent sigh of relief. There were not likely to be any objections from the bride's family, since they had arranged the match. The empty pews on his side would be peacefully silent. Margot was far too sensible to refuse, rather than say the vows. More importantly, she would never have gone to the trouble of leaving her shop just for the opportunity to embarrass him at the altar.

The success of the day was all on him. If he could manage to say the words, just as he practised them, there would be no trouble.

And then, the bishop began to read. 'Who can find a virtuous woman? Her price is far above rubies.' Why, of all topics, had he picked that one? He could not have chosen worse if he'd read all of Revelations. Stephen could feel the rage rolling from the woman at his side like a cloud of steam. She must think he'd suggested it as some sort of cruel joke. But now that they were in the midst of things, he could not demand that the officiant stop and chose a more suitable verse. He would find a way to make it up to her later. For now, they would have to brazen it out.

And then, things got worse.

The bishop began the vows. 'Do you, Stephen Xavier, take this woman…'

Do.

He had read the prayer book for hours, until he knew the entire ceremony by heart. Apparently, he knew it better than the bishop. The phrase was supposed to begin… 'Will you…?' And to that, he could answer effortlessly. But this sudden, unexpected move to the present tense made everything impossible.

He could answer, 'I will', just as he'd expected to. But would she think there was some doubt about his willingness of the moment? The more he thought about it, the harder it was to say anything at all.

The church was silent. The bishop had got to the end of his part and was waiting for an answer. It was his turn. He must say something, and say it immediately. 'Yes.'

For a moment, the bishop paused, as if about to correct him.

So Stephen chased the single word with a scowl of such ferocity that the man immediately turned to Margot and repeated her part.

At the end of it, she gave the same dramatic pause that he had done, while fumbling for his words. Then, very deliberately, she said, 'I do.'

The next few minutes were a nightmare. He staggered through the few sentences of his next speech, omitting some words, slurring others and making bizarre substitutions that turned sacred vows into nonsense.

The bishop watched in shocked silence. His soon-to-be wife stood frozen at his side. The back of his neck burned with the heat of Felkirk's angry gaze. There was no way to turn back the day like a clock and start it over again. So Stephen glared back at them all, daring them to challenge him out loud.

With one more slight hesitation, the bishop moved on to Margot's vows.

After a single, resigned sigh, she spoke them perfectly.

Now it was time for the rings. This would go better, he was sure. It sometimes helped when he could connect his statements to some solid object. He reached into his pocket and clutched the ring tightly in his palm, imagining the delicate ridges along the silver band and the amethyst set artfully between them.

She had designed it herself, at his request. He had asked her for a ring for the most beautiful lady in

England. Then he had suggested that she use her personal taste as a guide, hoping she would understand his meaning.

When she had presented him with the finished project, she'd admitted that she was quite proud of it. Then she had assured him that there was not a female alive who wouldn't fall at his feet should he offer it. When he presented it to her, here, on this most important of days, she would understand that this marriage was no mistake. It had been his intention all along.

And then, she would forgive him for the mess he'd made of things. Most importantly, she would not notice if he worshipped with self and not body, and endowed her with things and not goods. 'Til death was the most important bit. He barked the words, almost like a curse. But he got it out, once and clearly, sending the 'us do part' rushing after it.

There. Finished.

He had been too busy to notice her reaction. Apparently, she had lied when she had extolled the virtues of her work. There was at least one woman breathing who was totally unimpressed by the ring. The woman who had made it was staring down at it with disbelief.

For a moment, he still hoped that her expression would change to the surprised smile he'd been expecting. Instead, he saw disappointment, disgust and anger. He could feel the faint pull as her hand tried to escape his grasp, twisting as though trying to gain release from something particularly unpleasant.

He held even tighter, until the struggling stopped. It was an instinctive response and it embarrassed him.

He should not be holding the woman he had just promised to love and cherish like she was a prisoner on the way to the gallows.

But she had just promised to love him as well. It should not be necessary to detain her. None of this was as it should be. Nor was the cheek she offered him to kiss, before they turned to leave the silent sanctuary. They were married, just as he'd hoped it would be—yet it was all wrong.

Perhaps the worst was over. He had done his best to see that, despite the lack of guests, their marriage would be a festive occasion. For the wedding breakfast, he'd reserved the front parlour of the most fashionable hotel in Bath. The food was excellent. The fish melted on the tongue like butter. The ham was so thinly sliced as to be near transparent, but smoky and wonderful. The fruit bowls were heaped high with grapes, strawberries and oranges straight from Seville. He had chosen the wines himself, the most exclusive vintages from his own cellars. Even though the party was small, the cake towered above them, draped in real ivy and sugar roses.

Despite all this, Margot glanced impatiently about her and ate as if the food had no flavour at all.

'Is there somewhere else you wished to be?' he drawled, taking a sip of his wine. These words were clear and unhalting. Why was sarcasm was so much easier than normal speech?

'Yes,' she said, not bothering to elaborate.

Anywhere but here, he supposed.

'It is not as if there is any real reason for celebration,' she said. 'You are as trapped in this marriage as I.'

'For the sake of the others, we must smile and…' be polite…*gracious*… He gave up and shrugged, glancing in the direction of her sister.

'I do not see why,' she said, with almost masculine bluntness. 'They know the circumstances as well as we do.'

'Then for the strangers walking by on the street,' he said, with an expansive gesture that almost knocked over his wine glass.

'Because you had us seated near a front window on the most travelled street in town,' she said, obviously disgusted by his choice.

Because he was proud of his new wife and wanted to make it clear that their affair had been no casual flirtation with a woman of a lower class. He had fallen in love with Margot de Bryun and did not care who saw it. He shrugged again. 'Everyone loves a wedding.'

'Everyone,' she said. It was both a statement and a question.

'At least those who have never married,' he said, thinking of his own parents.

'But no one in your family, apparently,' she said. So she was thinking of them as well.

'This event is no concern of theirs.' At the last minute, he'd almost changed his mind on inviting Arthur. His brother owed Margot an apology. And the little sod deserved to see that his scheme, in the end, had come to nothing. If from spite alone, Stephen had forced circumstances around to the way he'd planned them to be.

It had been like trying to turn a barge with a birch twig. But, by God, it had been done.

'If we'd made our plans according to whom and whom did not have a legitimate stake in this union, we need not have done it at all,' she said. 'You had but to release me from my bargain with you and I could have returned to my shop as if nothing had happened.'

'Nothing?' he said. Was that what their love making had been to her, then?

'There was no harm done.' She took a hurried sip of wine. 'Despite my fears, there is no child imminent. While there has been a negative impact upon the business from my notoriety, I am sure, by next summer, it will be forgotten. To the next crop of holiday goers, I would have been nothing more than a merchant.'

'That is all that matters to you, is it? Your shop?' A normal woman would have lamented for her lost honour.

'It is my only source of income and therefore a primary concern,' she said, using the masculine logic upon him again.

'That is no longer true,' he reminded her. 'You are married. The value of the shop pales in comparison to the rest of my holdings.'

'The rest...' There was an ominous pause as she considered his words. 'Because it is yours now, of course. And what do you mean to do with this shop of yours, now you have gained it?'

It would have to close, of course. But only a fool would begin that conversation right after the wedding. 'Now is not the appropriate time to speak of it,' he said.

'When, then?' she said, looking up into his face with

more interest and intensity than she had during the ceremony.

'I will tell you when I have come to a conclusion.' The conclusion was foregone. But it must be delivered in a way that would not lead to a screaming row in a public room.

'And until that time, what am I to tell my employees? There are seven people who...' She paused. 'Six people,' she amended. 'After whatever you said to him the other day, Mr Pratchet has fled.' She gave him a sharp look. 'It was most unhelpful of you. The lack of a skilled metal worker could severely limit the business I am able to do. I am training up a clever girl who had been working the back counter and sweeping the floor. But what is the point to designing, if there is no one there to execute—'

'You could not stand Fratchet,' he reminded her, purposely mispronouncing the name so she would not hear him stammer.

'That is not the point,' she said.

'You are b-better off without him.' The man had been in the thick of the true conspiracy against her. And today, she took his side against Stephen.

She looked at him in surprise. 'Jealousy does not suit you, Lord Fanworth.'

'I am not...' he began, and felt an annoying prickle of irritation at the thought of Pratchet's smug and possessive attitude towards Margot.

'You are,' she accused. 'It is why you are keeping me here, in the middle of a business day, when I should be working.'

'It is our wedding,' he pointed out, in what he thought was a reasonable way. 'When else would we have had it but the morning?'

'Any time we wished. You had a special licence. You were not limited to the conventional place and time. We could have married quietly, in the evening.'

'I sought to honour you,' he said, gritting his teeth.

'By taking me away from my work? We are short staffed in the front of the shop. And if I am gone as well?' She took a deep drink of her wine and set her napkin aside, pushing away from the table. 'The clerks have no idea how to go on without some kind of instruction. Yet, here I sit, with you, nibbling cake.'

Only a few weeks ago, she had been eager to take time out of her schedule to talk with him. Why was it so different now? Perhaps it was because, when he spoke to her now, his voice sounded very like the one the Duke of Larchmont might use to put a tradeswoman in her place. 'You have known this event was coming. You should have readied them for your absence.'

'Do you question my ability to run a business that has been in my family for generations?'

'I question the need for it,' he said, even more annoyed than he had been at the mention of Pratchet. 'You are my wife. You can do anything you wish. Yet you speak as if you mean to leave in the middle of your wedding feast to return to that shop.'

'I do,' she said. 'Two simple words, Lord Fanworth.'

For such a small answer, it cut like a knife. Even at his worst, she had never mocked him, before this moment. She had never smiled as he stuttered, or grown impatient as he struggled and tried to finish the sentence.

She had saved it for this moment, when it was too late to get away. She had no right to speak so to the scion of one of the noblest families in Britain. 'You will return to my rooms as soon as the shop is closed.'

'To celebrate our wedding night?' She gave him another of her horribly blunt looks. 'At no time did I agree to that.'

'On the contrary. At the altar…'

'I believe the agreement already in place stated that I owe you two more nights, not a lifetime.'

'Things have changed.'

'Not as much as you seem to think,' she said. 'We married because my family left me no choice in the matter. But I like you even less than I did yesterday. If you insist, I will return to your rooms this evening. It will reduce the number of nights I must spend in your bed to one. I suggest you save it for a special occasion. A birthday, perhaps. Or Christmas.'

'Go!' His strength had returned to him in a rush of rage so strong it turned the command into a curse. But the relief was short lived. Suddenly, she chose to obey him, as a good wife should, and quit the room.

Chapter Thirteen

Margot stood behind a display in de Bryun's, tracing idle circles on the countertop with her finger. On the other side of the glass, gold wedding rings rested on satin, like so many shocked, round mouths and wide, round eyes. As if they had any right to judge her. What had just happened had definitely not been her dream of a perfect wedding day.

Of course, if she was truly honest, Margot could not remember ever dreaming of her wedding. She had not planned to get married at all. She had imagined herself, successful and alone. Not lonely, of course. Just, not married.

If someone had suggested that she might wed the son of a duke in Bath Abbey and follow it with a tasteful wedding breakfast in one of the most luxurious hotels in town, she'd have told them to stop spinning fairy tales.

Nor would she have expected to be devoid of wedding-night nerves, having dispensed with her virginity several weeks before the ceremony. In reality, this day was strangely anticlimactic.

The only real surprise was that it was possible to be even angrier with her new husband than she had been before. While he seemed fine with displaying her in a shop window at breakfast, there had been no sign of his family at either the wedding or the meal. He was ashamed of her.

To see her own ring placed on her finger, instead of some piece of family jewellery, was further proof that she was not worthy to be his marchioness. It was why, though she had sometimes dreamed of a proposal, she had not bothered to imagine a wedding. A union between them would not work.

Why did he still have that ring at all? Even after she had known him for the deceiver he'd proved to be, she'd assumed that he had bought her jewellery and requested her designs because he had some small respect for her talent. Even at the worst of times, it had done her good to think that the things he'd made adorned beautiful ladies of his acquaintance. Such a display would result in notoriety and more sales.

If he had kept the ring, what had happened to the rest of the things she had sold him?

'Will we be closing early today?' Jasper, the head clerk, looked hopefully at her.

'Why?' she said absently.

'Because of the wedding, your ladyship.'

She winced. 'Please, do not call me that.'

Now, the poor boy was utterly befuddled. 'I assumed, since it is proper… And you are not Miss de Bryun any more.'

Damn it all, he was right. She was no longer Miss de Bryun. But if she was not, then who was she and what name belonged on the shop window? She could not be Mrs Standish. When Fanworth had used his surname, it had seemed little better than a joke. But to become, without warning, a 'her ladyship' was too much to grasp on an already perplexing day.

She sighed. 'For now, perhaps it is better if you do not call me anything at all. Simply state your business and I will do my best to answer you.'

'I asked about closing,' he reminded her.

There was really no reason to stay open, when the shop was as desperately empty as it had been lately. This afternoon, the only potential customers had done nothing more than to peer in the window, whisper to each other and hurry away. 'I suppose there is no reason to stay here doing nothing. You can all go home, at least. Since I was gone the better part of the morning, I should be the one to stay to close up.'

Jasper paused for a moment, then said, 'If I may be so bold, miss, uh, ma'am. There is no reason that you should have to make up lost time in your own shop. Why do you employ us, if not to make your labours lighter?' And then, to prove that matters were well in hand, he presented the ledger with the day's only transaction neatly recorded, so she might total it with the cash in the drawer.

He was right, she supposed. While she had informed Fanworth that the place was in chaos without her, it had seemed to run quite well. 'Very good,' Margot said, not sure how she felt about the success. 'And now,' she called out, to the room in general, 'you are all released for the day. I will see you tomorrow, of course.'

But for how long? At least, for a while, it was still hers. Once Fanworth asserted himself, there was no telling what would happen to it.

If she was lucky, he would forget all about it. Now that they no longer shared pleasant conversations in the back room and she had persuaded him to stop walking by the window, he might have no reason to visit the place. If she was smart, she would give him what he wanted in bed and try not to goad him as she had today at breakfast. If she did not call attention to them, he might not care about her activities during the day. For all she knew, he might be planning that they lead separate lives.

She could keep her business. And he could chat up women on the street, laughing and talking with them, just as he used to with her. She had no clue as to the identity of the stranger she had seen with him through the window of the dress shop. But it seemed, now that he'd trapped her, Fanworth was cultivating a new favourite. Her cheeks had burned with shame and jealousy, as she had come into the church today. Did that woman call him Mr Standish? Or was he simply 'Stephen' to her? Or perhaps an affectionate 'Fanworth' as she touched his arm and stared up at him?

Why couldn't he simply have been a rake? If he had seduced her, and left her, she'd have been broken-hearted. It would have been awful, of course. But it would have been tidy. She could have put her finger on a day in the calendar when he stopped visiting. And perhaps some time later there would be a day where she stopped caring about it.

But, no. He had been a gentleman about it. He had pretended to love her. Then he had pretended that her honour mattered enough to marry her. And then he had gone looking for another woman, leaving Margot as a loose end, an unfinished job, a knot that would never be tied.

The bell on the door jingled and startled her from the unpleasantness. But it was not a customer, it was Justine. It was just as well. Margot did not feel like smiling or being polite or helpful. She felt like stomping her foot and throwing things.

Was it obvious from her expression? Without another word, Justine stepped behind the counter and enveloped her in a sisterly embrace.

'Such a greeting,' she said, trying not to sound as vexed as she felt. 'We have only just seen each other, you know. The way you are hugging me, it might have been years.'

'It seems that way,' Justine admitted. 'For I have only just left the company of your husband. After you were gone, he did not say another word. Only drank his wine and stared at us.'

Margot laughed. 'However did you escape?'

'Eventually, Will threw his napkin to the floor and made a very rude apology. Then Fanworth stood and we left.' She reached out and offered another hug. 'I am so sorry.'

'Whatever for? You were the one who suffered his bad temper, I was the one who abandoned you to it.'

'I knew he was bad,' Justine admitted. 'But when Will spoke to him, he came away thinking that perhaps a marriage between you would work out well. I had no idea he would drink so, on his own wedding day.'

'A bottle of wine at the wedding breakfast is not so very much. And I did give him reason to be angry,' Margot said, surprised to be defending him.

'If only the wine were all,' her sister said, with a disappointed sigh. 'I had no idea that he would arrive at the church so foxed he could not manage the vows.'

At this, Margot laughed. 'You thought he was drunk?'

'How else to explain the fact that he could not say the few simple words he had promised to?'

'He could not speak because he stammers,' she said, amazed that her sister did not know it already. 'Bs and Ds are especially bad. When he learned our last name…' The poor man had been tongue-tied. 'I gave him permission to call me Margot,' she said, remembering his smile of relief.

Then he had offered to make her Mrs Standish, for convenience's sake, if nothing else. They had laughed together over it. When he had left, she had blushed for the rest of the afternoon.

'That cannot be,' Justine said. 'We have all seen him, here, and in London, and no one has mentioned it before.'

'That is because he does not talk if he does not have to,' Margot said, stating the obvious. 'Have you never noticed how carefully he chooses his words? He avoids that which he cannot say. But when he has no choice, as in the church today…'

It must have been horrible for him. Then, over breakfast, she had taunted him with it. Suddenly, the anger inside her turned to shame. Whatever he had done to her, she had no right to attack him over something that pained him as deeply as this did, especially since he had no control over it.

Justine was still doubtful. 'How do you know of this, if none of us have seen it? Will's brother, Bellston, has known the man for years and has nothing to say about him other than to announce that he—' She broke off, embarrassed.

Margot gave her an expectant look.

'That he was almost as big a prig as his father, Larchmont,' Justine finished.

At this, Margot laughed. 'None of you know him as well as I do.' She stopped, surprised. She had said that without thinking. But if she was the only person who had noticed his stutter, it was probably true. Until the problem with the necklace, she'd have sworn that the real Stephen Standish was a complicated man, by turns roguish, funny, gallant and passionate.

And then, suddenly, everything had changed. Why had he turned so cold to her, treating her like a stranger? It would have made sense, if he actually believed any of the things he had accused her of…

Justine was staring at her, probably confused by her silence. 'Well, if you seriously think you know him, then perhaps there is hope. But my offer still stands.

If you think you have reason to avoid his home or his bed, then come to me. You will be welcome.'

'Thank you,' Margot said. 'But I think, for now at least, things will be fine as they are.' No matter how bad it might be, she would not be running to her sister with her problems. If there was anything to be done that would make a marriage easier between her and her new husband, it would have to be decided between the two of them.

When Justine left, it was time to close up for the evening. Margot looked with longing at the little flight of stairs that led to her apartments above the shop. How easy it would be to forget about the morning and simply climb them, to put her tea on in the little kitchen and go to sleep in her narrow but comfortable bed?

Only to have Fanworth come and haul her out of it, she supposed. Even if she had not promised to return to him, her discussion with Justine left her feeling unsettled. When he had been sweet and kind to her, she thought she'd understood him. Then he had been cruel. But she was still sure she understood his reason for it.

Now she was lost again. The laughing, kind Stephen Standish had been real. Given his unwillingness to reveal his impediment to the world, he'd never have paraded it before her, simply to get her to bed. But then, why had he changed? Had Mr Pratchet lied about his involvement? But then, where had the rubies come from?

Thinking about it made her head hurt. Or perhaps it was the lack of a decent meal. If she had swallowed her pride along with her share of the wedding breakfast, at least she might not be hungry.

If there was no supper waiting for her, she would insist that something be brought to her room. If she went to her husband's bed tonight, there was no reason to let nerves prevent her from eating. The worst was over. Her maidenhead was gone and what they were about to do was sanctioned by church and society.

And, if she was perfectly honest with herself, it might be enjoyable. Her whole body trembled when she thought of the last time she had lain with him. Despite what she had said to him at breakfast, she looked forward to doing it again, without guilt. It would be even better if there was a chance that she might find her way back to the Stephen she had fallen in love with.

Then she remembered the girl in the street. She might pine for their former familiarity. But it seemed he had moved on to another.

As she shut the front door of the shop and locked it, a black carriage pull forward, from the corner. 'Your ladyship?'

She glanced at the crest on the door and the colours of livery. She had not seen it before, but it must be Fanworth's. Her new family colours. She turned to the groom.

The man bowed. 'Lord Fanworth sent us to retrieve you. If you are ready, of course.'

She could argue that she preferred to walk, but what would be the point, other than to make life more difficult for this poor man? 'Thank you.' She allowed him to help her into a seat for the short ride to Fanworth's apartment.

And today, when she entered, it was through the front door. The look on Mrs Sims's face was still not what Margot would call welcoming. But at least the woman held her tongue as she took Margot's bonnet and cloak, and escorted her up the stairs.

Things had changed since her last visit. When the door opened, she had expected to see Fanworth's private sitting room. Instead, most of the furniture had been removed and his bed and dresser had been moved into the space they'd occupied.

Margot raised an eyebrow.

'Your room is through here, your ladyship.' The housekeeper led the way through the changing room, to what had been the master bedroom, then turned and abandoned her to her fate.

When that woman had said it was *her room*, it had not been a generalisation. All traces of masculinity had been scrubbed from it. The walls and the windows were hung with cream silk and the large bed had a matching satin coverlet and chiffon curtains that would be useless to keep out the morning light. Since she was often up before the sun, it probably didn't matter.

It appeared that the decorations had been chosen to remind her of the shop. If so, it was a confusing message. Was it to remind her that her new job lay here, in this bed? Or was it simply an effort to design a room to suit her tastes?

She opened the nearest cupboard and found the dresses she had ordered while shopping with Justine.

Apparently, the woman had saved time and sent them directly to her new home. Which meant the drawers on the dresser must contain the scandalous nightclothes that Justine had made for her wedding night.

When she had thought of this moment, over the last few weeks, she had envisaged her things stacked haphazardly in the corner of the room, a reminder that their owner did not quite fit in this new world that had been forced upon her.

She had been quite wrong. For someone she suspected of marrying her as little more than an afterthought, Fanworth had taken surprising care to make her feel welcome in her new life.

'Is it suitable?' He stood behind her, in the doorway to his own room, and had been watching her reaction. 'The entry to the hall is not yet finished. The carpenters were late.' He pointed to a place on the wall.

He meant a doorway, she supposed. But he had been careful not to say the word in front of her, for fear of a stutter. It made her strangely sad. 'It is lovely,' she said.

'They are setting a meal on the table in my room. If you wish…' He did not finish.

'Of course. Thank you.'

Once the food was served, the housekeeper disappeared, leaving them alone together for the first time in their married life. If she had expected Fanworth to relax, she was mistaken. If possible, he became even more quiet, as he ate from the plate set in front of him without so much as a clink of cutlery.

She tasted her own food, then set down her fork, reached for her wine and took a hurried sip. It appeared that Fanworth's cook was of the sort that was heavy handed with seasonings. The capon on her plate was so salty as to be practically inedible. She tried the carrots beside it only to discover where the pepper had been used. To make up for the two of them, the potatoes had not been seasoned at all, only burnt dry. She glanced at her husband who was close to clearing his plate without comment. 'How was your food?'

'Excellent, as usual,' he said, but made no effort to elaborate.

Either the man had no taste at all or she had been sent another subtle message of disapproval from the household staff. To test her theory, she reached for the dessert course, which was a shared pot du crème, garnished with berries. It was exquisite. She gathered it to herself and stuck in her spoon without bothering to fill her plate.

He watched her for a moment as if trying to decide if the behaviour had significance or was an aberration in manners worthy of correction. Then he reached for her plate, tasted her food and immediately spat into his napkin. This was followed by a torrent of perfectly pronounced cursing and the same foul look he must have given to her family over breakfast.

Then he rose and turned to the bell pull.

'No.' She put her hand on his arm to draw him back down.

'This cannot stand,' he said, waving his hand at her plate.

'It can wait until tomorrow.' She had almost said, *do not ruin tonight*. But she had no proof that statement was appropriate. It was quite possible that there was nothing left of the day to be salvaged.

He sat down again, still irritated. But since his mood was in defence of her, she did not mind it so very much. Then he switched their plates, offering her what little was left on his and setting a buttered roll beside it.

'Thank you,' she said, too hungry to pretend that his sacrifice had not been necessary. She tasted and found he was right. The food was excellent, if the cook liked and respected the one being served. That was some consolation. It would be far easier to deal with a tantrum in the kitchen than complete incompetence.

Fanworth's act of kindness was a silent one. He made no effort to comment further on the staff, the day, or his plans for the night. He simply stuck his spoon into the opposite side of the custard and ate.

It was clear he had no intention of volunteering information. If she wanted answers, she must find the questions that would most easily coax the truth out of him. He set down the custard bowl and took a sip of wine, watching her over the rim of the glass. She did not need words to guess what he was thinking about. His gaze had a confidence that had been absent in church.

She felt a low burn in her belly at the way his eyes travelled over her skin. And, for a moment, she actually wished she was wearing one of the new dinner gowns that would bare her shoulders so he might stare at them. Perhaps then he would feel as distracted as she felt. If she was not careful, by the time the meal ended, they would be in bed and she would have learned nothing.

She wet her lips. 'May I ask you something?'

'I cannot stop you,' he said, with the faintest of smiles.

She grasped one hand in the other, twisting her wedding ring off her finger and handing it back to him. 'Why did you give me this?'

'It was made for you.'

It had not been. She should know for she had taken the specifications herself. Though, if she was honest, she had been loath to let this piece go. He had encouraged her to create a ring no woman could resist and she had used her own tastes as a guide. But to wear it herself defeated the purpose. 'Surely there was some family ring that was meant for the woman you were to marry.'

She had almost said, 'For me.' But none of the Larchmont entail was intended for the likes of her. They both knew it.

He set the ring on the table next to his glass and went to his dresser. He returned with a wooden jewellery box, dumping the contents on the cloth beside her plate. Then he rooted through the pile with the tip of his finger before producing a ring. 'This.'

She picked it up and examined it with the critical eye of a jeweller. The setting was too large for the stone, which was an inferior grade of opal so old it was losing its fire. Opals were bad luck in wedding rings, for exactly that reason. If the lustre signified the spirit of the wearer, this spoke of a fading soul.

'Ugly, isn't it?' he said.

'It is,' she agreed, unable to lie.

He reached forward and gathered her hand in his, then picked up the ring and slipped it back on to her finger. 'This is not.'

So it had not been an insult at all. 'When you bought pieces from me, what did you do with them?'

He went back to his dresser and retrieved another box, this one a lustrous ebony. When he opened it, the pieces she had sold him were nestled in the white-silk lining.

'You did not give them away,' she said, numb with disappointment.

'Who would I have given them to?' he replied with a half-smile rather like the one she remembered from the shop.

'You spoke of an actress, a mistress, cousins…'

'I needed a reason to frequent the shop,' he said, as though pleased with his own cleverness. 'I saved them. For you.'

No one had seen them. No one at all. She had worked so hard to make them perfect, knowing that the woman on the arm of a marquess would draw all eyes in a room. They would see her jewels and whisper. Then they would come to de Bryun's.

And all this time, they had been hidden in his bedroom, invisible. Now he was staring at her, as though waiting for her to be grateful for the gift.

'They were meant to be worn, not locked away in a box,' she said softly. 'I'd hoped that people would admire them and ask about the jeweller. It would bring more business.'

'People will see them now,' he said. 'On the Marchioness of Fanworth.'

Then she might as well put them back in the box and take them to the shop for resale. She had no time to parade about Bath in the evenings like a walking advertisement.

'You never wear j-jewels,' he added. 'You should.'

'I am surrounded by them all day,' she said, with a sigh.

'Exactly,' he said, as if they were in some way finding a common ground. 'Yet you act as if you are not worthy of them.'

How could she explain that it had never been her desire to wear the things she made? Granted, the ring was attractive. She had designed it to be so. But she had never imagined it on her own hand.

He took her silence for assent and reached into the tumbled pile of jewels, slowly drawing forth a string of pearls and draping it around her neck. It was a long rope with a gold and diamond clasp in the shape of joined hands. It was beautiful, of course, but it did not suit her. Even when wrapped three or more times about her neck it would still be too long for the modest gown she was wearing.

'Where is the lace?' he said with a slight frown, tracing the neckline with a finger.

He meant Justine's fichu, she supposed. 'I left it at the shop. It was in the way.'

'It was lovely.' He shrugged. 'Not as lovely as you, of course.' Then he took her by the hand and pulled her to her feet, to stand before a full-length mirror beside his bed.

And so it was to begin. She had convinced herself that she was not nervous. It had been a lie. A few compliments and a touch of his hand, and her pulse was racing. Knowing what was to come had removed the fear from her wedding night. But dread had been replaced with eager anticipation.

He stood behind her now, loosening the back of her gown, until her shoulders and throat were bare and the pearls could rest against them.

'Luminous, like moonlight,' he said, tracing them with his finger. 'But they are no match for your skin.' He placed his palm flat on the beads, rolling them against her bare throat.

Despite her unwillingness to wear them, she enjoyed the feel of the pearls pressing into her flesh and the roll against her tired shoulders. He released the loop he had been holding and let it slither under the bodice until it swayed between her breasts. Then his hands were behind her again, undoing more hooks and laces until she stood bare before the mirror with her bodice, stays and shift bunched at her waist.

He took up the pearls again, rolling them up the slope of one of her breasts, sliding them back and forth across her nipple. 'Now tell me, how do you like your own work?'

They were not really her work at all. Though she had made the clasp, the oyster had supplied the majority of this perfection. She had but given them order. But words failed her. Her reflection showed a ring of pearls about her breast. As he tugged on it and as the loop tightened, the skin around her nipple tightened as well. His hand cupped the other breast from beneath, the tip of it pinched firmly between ring and last finger.

He pressed kisses into her shoulder, until his lips rested warm against her ear. 'I want to take you wearing nothing but pearls.'

He had not stuttered. How strange. But everything about this was strange. She was staring at her own body in a mirror, watching him touch it, hardly daring to breathe for fear he would stop. Now she was helping him as he pushed the skirts to the floor. He settled her own hand to the wet place between her legs so that she could touch herself as she watched the pearls sway against her belly.

It was wicked. It was decadent. And she loved it. She rubbed her back against the wool of his coat for it seemed to heighten the sensation of her own hand to know he was there, hungry eyed, watching her pleasure herself. Her breath caught in her throat as the first tremors of arousal began.

Suddenly, he released her to fumble with the buttons of his breeches. Then he thrust into her hard, over and over. His hands came back to her breasts to hold her so tight to his body that her feet barely touched the floor.

Her self-control snapped, and she reached behind her to clutch at the back of his thighs. Her body tightened to grip his shaft, as if she could draw him into her very soul and keep him there for ever.

It was over too soon. His fingers relaxed their grip on her and his head lolled forward so that his hair brushed against her arm. Then he gave a final sigh of satisfaction and scooped her up in his arms to carry her into the other room and drop her on the satin coverlet.

Without a second thought, she held out an arm to welcome him into her bed.

He shook his head. 'Only one time left. I must be careful.' But he did not leave. And then he smiled.

She had been angry with him this morning. In turn, he had been furious with her. It was possible, once they regained their senses, that they would be right back to sniping at each other.

But that did not alter the fact that she wanted more.

She ran a finger along the rope of pearls, tracing them from her neck to the low point where they settled on her belly. Then, she spread her legs.

He stared at her for a moment, doubtful. 'I suppose I could stay. For a while.'

She nodded. Then she smiled as he began to remove his clothing. He looked rather undignified, standing over her with his breeches hanging open. But it would not last. The Marquess of Fanworth was never without his dignity. She would cherish the brief loss of control, for she might not see it again.

Now he was fully nude. The sight of him made her forget that she longed for vulnerability. Like this, he was invincible. The long smooth flanks, narrow waist and strange ridges of muscle made her long to touch and to submit. If she could capture such fluid power in gold, she would worship at it, like a pagan.

She smiled to herself at the ridiculousness of the idea. But the sight of him stirred something in her, other than simple lust. It was the strange, creative rush she got, right before a new idea. Tomorrow, when she got to the shop, she would take up her sketch pad and see what resulted.

But for tonight?

He was climbing up on to the bed with her, lying on his side, his head leaning against his bent arm. Then, he leaned forward and kissed her. It was more tender than passionate and his smile was achingly familiar. It belonged to Stephen Standish: the man she loved.

His free hand reached to brush the hair from her face. 'Lady Fanworth,' he said softly, 'you are temptation incarnate.'

If that was so, then for a change he was at her mercy and she could do as she wished with him. So she slipped the pearls from about her neck, wrapped them loosely around his manhood and stroked.

Chapter Fourteen

Stephen awoke the next morning to the smell of lavender and the feel of satin against his cheek. It took him a moment to realise that he was face-down in the pillows of his wife's bed. He had requested the linen be pressed with flowers and chosen the coverlet himself. It was to be the sort of gentle bower his beloved deserved.

Despite his careful planning, she had left him again, to go to that damnable shop. It had never occurred to him that, when offered wealth, title and a life of ease, the woman he married might continue to work. It was a nice enough shop, he supposed. He had found his visits to the white-velvet salon to be relaxing and pleasant.

But then the place had not been his rival. When he thought of it, he felt something very like jealousy. It was clear that she loved it more than she did him. And she gave no indication of changing her mind on that point.

The current situation could not continue. He had no real wish to command her to give up her work and stay in his home. If she chose to do so of her own accord, life would be better for both of them. But to achieve that, he must give her a reason to stay.

His intent had been to wake before she did and be ready to stop her as she passed by his bed on her way to the door. If she could be tempted with the pleasures of the marital bed, she might forget all about the desire to rush away from him, just to stand behind a glass-topped counter, smiling at strangers.

He had intended to do that. Instead, he had over-slept. To be fair, she had exhausted him. One of her silk stockings was tied about his wrist in remembrance of a point during the previous evening when he had tried to leave her. His other hand clutched those infernal pearls.

He set them gently on the pillow, as if they were a dangerous weapon that could discharge at any moment. He had thought to tease her with them. But she had turned the tables upon him, binding him with them until excitement made the tightness a mix of pleasure and pain. Then she'd released him and he'd surged into her, desperate for relief.

At least she seemed to have forgotten her threat to hold him to their earlier agreement. If she meant to set a strict limit of four encounters, they would need to reason like Jesuits to explain last night. At the very least, he would insist that some of the things they had done to celebrate their wedding could count for a half, or perhaps a quarter of a whole.

Of course, some had been so delightful they should be counted twice. If some creativity was not used in the accounting, the rest of his marriage would be had on credit.

He hoped that her ardour was a sign that her resolve

was weakening. If she would warm to him enough to listen, he was more than willing to apologise for the trouble he had caused her. She would be more likely to believe him if he could have got Pratchet to retract his slander. But there was no hope of that. Stephen had taken too much pleasure in frightening him and, as expected, the little man had bolted.

The alternative was to force Arthur to explain himself. But if his brother wanted revenge for his damaged nose, it would be most unwise to introduce him to Margot.

He'd find another way, then. But damned if he knew what.

It had been an interesting night.

Margot stood behind the counter, staring off into space, unwilling to wipe the small, secret smile from her face. It was clear that marriage had advantages. She had filled several pages of her sketchbook with ideas for new designs, including a fob chain with links that reminded her of the crook in her husband's elbow.

Then she set Miss Ross up with the form and the heaviest gauge of gold wire, teaching her how to twist as she wrapped it to add character to a plain chain. It was a simple enough construction and it would be a useful skill for the girl to form and cut links and solder them back together.

Perhaps some new designs in the front window would help to draw trade. She had been an object of curiosity when she was Fanworth's mistress. People came to the shop so they might gossip about her. Many of them made purchases so their motives might be less obvious.

But the moment that it was announced she was to be his wife, the crowds had dispersed. The world could not decide what to do with a marchioness who was in trade. Were they to scrape and bow to her, or should she do it to them? So far, society had decided she was neither fish nor fowl, therefore, it was best to push her to the side of the plate and ignore her.

But just now, there was a fashionable lady, passing by on the other side of the street. Perhaps she was in need of a gift for a lover or a husband? Then the woman passed from shade into sunlight and adjusted the angle of her parasol so Margot could see her face.

Not her.

She needed customers. But of all the women in Bath, this one must just keep walking. It was the beautiful woman who had been speaking with Fanworth, the week before their marriage. More importantly, she was the one to whom Stephen had had been speaking.

Even during last night's intimacy, when speaking to her he'd seemed to navigate with caution. He had spoken little, but when he'd smiled, he'd seemed almost like his old self. It had been going so well that she hoped, just maybe, he might relax and be the man she once loved.

But at the sight of this woman, Margot's confidence slipped. He might have married her, but that did not mean that he intended to open his heart to her. If there was to be a relationship between this woman and Stephen, it was not her place to comment on it. Perhaps, if he was distracted, he would be less likely to interfere in the shop. Perhaps he would forget about her, and it, and things could go back to the way they had been.

Suddenly, that prospect did not seem nearly as inviting as it would have, before last night.

And now the last woman in the world whom Margot wished to see had crossed the street and was passing by the shop again, pausing at the front window to stare directly in at her.

Margot offered a polite smile in response. It would not do to scowl at a potential customer. Nor would it help either of them if she admitted recognition of the woman who was likely to steal her husband's attention, just as she realised she still wanted it.

The young lady came very near to passing by again before turning back, as though she wished the nerve to enter, but hadn't quite mustered it. She was young enough to be unsure of herself. Now that Margot could see her clearly, it was plain that this girl was no older than herself. Young and lovely, with smooth brown hair, large clear eyes and the limbs of a colt.

The maid following patiently behind her spoke of a family rich enough to make sure there was money in her pocket for frivolity.

Margot forced another, even brighter smile through the glass, holding her breath. *Go*, Margot willed silently. *Or come, if you must. But do not linger in the street, staring at me. You will embarrass us both.*

The girl smiled as well. She hesitated for a moment longer, then made her decision and reached for the shop door, giving it a sharp pull. The brass bell clanked and she looked up in alarm, as though fearing she'd caused an affront.

'Welcome,' Margot said softly. 'May I be of assistance?'

'Are you Lady Fanworth?' the girl asked hopefully.

Margot took care to hide the chagrin at hearing the unfamiliar title. Then she offered a brief nod.

'I attempted to call on you at home, but they told me that you would be here.' She pulled a card case from her reticule and searched around her for some servant who she might hand it to. Then she put it away again, still torn between etiquette and the simpler rules that should preside here. 'I am Louisa,' she said. When the name had no effect, she added, 'Standish. Fanworth's sister.'

Of course. It was why they had been so well suited, when they had stood on the street together. And why he had talked easily and laughed with her.

But it did not explain why he'd said nothing of the meeting. And why had she not come to the wedding if she had been here in Bath, all along? The hurt came back, fresh and sharp.

She swallowed it and put on her most neutral smile. Louisa Standish was here, now. The least Margot could do was pretend that it was a normal meeting. 'Come in Lady Louisa. Please. Sit down with me. Perhaps a glass of lemonade, or perhaps a ratafia, in the back salon.'

Lady Louisa gave her a hopeful smile. 'You have the time?'

'For you? For family?' Margot added, the words thick on her tongue. 'Of course.' She held back the drapery and escorted the girl to the same *chaise* that her brother had so often enjoyed, and snapped her fingers to an idle clerk, indicating that refreshments must be brought.

Then she stared at Lady Louisa for a moment, trying to clear the haze from her brain. What was she to make of this visit? It was too late for the girl to upbraid her for angling after a man so far above her station. But there was nothing in her manner that suggested that was the reason for the visit. Still, it was strange that their first meeting was here and not in the Abbey.

Louisa looked at her with an equally dazed expression. 'We are all very curious about the new member of the family, but rather at a loss as to how to proceed,' she said, with the shyest of smiles. 'Well, Mother is. She very much wants to meet you. But without my brother's permission, she cannot. And, of course, he will not give that.' She gave a little shake of her head, to indicate that there was nothing to be done with some people. 'In my opinion, Fanworth can hardly be blamed for any of it. But, since they have all but forgotten about me, I decided to take matters into my own hands.' She extended her hands outward in a gesture that said, 'Here we are'.

'Blamed for any of what?' Margot gave up trying to pretend that any of it made sense to her.

'Why, not inviting the family to your wedding,' she said, as though it must be totally apparent.

Margot sniffed. 'I understand that your family is probably mortified. But if he was so embarrassed by me, he really needn't have bothered with the wedding.'

Louisa's eyes grew wide. 'Is that what you thought? Oh, dear.' She shook her head. 'And he allowed you to labour under this misapprehension.' She shook her head again. 'Stephen is my favourite brother, Lady Fanworth. In fact, he is my favourite person in the entire world. But you must have noticed how stubborn he is and how proud.'

'It is why he does not speak,' Margot agreed.

'I had hoped he would, at least, speak to the woman he chose to marry.'

He had. Once. What could she tell her husband's sister that did not make it sound as if she did not know the man at all? For she was beginning to think, perhaps she didn't. 'It was all very rushed,' she said, striking a path between explanation and apology. 'And certainly not the wedding that either of us expected to have.' She glanced around the shop, angry that they might expect her to be ashamed of all that she had accomplished. 'But I am sure I am not the woman that Lord Fanworth expected to present to his family.'

'On the contrary,' Louisa insisted. 'He spoke most highly of you and was eager for us to meet, even though he did not wish me to attend the wedding. He extolled your beauty, your wit and your talent. He said we would get on famously, once he had found a way to introduce us.' She smiled. 'It was a great relief to know that his heart was engaged. I have never seen him so effusive.'

'He was effusive?' It explained the animated conversation she had witnessed in the street. But it had never occurred to her that she might have been the topic discussed. It was even more surprising that he had been numbering her many good qualities. Given that, it made no sense that he should prohibit his sister from attending, if he was so very fond of the pair of them. 'I am afraid I still do not understand. If I am such a catch, then why did you not at least take breakfast with us yesterday?'

Lady Louisa gave her a sad smile. 'It is simple. He is not ashamed of you, Lady Fanworth. He is ashamed of us.'

'Of you?'

'Well not me, perhaps,' Louisa admitted. 'We really do get along brilliantly. But I could not come without Mother. Mother would have insisted that Father be invited, before she was willing to attend. She still hopes there is a way to mend this breach between the duke and his heir.' Louisa shook her head as though contemplating the impossible.

'My husband does not get on with his father? If anything, society seems to think they are two of a kind.'

'Heavens, no. They are both proud, of course. But that is because of Father's continual reminders that the Larchmont title is one of the oldest and most respectable in Britain. Nothing must be done to embarrass the family.' Louisa frowned. 'Although he claims to want the best for his heir, he actually wants the best *from* him as well. Nothing less than perfection will do.'

'And Stephen is not perfect,' Margot said, hating even to mention a thing which did not really matter.

'When Father is disappointed…' Louisa gave her a tight, little smile '…it is best to just avoid him. Since he is frequently disappointed in Stephen, my brother refuses to have anything to do with him.' She whispered the next, as though it were part of some shameful secret. 'The stammering is really so much better than he used to be, now that they do not talk. When Stephen was at home, if he made even the smallest mistake, Father would badger him until he could not talk at all.'

It was a horrible story. But it explained why the church had stood empty on their wedding day. 'So there could be no duchess without a duke, and no you without the duchess.' She thought for a moment. 'But I understand you have a second brother, as well?'

Louisa nodded. 'At the moment, there is a disagreement of some kind between my brothers. Fanworth was adamant that he did not want to see Arthur at his wedding. And Arthur does not want to be seen by anyone until the bruises have fully healed.'

'Bruises,' Margot repeated, still confused.

'Stephen struck him,' Louisa said with a little giggle. 'I think his nose is broken. And both eyes…' She gulped back a full laugh and took a ladylike sip of her drink to clear her throat. 'I do not know exactly why. But I am sure that there was a good reason for it. Fanworth likes to pretend that he is gruff and imposing. But he is not usually moved to violence. And Arthur?' Louisa sighed. 'Arthur frequently deserves to be hit. At one time or another, we are all disappointed in him. Yet, Father seems to like him best of all. There is no pleasing some people and that is that.'

'You seem to have a most unusual family,' Margot said, as politely as possible.

'Perhaps that is true. Some say the upper classes are prone to eccentricity. If so, there are few houses that can compete with Larchmont.'

'If your father is so set on perfection, I suspect it makes your brother's choice of wife all the more unacceptable,' Margot said, resigned to her role.

'Perhaps you did not understand my meaning,' Louisa said with another little sigh. 'There is no woman likely to find acceptance in a family led by my father. The fact that she was chosen by Stephen would be reason enough for him to find fault.' Then she smiled. 'For my part, I love my brother very much. If he loves you, that is reason enough for me to love you, as well.'

Now Margot should explain that it was not a love match at all. Despite what Louisa had told her of their conversation, she suspected her husband barely tolerated her when she was not in his bed. But when she was? Her skin grew hot at the thought of the previous night's sport.

Perhaps that was a solid basis for a marriage and the rest did not matter. And to see this lovely young woman smiling before her and holding out the family olive branch was too tempting. 'If you welcome me, of course we will be friends,' Margot said cautiously.

'Or sisters, if you wish,' Louisa said, with a hopeful smile.

'I already have a sister,' Margot responded, then noticed the other woman's smile falter. 'But that is no reason that I cannot have another one.'

Louisa smiled again. 'I have never had one. And few friends because...Father,' she said as if that explained it all. 'Mother is a dear, of course. But there are times it would be nice to have someone nearer my own age.' She glanced around her. 'Even if you are so often here.'

'I work here,' Margot said, testing her reaction to the word. 'But since I am the owner, I could be a bit more free with my time.' Hadn't Jasper suggested such a thing just yesterday? Perhaps the world would not end if she was not here from dawn to dusk. 'When your brother used to visit here, I spent many happy hours talking with him.'

'Talking. With. Fanworth.' Louisa's first expression was one of incredulity. Then it settled into a warm smile. 'Of course. I think this makes everything much clearer. When Mother heard how beautiful you were, she was rather worried.' She stood, ready to take her leave. 'But I will tell Mother that you have talked with Fanworth, for hours at a time. It will set her mind at rest.'

Margot stood as well and returned a smile to this rather cryptic remark, not wanting to think too hard on what the duchess had assumed about her character. 'Thank you for your visit. And your kind words.'

'And thank you, for the sake of my brother.' Louisa smiled again. 'I will come again, soon. If that is all right.'

'Of course.' Margot escorted her to the door. As she waved goodbye and watched Louisa and her maid stroll down the street, she felt more hopeful about her future than before, but no less confused.

Chapter Fifteen

Stephen spread the afternoon mail out on the writing desk in the salon and sighed. The packet of letters was not as large as he would have hoped. After his recent marriage, there should be invitations to balls, routs, or at least a dinner or two. Most importantly, there should be something addressed to Lady Fanworth.

Hopefully, Margot would not notice the degree to which she'd been snubbed. So far, the only event they would be attending was the hastily arranged reception Justine was hosting to celebrate the wedding and to welcome her brother-in-law, the Duke of Bellston, to Bath.

His parents would be in town by then. If they attended, it would give him a chance to introduce the family on neutral ground. Mother would be charming wherever they met her. But Larchmont was more likely to be civil if another peer was present. Much to his father's annoyance, the Bellston title was the older and respect for tradition would force him to be on his best behaviour.

If the rest of the town did not see this party as a reason to welcome them, then they could all be damned. Since the majority of the *ton* followed the Regent to Brighton, it hardly mattered what people thought here. They would manage well enough until it was time to retire to Derbyshire and by the London Season, it would be old news.

But while he could ignore the snubs of strangers, he would not abide dissension in the staff. When he had come on holiday, he'd brought Mrs Simms, and the cook along with him. He liked his comforts and, in Derbyshire, those two women fussed over him like two hens with a single chick.

But it appeared that his marrying a woman of a lower class did not meet with their approval. Worse yet, he had entertained her in his home before marriage and they knew for a fact that she was not as virginal as her snowy-white gowns.

The insults to his wife were subtle, but frequent. Mrs Sims had been able to keep her own counsel while he'd entertained Margot as a mistress in the house she managed. But her patience had come to an end the moment he announced he would be marrying her. At any mention of the wedding or the bride, Mrs Simms had taken to sniffing in disapproval. She had done it so often that he had enquired of her whether she had a cold, or some chronic condition that affected her breathing.

Cook was little better. Lady Fanworth's portion of last night's wedding supper had been practically inedible, as if she thought that it might be possible to starve the interloper out of the house. It was only Margot's kind-heartedness that had saved the pair of them from a dressing down worthy of Larchmont at his most temperamental.

As it sometimes was with servants, the lady's compassion was greeted with more contempt than obedience. And now they were growing so careless as to be gossiping in the front hall, oblivious to the fact that the master of the house was listening to every word.

'I suppose it will be dinner in the bedroom, again,' said Cook in a disgusted voice, 'while a perfectly good dining room stands empty.'

'Herself is too busy to use it,' Mrs Sims responded, equally annoyed. 'Down to that shop, dawn until dusk.'

'Perhaps I should ask her to stop at the grocer's on her way home,' Cook said with an evil chuckle.

'It makes more sense than that we be waiting on her,' Mrs Sims agreed. 'A tradesman's daughter. No better than us, really. The duke will never approve. Of course, her Grace's blood is as blue as the Princess Charlotte's.'

Stephen rose, throwing down the letter he had been holding. By God, he had heard more than enough. They had served in the family since before his birth. But he would sack the pair of them if this was how they behaved when he was not in the room.

'Ladies.' Margot had heard as well. She had come home hours earlier than usual, totally unprepared for a household contretemps. If he'd handled the problem last night, as he should have, he might have saved her from this embarrassing encounter.

'Your ladyship,' both women responded in unison and there was a moment of silence to cover what must have been the most hypocritical curtsies ever performed.

Stephen waited for his wife's response. Had his mother ever been in such a situation? He doubted it. She held the staff in check as Lord Nelson held the Navy. But then, she was past fifty and had been the daughter of an earl before becoming a duchess. If his sister had been presented with such a problem, it would have reduced her to tears.

And Margot was barely older than Louise.

'Despite the concerns you voiced a moment ago, dinner will be in the dining room tonight,' Margo said. 'And so it will be on any evening I arrive before six. I trust that it will not be necessary for me to run errands, since Fanworth assures me that his house is very well managed.'

Liar. They had never discussed such a thing. He smiled.

She sighed so heavily that he could hear it from where he sat. 'But I begin to wonder if that is the case. Last night, the capon you left for me was practically inedible. It was as if someone had upended the salt cellar over it. There was too much pepper in the carrots and the potatoes were bland. Fanworth shared his plate with me and neither of us got enough to eat. See that it does not happen again.'

'Yes, your ladyship,' said Cook, properly chastised.

'And before we go any further, Mrs Sims, I must

correct your other assessment of me. I am not a tradesman's daughter.'

'You are not?' Now the woman was torn between bravado and confusion.

'I am something far worse.' It was said in a sweet and youthful voice that hardly matched her matter-of-fact tone. 'My father has been dead for over twenty years. I own and run the business alone. I am in trade myself, Mrs Sims. As such I am accustomed to dealing with employees, both hiring and firing.' She took another dramatic pause. Then she continued. 'Perhaps other young ladies of my age would be intimidated by your obvious mastery of the household. But I am not. I respect it, of course. And Fanworth adores you. It would be a shame to have to replace either of you. But I will do so without hesitation if you are unwilling or unable to take my instructions.'

'Of course, your ladyship.' There was a kind of grudging respect in Mrs Sims's answer, as though she had not expected the new lady of the house to have such starch in her.

'Very good.' Through it all, Margot's voice had lost none of its cheerfulness. 'Dinner at seven, then. Send up a maid, for I intend to dress. And remember, do not over-salt the meat.'

'Yes, your ladyship.' This answer came in unison, as both women acknowledged her authority.

Then Margot was gone. The sound of her slippers pattering up the stairs was light, youthful and unladylike.

Stephen smiled and settled back into his chair.

* * *

As requested, dinner was served promptly at seven. Lady Fanworth looked well satisfied with herself and sent her compliments to the cook on an excellent meal. Then she smiled at him more warmly than she had in weeks.

Stephen smiled at her in return. For all he cared, they might have been eating gruel. He'd still have proclaimed it ambrosia. To see her smiling across the table at him was the fulfilment of the dream he'd harboured since the first day they met. And no part of that fantasy had prepared him for the sight of her, dressed for dinner.

Perhaps Bath society thought they could spurn her, as a lower-class woman who'd got above herself. But they had not seen her like this. She was perfection: her beauty unrivalled, her grace unaffected and her smile so warm and genuine that one could not help but be drawn to her. One had but to speak to her for a few moments to learn that her personality matched her looks. God made a woman once or twice in a generation who was fit to be a queen. It was only natural that Stephen should wish to make her a duchess.

And on a much more personal note, it was dizzyingly erotic to see her perfect shoulders displayed above the low neckline of her green-silk gown. He had kissed those shoulders. She wore the pearls around her throat to remind him that they had done far more than kiss. They would do so again tonight. He was, truly, the luckiest man in England.

She was staring at him as if she knew a secret. Her

sea-green eyes were bottomless. He could gaze into them for the rest of his life, floating, sinking, lost in their depths.

She had spoken.

He had not heard. He dragged himself back to reality. 'Excuse me?'

'I said, I had a most interesting day at the shop today.'

'Really.'

'Your sister came to visit me.'

He could not even manage am abbreviated answer. All words were shocked out of him and he could do nothing but stare at her in silence.

'She is perfectly charming. You should have introduced us sooner.'

He nodded. Of course he should have. He had attempted it. It had not been his fault that he had failed.

The smile that she was using on him was dazzling, as though she knew how easy it was to beguile him. 'We spoke of you, of course. And of the rest of the family.'

They talked about him. Of course they had. What other common subject could they have? It was rude to tell him of it. But what had he to fear? Of all the people in the world, he could trust his sister to be kind. And, of course, he could trust Margot.

I do. Two simple words, Fanworth...

He had managed to forgive her that. She had been angry. But he had given her reason to be. If he wished her to forgive him, he could not rage at her over every slight. Last night, he had trusted her with his body and been well rewarded for his faith.

But that had not involved conversation.

Now, her smile looked positively smug. Could he ever truly trust a woman who knew his greatest weakness and mocked it on their wedding day? She might sound sweet, but today that honeyed tongue had put the servants in their place with just a few words. He had admired her ruthlessness. But then, she had been using it on others.

'Fanworth.' She waved a hand in front of him, to gain his attention. 'Stephen.'

It was only then he realised that she had continued speaking and he had not heard a word.

'Excuse me?'

'I asked if you were enjoying the dinner.'

'It is fine,' he assured her.

She gestured to the plates on the table. 'Do you have a favourite, perhaps?' She was trying to persuade him to speak.

He looked down at the dishes set before them. Duck in burnt butter. Pickled beetroot. Potted pigeon. Pears in puff paste.

It was a trap.

His father might use force and shouting to make his point. But his wife was a subtle creature. Now that he had taken her into his life, there were a hundred ways she could find to make him miserable. If there were any weaknesses she had not already guessed, she was likely to learn the rest from his sister. And he had no one to blame but himself. He had been the one to court her, accuse her and seduce her. He had made her his enemy.

He had created his own hell.

He said nothing. To speak was to give her ammunition. Instead, he tossed his napkin on the table and left the room.

Chapter Sixteen

Margot crumpled the note in her hand. She had not seen her husband in days. And now he chose to communicate in writing. It was outside of enough. The worst of it was, she had no idea what she had done to make him angry again.

In her opinion, things had been going quite well. They had proved they were more than compatible, once the lights were out. And after speaking with his sister, some of her reservations about the marriage had been laid to rest. There was still much to discuss, of course. She still did not understand the matter of the necklace.

But to discuss, both parties had to speak. And for some reason, he had gone from speaking little, to not speaking at all. She had no idea what she'd done to cause the change.

She'd returned home early, specifically to please him. They'd dined at the table and she had dressed in a manner befitting the wife of a great man. If he could find nothing good to say about her, the least he could have done was remark on the food. The cook had outdone herself and the quality of her portion had been the equal of his. A single taste of her plate would have proved to him that he would not have to involve himself in domestic strife or the running of the house. She was perfectly capable of managing the staff on her own.

Her efforts to please him had been for naught. He'd stared at her over dinner as if he'd never seen her before. Then, with no warning and not a word of explanation, he had got up from the table and abandoned her.

She had assumed that they would have time later, in bed, to talk. She had even planned to playfully remind him that he was still entitled to one more night of her company. But he had not been in his room when she had gone to bed. Even though she'd arisen early the next day, he was not there. It looked as if he had not come to bed at all.

And so it had gone, for several days. To question the staff about the location of her husband after only a week of marriage would embarrass her in front of servants that had only just come to accept her as mistress. And as it had repeatedly over the last few weeks, she felt the creeping suspicion that he'd got all he wanted from her, and had lost interest.

Now, this. A curt note reminding her of her sister's reception, this evening, and his request that she be dressed and ready to accompany him at eight. Apparently, though they did not speak in private, they were to be a happy newlyweds in the eyes of the world.

And he expected her to be the beautiful ornament suitable to a man too proud and well born to have an ordinary wife.

If he meant to escort her in silence, it would be an even greater ordeal than she had expected. Margot had more than enough time to visit with Louisa, since customers continued to avoid the shop. But this morning, the girl had informed her, as gently as possible, that the family would not be attending this evening's festivities. It was quite possible that her visits to the shop would end, as well. Now that the Duke and Duchess of Larchmont were in Bath, they would expect their daughter to stay with them and not with the cousin she had been visiting. Since it had been decided that Larchmont and his lady would not be attending the reception, Louisa had little choice but to remain at home with her needlework.

So, his family was not willing to celebrate the union. If the ledger book told a story, the rest of Bath meant to avoid her as if she had some contagious disease. If no one liked them, then why were they bothering to play-act their happiness? Perhaps she would simply ignore his command and pretend she had forgotten the invitation. She would work later than usual, even if it meant sitting in an empty shop.

Then she remembered Justine, so eager for her happiness that she had orchestrated the wedding, and the party to celebrate it. If the evening was a poorly attended disaster, it would be up to Margot to console her sister, thank her for her efforts and pretend to be happy, just as she planned to do in her marriage. And, if Fanworth wished for nothing more than a beauty, she would give him what he deserved.

She arrived home even earlier than necessary and ate a hurried supper alone before giving herself over to the ministrations of the maid whom her husband had hired for her. The gown they chose was the green of spring leaves, with a deep hem embroidered with white-and-gold flowers. The maid dressed her hair so that tendrils wound down about her face like so many vines in an overgrown wood. Margot had to admit, the finished look was striking. There was something faintly pagan about it, as though a nymph had been dragged from the woods and forced to marry well.

She smiled at herself in the mirror. If the town gossiped that Fanworth had married beneath him, at least there would be no question as to his reasons. And she had just the jewellery to match it. She directed her maid to get the ebony box from my lord's room.

As the door to the connecting room opened, she could hear him on the other side of the suite, swearing quietly as his valet dressed him. It surprised her that the son of a peer had such a diverse and vulgar vocabulary. But he used it with confidence, for there was not a trace of a stammer as he complained about the tying of his cravat.

The cursing ceased as her maid entered and requested the jewels. There were a few more moments of profound silence. Then Fanworth stood in the doorway, cravat still hanging untied about his neck, shirt open at the throat and the ebony jewellery box in his hands. He was staring at her with the same hungry expression he'd had at the dinner table, before everything had gone wrong.

Perhaps he had only wanted her for her beauty. Then she would desire him for his handsomeness. She was sure that, at this moment, they were both thinking the same thing. If they dismissed the servants, she could go to him, lick once against the bare skin of his throat and they would not leave the house or the bed until morning.

He stepped forward and the spell was broken. When she reached for the jewellery box, he held it just out of her reach. 'Allow me.'

Only two words. But they were the first she'd heard from him in days and they struck right to the heart of her. With a casual flick of his finger, he opened the box, reached into it, and removed the necklace she wanted: a narrow band of gold leaves, set with pavé emeralds. His fingers trailed along her skin, circling her throat as he fastened it.

Why could he not speak to her the way he touched her, as if she were the most precious gift in the world? Now he was affixing the matching drops to her ears, his index finger drawing lightly along the shells before settling on the lobes, sliding the wires into place.

She turned to look into the mirror, if only to distract herself from his touch. Her throat tightened at seeing her work reflected back to her. At last, these pieces would be worn in public, just as she had intended. She would see, first-hand, if they were admired.

Fanworth reached out and took her gloved hand,

kissing the knuckles before slipping a bracelet on her wrist. It was the emerald viper he had bought on the first day.

She looked down at it, worried. 'Surely this is too much.'

He shook his head and smiled. 'Eve needs a serpent.'

Did he still think her a temptress? If so, he had been resisting well enough lately. But he was right. The bracelet did go well with the gown. And then she remembered the story. 'Eve was…' Not wearing a gown.

His glance swept her body as though he could see through the silk to the woman beneath. 'Later, you may keep the bracelet on,' he said, smiling again. Then he returned to his room to finish dressing.

While the assembly room was hardly full, it was not the barren wasteland that Margot had feared. The Duchess of Bellston greeted her with a warm kiss upon the cheek and compliments on both her marriage and her appearance. The duke smiled and kissed her hand, then exchanged properly sombre greetings with Fanworth as they took their places in the receiving line.

Though she had been to a few routs with her sister, Margot had never been in such high-born company, much less an honoured guest. Then, she remembered her husband held precedence over all in the room but the duke. She must learn to behave as the duchess did, polite, friendly and confident in her place.

If any guests came with the intent of offering a snub, they were properly subdued by the obvious warm relationship the new marchioness had with Bellston and his duchess. Some even dared to enquire, politely, if the jewellery she was wearing was from her own shop.

She acknowledged that it was so. She had designed it herself. In response, she saw speculative looks on the faces of some of the ladies, as though trying to decide if the social awkwardness of greeting the Marchioness of Fanworth from across a shop counter was greater than their desire to be the first of their friends to own one of her pieces.

Beside her, Fanworth greeted both the ladies and their husbands with a cool smile and as few words as was possible. When compared to his disdain, she looked all the more approachable. And to her surprise, the looks cast at her by some of the ladies in the room changed from suspicion to pity. They seemed to be imagining how difficult life would be, in the presence of such a cold and unfeeling husband.

She had been thinking such a thing herself, only this morning. But then she remembered their wedding. There was a lull in the crowd and she glanced at him now, noting the slight frown that creased his forehead and the way his lips pinched in the tightest possible smile. He was not sure what might escape should he relax and speak freely.

This continual wariness must be as exhausting for him as it was frustrating for her. And it must be very lonely. Without thinking, she reached out and touched his sleeve to remind him that she was still by his side.

He started, looking down at her, as though he had forgotten her presence. Then, ever so slightly, his brow seemed to relax and his smile became less threatening. Perhaps she was more to him than a warm body in his bed. He had chosen her to be his life's companion.

When he had visited her in the shop, he had willingly shared his soul. If he could not manage a few simple hellos at a time like this, there was no way he'd have been so open to her, just to bed her. He had loved her, just as she thought. For this union to succeed, they must find their way back to that place of communion.

The first step would have to be hers. She let her hand remain in the crook of his arm. Let him think that she needed his support, if it was easier for him. Perhaps it was true. But it was equally true that they needed each other.

In response, he moved an inch closer to her. And at the approach of the next gentleman in line, his other hand covered hers. The man in front of them bowed and, though he was a stranger to her, greeted her with an overly familiar smile.

She felt her husband stiffen again, as he made the introduction. 'Lady Fanworth? Lord Arthur Standish.'

She should have recognised him without Stephen's help. Now that she had reason to look for it, the similarity between the men was marked. But the younger brother's good looks were spoiled by the fading blue circles under his eyes and a nose which was still a little swollen.

'How do you do?' she said, offering a hesitant smile.

'Not as well as you, I think,' Lord Arthur said. Unlike her husband's superior smile and distant manners, there was something wolfish about Arthur. She suspected, if he should grin, he would show far too many teeth. Then, as suddenly as he had come, he disappeared into the crowd and they were greeting the next couple.

Once the majority of guests had arrived and the line dissolved, Stephen parted from her with little more than a light touch on her hand and a sympathetic smile. Apparently, she was to be left to her own devices while he did whatever it was a marquess did at such gatherings. If his current behaviour was any indication, they stood disapprovingly against a wall, avoiding other people.

She looked back at him and frowned. Something would have to be done about that. But now was not the time to find a solution. At least he had his brother to talk to. Lord Arthur was beside him, speaking to him as though there was nothing unusual in his behaviour.

It was wrong of her to take such an instant dislike to a person. But there was something about her husband's brother that unnerved her. When he was not at her husband's side, she found herself searching the rest of the room for him, as if she feared the mischief he might create if he was not always in sight. When she could not find him, the raised hairs on the back of her neck told her that he was somewhere nearby, watching her.

Perhaps she was right. After she had not seen him for some time and was almost convinced that he had left the room, he appeared before her wearing the same predatory smile he'd shown at their introduction. 'Lady Fanworth.'

No matter what her feelings, this man was her husband's brother. She had little choice but to respond politely. 'Lord Arthur.'

'It is a shame that it has taken so long for us to meet. We are family, after all.'

'You are Stephen's brother.' It was hardly necessary to state that fact. But somehow, she could not muster a warmer acknowledgement of their connection.

'That I am,' he agreed. But the way he was looking at her was not in the least bit brotherly. 'I must admit, Stephen has excellent eyesight, if dubious taste. You are the most handsome woman here.'

An insult wrapped in a compliment did not warrant a response, so she remained silent.

'It is a shame we have not met before now,' he said. It was an innocent statement, but the ironic glint in his eye said something far different.

'I suspect there is a reason for it,' she said, glancing out over the room and taking a sip of her wine. If he had truly wished to meet her he could have searched her out, just as Louisa had.

Arthur laughed in surprise at her sarcastic response, but he did not leave. 'Perhaps it is because I do not frequent any but the best merchants.'

It was one thing to insult her and quite another to insult the shop. 'Then it is fortunate that I do not need your patronage,' she said.

'Of course you do not,' he agreed. 'You have married well enough that you need no one's help.'

'It was not my plan to do so,' she said.

'Of course not. We have my besotted brother to thank for this union. I told him it was unwise.'

And it appeared he had got a punch in the nose for his trouble. She glanced across the room at her husband who stood as impassive as a statue against the opposite wall. 'Fanworth has a mind of his own.'

'Would that he was less stubborn. He has overstepped himself, this time. Larchmont will never accept you.' He looked her up and down again as though the flaw in her character were somehow worn on the outside, for all to see.

'What's done is done,' she said in response. 'He cannot exactly *un*-marry me.'

'I suppose not.' Now he was quite obviously admiring her body. 'If I were married to you, an annulment would be impossible. And I have heard that the lower classes do have a greater appetite for certain things than the milk-and-water misses you find at Almack's.'

When one had customers, one grew used to accepting insults with a smile and not responding to them as they deserved. But Louisa had been right. Lord Arthur Standish deserved to be struck, hard and often. Before she could stop herself, Margot had given him a hard slap to his broken nose.

With a curse that was heard by half the people in the room, Arthur doubled over, cupping his offended proboscis in both hands. All conversation stopped as heads snapped to look in their direction. And then it began again. The crowd swirling like stirred tea as those who had seen informed those who hadn't that the new Marchioness of Fanworth had raised a hand to her husband's brother.

Arthur straightened, glaring at her and mopping at

the trickle of blood that dripped from his re-injured nose. 'Pratchet was right. When I sold him the rubies he said you were every bit as stubborn as Stephen. Since neither of you would choose the sensible course, I hope you are both satisfied with the results.'

'Infinitely.' Margot felt the reassuring touch of her husband's hand on her arm. 'So nice to see the family represented, Arthur.' There was a long ironic silence. 'If you will excuse us?' Then, with a gentle tug on her elbow, Stephen led her away.

Catastrophe. Fiasco. Calamity.

When one had the time to think, there were many words to describe the evening other than disaster. Judging by the way Margot was slumped in the carriage seat opposite him, she had thought of all those and more.

In Stephen's opinion, it could have been far worse. It was fortunate that they'd not met his parents, as he'd expected. If Arthur was any indication, he had been naïve to assume Larchmont capable of good behaviour. More likely, he'd have thought it good sport to humiliate Margot as Arthur had tried to do. While she'd proven capable of handling difficult servants and annoying younger brothers, the duke would not be so easily dispatched.

Her victory tonight had not come without cost. After Arthur had gone home to tend his injury, Stephen had remained by her side, to make it clear to the crowd that his sympathies lay with his wife. But as the evening wore on, she smiled less and spoke hardly at all. It was as if, by marrying her, he'd infected her with his own form of misery.

She had not said a word to him since they'd departed the assembly rooms, staring out the window of the carriage without really seeing the streets they travelled. 'I am sorry,' she said suddenly, not turning her gaze to meet his. 'So very sorry. I never intended… It just happened.' Her hands gave a helpless flutter, then covered her face.

'I understand,' he said.

'Louisa was right.' The words came muffled from between her fingers.

'How?'

'She said you had struck your brother. But that he sometimes deserved to be hit. I did not give it much thought. And then…he began speaking to me…' She shrugged, unable to continue.

'Normally, when we Standishes strike each other, we do so in p-private.' The truth sounded even worse when stated thus.

But she looked up at him, with a surprised smile. What had he said to put such hope on her face? 'You are not angry with me?'

'I am angry with myself,' he admitted. 'I should have kept him away from you.' He reached across the space between them and gave her hand an encouraging squeeze. 'What did he say?'

'I will not tell you,' she answered, with a stubborn shake of her head. 'Or you would likely want to hit him a second time.'

'I will do so anyway, if he annoys you again.' And

he would do so, gladly. When he looked at her, he felt a fierce wave of protectiveness. It was as if he had been given a fragile ornament to hold, only to see his brother try to snatch it from his hands and destroy it. Now, he must do whatever it took to teach Arthur that this was not some playroom tussle over a toy.

'Why did you hit him the first time?'

'Eh?' His lady wife was looking down at the hand that held hers, rubbing her thumb along the inside of his wrist. It was a simple touch that probably meant nothing at all to her. But at this gentle friction, he could hardly remember his own name, much less hold a conversation.

'Why did you strike your brother? Louisa said it happened before we were married. She said you would not have him at the wedding. And tonight, there were still bruises.'

Had Arthur lied about the reason, implying he was some sort of bullying brute? He chose an answer that was vague and dismissive. 'He meant to cause trouble between us.'

'It was about the rubies, wasn't it? Tonight, after I slapped him, he admitted he was the one who sold them. I was wrong about you.'

'And I you.' It seemed he took the first deep breath in ages. If she knew this much of the truth, the rest was child's play. He took her other hand and gathered them both to his lips for luck before speaking. 'The day I realised you b-blamed me for the theft, I spoke to P-Puh-Pratchet. He ran off, or he might have explained it all...' He squeezed her hand again. 'It was Arthur, all along. When I showed him the necklace you had made, he'd said you must have stolen the stones. Sold them b-back to me as a joke…' His words were full of embarrassing halts and stumbles. But she did not seem to notice. She was leaning forward, listening patiently, just as she used to.

He kissed her hands again. 'I was angry with you for no reason. I had to marry you. I mean, I wanted to marry you. From the first. B-But now, I had to. Quickly. To make up for what I had done. And you would not speak to me.' He was making a mess of it again. It was what came of speaking without preparation. He was getting ahead of himself.

'And you hit Arthur?' she prompted.

'After P-P-Pratchet. Before the wedding. B-because he deserved it.'

'Why would he do such a horrible thing?' Why indeed? She had done nothing to deserve such elaborate plots against her, other than to sell him a few pieces of jewellery.

So he told her the greatest truth of all. 'Because I loved you. We are…not of the same class. It d-does not matter to me. But Arthur wanted to p-put me off you.' He didn't feel it was necessary to also mention his brother's gambling debts.

'I see.' She glanced around her as though waking from a dream. 'Well that did not turn out as he expected.'

For a moment, Stephen froze, amazed at the lack of anger in her response. Then he pulled her across the carriage to him so that she sat half beside him, and half in his lap. 'No, it d-didn't,' he agreed. 'And I am glad.'

And then he kissed her. Suddenly, things were exactly how he had imagined they would be, when he had courted her in the jewellery shop. She relaxed and let the kiss happen, responding gently, playfully against his barely open lips.

There was no need for passion, although he certainly felt it, whenever she touched him. But they had a lifetime to indulge it. Instead, they shared the sweet kisses of old friends who had finally become lovers. He wrapped his arms gently around her, wishing that it could be this way for ever.

She started suddenly and pulled away. 'There is something I must say, before…'

Before. So there was to be an after, tonight. That was reason enough to smile. 'What?'

'At the wedding breakfast. I did something unforgivable.'

'Let me decide that,' he said, still holding her close.

'I mocked you,' she whispered. 'There was so much I did not understand. I thought I had been tricked into marrying you. And I was angry. You had already apologised and I had not listened. But no matter about that. I never should have mocked the vows you made to me. Especially since you meant them.' This last was said with a kind of wonder as though she still could not quite believe that what had happened was real.

'I d-did,' he said, annoyed that he could still not quite manage the words. 'I love you.' That was much easier. He must remember to say it often. 'I love you.'

'Then what I did was all the more horrible. I know how hard it can be for you to speak. I swear I will never do it again.'

When he stared at her lips, he quite forgot what it was she was apologising for. 'Forgiven,' he said, using it as an excuse to kiss her again. And again.

'Thank you,' she said with a sigh of relief that made her soft and pliant in his arms. She rubbed her cheek against his, giggling as the stubble scratched her. Had he ever heard a sweeter sound than the laughter of a woman who did not mind his flaws? Then she whispered, 'I dreamed of this. Of you. But I could never have imagined how wonderful it is to be yours for ever.' Then, she leaned forward to kiss him again.

It was what he'd longed to hear, since the first moment he'd seen her. So he settled back into the squabs and kissed his wife in return.

Chapter Seventeen

Could happiness be so simple as this?

Her husband loved her. And she loved him in return. His family objected, just as she had known they would. But as she had told Lord Arthur before slapping him, Stephen had a mind of his own. Efforts to part them had only bound them more tightly together. All that mattered to him was their love.

But had she told him of her feelings? They had said a great many things, while in the carriage. It was the first time they'd really talked in ages. But had she said those three, specific words that had meant so much to her when he'd said them?

They were already at home, in their respective bedrooms as maid and valet helped them out of their evening clothes to prepare for bed. She could hear Stephen's good-natured cursing from the other side of the suite, as he tried to decide if a shave before bed was appropriate.

She smiled as her maid helped her out of the ball

gown and into the nightgown that her sister had made for her. Then she called out, loud enough for the whole house to hear, 'Do not bother with a razor. I love you, Lord Fanworth, down to the last whisker.'

There was a moment of silence, followed by a hearty laugh. 'As you wish, Lady Fanworth.'

Margot glanced in the mirror and let out a laugh of her own. 'Are you sure it fits?' she whispered to the maid. 'It is...' The word she was looking for was indecent. The lace yoke was cut so low that her nipples peeped between the gaps in the silk flowers.

The maid nodded, then grinned at her. 'It is very pretty, your ladyship. And I think Lord Fanworth will like it very much.'

Apparently so. He had heard this interchange as well and had manoeuvred himself so he might stare at her through the open doors of the changing room.

His valet was there as well, framed in the doorway. His eyes were fixed rigidly on the floor as he removed my lord's boots.

Before marriage, Margot had managed quite well in two rooms with no maid. How things had changed. It was a shock to admit it, but even with the new door, the situation in Fanworth's house seemed rather cramped. If he wished her to dress as a lady and maintain a shred of modesty in front of the staff, there was no way to share a changing room with her husband and a servant a piece.

A short time later, Stephen dismissed his valet and appeared in the doorway of her room. He was wearing the same dressing gown she had borrowed on their first night together. Despite the sheer gown she was wearing, her skin grew hot at the sight of him.

He glanced at her maid with a raised eyebrow and made a little shooing motion to signify that the girl was dismissed.

'We are not finished combing out my hair,' Margot argued.

'Let me help.' He said it as if there was no greater joy than to wait upon her. Then he took his place behind her dressing table and picked up a silver-handled brush, drawing it slowly through her curls.

Her eyes met his in the reflection of the mirror. In reflex, her nipples tightened with desire.

He noticed and smiled. Then he quickly plaited her hair and offered his hand to lead her to the bed. They had not gone two steps before she had pressed herself against him, demanding and receiving a kiss. The rest of the short journey was a staggering, stumbling laughing tangle of bodies that collapsed as their knees made contact with the mattress. Only then did he part from her long enough to look into her eyes.

'Your maid was right. I like this. Very much.' His fingers danced over the lace yoke of her gown, touching skin through the netting.

'You heard?' she said.

'It was impossible not to. We are rather cramped,' he admitted.

'And I suppose your valet heard as well?' Worse yet, he might have seen her.

Stephen kissed her ear. 'Barker does not see or hear anything I do not wish him to.'

How like an aristocrat, to think that he controlled the senses of his household. 'All the same, I would feel more comfortable if we could seek out larger apartments, so that the poor man will have nothing to ignore.'

Her husband did not answer immediately. He had become distracted with the lace again, trying to taste her breasts through the mesh. When he finally raised his head, they were both quite out of breath. 'Do not worry yourself over it. Summer is half over. We will not be here much longer.'

Suddenly, she was not the least bit distracted by his attentions. 'And where are we likely to go?'

'Where does anyone go? London, for the Season,' he said, taking one of her hands and kissing her arm from fingertips to shoulder, lingering for a moment to toy with the bracelet still twined about her wrist. 'And my home in Derbyshire for autumn and Christmas. The house there has all the room you could want.'

'But my work is here,' she said. She had waited patiently to be of age so that she might return from school and take up the family business. She had no intention to quit it in little more than a year. 'I have a shop to run.'

'We will be shutting that, at the end of summer, when we leave,' he said, as though it was something that had been discussed and agreed upon.

'Will we?' she said.

'It is only common sense,' he responded, completely oblivious to her rising temper.

'Is it?' she said.

'What else would we do?' He was undoing the little pearl buttons at her throat, preparing to remove her gown.

What else would they do? She was not sure she had an answer to that. But she had hoped, when the time came, she would have some part in making the decision. She prepared her argument.

And then, she noticed, for the first time in ages, he had been speaking freely and ignoring the small stammers, just as she did when she listened to him. If she chose to fight him, now of all times, she might lose this closeness, yet again.

He had said they would not leave until the end of summer. That meant she had time to persuade him. And judging by the solid feel of his member pressing against her leg, she had means to persuade him that she had not yet exercised. She reached to his waist and untied the sash of his dressing gown. 'Lord Fanworth?' she said, teasing his lips with hers.

'Lady Fanworth?' he responded, capturing them so he might kiss her.

She pulled away. 'Do you love me?'

'Did I not tell you so?' He seemed surprised that she would ask.

'I wish to hear it again,' she said.

'I would rather show you,' he said, stripping the gown over her head and tossing it to the end of the bed.

She placed her hand lightly on his lips, stopping them before he could kiss her again. 'But first, you must say the words. It is our fourth night together, after all. If you wish me to release you from our agreement…'

He growled. 'By morning, you will beg me to re-negotiate.'

'But tonight…' she reminded him. 'Arouse me with words.'

He gave in without further struggle. 'I love you. I worship you. I adore you.' He paused to kiss his way down her belly. 'Since the first moment I met you, I have been yours to command.'

To test him, she spread her legs and guided his lips to where she most wished to be kissed. And as he promised, he worshipped her. Tomorrow, she would hold him to his promise and command that they keep her business. But tomorrow was a long time away. For the moment, she was lost in the present.

Chapter Eighteen

The next day, Margot glanced around the shop, as if she had never seen it before, trying to memorise every last inch of it. She meant to broach the subject of its future tonight, at dinner. But if Stephen was adamant that it was just a brief diversion to be cast aside at the end of summer, she must savour every moment here.

She smiled grimly. Of course, if he thought such nonsense, he did not know her as well as he thought. With the servants she had been firm. With Arthur she had been violent. But with her dear Lord Fanworth there was a much more pleasurable way to work him ’round to seeing things her way.

She had no intention of closing, now that business was increasing again. After the previous evening’s party, she’d had a steady stream of customers interested in seeing the source of the jewels that had been worn by the notorious Marchioness of Fanworth.

To ease their minds about a titled lady in trade, she had retired to the private salon and plied them with tea and cakes, before selling stock and taking orders. By mid-afternoon, she had rough sketches for several custom projects to give to Miss Ross so that the girl might practise carving wax for the moulds. The front counter had sold so many buckles, hairpins and snuff-boxes that it had needed restocking twice. It was the most profitable day she'd had all season.

Fanworth would be appalled.

She smiled. It was good that she had not followed her first instinct and flatly refused to obey. After an hour in her gauze-draped bed, he showed no interest in discussing the demise of her life's dream. After a week, it was possible that he would not even remember having suggested it. And after a month, she would convince him that it had been his own idea to relocate permanently to Bath.

Such a complete victory was unlikely. But two months ago, she'd not have believed that a marquess would fall in love with her. The world was a strange and miraculous place.

There was a sharp clang from the brass bell as another customer entered the shop. 'I wish to speak with Lady Fanworth.' The gentleman at the front counter spoke in a voice so commanding that it carried all the way to the back of the shop. Margot did not need to see him to know that he was used to being obeyed. She got up from the divan, smoothed her skirts and went back to the main room.

But once she had seen him, there could be no doubt as to the identity of the man at the counter. The Duke of Larchmont was an older version of her husband.

He had more than a touch of grey at his temples and leaned on an ivory-handled walking stick as he glared down into the cabinet of her best work as though it were nothing but tin and paste.

It would have been a lie to say he looked welcoming. But she doubted that he was as bad as the world seemed to think. After all, everyone had been quite wrong about Stephen. It was proof that she must meet the man before forming an opinion of him.

She suspected Arthur was wrong as well. If the Duke of Larchmont did not mean to accept her as daughter, he would not have troubled himself to come to the shop. He had but to ignore her to make his feelings known. If he had come to make the first move of welcome, she would be sure to give no objection.

'Your Grace.' She swept down into her lowest curtsy, averting her eyes.

'Get up, girl, and let me have a look at you. Do not think you can win my favour by bowing and scraping.' When she raised her head to look at him, he was examining her through a quizzing glass as she might look at a stone with her loupe. She remained still as he walked around her in a slow circle, continuing to treat her as if she were an unfeeling, inanimate object.

When he reached the front of her again, he gave a resigned nod. 'I can see why Fanworth took it into his head to marry you. At least the children will be attractive. It does not matter for a boy. But there is little reason to have a girl, if she is not pretty.'

She bit her tongue to keep from explaining that the gender and appearance of her unborn children were not things that could be planned or predicted. Even if they were, it would not be left to him.

He sighed. 'I suppose it is too much to hope that you have wits.'

'I like to think so, your Grace,' she said, struggling to be polite.

'You have learning? Languages?'

'French, of course,' she said. 'My mother spoke it.'

'Immigrants.' His lip curled. 'And manners. Did she teach you those?'

She tried not to think of the blow she had struck when last trying to prove her worth and gave a polite nod in response.

He nodded back. 'Better to remain silent, as Fanworth does. Especially when you are lying.'

'I assume you are referring to last night's altercation with Lord Arthur,' she said, as calmly as possible. 'He was not behaving as a gentleman.'

'We are discussing your behaviour, not his,' the duke replied.

If he expected her to apologise, he was about to be disappointed. 'If such rudeness is customary from him, next time I will be prepared for it and refuse to acknowledge him, should he speak to me.'

The duke laughed. 'Just as my son does to me. The two of you are very well suited.'

'Thank you,' she said.

'It was not meant as a compliment.' He set his stick across the glass of the counter beside them and leaned forward, glaring into her eyes. 'It is too late to be rid of you, short of bundling you into a sack and throwing you into the river like the mongrel you are. But the least you can do is to refrain from embarrassing the family further than you already have.'

'I have no wish to bring shame upon my husband,' she said. It fell short of allegiance to the Larchmont name, but it was the best she could manage.

'That is more than he can manage for himself,' the duke said, with a sneer. 'And not nearly what is required, if you are to be the future Duchess of Larchmont. I expect you to deport yourself as a lady and not behave like some common tradeswoman.'

She hoped that he meant something simple, like being dressed by the right modiste or not slapping members of the immediate family in public. 'I will do my best to behave in a way that honours your name, your Grace. Last night was an aberration and it will not be repeated. Give me time and I will prove to you that the manners of a common tradeswoman are no different from those of a well-born lady.'

'I have no desire to learn anything of the manners of your class,' he said with the sour frown of someone who has seen something awful in the gutter. 'For as long as there has been a Larchmont, there has been no such creature in this family. There will not be one now.'

He put his full weight upon the counter and leaned forward until his face was inches from hers. 'You will close this shop, immediately. Then you will retire to Derbyshire for as long as it takes for your past to be forgotten.'

Was she really so repellent a choice that she must be hidden away from society? Even her husband did not demand such extreme measures when planning for the future. She took a breath, being careful to control her temper. 'I am sorry that our marriage displeases you, your Grace. But I cannot simply close the shop with no notice. There are employees to be provided for, creditors to pay, stock to liquidate… Even if I wished to, it is more complicated than just closing the doors and walking away.'

'I beg to differ.' Without warning, he shifted his weight and pushed down, hard, on the cane resting on the countertop. The glass under it cracked from end to end with a musical clink.

One of the shop girls let out a frightened shriek and Jasper took a step forward, as if fearing he might need to protect her from further violence.

Margot held a hand up to stay him and calm the girl.

The duke ignored them all and picked up the cane. Then, he stared down at the ruined glass. 'This is only my first visit to your little shop. But it is obviously a very dangerous place. There is no telling what might happen to the staff, or the customers, should it remain open. As I said earlier, you must close it immediately.'

She stared down at the glass as well. When she had imagined incurring the displeasure of the peer, she had thought it would be a genteel punishment: a direct cut or a few harsh words. She would never have imagined vandalism and direct, physical threats.

It had been naïve of her to think that anything good would result from this meeting. The Duke of Larchmont punished her husband for an imagined weakness and doted on Arthur, who had not thought twice about sending an innocent woman to the gallows for a theft he'd committed. To find that such a man was warped by pride and the need to control others should not have been a surprise.

And now, he cupped his hand to his ear. 'Perhaps I am going a trifle deaf with age. I did not hear an answer.'

She had not answered, because there was no point in reasoning with a madman. For now, she needed to do what she could to get him from the shop. Then, she needed time to think. Once again, she bit back the things she really wanted to say, and managed, 'I understand, your Grace.'

'See that you do.' With that, he gave a single, sharp tap at the centre of the crack. The ruined glass plate shattered, the shards falling to cover the diamonds on display beneath.

Chapter Nineteen

Something had changed.

After the previous evening, Stephen assumed that almost all the difficulties between them had been sorted. She knew the truth about the rubies. He had been able to speak freely again. They had shared her bed. And that had been after he'd mentioned his plans to take her away at the end of the summer.

He was still awaiting the argument on that subject. He'd win it, of course. There could be no other result. But for such a tiny armful of woman, Margot was surprisingly strong willed. That she had accepted his words without question or contradiction made him suspicious.

But last night, he'd had no desire to question her on her feelings. Talking had been the last thing on her mind as well. And it would have taken more strength than he possessed to resist the new Lady Fanworth when she was dressed in nothing but a thin lace gown and an emerald bracelet.

She was almost as alluring now, seated across the

dining table from him in blue silk. The lace and sequins on the bodice drew his eyes to the gentle slope of her breasts, firing his imagination for what might happen when dinner was finished and they had retired for the night.

But there was no sign that she was having similarly pleasant thoughts. She was thinking about something, he was certain. She stared down into her plate with a slight frown, but did not eat.

'Is the food not to your liking?' He had thought the matter settled.

'No,' she said. 'It is delicious.' Then she picked up her fork and began to eat, as though seeking an excuse to avoid conversation.

In an effort to distract her, he questioned her about her day. She answered in monosyllables, if at all. It was a strange inversion of the last weeks, where she had been the one to talk and he had evaded. Now, when at last he was ready and eager to speak with her, she spoke as few words as possible.

Then, he noticed the handkerchief wrapped tightly around one of her fingers. 'What happened there?'

She looked up, startled. 'There was an accident. In the shop. Broken glass. As I was cleaning up, I cut myself.'

Hs stood up and went to her side, taking her hand gently in his and unwrapping the cloth. 'Does it hurt?' It did not appear to be deep, but she looked near to tears.

'It is all right,' she said.

'You work too hard. You must take better care of yourself.' He kissed the finger and wrapped it again.

'I have been thinking that, as well,' she said and took a deep breath. 'In fact, I think you are right about giving up the shop.'

Of all the things likely to come out of her mouth, he had not expected this. 'At the end of summer,' he reminded her, feeling uneasy.

'Or sooner,' she said. 'Tomorrow is Sunday and we are closed. I do not have to worry for a day or two.'

'You do not have to worry at all,' he assured her. When he had first decided that they must marry, hadn't that been his fondest desire: that she should never have to worry about anything again?

But she did not seem to hear his reassurance. She was staring down into her plate again, poking listlessly at the food with a fork. 'Perhaps, next week, it would be possible to find Mr Pratchet… He wished to own it. I might sell it to him. Or not…' The words were fairly pouring out of her, now that she had begun to speak. But she did not seem any happier for her decision.

'Before we married, you were quite adamant about Mr Pratchet not taking control. This is quite a change of opinion,' he said cautiously.

'I can think of no one else,' she said, setting her fork aside as though she had lost her appetite. 'Justine would not want it. Her memories of the place are quite horrible. When it came fully into our control, she wanted to close it and forget it had ever existed.'

'Women are not meant to run businesses,' he said, repeating what he had always assumed to be true.

She gave him a tired look, as though she had heard the words too many times before. 'Perhaps not. But there was little choice in the matter, since my father had daughters and not sons.'

He started to speak, and then stopped. Logic dictated that if a business owner had daughters, then the business should fall to the men they married. But that would have meant that she should have married Pratchet, who wanted the business more than the woman, and not a man who wanted her, but had no need of a jewellery shop. Perhaps that was the logical argument. But when it ran contrary to what he had wanted to do he'd had no problems ignoring it. Why should it be any different for her?

'We sisters knew that some day the business would fall to us and we prepared accordingly. We had played in the shop since we were little. And though Mr Montague was a horrible man, he was an excellent jeweller. He taught us everything there was to know about the stones, the metals and the making of jewellery. We learned our letters and our numbers.' She smiled faintly. 'Arithmetic works just the same for a woman as it does for a man. If you were to examine my bookkeeping, you would find it kept in a reasonable hand and totalled properly at the bottom of the ledger.'

Then the smile was gone again. 'But Mr Montague really only wanted the money. And Justine wanted her freedom. I was the only one who really cared about the shop. I planned for years so that I might be ready to take it on. And I have done well. Or, at least, I did. If I cannot have it…'

She spoke of the place as if it were a living thing. And a precious one, at that. It was not just some stray dog that could be put out when it became too inconvenient to keep. By the look on her face, she would be no more willing to abandon a child then she would shutter the windows and lock the doors of de Bryun's.

'Are you quite sure you are ready to leave it?' She had come to the decision on her own, just as he'd wished. Why did it not make him happy?

'You wish me to close it, do you not?'

'Well, yes.' He did. Or, at least, he had. Now, he was not so sure. 'But when we have discussed it before, you have been quite adamant on the need to ensure the livelihoods of your staff.'

'I must see to their safety as well,' she said. It was an odd statement, after the assurances she had given him about the minimal risks involved in her job.

'You promised me before that if you were worried for your safety you would let me protect you,' he reminded her.

Hope flared in her eyes for a moment. Then the look of misery grew deeper, as she became even more obedient. 'Of course. But as you pointed out to me, yesterday, it will be difficult to run the place with the responsibilities I am likely to have as your wife.'

'That is correct.' He thought of his mother and what she did to fill her days. She called on friends in the morning. In the afternoon, she sometimes shopped. She went to dinners in the evening. When they were home, she might visit the sick and the poor. If she stopped doing any of those things, it would not have mattered one whit to the duke, or the people around her. She kept busy. But he would hardly have called what she did 'responsibilities'.

But Margot had pointed out to him on several occasions that she already had them. It was ludicrous to insist that she accept idleness for propriety's sake. 'Perhaps there might be a way to keep it open part of the year. Summering in Bath does not conflict with a London Season.' What was he saying? Hadn't it been his wish that she stop work and devote herself to him? But now that she was considering it, he felt no happier about it than she did.

She shook her head. 'It is better to make a clean break of it. I cannot ask my staff to work half a year, and wait for me to return. It would not be fair.'

'I see.'

'And there is your family to consider,' she said.

'My family?' It was strange that she would think of them, since he spent little enough time considering their feelings. 'If you are thinking of yesterday's meeting with Arthur, put it from your mind.'

'It is not that,' she said. 'I am sure your father would prefer that there not be a shop girl in family.'

'My father?' Stephen laughed. 'My father can go to hell and take his opinions with him. When he does, I will be Larchmont. And I do not care a fig if my duchess has a shop.'

'You don't?'

'I don't.' Perhaps it was just a contrary wish to do the thing that would most annoy Larchmont. Or perhaps it was that she was smiling at him for the first time all evening.

He put an arm around her shoulders, drawing her out of her chair and away from the table. 'It is plain that talk of closing de Bryun's upsets you. We can discuss it tomorrow. Or some other time.' There were weeks left before the season changed and they must leave for home. 'But we will find a way to handle it that will be satisfactory to all concerned.' He kissed her cheek.

And as they always did, when he was this close to her, troubles did not seem so important. 'All that matters is that we are together.' He kissed her again. 'Although I do not know what I shall do with my nights, now that I have used up all my time with you. Last night was four, was it not?'

This actually coaxed a grin from her. 'Nothing happened on the second night. I do not think we should count it.'

'On our wedding day, you suggested I save my last visit to your bed for a special occasion. Christmas, perhaps. Or my birthday, which is in March.'

'March is a very long time away,' she said.

'It is,' he agreed.

And quite suddenly, she was in his arms, clinging to him so tightly that it would have taken all his strength to part from her. 'Then let us make the last night last for ever,' she whispered. 'Just promise me, that, no matter what might happen, we will not be parted.'

'Never,' he agreed.

'Then it will be all right,' she said, as he manoeuvred them towards the stairs and bed. 'As long as I have you, the rest does not matter.'

* * *

Margot awoke alone the next morning in her husband's heavily curtained bed. Just beyond the velvet, Stephen was assuring his valet that he had no intention of leaving the chamber until evensong, if then. Breakfast should be brought to the room. Tea as well. Nothing else was required from the servants for the rest of the day.

And then the bed curtains parted again and he returned, throwing himself back on to the mattress. 'There. Sorted. I will make the night last for ever, just as you commanded. Come to me, my love.'

She did not need to comply, for the force of his return had bounced her to his side. His arms were about her again and she felt warm and protected. The slight throbbing in her cut finger made her snuggle even closer to him. Perhaps there was madness in his family. Stephen seemed quite normal, as did Louisa. But Arthur and the duke… She shuddered.

'Cold?' He pulled the comforter over them and she did not have to explain. 'Let me take care of everything.'

'That would be nice,' she admitted. Not even the duke could harm her, if she was with Stephen. Though he had wished aloud that she could be thrown into the river, she doubted that he was liable to carry out the threat.

It annoyed her that one visit from the man had left her ready to give up. But, in her defence, it was one thing to stand up to the likes of Arthur and Mr Pratchet, and quite another to stand alone against the wrath of a peer. Larchmont had almost infinite power and wealth, and he had already taken a dislike to her.

He was also quite mad. The interaction with him had shaken her more than she'd expected. There was something in his eyes that hinted a broken counter was the least of her worries, should she have further dealings with him.

Stephen noticed her mood and made a soft, shushing sound in comfort. 'What is it that troubles you so?'

She should tell him about the visit from the duke. She should have told him immediately after she had returned. But it seemed there was trouble enough between father and son, without her adding to it. 'Nothing, really.' Perhaps, when she had got over the shock of his first visit, she could seek out Larchmont and assure him of their plans to leave Bath. Then she could explain to Stephen that any potential problems with the family had already been settled.

'You are not worrying about the shop again, are you?' He pulled her on top of him. 'Stop it immediately. I have found a solution that will satisfy us both.'

'Really.' It was probably the plan to stay in bed with him until she no longer cared. That solution was impractical, though it had certain advantages.

'You must appoint a manager. What's the fellow with the ears?'

'Ears?' To the best of her knowledge, all men had them. Even the man currently easing her into a more comfortable position on his torso sported a pair.

'The tall chap in the front of the shop, with ginger hair and…' Stephen cupped his hands to the sides of his head and flapped them.

'Jasper,' she said, embarrassed at noticing a resemblance.

'Train him up on the running of the shop, just as you said you are training a girl to do the goldsmithing. You might continue drawing your designs wherever we go, just as other women sketch flowers. Then you might visit Bath periodically to deliver them and be sure that things are running smoothly. We could return in summer, of course.'

Jasper was the only clerk she had retained from the dark days when Mr Montague had run the shop. He knew more about it than anyone, other than herself. There had been only a small amount of disruption on the days she had been late this summer.

And Jasper had been the one to encourage Miss Ross to take over the workbench. Margot might not have come to that decision without his help, since she had been set to advertise. But it appeared that it had been a wise one.

'You are thinking about it, aren't you?' Stephen gave her an encouraging smile.

She nodded and smiled back.

'While I would not normally encourage a woman in this position to think of another man, today I will allow it.'

She glanced down to notice that she was straddling her husband in a way totally inappropriate to be discussing business. 'You are sure you would not find it embarrassing to have your family associated with trade?'

'It is not as if my name is on the door. Nor do I mean to stand in the window hawking watch fobs to a holiday crowd. And I have never been ashamed of you.'

It was true. He had been vexed with her, he had lusted after her and perhaps, for a time, he hated her. But he had never given an indication that she was an embarrassment to him.

And Larchmont was not embarrassed, so much as angry. She would assure him of her plan to distance herself from contact with the customers, and remind him of Justine's relation to Bellston. Her sister still owned half the business and no one remarked on it at all. 'So we might not have to close the shop at all,' she said thoughtfully.

'Not if you do not wish to.'

'I do not,' she said, relieved to be able to speak honestly.

'Very well, then.' Her husband lay back upon the pillows, and placed his hands upon her hips to guide her. 'You may now reward me for my brilliance.'

Chapter Twenty

Margot had married the most brilliant man in England. It was an overstatement, perhaps. But not by very much.

When the shop had opened again on Monday, she had pulled her senior clerk aside and made her proposal to him. His eyes had widened, just as she suspected hers had, when Stephen had made the suggestion to her. It was as though he could suddenly see possibilities that had not occurred to him before. But rather than accepting out of hand, he had requested that they go into the office and discuss things in detail.

As an employer who was used to being promptly obeyed, she had found it annoying. But as a shop owner searching for a competent manager, she had been secretly pleased. He had wanted to negotiate not just a rise in pay, but hiring of additional staff, changes in the scheduling and the implementation of several of his own ideas as to the display of stock. While he might not know the craft as well as she did, it was clear that he understood the running of the business.

The next day, as they had arranged, she arrived several hours later than usual to find Jasper, now called Mr Suggins, wearing a smart black suit and smiling over the counter as he welcomed customers to de Bryun's. The shop was immaculate. The staff was tidy as a paper of pins. The transactions were recorded correctly in the accounting book. There was very little for her to do, other than work with the more exclusive customers and guide Miss Ross in the casting of a hand clasp for a necklace.

Since she did not have to stay late to lock the doors, she was home in time to dine with her husband. After, she climbed into his bed, secure in the knowledge that she did not have to rise from it before the sun was fully up. While she did not precisely enjoy turning the minutiae of business over to another, she could become used to it.

How things had changed in just a few days. A week had passed and she was enjoying a cup of tea in the private salon, doodling designs for a series of bracelets and actually looking forward to the time that she could go home to Stephen.

Suddenly, her peace was disturbed by the clank of the bell and the crack and bang of the shop door swinging wide on its hinges to strike the frame before slamming shut. While it was inappropriate to scold a customer for carelessness, this one should use more caution, lest he break the window glass.

Broken glass.

There was no need to look into the front of the shop. She knew who had come. And all her plans for their next meeting, to stay rational and pleasant and have a discussion, had fled out the door before it could shut.

He was asking for her again. He sounded reasonable. It was a lie, of course. Reasonable men did not break things to prove a point. Perhaps, if she stayed still, like a rabbit in a thicket, he would not realise that she was here. Maybe he would go again.

Dear, sweet Jasper was lying for her, denying she was in the shop. But it was not working. 'Now see here, your Grace, you cannot simply barge into the back rooms.' It was very brave of Jasper to try to contain the man. If they both survived this, she would thank him.

She could hear the duke's wordless response to opposition: the splintering of breaking glass.

She was up and moving before the last pieces hit the floor. If she wished to prove herself worthy of the Standish name, she must not let him find her hiding in a back room like a coward. When she arrived in the main room, the last of the customers were scurrying out the door and Larchmont's cane was poised and ready to strike the next mirror on the pillar beside him.

'Stop this nonsense immediately, your Grace,' she said. Then followed the demand with a curtsy so that he might not notice her shaking knees.

'Nonsense, Lady Fanworth?' He said her name with

scorn, as though doubting that lady was the correct term to use. 'There is nothing nonsensical about my behaviour. It is a result of the surprise I feel to see you still here, after the perfectly reasonable request I made, on my last visit.' He was smiling at her as though nothing was wrong. Even with their limited acquaintance she was sure that the expression did not bode well.

'I discussed the future of de Bryun's with Fanworth,' she said, with more confidence than she felt. 'And we immediately turned over its management to my assistant. I will remain as a silent partner, until we leave Bath in a month.' It was an exaggeration. But she hoped it would do.

'You d-d-discussed it with Fanworth?'

He was laughing at Stephen. She had not liked Larchmont before. In truth, she was terrified of him. But this was the first time she could describe her feelings as hatred. 'Do not talk about my husband in that way,' she said, unable to stop herself.

'He needs his wife to defend him, now?' Larchmont's lip curled in disgust. 'I knew he was a fool. But I did not think him a coward, hiding behind a woman's skirts.'

'Stephen is perfectly capable of defending himself,' she said. Anger was good. She sounded stronger, and thus she felt stronger. She lifted her chin and straightened her spine. 'But if he is not here to do so, I will not stand in silence and listen to you speak ill of him.'

'You have spirit,' Larchmont said in a tone that was almost admiration. 'That is a shame. It would go easier for you if you did not.' Then he lashed out with his cane and broke another mirror as a punishment for it.

She did her best not to flinch as the glass crashed to the floor. 'I understand that you are displeased with Fanworth's choice of a wife. There is no need to destroy the shop to make your point.'

He glanced around him and then said, in a voice silky with menace. 'Apparently, there is. I told you to close the place. And yet, a week later, here we are.'

'I am removing myself from the business,' she said. 'I will be gone from Bath in a month. I will rusticate in Derbyshire. Surely that is what you really want.'

'Do not tell me what I want,' he said, tapping his cane on the floor. 'What I told you to do was to close the doors.'

She glanced past him to Jasper, who turned the sign in the window to read 'Closed'. It would do no good to anyone should strangers wander in and witness the duke's temper. And they might yet save a pane or two of glass by mollifying him. 'But, your Grace, as I told you before, it is not so easy as that.'

'"But, your Grace,"' he repeated in a mewling voice. 'Do I need to turn the key in the lock for you?'

'There is more to it,' she said, as patiently as possible. 'There are still orders that need to be filled. And taxes to be paid. I cannot just turn the staff out in the street.'

'Trifles,' he barked, waving his stick wide. 'I gave you a simple instruction. You disobeyed.'

His tone implied that punishment was inevitable. He wished to break things. Most of all, he wished to break her. She could deprive him of that, at least. 'I obey only one man and he is your son. And I do not think Fanworth agrees with your plans for this shop.'

That was all it took to drive Larchmont the rest of the way to madness. The cane came down hard on a glass display table by the door, striking a vase full of flowers so hard that it shattered against the opposite wall. When the cane came up again, it hooked the chiffon curtain, tangled briefly with it before bringing it to the floor.

Jasper gathered the shop girls and herded them from the room, shutting them in the office for their own safety. Then he came back to defend her.

She caught his shoulder before he could attempt to stop Larchmont from further destruction. If he raised a hand against a peer, he would be lucky not to hang.

He wordlessly accepted her caution, but positioned himself in front of her to protect her from flying glass as the cane rose and fell, over and over. They had repaired the front counter since his last visit—now it was ruined again. A backswing hooked the leg of another little side table, sending a display of perfume bottles crashing to the ground.

'Enough,' Jasper said, unable to remain silent. 'You have made your point, your Grace.'

He glanced at the boy with a raised eye brow. 'No more? I do not think she is convinced, as of yet.'

By the time he was sure, she had lost three more mirrors and a second display case. And, as always when one was dealing with a member of the peerage, there was little she could do but watch it happen.

He took a deep breath, as though the exertion had winded him, then smiled and leaned upon his cane again. 'There. I feel much better about the place now. You must shut the doors, if only to clean up the mess. If you open them again, I will return and do just as I have done today.'

'That will not be necessary,' she said. Louisa had been right. It was best just to avoid the man if he was in a bad mood. Her husband avoided him as well, probably because his behaviour was dangerously unpredictable. But no one had told her what to do if the mad peer sought you out.

'I suppose you will go running to your husband over this. If he is smart, he will do nothing, just as he normally does. He has learned to hide from me. I allow it, as long as he keeps his mouth shut in public. But if he crosses me on this, tell him I shall dog his steps about town, until he reveals himself as the stammering idiot he is. He deserves it, for bringing you into the family.'

She had assumed that if she married above herself, she would meet with some objection. It had not mattered to her until now. What harm could snubs and unkind words do her?

But she had never imagined physical violence. Nor did she want to see her beloved humiliated in public, made to suffer for loving her. This madness had to stop, even if it meant the loss of the one thing that had value to her. 'It will not be necessary to bring Fanworth into this,' she said, grinding her teeth to stop them from chattering. 'From this moment on de Bryun's is no more.'

'Very good,' Larchmont said, smiling over the destruction as if it was an improvement. 'Now that we have settled this matter, we must see if you can persuade me that you are worthy of my name. If not? Further corrections will be necessary.'

She did not hear him go. In truth, she did not hear much of anything for a time. Fear blotted out all other senses. But as her knees gave out and she sank to the floor, her last coherent thoughts were of what he might do to her the next time she failed to live up to his expectations.

Chapter Twenty-One

'Lord Fanworth.' Mrs Sims poked her head into the salon, where Stephen was reading. Her normally placid expression was replaced with worry. 'A girl is here, from the shop. There has been some sort of trouble.'

He set aside his book with a smile. 'What sort of trouble? Has someone lost an earring?' His smile faded, when he saw the girl, a petite brunette, her starched de Bryun's pinafore rumpled and her face stained with tears.

'Tell me all.'

But the girl, Susan, could barely get out a sentence around her tears. 'A madman came into the shop. Everything is broken.'

Stephen seized her arm. 'Lady Fanworth. Was she hurt?'

'I do not think so.'

The girl was useless, if she could not reassure him. 'The carriage. How soon can it be ready, Mrs Sims?' Any delay would be too long. It took him only a moment to decide that the girl should wait for it and guide it back, with the driver and two stout grooms. He would set out on foot.

Without the bother of a vehicle, it took only a few minutes to cross the Circus and run down George Street to Milsom. But when he reached the shop, he found the shades pulled, the sign turned to 'Closed' and the door tightly locked against him.

Damn it to hell. Why had he not asked her for a key? At a moment such as this, he should not have to be left pounding on the doorframe.

The door opened a crack and a girl who he had not seen before whispered, 'We are closed, sir.'

'Not for me.' Had it really been so long since he had been here that the staff did not know him? He forced his boot into the crack in the door before she could shut it again.

'Lord Fanworth.' The ginger with the ears appeared from behind her and opened hurriedly. 'Of course. Come in.'

'Where is my wife?'

'Safe, my lord. But shaken.'

The room was in chaos, the floor littered with broken glass and scattered jewellery. It was silent other than the clank and tinkle of the cleaning in progress and the quiet weeping of one of the younger shop girls. The boy led him through the midst of it, to the private salon where Margot sat on the white-velvet couch, twisting a handkerchief in her hands.

'What has happened here?'

'Nothing,' Margot stared towards the wrecked front room, dry eyed and impassive.

'A robbery?' If that was the case, he should never have allowed this to continue. Or at least he could have posted a man to keep her safe.

She was shaking her head. 'An accident. Nothing more.'

'An accident.' It looked as if a whirlwind had got in through the front door and jumbled the contents of the room.

'Nothing of importance,' she said hurriedly. 'But we will be closing the shop after all. If I must replace all of this…' She swept her hand about the room and gave a light and very false smile. 'It hardly seems worth the bother.'

'Closing?' Had they not just agreed that closing was not necessary? He turned his attention to the new manager, hovering at his wife's side. 'Enough of this. What really happened?'

Jasper, the ginger, wet his lips for a moment, as though weighing the punishment he might get for speaking against the one he was sure to get if he did not. And then, he said, 'His Grace the Duke of Larchmont wishes the shop closed immediately.' He glanced around him. 'He was most adamant.'

'Thank you for your honesty.'

He turned back to his poor, shattered wife and sat down beside her on the soft white velvet of the sofa. 'This was not the first visit, was it?'

She shook her head.

'The night you came home with the cut finger.'

'He cracked the glass of the showcase with his cane.'

'And why did you not tell me, then?'

'I thought you agreed with him,' she said. 'And then I did not want to make more trouble between the two of you. After what happened when I met your brother…I wanted to do better this time.'

'My father is not like Arthur,' he replied. But she had learned that through bitter experience. 'And you do not need to be better. None of this was your fault.' It was his. He had known what his family was like. He should have protected her.

'I thought our plan for a manager and leaving at the end of the season would be a reasonable compromise. I assumed, when I told him… I was wrong,' she said, looking at the mess around her. 'Perhaps if I had not provoked him…'

How often had he thought that when growing up? It would do no good to explain to her that she provoked him by her very existence, much as Stephen did, himself. 'You did not provoke him. There was nothing you could have done,' he said.

'Perhaps the shop was a mistake, after all. I should have known better. Everyone told me not to take this job upon myself. But I was so sure I could manage. And now, look at it.' Her voice was almost too calm, as though she still did not, could not, truly understand what had just happened.

He remained calm as well. It would not do to frighten her again, while she was still recovering from Larchmont. But inside, his blood boiled at the years of injustice. He had felt as she did now, when faced with his father's random displays of temper. He'd choked on the fear and anger, letting it muzzle him.

No longer.

'It is over,' he agreed. 'You will never be treated this way again. Wait for me here. I will return shortly, with the carriage.'

He strode into the main room, glaring at the frightened clerks. Jasper, the ginger, had opened the cash box and was paying off the staff before releasing them. 'Do not dare!' he barked.

Jasper slammed the box shut and jumped away from it, as though afraid that Larchmont's violence ran in the family.

'Clean up the mess. Find someone to repair the mirrors. We will open tomorrow, as usual. Nothing has changed.' He added a second glare to show that it hadn't. 'And find Lady Fanworth a cup of tea.' Then he unlocked the door and went out into the street.

When in Bath, the Duke of Larchmont always let the same house in the Royal Crescent. Woe be unto any who dared take it ahead of him. The landlord would gladly put another tenant out into the street to avoid angering the peer. It was just one more example of the duke's disregard for the needs of others and the terror he evoked in those that had to deal with him.

And today it would end.

Stephen rapped once upon the door, then opened it himself, not waiting for the startled servant reaching for the handle on the other side.

'I wish to see Larchmont.' The footman quailed in front of him, clearly used to the tempers of the family.

Without waiting for an escort, Stephen walked down

the hall to the small salon and paced in front of the fireplace. It would not do to lose a single drop of the rage he carried.

'What is the meaning of this?' His father stood in the doorway.

'You know damn well,' Stephen said.

'Do not use that language with me, whelp.'

Larchmont hated blasphemy almost as much as stuttering. Stephen grinned. 'I bloody well will. Now, let us discuss your damned visit to my wife.'

His father was smiling. Stephen had come to dread that expression as a warning of disasters to come. 'You do not wish me to become acquainted with my new daughter?'

'Until you can behave like a bloody gentleman and not some drunkard, I forbid you from visiting her.'

There was actually a pause before he could respond to this, as Larchmont tried to decide which made him angrier, the insult or the command. Then, he laughed. 'You? Forbid me? You have no authority over the family, boy. And less than none over me. It is clear you cannot control your tongue, or your wife. Someone must step in and protect our honour.'

'My wife needs no controlling.'

'In my opinion…' his father began to speak, brandishing his cane.

'No one has asked for it, you lick-fingered old fool.' Stephen reached out and snatched the stick from the old man's hand.

There was a moment of absolute silence. And then

his father staggered from the loss of the stick. 'How dare you.'

Stephen sneered back at him. 'Do not think to feign weakness where none bloody well exists.'

'I have the gout,' his father shouted back at him.

'Damn your gouty leg to hell and back. You can stand well enough when you are using this to strike people and break things, you miserable bugger.'

The older man watched the stick in his hands as though waiting for the blow that had been years in the making. When it did not come, he smiled again, still thinking he could regain control of the situation. 'I am strong enough to deal with that fishwife you married. And you. You are a full-grown man and still quail before me.'

'Do not confuse silence with fear,' Stephen said.

For a moment, Larchmont himself was silent, as if he had finally recognised the threat right in front of him. Then he said, 'What I did was necessary, for the good of the family—'

'Not my family,' Stephen interrupted.

'Something had to be done,' Larchmont argued. 'The future Duchess of Larchmont cannot be allowed to associate with half the people that come into that place, much less wait upon them like a menial.'

'The only one she cannot associate with is you,' Stephen said, looking at the stick in his hands.

Larchmont watched it as well and smiled. 'Since you do not have the nerve to strike me, I fail to see how you will stop me.'

Stephen twirled the stick in his hand. 'I will damned

well tell Bellston that you are as mad as King George. When he hears that you threatened a member of his family…'

'A distant link, at best,' Larchmont argued.

'He is closer to her than to you,' Stephen replied.

'We sit together in Parliament.'

'Because he is forced to,' Stephen said. 'There is not a man in England who would sit with you by choice, you miserable cod.'

Larchmont scoffed. 'I do not need friends.'

'It is better to have them than enemies,' Stephen said. 'And you have one of those, right here in the damned room.'

'You are not allowed to say such things. You are my son.'

'D-D-Did I not speak clearly, you old tyrant?' For once, Stephen enjoyed his stutter. 'I am your enemy. What in bloody hell did you think I would become when you raised a hand against the woman I love?'

'Her useless shop, only,' his father corrected. And for the first time in his life, Stephen felt the man give ground in an argument.

'Her shop is as much a part of her as her head or her heart. Threaten it again and I will walk the streets of Bath in a coronet, selling snuff boxes.'

'It is a blot on the family.'

'Not as sodding big as the mess I will make, if you annoy me,' Stephen said, smiling his father's smile back at him. 'I will introduce Margot to the Regent. Have you seen her? One look, and he won't give a tinker's curse who her father was. She will tell the story of your irrational violence…' Stephen smiled, imagining the scene. 'Prinny's had experience with difficult fathers. He'll bleeding sympathise.'

'You wouldn't dare.'

'Should I go to the tattle sheets instead?' The thought made him grin. He spread his hands in the air to picture the words, 'Mad Larchmont runs amuck in Bath!'

'I am not mad!'

'You cannot prove it by your behaviour, you bum-legged Bedlamite.'

'If you try such a thing, I will…I will…' Without even realising it, Larchmont was searching for the cane Stephen still held.

He held it out towards his father, giving him the barest moment of hope before snatching it back and snapping it over his knee. Then he tossed the pieces in the fireplace. 'Now what will you do? I think you are too old to hit me with your bare hands. But if you wish to try, I will defend myself.' The words were sweet, like honey, and he had no trouble speaking them.

'You would strike an old man?' Suddenly his father was doing his best to look feeble.

'If the only way to get through your thick skull is to crack it,' Stephen said. What he felt was not exactly pity. But it was different from the anger he'd felt so long when thinking of Larchmont. 'Or I will humiliate you, just as you always said I would. You fear for the family reputation? I will happily destroy it, if you force me to.'

'You have done that already, by marrying that…that woman with her infernal shop.'

'If that is all it takes to ruin us, then I fault you for creating such a fragile honour.'

Perhaps he did not have to strike the man. Showing him his faults had caused an expression as shocked as a slap.

It was enough. For now, at least. He bowed. 'And now, your Grace, I must go. Back to Milsom Street. I suspect they still need help with the cleaning up.'

Chapter Twenty-Two

'Must we be here?' Margot stared out over the crowd in the assembly room, who all seemed to be enjoying the last ball of the season more than she was.

Stephen shook his head, smiling. 'What sort of woman are you, to turn up your nose at balls and dancing? It is positively unfeminine. Next you will be telling me you do not like jewellery.'

'You know I will not. I am simply tired. I swear, I have worked harder in the last month than I have all year.'

'Because, as always, you take too much on yourself,' her husband scolded. 'You must trust Mr Suggins to do more. And you may always ask me for help. I will put on an apron and work for you.'

She smiled, remembering Stephen's ineffectual attempts at sweeping the floor on the day that the shop had been destroyed. Until that day, she had not thought a broom a particularly complicated tool. But it was clear that he had never used one in his life. Or perhaps he had only been trying to make her laugh. She kissed him on the cheek. 'It is enough that you paid for the new glass and the curtains.'

'And the painters and woodworkers,' he reminded her.

She shrugged. 'Since so much work needed to be done, I felt it was time for a few changes to the rest.'

'I consider it an investment in our shop,' he said, smiling at her.

'Our shop,' she repeated. At times, she still found his change of heart to be rather amazing. But he had returned from talking with his father that day and informed her that the shop was to remain open with the full support of his family. While she suspected that was an exaggeration, she'd had no further visits from the duke.

'You will rest tomorrow, in the coach to Derbyshire,' he said, kissing her hand. 'I know you are not looking forward to the trip. But I assure you, you will enjoy the place, once we have arrived.'

She smiled and nodded. It was plain from his expression, when he spoke of it, that the pleasure of the summer holiday was wearing thin for him. She must learn to be as supportive of his interests as he was of hers.

'But you say you are tired. Do you wish refreshments?' He gave a shallow bow to indicate that it was his pleasure to serve her.

'It would be nice,' Margot admitted, for the heat from the crush of bodies in the room was oppressive.

'Stand here and wait for me. I shall return in a moment.'

'Or I could accompany you,' she said. The spot he had chosen for her was out of the common path, near a back wall of the assembly room. If she remained there, she would not see a single person of her acquaintance.

'Wait,' he insisted.

'I will be over there, by Louisa.' She pointed across the room to where her sister-in-law was surrounded by a flock of gentleman eager to procure a last dance before summer ended.

'Later, there will be time to speak to her,' Stephen said. 'For now, you must stay here.' He pushed her even deeper into the shadow of a potted palm.

'Are you trying to hide me from view?' Margot said, hands on hips. 'Because I cannot think of a reason you would wish me to stay here.'

'I am trying to surprise you,' he said with exaggerated impatience. 'And you are making it damned difficult.'

'Then I will hide behind the palm tree, just as you wish, Lord Fanworth,' she said, blowing him a kiss as he walked away.

It took only a moment for her to realise why he had been so particular on her exact location. From the other side of the plant that hid her, a voice called out, 'Larchmont!' It was the Duke of Bellston, greeting the other peer in the room.

Another duke, perhaps, but not an equal. The Bellston title was one generation older than Larchmont's. Despite all the family pride he professed, her husband's father ranked beneath the younger, and far more pleasant, Bellston.

Although she doubted he would make a scene in front of the other peer, as Larchmont approached Margot shrank even further into her concealment. Stephen had sworn that she never need see the man again. He had also assured her, if they did meet, the duke would behave as a gentleman. And that seemed almost as unlikely as her husband using a broom.

'Bellston.' The answering greeting was delivered with the minimum of courtesy. If this was the way Larchmont behaved in public, it explained why her husband was thought rude, when he did not speak.

'So good to see you this evening,' Bellston said, sounding positively gleeful. 'I was just saying to Penny that it has been too long since we've seen you.'

'Yes, dear.' Her Grace, the duchess, was not nearly so convincing a liar as her husband.

In response, Larchmont said nothing.

'I trust the waters have helped with your foot,' Bellston continued.

'There is nothing the matter with my foot,' Larchmont announced.

'Of course not,' soothed Bellston. 'So I assume you carry that handsome stick as an ornament. May I examine it?'

Margot put her hand to her mouth to keep from laughing. It had surprised her when Stephen had made this very specific request for a gift for his father. Then he remarked that the old cane had met with an accident. She suspected the accident was similar to the one that had happened to Arthur's nose.

A moment passed as Larchmont relinquished his cane to the younger man.

'Do not worry,' Bellston drawled. 'I will return it to you, if you feel unsteady. I only wished to see the markings on the head. That is your family crest, set in the mahogany, is it not?'

Larchmont grunted in acknowledgement.

'And a wolf at the head, pewter or silver?'

'Silver, of course,' snapped Larchmont, as if no lesser metal would dare contact his skin.

If he was so sensitive to base metals, it was a good thing he did not know about the lead shot she had hidden at uneven intervals down the length of the wood. Though Stephen had remarked that the old ebony cane handled like a rapier, this new one was fit for nothing more than support. It would prove horribly balanced, should one attempt to wave it about, or strike out with it.

'Are those rubies for the wolf's eyes?' asked the Duchess of Bellston. 'How very clever. They are set inside the mouth as well. The beast looks quite savage, does it not, Adam?'

'Ravenous, my dear,' her husband agreed. 'Tell me Larchmont, where did you purchase such a marvellous stick?'

'It was a gift,' the man admitted, sounding rather like he was going to choke upon this act of kindness.

'From de Bryun's, I suppose,' Bellston said. 'We buy all our jewellery there, because of the family connection.'

'Margot is very talented,' agreed the duchess. 'She

has redone the hideous Bellston ring for me so that I almost enjoy wearing it.'

Almost? Margot shrugged. But it was exceptional praise from the duchess who had simple tastes for such a great lady.

The conversation continued in a similar vein, with the younger couple extolling her talent until she was quite embarrassed to be eavesdropping and Larchmont became frustrated enough to leave.

'Did you like your surprise?' Stephen had arrived and was holding a glass of lemonade out to her.

She nodded, taking a sip.

'I doubt if he will ever admit it aloud, but he is quite enamoured of the cane,' Stephen said.

'However can you tell?' He had not said two words about it, just now.

'I have seen the care he takes that the crest is visible, when he walks with it. Family pride, you know.' Stephen looked across the room at the retreating back of his father. 'And now we must go to your next surprise.'

'Two in one night,' she said. Although she was relieved to see that he was leading her in the opposite direction from the one the duke had taken.

They worked their way through the crowd to a quiet terrace at the back where several invalids in Bath chairs were enjoying the music. Seated amongst them, on a low couch, was a pale woman in her middle years. She was obviously beautiful and just as obviously frail. Around her neck were the rubies that had been the cause of Margot's greatest trouble and her greatest joy as well.

'Mother.' Stephen bowed and then bent forward to kiss the woman on both cheeks. 'May I present my wife?'

Margot swallowed nervously, propelled forward by her husband's hand at the small of her back.

'Come closer, my dear.' The Duchess of Larchmont gestured to her, reaching out to take her hands. 'Let me look at you.'

Margot had known the moment would come when she would meet her husband's mother. Despite his assurances that she was very different from Larchmont, she had not known what to expect. Her plan had been to be friendly and polite. But now, face-to-face with the great lady, the best she could manage was an awed curtsy. 'Your Grace.'

'She is a rare beauty, Stephen, just as you said,' the duchess announced, pulling Margot forward to sit on the couch beside her. 'There is no need to be so formal.'

'I scarce know how else to be,' she whispered, for a moment shocked into honesty.

'You must treat me as you do your own mother,' the duchess said firmly.

'I do not have a mother,' she said, and then corrected herself. 'At least, I have not had one since I was very small.'

'How sad,' said the duchess. Then she smiled. 'But I understand you honour her by continuing with your family's work.'

Somehow, Margot doubted that the duke described what she had done in quite that way. But for the duchess, she settled for a simple, 'Thank you. You are too kind.'

The duchess gave a small nod of her head and touched the necklace at her throat. 'And I see you are admiring my rubies.'

'They are magnificent,' Margot agreed.

'I was so glad to hear that Stephen had them reset for me.'

For a moment, Margot hovered on the edge of fear. It was rare to see her work after it left the shop. And even stranger to see it in this way.

The duchess touched the necklace again. 'It is strange to lose something so precious and have it returned looking even lovelier. See how clever the work is on the gold. And Stephen has promised me that I shall meet the designer here tonight.'

Her first impulse was to turn and run. But she felt her husband's hand at her back, holding her in place. 'And so you shall, Mother. It is none other than my Margot.'

His mother's eyebrows raised in surprise. 'You?'

She could manage nothing more than a small nod of her head.

'Beautiful and talented,' the duchess said. 'When I heard that Stephen had married a shop girl, I did not think that could be right. But to find a lady with such a rare gift? That is entirely a different matter.'

Margot wanted to correct her. When she took on the shop, it was never with the intent of being anything so grandiose as an artist.

But Stephen was speaking and there was no time. 'Yes. It is. When I first chanced upon her work, I had to know the person that had executed it. You can hardly blame me for losing my head.'

He spoke glibly today, without a sign of the halt that she sometimes heard. But it bothered her to think he would lie so easily and to his own mother.

'She has a special room at the back of the shop, where she entertains her more prestigious customers,' he was assuring his mother.

'So it is hardly like going to a common shop, then,' his mother agreed. 'It would be more a meeting of equals. So much nicer than tramping down Bond Street with the rest of London.' She glanced at Margot. 'You do have a shop in London, do you not?'

'Only the one in Bath,' she said softly.

'Well, that will not do,' the duchess said, with a frown. 'When you are in London for the Season, you must speak to Stephen about finding a property.'

'What would happen to the shop in Bath?' she said, not wanting to seem ungrateful.

'I suppose then you shall have two shops,' Stephen said, with a smile.

'Two,' she repeated, in wonder.

'And we must convince the Regent to give her a Royal Warrant,' the duchess continued. 'I have but to show him the rubies.'

'And Larchmont's cane,' Stephen added. 'She did that as well. And work for Bellston…'

'Really.' His mother gave an impressed nod. 'Then certainly, she must have a Royal Warrant. You must design a birthday gift for Prinny, my dear. One smile and he will be eating from your hand.'

'And buying your jewellery,' Stephen added.

'Of course,' she said, barely able to whisper. If she

was to be a marchioness making jewellery, then why would it not be fit for a prince? Then she looked from her husband to his mother and back again. ‘But what if he does not think it proper for a woman to be in trade?’

The duchess smiled at her. ‘Then, my dear, we will remind him of Lady Jersey and the Duchess of St Albans. Some of the biggest banks in England are run by women, you know.’ She gestured to Margot to lean closer, so that she might whisper in her ear. ‘That is the problem with men, my dear. They think so small. But we love them, so what can we do?’

Margot looked to her own dear Stephen and smiled. ‘Indeed, your Grace. What can we do but love them?’

* * * * *